D0390047

Hot Cross Buns

Judy Rogers and Sarah Porter

Penned Press

Penned Press

October 2012

Published in the United States by Penned Press
Spokane, Washington

This is a work of fiction. All incidents and dialogue, and all names
and characters, with the exception of a few well-known places, are
products of the authors' imagination and are not to be construed as
real. Where similarities to real life appear, the people, situations,
incidents and dialogues are entirely imaginary and are not intended
to depict any actual events or persons.

Cover design by Susan Aldworth

Cover photo by Cynthia Waltho

Library of Congress Control Number: 2012917989

ISBN-978-0-9882567-0-5

Printed in the United States of America.

First Paperback Edition

To
Ann Porter Brown
Our Muse

HOT CROSS BUNS

Hot cross buns!
Hot cross buns!
One ha'penny, two ha'penny,
Hot cross buns!
If you have no daughters,
Give them to your sons
One ha'penny, two ha'penny,
Hot cross buns!

English folklore includes many superstitions surrounding the Easter tradition of baking hot cross buns on Good Friday. Our favorite is that of sharing a hot cross bun with another will ensure friendship throughout the coming year, particularly if:

"Half for you and half for me,
between us two shall goodwill be."

ACKNOWLEDGMENTS

Mary Harnetiaux, Suzanne Harris, Nancy Long,
Bev Goddard, Pat and Jerry Stebbins, Gayle Ogden,
Marilyn Dreis, PJ Watters, Carol Gallagher,
Elisa Ferraro, Shannon Shields, Patty Porter Rood,
Marny Gaylord, Coleen Keenan O'Brien,
Annabel Armour, Art Fox, Shannon O'Brien,
Katey Treloar, Joe Brown, Gail Stevenson,
Julie Honekamp, Vee Sutherlin, Mina Gokee,
Marian Durkin, Lynn Kimmel, Kristi Blake,
Debbie Detmer, Kathie Burch, Trish McFarland,
Jeanne Ager, Jan Karel, Terry LaLone,
Cam Magnuson,
and
Michelle Grabicki Grover, our copy editor.

Chapter 1

Ellen Kirkpatrick felt like a moth caught behind a closed window screen. Trapped, scared and begging for flight.

"Mom, I'm moving to Los Angeles."

She tried to focus on the words coming from her daughter's mouth without much success. With Molly sitting just a few feet away, Ellen should have been able to hear her daughter's startling message. But the insistent, high-pitched hum of anxiety vibrating through her head made concentration nearly impossible.

Moving on. That, Ellen got! The rest came in fractured syntax—something about Los Angeles and Jesuits and immigrants—all jumbled into the horrific fact that her Molly was leaving. Only when Ellen was finally able to shift from fear to anger would she be able to digest the actual words Molly had spoken. That's how Ellen processed grief. That's how she managed to live through the death of her husband, Sam, and that's exactly what she would do now, and damn it, she would make it work.

"Molly! Will you zip it for two seconds and let me catch up?" She heard the words. They were hers. A breakthrough! There, she was mobile again and she was angry. This mourning routine was woefully familiar.

"You haven't heard a word I've said, have you?" Molly shot back defensively. She knew this fear and anger cycle as well as her mother did but was disappointed to see it resurface. It'd been such a nice holiday.

"Well, I certainly heard the first part. You're moving to Los Angeles? Of all the god-forsaken, Botox-riddled places, you pick LA? Why not Calcutta? I hear they need some help since Mother Teresa died."

Molly's blue eyes began to water. She felt the full gamut of emotions she'd been dreading as she broke the news to her mom she was leaving Spokane—leaving home, leaving her—to discover her own life. Loss, guilt, fear. They all queued up in her leaky tear ducts ready to squirt across the table at her mom's red face.

"I am, mom. It's time," Molly said tearfully and emphatically. "I'm sorry. I'm not deserting you. I'm picking up my life where I left off before dad died. I wanted this time with you. I needed it. But I have to move forward. Isn't that what dad would want? And you, too, right? That's how the two of you raised me."

They were sitting at a small table tucked into a corner of Ellen's burgeoning bakery, The Manito. For almost two years, bringing the bakery to fruition had been the salve she needed to heal the wounds left after Sam died. Ellen got up and walked around the table. She leaned down to hug Molly and a deep reservoir of love doused the hot flames of anger. Was she sad? Yes. Was she scared? Yes. Was she proud of her daughter? Yes.

She kissed the top of her daughter's head. "God, I hate it when you're more mature than I am."

"Me too," Molly said, simultaneously hoping she was as sure about her decision as she sounded.

. . .

A small photo of Sam was tacked to the cluttered corkboard in Ellen's cramped bakery office. Receipts and orders framed a tanned angular face smiling at the photographer. Ellen could see so much of Molly in Sam. She wondered how she could still get so annoyed just looking at that face after this long.

In their nearly quarter of a century of marriage, perhaps Sam's most remarkable physical feat was dropping dead at the age of forty-eight. He was one of those tragic stories, a man who had a fatal heart attack before his age-appropriate time. His heart disease was apparently invisible, because at that time, Sam was the epitome of middle-age physical fitness. When, in cardio-speak, the "heart event" occurred, Ellen was utterly and unconditionally unprepared for the choking finality. They'd been together since meeting in a history class at Gonzaga University. Soon after, she agreed to a first date, and it was the last date she'd had with anyone other than Sam. A little over a year later, they married and then Molly, their only child, burst onto the scene. Ellen and Sam shifted smoothly into zone defense, and their parenting routine turned into a tag-team sport during the many nights, weekends and summers when Sam studied for his master's in engineering and Ellen her master's in counseling. Looking back, it was worth the struggles. But through it all, Ellen knew she and Sam would be as good together in their golden years as they were in the paper plate and Top Ramen days when most of their money went toward tuition and diapers.

Ellen thoroughly enjoyed being a mom, but she had to admit looking forward to more time alone with Sam. It was their turn, their time. Since Sam's death, Ellen often debated the concept of time. Some say time is of the essence. Others believe we have all the time in the world. In Ellen's opinion, time is the ultimate gamble. A total crap shoot.

Instead, now Sam was gone, and Ellen had taken early retirement from her counseling position at Lewis and Clark High School to open The Manito, a bakery and coffee shop. Why not take the 'a' out of avocation? NPR's Morning Edition (she sorely missed Sam and Bob Edwards) had recently done a series about people who reinvent themselves. Secretly, she was tempted to fire off an e-mail with herself as a story idea.

Sam's life insurance policy from his engineering job at Avista Utilities provided just enough financial capital for the bakery. The sale of their Comstock Park 1950s brick rancher and their savings account gave her a small but adequate landing strip. The two apartments on the second floor above the bakery became home for Ellen and Molly. "We raised a great girl, Sam," Ellen said to the smiling face in the photo. "Now if I can just figure out a way to live my life the way we raised her to live hers."

She got up from her small desk and headed toward the door to the kitchen. She stopped to look at Sam's photo again. "Would it have been so bad if we'd enabled her just a little? Made her just a smidge co-dependent?" she asked the smiling face. The idea made her laugh at herself, which is what she needed right now. She rolled up her sleeves, ready for some serious baking.

. . .

After breaking the "I'm leaving" news, Molly went for a long run while Ellen put the finishing touches on a five-pie special order. Baking made her feel somewhat less vulnerable. Preparing a no-fail pie crust was helpful, but nothing compared to the lift of spirit she received a few minutes later when her friend, Louise Marie Ross, came bounding through the back door of the bakery.

"Hi Lou! How was your trip to South Bend?" Ellen asked.

"Couldn't have been better. Peyton's reunion with his Notre Dame Baseball teammates was great therapy for him. We also saw the first preseason exhibition game of the football season. For a couple of jocks, it was hog heaven. Oh, and by the way, I met a young man I want Molly to marry."

Lou had been close friends of the Kirkpatricks since Lou and Ellen's first day on the job at Lewis and Clark High School in the early '80s. While Ellen and Sam were studying at Gonzaga, Lou was 20 miles west of Spokane at Eastern Washington University majoring in secondary education. She and Ellen considered themselves lucky to land positions right after graduation. The two novices reported for duty that first day in September: Lou to her job as a world geography and American history teacher and the new coach of the girls' softball team, and Ellen as a guidance counselor at Lewis and Clark High School. An all-state softball player in high school, Lou brought skill and team spirit to her new job. Ellen was immediately drawn to her enthusiasm, and the two quickly became steadfast friends. Open, funny, athletic and positively ebullient about almost everything, Lou helped Ellen get through her tentative first year and every year since. When Lou married the funny and handsome Peyton Ross, a Lewis and Clark physical education teacher and head baseball coach freshly graduated from Notre Dame, it was Ellen and Sam who stood up for them and stood by them from then on. Until, of course, Sam quit standing.

When it was confirmed Lou and Peyton could not have children of their own, the two families fell into a natural pattern of raising Molly together. The five of them spent summers together at a shared cabin on Lake Coeur d'Alene just thirty minutes east of Spokane in North Idaho. They traveled en masse to Mexico, Ireland, Australia and Canada. Ellen and Lou were sisters by choice, and Lou became a second mother to Molly.

"Anyone I might happen to know?" asked Ellen, still amused Lou had taken on the role of matchmaker for Molly about a week after she was born twenty-four years ago. First there was the high school chess team captain, whom Lou swore would become the second Bill Gates. Sadly, he became a missionary in Ghana. Then there was the Robert Redford-handsome ski bum who lived off a trust fund the size of his parents' Big Sky, Montana, ranch. Alas, he was disowned when his parents discovered he had a wife and kid tucked away in Jackson Hole, Wyoming. Lou's credibility as a Yenta took a big hit on that one.

"No, you don't know him, but the karma is strong on this one, trust me." Lou shot out a list of attributes in rapid-fire succession. "Early thirties, single, handsome, Notre Dame graduate, Harvard Law, and now an attorney with the federal government in Chicago."

"Chicago. Hum. That makes sense considering Molly lives four states west of the Windy City," Ellen said with sarcasm, a trait more typical of Lou than herself. She'd always been the more even-keeled of the two and got a charge out of poking holes in Lou's latest schemes. Ellen smiled. She'd been down this road with Lou before. She didn't want to burst Lou's bubble by telling her Molly was leaving Spokane.

"It's called Facebook, e-mail, Twitter and blogging, El." Lou slid a piece of paper with an e-mail address on it across the countertop in Ellen's butter-infused bakery.

Ellen looked skeptically at the tiny piece of paper. "And where did you meet this fine young man who's theoretically my son-in-law-to-be?"

"Here's where my credibility is rock solid," Lou declared. "I met him when Peyton and I were visiting Father Joe last weekend before the football game. He stopped by his apartment to say hi. I'm here to tell you, El, this kid's the real McCoy. Try this shirt on for size. He graduated in the classics—just like Molly! Besides, my faith in Joe's judge of character is unwavering."

"Can we trust a priest on issues of romance?"

"Oh for God's sake, give me a break!"

"I'm just kidding, Lou," Ellen chuckled. "Wow, you really are on a roll."

"Of course, we can trust him. And mark my words, you'll be thanking Father Joe O'Brien when your first grandchild is born."

"And what is…"

Lou jumped in. "Liam. His name is Liam. Liam O'Connor."

"Ah ha, Irish to the bone." Like a lot of Lou's previous match-up attempts, the kismet sounded too good to be true, but definitely more promising than an antiseptic chess player. Lou admitted to herself her batting average in pigeonholing a perfect match for Molly was a dismal zero, but she refused to stop. She loved the kid and a home run was imminent.

. . .

"Hi Lou," Molly mumbled as she walked across the kitchen to grab a bottle of water from the giant commercial-size fridge. Lou noticed the greeting wasn't signature Molly. Her pink, post-run cheeky glow didn't hide the obvious. Something was wrong. A quick glance at Ellen's face verified her assumption. She looked as shit-scared as she did the first day she put Molly on the school bus.

"Hi Molly, how was your run?" Lou asked.

"Fine," Molly mumbled. "Hey," she perked up, "want to go for a short one?"

"A run? You just got back from a run, Mol. And so did I, hence I need to get home and shower the stink off this old body."

"Come on, just a short one. Don't act your age. Let's go."

Lou looked at Ellen and shrugged her shoulders. What the hell's going on here? When Ellen didn't offer any clues, she decided to roll with it.

"If you're going to pull the age card, okay, sure." She was talking to Molly but still looking at Ellen, who at the moment was acting far too occupied pouring thick, golden pecan filling into a perfect pie crust shell. When the door shut behind Molly and Lou, Ellen tossed the wooden spoon into the sink like she was putting every mouse in the neighborhood on notice.

Lou was point-blank in her investigation as they ran along the meandering trails hugging the basalt bluff of Spokane's South Hill. It really didn't take much investigating, however, because Molly was eager to get the news off her chest.

"Lou, I've got a great job offer in LA," said Molly. "Well, great in a way that the work is meaningful and engaging. But quite frankly, the pay sucks."

"And—let me take a wild guess—you told your mother, and she didn't take the news too well." So that's what the Twilight Zone vibes back at the bakery were all about.

"Lou, she's so hurt. I hate the thought of leaving her alone, never mind taking on the weight of the bakery without me." Molly also knew now that as long as she stayed in Spokane her dad's death would remain center stage in her life. She had begun to wonder when his death would lose the "recent" adjective.

"Get real, Molly. You're fresh out of college and need to explore life beyond schlepping flour and grinding coffee beans. Getting the bakery launched was the perfect medicine you and your mom needed to get your feet back under you after your dad died, but it's your Mom's gig of choice, not yours. You've got every right to do what you want. Besides, Peyton and I will always be here for your mom."

Lou stopped running. "Molly, who knows, someday you may want to run the bakery, but you've got to get out of SpoVegas to figure out who you are and what you're made of. Now, tell me more." Lou was a great coach, on and off the softball field.

"Well, a while ago I met with Father Pat—he was one of my GU profs—about my options. You know, could I get a job anywhere with my degree? Should I, God help me, think about graduate school? Anyway, he told me about this program, and, well, I applied and was accepted. I'll be helping Mexican immigrants navigate their way through the maze of red tape and obstacles of trying to obtain U.S. citizenship. None of these people speak much English, so at least I'll put my Spanish to work."

"Woo-hoo!" Lou pumped her arms above her head. "So that minor in Spanish and semester abroad in Guadalajara, primarily at the beach perfecting your tan, will finally pay off!" Lou teased.

"I start in two weeks, Lou."

Ah-ha! Lou thought. One more reason for Ellen to look like the kitchen rug had just been pulled out from under her. "So soon? Where will you live? Does that mean you won't be home for Thanksgiving? What about Christmas?" Lou dreaded the idea of their family traditions being lost.

"Thanksgiving, I'm thinking not. Christmas, I'm more hopeful. I won't know all the details until I get to LA. Father Pat has arranged for me to stay with the Sisters of Providence at their retreat house just outside Los Angeles. The Jesuits and the Sisters are partnering in their mission of operating a community center called El Centro where I'll be working. Like I said, I don't get paid much but I have access to a car, my own room, three squares and a small stipend for one year. Oh, and I forgot the LA Transit pass." Molly smiled. "That was the deal closer for me."

"Amen, sister. Who could resist a sweet deal like that? Does this have anything to do with your break-up with Randall?"

"And Winston and Anders and Peter and..."

Lou cut her off. "I need to tell you about a young, eligible lawyer I met when Peyton and I went to South Bend last weekend."

"Lou, you're my second mom but not my Yenta, please!"

Ignoring Molly's plea as she had Ellen's, Lou blew right by the objection.

"Liam O'Connor. Notre Dame grad who majored in THE CLASSICS and earned a Juris Doctoris from Harvard Law. Doesn't that intrigue you a little? Come on. Make an old Yenta happy."

"Lou, I'm really done with relationships for now. That's part of why I'm taking this job. If you're still matchmaking in a year, we'll kibitz on it."

"You've got yourself a deal. I have no intention of giving up. I have a strong feeling about this one. Now let's get back to your mom."

. . .

Ellen knew Molly suggested a run so she could tell Lou her news. The fact that Lou also agreed to stay for dinner confirmed to Ellen what a solid friend she was. Lou would provide a good cushion between Ellen and Molly's untidy heap of flailing emotions.

Molly made dinner in her apartment—Ellen's favorite of flank steak, tortellini salad tossed with pine nuts, parmesan and cranberries, and thick slices of Ellen's dense peasant bread with sweet butter. Lou had gone home to shower, change and returned with wine—Barrister's Rough Justice Merlot. For dessert, Molly arranged several varieties of dark and milk chocolate broken into asymmetrical, angular pieces with pear slices along with a dessert wine.

Molly set the table with three different place settings of mismatched Spode Blue, Pink and Brown Willow and real silver she bought randomly as she searched for furniture and decorative pieces for the bakery. She had a gift, not unlike a Picasso, where a sense of disorder is used to create a masterpiece.

"Mangia bene!" the three women saluted each other and enjoyed Molly's dinner, despite the mass of apprehension clouding the atmosphere. Finally, Lou threw Ellen a quick pitch. Her coaching instincts told her to take control of the field with a strong first play.

"So our girl is headed to LA-LA land! Have you ever been to Los Angeles, El?" Lou started right in, trying to sound casual.

"I told Lou about my job in Los Angeles, Mom," said Molly, diving head-first into the deep end for the second time that day.

Ellen studied the Blue Willow pattern on her dessert plate and took one last sip of wine. She sighed deeply before finally looking up.

"Don't worry, Molly, I'm not going to fall apart again," Ellen said. "It's okay, I get it. I'm sad. I earned that right by virtue of being your mother. And, I'm not ready to defy the Jesuits. Boy, you really know how to stack a deck."

"Are you sure it's okay?" Molly asked pensively.

"Sure, I'm sure," Ellen said with a wan smile. She tried to sound encouraging but knew it was a farce. "Now, if you two don't mind, tonight's party is over for me. I've got to get up and make huckleberry scones and a fresh batch of granola for the breakfast crowd. They're depending on me."

When Ellen was completely alone in her apartment across the hall, she collapsed into her over-stuffed chair, pulled a blanket over her head, and cried. All the tears she held in reserve after Sam's death flowed freely until the reservoir ran dry. She fell asleep wrapped in the big, soft hug of Sam's favorite chair but awoke a few hours later, unsettled and agitated. Knowing that going to bed would be an exercise in futility, she decided to get started in the bakery.

Chapter 2

Liam O'Connor looked at the leaning tower of legal work on his desk and considered skipping the surprise party he wasn't supposed to know about. His current girlfriend, Stacie, although easy on the eyes and enthusiastic in bed, was easily not the sharpest knife in the drawer.

Stacie Dearborn was from a late-model, upper-tier Chicago family. Her parents made sure Stacie had every opportunity that money could buy, including admission to Notre Dame through an anonymous, albeit obscenely generous, contribution to the President's Campaign for Excellence. In turn, Stacie excelled at ND parties and cheerleading. Both skill sets were more than adequate preparation for social climbing and a "Bring It On!" career in the world of fashion merchandising. She traveled in Chicago's HOV (Highly Ostentatious VIP) lane where Liam could hold his own, but didn't always relish the ride. Their social lifestyle was fast-paced, and the sex was always good, but he wouldn't set a personal goal of becoming the youngest, non-legacy member of the Oak Park Country Club.

Oh, to hell with the growing piles of work on his desk. Yet another curse of a government job with the never-ending work and legal problems of the unwashed masses to sort out.

"I'm only thirty-three once," he said out loud. "Get your game face on, Liam, and let's get this party started."

Liam sorted the papers on his desk into random piles of project-focused work. He could find any document he needed within about fifteen seconds. He had a photographic mind, a gift he'd thanked God for many times. But if a truck hit him tonight, it would be up to God to help the poor sot left behind to sort it all out.

He grabbed his jacket, pushed his fingers through his reddish blond hair and called it good. Liam didn't bother to a great extent with his appearance. With his tall, athletic build, he naturally looked good in clothes. In business suits, he was loyal to Brooks Brothers, but for off-work attire, he was loyal to Mr. Levi Strauss, old t-shirts and whatever hoodie was clean enough to wear. Stacie, on the flipside, was haute Chicago couture chic. She was always pushing him to wear the general look of some Jersey hustler. Not likely.

But he was fond of Stacie. She had a sweet side, a sexy build and, he had to admit, the life he had outside work was never boring because of her "Neverland" approach to partying and event planning. Looks, style and being seen with the right people were everything to Stacie, but her life was like a checkers game, and he preferred chess. He wasn't sure why she hung onto him so ardently. He knew the Notre Dame/Harvard combo had some appeal because she pulled it out like a trump card when she felt the need to. But it wasn't like he was a rising star—you know the type, just "one big case" from making partner status in one of the larger law firms in the Windy City, although he reluctantly admitted to himself he might someday like the challenge of corporate law.

Arriving a few minutes after seven o'clock, Liam walked into Ruztik Restaurant on the thirty-fifth floor of the Logan Building.

"May I help you?" asked the hostess.

"Yes, I'm meeting Stacie Dearborn. Has she arrived yet?"

The hostess smiled knowingly and asked Liam to follow her. The Ruztik's décor was shades of beige, black and brown with splashes of red in the Jackson Pollack-style oil paintings and several impressive Chihuly knock-off glass pieces. This was the newest of Stacie's see and be seen hangouts.

"Surprise!" Stacie was sitting at a table in the bar with two frosted martinis and a plate of a dozen raw oysters on the half shell.

"Just us? How nice, Stacie!" he said in all honesty as he sat down.

"This is just the start. I have the most fabulous night planned for your birthday. Just sit back, relax and enjoy the evening."

She gave him two quick kisses on both cheeks, Euro-style. When they settled into their seats, Stacie raised her martini for a toast.

"To you, darling. Happy birthday!"

Over his glass, Liam noticed she personified the martini she delicately sipped. Her highlighted blonde hair was swept up in an Audrey Hepburn chignon. Her slim, figure-hugging sheath dress was an amazing shimmery charcoal gray that gave her an ethereal sophistication reminiscent of Grace Kelly in High Society. Her jewelry, frosted emeralds and diamonds set in platinum, dangled from her ears and her wrist and mimicked the green of her eyes. A very large ruby ring dominated her right ring finger. Ah yes, the perfect martini with olive accessories. He marveled at her high-heeled, sharply pointed strappy shoes with no, God forbid, pantyhose on her long, expertly tanned legs. He was, as ever, amazed at her attention to detail. Ironically, he preferred her in her well-worn Sunday Notre Dame sweatpants and a t-shirt. But, what the hell? He appreciated her efforts, even though he knew it was more for her sensibilities than his.

"You look fabulous, Stacie. How was your day?"

"Great. I took the day off to plan…well, you'll see," she said with the second Cheshire cat smile he'd seen in less than ten minutes. "Have you ever played Truth or Dare?"

"Hmmm, not since I was twelve. Lydia Prentiss dared me to French kiss her. I took her dare and was sure I'd gotten her pregnant. That kiss officially kicked off my sex life."

"You've come a long way, Romeo."

"I still need lots of practice," he leaned over toward her in a whisper. "What do you say we go back to my apartment, and I'll brush up your Shakespeare?"

"Not yet," she giggled. "We've got more stops to make

before this night of natal revelry is complete. Come on and finish your martini, and then let's move our Canterbury tails."

Wow, that was an uncharacteristically clever comeback for Stacie, he thought. She's full of surprises tonight.

A limo was waiting for them. Oh shit, thought Liam, this feels like a Lindsay Lohan smack down video. But he quickly adjusted his attitude, decided not to say anything and tried to get into the "Livin' Large with Stacie" program for the night.

The limo driver popped a bottle of Dom Perignon as they were getting comfortably seated in the car's luxurious leather. Stacie poured two glasses and toasted to Liam on his thirty-third birthday. He toasted her beauty and style as the limo wound around Lakeshore Drive to face the muted lights of sunset descending on Lake Michigan.

When Stacie closed the privacy window between the backseat and the driver, he stopped paying attention to where they were going and concentrated on other things that were offered to him.

"We are approaching the Oak Park Country Club, Miss Dearborn," the limo driver's voice announced through the speaker system.

"Oh Liam, darling, do get off. I have to pull myself together and fast."

He did as he was told. By the time the limo pulled up under the portico, Stacie's hair and makeup were perfect again. She made an elegant exit from the limo to the appreciative stares from the valets and excessively sanguine greetings from several town and country clubbers.

Waiting at the opulent entrance of the Club, which Liam always thought of as socially antiquated, were Stacie's parents, Jim and Marge Dearborn. Cripes, they looked like gargoyles. You're so vain, he chuckled to himself, you probably think this birthday's about you.

"You've already had your appetizer course. We're your dinner course!" greeted Marge with an overly perfumed hug.

Ugh.

The hug was followed by a strong, golf-grip handshake

from Jim. "How does it feel to be thirty-three years old, Clarence Darrow?" Mr. Dearborn got a big kick out of his own jokes.

"Never better!" Liam returned with an appropriate country club chortle.

"I'd like to talk to you on the 'QT' later, Clarence," said Jim in a quiet voice.

"Right, sir. And feel free to call me Liam."

"Cigars after dinner, old man."

"Roger," confirmed Liam.

"Who's Roger?" And with that Jim turned to catch up with the ladies, laughing heartily at his joke.

These people are outrageous, he thought to himself. Geez, he'd really have to pull himself together to get through this dinner. Not for the first time he wondered if good sex and an active social calendar were really worth the accompanying baggage. Quid pro quo? Legal terms are always so much more meaningful when they apply to real life.

As always, dinner conversation with the Dearborn's centered on Stacie. How cute she was as a little girl. How popular she was in high school. Did you know she was Homecoming Queen her senior year? How she excelled in college? Oh, yes, you went to Notre Dame too, didn't you Liam? Funny how you and Stacie never met until after college. Oh that's right, you were at Harvard when Stacie was in college. And now her career in the big-time fashion world was going so well! The conversation followed its usual progression as it had every time Liam was in the company of the Dearborns. And the funny thing was Stacie never seemed to tire of the subject of Stacie.

After the last of the white-gloved servers brought coffee and crème brulee for dessert, Jim said, "Cigar time, Clarence old boy."

"Yes sir, Mr. Dearborn."

They stepped into the designated smoking room. The Club had banned smoking from its facilities as the nonsmoking trend became politically correct, and not a moment sooner.

Some older members weren't ready to relinquish their "puffed up" rights and privileges. The smoking room was the peace pipe, so to speak, putting the last of the Mohicans on the smokers' reservation.

And then, there were the nouveau cigar smokers, like Jim Dearborn. The man had recently installed a humidor in the room next to his wine cellar. Hard to believe.

"Call me Jim," he said, lighting up his cigar.

"You bet, sir, as soon as you start calling me Liam," he replied between his teeth as he lit his own cigar.

"Okay, Liam. Let's have some honest talk, shall we?" said Jim in all seriousness.

Liam sat up and steeled himself for a lecture coming his way that would have all the subtlety of a heat-seeking missile.

"At your ripe old age, I imagine you're starting to get serious about things. Things like marriage, career, investments and retirement...the really important things."

Not surprisingly, Jim didn't wait for a reply before he continued. "As you can probably tell, we are very fond of our little girl, our precious daughter, Stacie." As if Liam didn't know whom he was talking about. "Her mother and I would like to see her settle down with a man who can give her the life she deserves. We've spoiled her, I know. But she's still as sweet as those happy days when she would climb on her daddy's lap for a hug. The question becomes, 'Who's her daddy now?' She seems to have chosen you, Liam. Can you provide for her? Quite frankly, Marge and I are ready for grandchildren."

Liam puffed on his cigar to buy a little time.

"I'll give that some serious thought, sir."

"I'll give you something else to consider, Liam." Jim leaned closer as if to give him an insider stock tip. "The law firm that handles my company's business is looking for a corporate attorney. I suggested they take a look at you."

"Thank you for your vote of confidence, sir."

"Jim."

"Right, Jim."

"So, as I was saying, I've taken the liberty of talking to Osbourne, Wainwright, Nelson about you. They've done a bit of research. Can't be too careful, you know. Anyway, they like what they see, Liam. Harvard Law speaks volumes. They want to talk to you next week. Do you think you can carve some time out of your government job to take a look at how real law is practiced?"

Ouch. That last comment doesn't even deserve a response, Liam thought. Keep your head and get out of this room as soon as possible.

"Well, Jim. That's a tempting offer."

"Great. Call me at my office Monday morning, and I'll give you all the particulars."

"I'll do that."

As they walked back to the table where Stacie and Marge were talking, Jim put his arm around Liam's shoulder and gave him a fatherly pat.

"Let's keep this conversation between ourselves for now."

"Whatever you say, sir."

"Jim."

"Right, Jim."

They went their separate ways, which at the moment Liam was wishing was a continent apart. Jim Dearborn, Armani suit and all, was too hip-slick-cool for his late middle age. Stacie, unfortunately, would never agree with the way he'd sized up her dad.

"That was fun!" she said as their limo pulled away from Club.

Liam chose not to comment.

"It's almost ten o'clock. We're right on schedule."

"There's more?" he asked.

"Time for some après-dinner drinks, n'est-ce pas? I thought we'd stop back by the Ruztik on our way home. Besides, my car is parked there."

"I took the early train this morning, Stacie. I'm pretty close to running on empty."

"You're staying with me tonight, lover. I'm looking

forward to some Shakespeare Truth or Dare tonight. Have you read *As You Like It*?"

After disembarking the limo, they rode the elevator up to the Ruztik, where the interminably long evening began, and the same hostess was waiting for them with the same smile seemingly frozen in time. She led them past the late-night diners to a small room in the back.

A chorus of dazzling people erupted as the lights were flipped on. "Surprise!"

Damn.

Chapter 3

Some say when a person sneezes, their heart stops.

This morning's first of several brain-jolting sneezes shook Ellen all the way down to her size eight Birkenstocks. And, like every other morning, she envisioned her heart squinting up at her nasal cavity begging for a reprieve. Alas, there was none. Who would have thought her dream of opening a bakery would come with a mild flour allergy after all the baking she'd done growing up?

Ellen Kirkpatrick calculated she'd bagged the sum total of 1,598 heart-stopping flour-induced sneezes since opening The Manito bakery and coffee shop of which she was the proud owner and co-founderess. Still, she couldn't reconcile the fact that almost two years ago a heart-stopping event of a different kind had prematurely killed her husband.

Ellen sighed. Even so, she had to admit that it felt good to look out at her bakery's early morning tableau of dark oak tables, eclectic assortment of chairs, deep comfy couches, and junk-shop art. Itching for a neighborhood Starbucks alternative for years, a steady stream of Spokane's South Hill-ites began trailing through the door. The day typically started with the early-to-work crowd. Then, about eight in the morning, small children still in their jammies munched on The Manito's breakfast cookies designed with their young palates in mind, while the moms took in a good dose of caffeine and adult conversation. As the day progressed a blend of locals concentrated over books, laptops, or newspapers. It became a neutral location for family consultations or a quiet den to read correspondence or write letters. It was private without threat of loneliness and there was a constant flow of good pastries and coffee. Later in the day, The Manito became a haven for after-school snacks and high school homework.

Located smack dab in the middle of one of Spokane's oldest, family-laden neighborhoods, the bakery had once housed the Manito Grocery. Like most neighborhood markets that dotted corners around every city, it was supplanted by impersonal supermarkets. The Terrazzo-floored, fluorescent-lit, behind-the-times local market had hung on longer than most of its contemporaries, mostly because of its famous butcher and free home delivery. Cold cash rarely changed hands. "Sign for it" was as good as gold. Buying the defunct grocery turned out to be the kick-start Ellen needed back into a real life—a life alone.

Was baking an unacknowledged passion she'd suppressed for years while working as a high school counselor? Not likely, but Ellen knew good pastries. Her French-to-the-core grandmother's baked delicacies had been a basic food group in Ellen's youth. While some kids teethed on stone-flavored teething biscuits, Ellen enjoyed her grandmother's rendition of the granite pucks. What a difference a touch of clove made in soothing those tender gums. Ellen recalled spending many nights and weekends at her grandma's, the two of them elbows deep in new recipes. This was how her grandma sheltered Ellen from ugly realities of her mom's alcoholism and many lost weekends. These feelings of stability and security were likely motivators to cash-in her past and start anew with The Manito after Sam died.

So Ellen prayed to the patroness saint of baked goods, Our Lady of Hot Cross Buns, for stamina and guidance. As fate and luck would have it, the South Hill was in desperate want of good pastries and her prayers were answered.

Catching a glimpse of herself as she hoisted another sheet of Thin Thigh Muffins into the oven, an admitted oxymoron that sold like crazy, she noticed her deep auburn hair already wore its daily dusting of flour. A tomboy at heart, she'd given up on glamorous by seventh grade at St. Augustine's grade school, located just a few blocks from The Manito. But clearly there was a middle ground. There was no need to go through the day looking like "Cousin It" from The Addams Family. She pulled a bright yellow and green flower print bandana out of her back pocket and tied it haphazardly around her head. Done. Next up, scones.

And so the rhythm continued, and she plunged her strong fingers and forearms into a heap of dough that reminded her of an old woman's legs. When she added huckleberries to the dough, varicose veins started to appear. Sometimes, she felt bad that her baked goods might contribute to unsightly curds that suddenly appear on unsuspecting middle-age women. More's the pity, she thought, artfully folding the twenty-pounds of dough into itself over and over again. One day, countless Spokane South Hill women would don their tennis togs, glance in the mirror for a final check and, lo and behold, see something startlingly imperfect. Upon closer inspection, the dimples and curds (yes, cellulite) would announce themselves. It would be a life-changing moment, hitting harder than a smoking two-handed return. That curd-like moment had eluded Ellen, for now anyway, and her slim figured-favored gene pool should keep it in abeyance for a while longer. She hoped.

Scones successfully in the oven, Ellen looked out into the bakery past the front counter and reflected on the time she'd invested into its renaissance. She'd poured every waking hour into it, with Molly as her trusted co-pilot. She looked through the slight fog of flour that settled over her bakery every morning and wouldn't dissipate until it was sucked out the front door with the arrival of her early morning customers. Until then, she admired the pastry case lights that created a dream runway for her Pacific Northwest French pastries.

With well-earned satisfaction, she flipped the sign hanging on the glass front door to OPEN and waited alongside her young, eager employees for the first customers of the day. And then she sneezed again.

Molly had popped out of Ellen's uterus hollering, and she kept hollering for seventeen years. She may have hollered well past that, but while she was away at college, Ellen and Sam took out their ear plugs and savored the quiet solitude of their empty nest. Amazing, they thought, how such a gentle soul as Molly could be so loud.

When Molly chose to stay in Spokane and go to Gonzaga University, Sam especially worried she'd never leave the nest and break out on her own, but as it turned out, three miles may as well have been three thousand miles as she rarely visited home.

Over Thanksgiving her freshman year, they recognized the changes in their daughter instantly. Ellen and Sam saw a young woman full of contradictions, yet somehow anchored, steady and dependable. In young adulthood, she could go toe-to-toe with the best of them, but maintained a quiet, self-effacing youthfulness her friends cherished. Molly matured into a rarity among most twenty-four-year-olds, which made her all the more attractive and endearing. Even her much-hated Coke-bottle glasses, which she still had to wear if her contacts weren't in, made beautiful women pale. On Mol, as people close to her nicknamed her, they just reinforced her down-to-earth personality. Perhaps wearing glasses since she was five kept her humble and unimpressed by her natural beauty and sharp intellect. No one would guess Molly had been a feverish renegade in her junior high years. Funky, earth-toned knit hats resembling mutated Shriner's fezzes were her standard logo-wear through middle school. Her mom finally resorted to paying Molly—the young, upstart fashion plate—fifty cents a week to trade in her long johns for tights.

People liked Molly for her wonderful mix of kindness and strength. She was slender in stature, but prodigious in personality. To this day, she was a girl you'd glance at once, maybe twice. But when she spoke, you couldn't look away. At one hundred twenty pounds, her straight-legged Levis hung amazingly well on her, and the hand-knitted sweaters she started fashioning in high school were style statements by the time she hit college. She inherited Ellen's mother's square jaw and fine, straight freckled nose that even Ellen envied. Her long, dark brown hair was usually caught up in a haphazard, careless knot.

Molly was at an age when it was still a romantic notion to run away to experience something bigger, better or different. She loved Spokane for its small big-town feel. It was a perfect place to grow up. It was a great city during her college years, but by her senior year at GU, she started feeling cloistered. She was ready for a new challenge. In addition, several disastrous relationships during high school and college had made her barn sour toward men. After the last blowup with Randall, the scrawny chimp-like rock climber hell bent on getting himself killed, she was not eager to seek another relationship. She'd been satisfied, until recently, helping her mother launch The Manito. The look of the bakery and the two apartments on the second floor—early eclectic meets Spokane shabby—were all her doing. In truth, Molly had more interest in ambience than anise. Now that the bakery business was up and running, it seemed the right time to move on.

Chapter 4

As promised, Liam called Jim Dearborn's office the following Monday morning. Truth be told, he was mildly intrigued about interviewing for a job with one of Chicago's largest law firms. Practicing in the corporate battlefield of law had been the furthest thing from his mind at Harvard. Social justice defined his personal philosophy and professional values. Therein his chosen practice of law followed. He was the top student selected for an internship with the federal government specializing in immigration law and migrant worker cases. After graduation, he was hired by the federal government and assigned to the Chicago office in his late twenties. Now he was responsible for the Midwestern regional office.

Stacie really didn't understand why he spent his valuable time and greatest income-producing years earning a government-level salary, but that was to be expected considering she had never been able to comprehend his morally-strong, yet economically-modest childhood. She reminded him often that he graduated magna cum laude from Notre Dame, was in the top two percent of his class at Harvard Law, and co-editor of the law review. Stacie strongly and repeatedly argued in favor of the amalgamation of his brains and her looks and ambition. In her words it was "a killer combo." More subtly, she reminded him they would produce beautiful, brilliant children. It was clear what she hoped his contribution to their gene pool would be. Though he rarely thought about it, he knew he was considered moderately handsome. Stacie wouldn't be seen with him otherwise. But, he was not Sean Connery or George Clooney beautiful. So their killer combo allowed Stacie's plumage to flash and be appreciated in full living color.

"Good morning, Dearborn Manufacturing, may I help you?"

"Yes, this is Liam O'Connor calling for Jim Dearborn."

"Yes, Mr. O'Connor. Mr. Dearborn is expecting your call."

Liam waited patiently on the phone for an inordinately long time. He was just about to hang up when Jim Dearborn came on the line.

"Liam. Glad you called. I just got off the phone with Mel Wainwright. I took the liberty of making an appointment for you. Osbourne, Wainwright, Nelson is in the Poole Building on the corner of State and Madison. You know it?"

"Yes, I do."

"Good, they're expecting you at four this Thursday afternoon."

"I'm checking my calendar right now."

Geez, this guy has a lot of nerve, thought Liam. It was an odd coincidence, though, because he had nothing on his calendar after three that day. That, literally, was the only block of free time he had all week. Odd.

"Looks like it will work. Should I call and confirm the appointment?"

"Not necessary, old boy. I told Mel you'd be there unless I informed him otherwise. You'd better start cleaning out your desk because you're headed out of the farm league and into the majors." Jim Dearborn, as always, laughed hardest at his own cleverness, and he seemed to enjoy this comment enormously.

"Got a call waiting. Break a leg on Thursday." The phone line went dead. Thursday? Liam had a lot to think about between now and Thursday.

The phone rang and jolted him back to the present tense.

"Hi Liam! Dad says you're on for an interview with his law firm on Thursday. I'm uber-excited. This could be so great for you, and for us."

"Hi Stacie."

"I don't have any plans tonight, lover. Why don't you come over, and I'll pick up some dinner and a movie?"

"Okay, but I can't get there until about eight-thirty. I'm rowing with my crew tonight."

"Perfect. Tiffany wanted to meet me for drinks after work. We'll both get to my place at about the same time. We're going to a new spot called The Icon. I've heard their Grape Nehi martinis are fabulous. Have you heard of it?"

"In all honesty, I can't say that I have," replied Liam.

. . .

Liam needed to talk to someone.

The interview at the law firm of Osbourne, Wainwright, Nelson had gone well. Too well. Liam, as he did with most everything in his life, had approached the interview with the intent to give it his best and win. Why else would he waste his time, or theirs? And then, damn if he hadn't just hung up the phone with Mel Wainwright who said an offer letter from OWN would be delivered by courier within a week. Mel said he was looking forward to working with the newest, and in his words, brightest member of the firm. Holy shit, he landed the job. He'd gone in there with the spirit of a conqueror, but in his mind it was more of a chess game than a sincere career move. And Mel did drop a figure of $150,000 a year with bonuses and a fast track to partner. That figure immediately doubled his current salary. Bonuses were how corporate lawyers could afford new cars, luxury condos, sailboats and country club memberships. Flagrant, yes, but tempting nonetheless.

After a few attempts, he finally got Joe O'Brien—he'd learned early on Joe rarely used his religious prefix—on the phone. Joe had just returned from a Notre Dame Football game against the University of Washington in Seattle. In addition to his priestly and academic duties, Joe traveled with the team to remind the players that God, himself, was a key member of the Fightin' Irish and on their side (case in point,

ND 34 – UW 12). Yet another part of his job description was to raise funds for the University. A visit with Notre Dame alumni chapters and wealthy individuals in the Washington state area was always important to say thank you and remind alumni and friends how much their continued contributions were needed at the Mothership.

Joe suggested that Liam come to South Bend in the late afternoon on Sunday. Liam could take in the early-evening Mass at his old dorm, Morrisey Hall. Afterwards, they could call out for food, and talk.

. . .

As planned, Liam took the commuter train on Sunday from Chicago to South Bend. He could have driven his car, he supposed, but chances were they would end up tipping more than a glass or two of good scotch, and he wouldn't want to risk a DUI on the drive home. The good Fathers, Joe in particular, loved the single malts. Liam purchased an eighty-dollar bottle of Lagavulin for the occasion knowing the smoky, peaty aroma made it a particular favorite of Joe's.

He stopped by Joe's apartment about four-thirty, dropped off the scotch and walked with him to five o'clock Mass at Morrisey Hall. It was good for Liam's soul, and soul searching, to be back on campus where he began his journey toward adulthood. The only son of a machinist and a house cleaner, who both died before he graduated from college, Liam had turned to Joe for advice and counsel. The priest had never failed him. This was, after all, one of the elite higher-education homes for unwed Fathers. And Liam was now in dire need of Joe's parental counsel.

The gospel was Matthew 7:1-2 – Do not judge that you may be judged. For with that judgment you judge, you shall be judged; and what measure you measure, it shall be measured to you. Joe's homily hit the bull's eye. Spiritually, Liam was home.

Joe, in his own right, truly cared for this young man who

had been one of his brightest and most interesting students. A secular father-and-son relationship had naturally begun when Liam lost both parents his junior year. Mr. and Mrs. O'Connor were a hard working, middle-class couple who saved every dime they could to enroll Liam in a Catholic high school and then Notre Dame. Scholarships and work-study jobs took care of tuition, but the total cost of room and board was very expensive for his parents. Liam picked up extra work on campus enabling him to finish school after his parents died. As his dad always said, "The kid isn't afraid of a hard day's work."

Joe enjoyed their debates, the discussions of great works of literature—and the not-so-great ones—and the never-ending dissection of life's struggles. Joe had already deduced the latter was today's topic. It was, after all, Joe who encouraged Liam to apply to Harvard Law and followed his legal career with more than a passing interest.

After Mass, Joe called his favorite Italian spot, Luigi's, and ordered two calzones with the works and Caesar salads. When the order taker on the other end of the phone realized he was speaking with Joe, he promised to personally speed up his order with delivery guaranteed in thirty minutes or less. Joe's apartment was in Halbert Hall where he had been elevated to the status of Father Superior and was responsible for retired elder statesmen of the local tribe of Holy Cross Fathers. He no longer taught English, which was a shame as he was Notre Dame's most popular professor since the school initiated student evaluations. His love of books was visible throughout the few rooms he called home.

"I'm so sorry to hear about your mother," said Liam. "I was hoping to make it to Cleveland for her service. I should have been there."

"No apologies necessary," Joe said sincerely.

"That's kind of why I'm here. To get my priorities collated."

Joe smiled and thought, not for the first time, how kids like Liam made his job easy. They were the reason he could perform one of his hardest jobs, asking for money. Alumni were encouraged to put the university and her students in the same standing as family and heirs. When Joe visualized Liam, and students like him who had accomplished so much despite life's many challenges, it was easier. He had a similar personal history and experience, but of course asking for one's self was rather knotty.

"Take it from the top, my friend."

Liam started with the job offer and how he got there. Joe was familiar with Jim Dearborn, and he knew Stacie, both as a former Notre Dame student and as Liam's girlfriend.

"If I take this job, I'll be taking the directive from Jim Dearborn to practice lucrative corporate law, marry his daughter, join the Oak Park Country Club, become a scratch golfer, smoke cigars and start producing grandchildren."

"Is that what you want?"

"Yes and no. I don't know."

"What's the yes?"

"Yes, I do want to marry and have children."

"And the no?"

"My gut tells me this isn't my package. This dream being pushed my way is not my dream, it's Stacie's. And I don't know if I have the chutzpah to work for Osbourne, Wainwright, Nelson. Up until now, I've never considered this kind of career move."

"Do you remember reading *The Fountainhead* by Ayn Rand in my English Lit class?" Liam nodded. Who could ever forget that rich man, poor man novel?

"Let me find it for you." Joe walked over to his bookshelf.

"How do you find anything in that mess?" Liam asked. "You need a librarian."

"How do you find anything on your desk?"

"Touché."

Joe handed Liam the book. "You can read it on the airplane. Meet me this Friday morning at ten at O'Hare."

"Why the airport?"

"Because you're going with me to Los Angeles to see Notre Dame play UCLA. LA has a number of Notre Dame alumni chapters, and I'll need your help, even if it's just moral support. Besides, you should get out of Chicago-land for a few days. A change of scenery will do you good."

The Luigi delivery arrived, and they devoured the best calzone Liam could remember since college days.

After dinner, they booked Liam on the same LAX flight as Joe. They also secured him a room at The Westin, game headquarters in downtown LA where loyal Irish fans had discount-rate rooms, pep rallies, happy hours, inside game tips from the coaching staff and all of the excitement an Irish football game can muster.

After his third slug of Lagevulin, Liam noticed it was after nine o'clock and called a cab. "I'd better get going if I'm going to make the next commuter train. And now I'll need to compact five work days into four. That leaves little or no time for Livin' Large with Stacie this week."

Joe just nodded in agreement.

The cab driver arrived and they said their goodbyes. As Liam walked out the door, he suddenly stopped and turned back to Joe.

"You said on the phone you had something to discuss with me?"

"It'll wait until Friday. But a small piece of parting advice, ol' boy. Postpone any decisions with regard to the job and the country club for a week or two."

"Roger."

Joe offered a thumbs up.

Liam was so glad when he didn't reply, "Who's Roger?"

Chapter 5

The Manito's two large adjoining rooms offered seating at mismatched antique tables and randomly arranged chairs where patrons enjoyed double-nonfat-grande lattes and their sweet, sumptuous carbohydrates. The wall art groupings ranged from a country scene of Provence at sunset, to Chief Joseph in full headdress praying to the gods on a brown and white pinto at sunrise.

Business was brisk in a breakneck way between seven in the morning and two in the afternoon. And although Ellen experimented with the hours at first, trying afternoon high tea, her patrons eventually determined the hours by being there, or not. Her favorites among the bakery's eclectic group of regulars was a group of ten or so—depending on tee times, travel schedules and doctor appointments—retired men ranging from age sixty to well into their eighties. This alphabet soup mix arrived every morning at seven, even on Saturdays and Sundays. It wasn't long before her younger, professional male customers gravitated to the older, retired gents. These included bankers, accountants, professors, trust funders, lawyers and an architect. The group's demographic makeup made for lively conversation, heated debates, and even some man gossip that Ellen learned could be twice as hen-like as women's.

And then there was Dr. Jack Doyle, one of the newer members of this good old boys coffee klatch, most often referred to as simply the coffee boys. Despite her silent jousting between sadness, fear, pride and exhausting work, Ellen took notice of Jack the first time he walked in the bakery.

Of course, she didn't know she had taken notice until Lou noticed.

"Do I need to take a picture of your face when you look at him?" Lou said. She was seated at her regular perch in the kitchen after the morning rush subsided. "I hate to break it to you, but your eyes are very telling, deary."

"What? Huh, really?" was all Ellen would commit to.

"El, listen to me. It's okay. Sam is not going to reach down out of the heavens and strike you down like a bolt of lightning. Molly is moving on. You have permission to do the same."

Ellen kept her face focused on measuring oats destined to become granola. Lou was right. Sam wouldn't expect her to live the life of a stoic lonely widow, but still…

Lou interrupted Ellen's familiar slide toward relationship guilt. "Even so, my keen instinct tells me Jack Doyle may be a little too complex for you, El. Maybe you could get your feet wet with someone a little less complicated. He reminds me of a jigsaw puzzle you can work on all winter and never finish."

Ellen started pushing Lou toward the back door. "What do you know? Shoo!" Lou's self-appointed role as Ellen's alter ego was getting out of hand. But always insistent on getting the last word in, just as the door was shutting behind her, Lou said laughingly, "And besides, you know what the coffee boys call him? Mr. Darcy! I rest my case."

With Lou gone, Ellen returned to her oats, but not before she took a quick peek out front at Jack Doyle, who was coolly chatting it up with the boys. What in God's name am I doing, Ellen wondered, feeling embarrassed? Nothing, I'm doing absolutely nothing.

. . .

Jack had arrived that morning, ordered his usual Shot in the Dark—two shots of espresso added to a venti drip coffee—and joined the coffee boys. Today's round table topic: why men, most men anyway, don't have friends the way women have friends. Who knows who teed up this morning's high-brow chatter, Jack thought. It was kind of a girly-boy issue for this manly group. Tanner, the only male in the mix who wouldn't wet his pants should anyone so much as hum "Feelings," was probably the culprit, Jack accurately suspected.

Tanner had three college-age girls and a wife—the original wife, not a second or third variety so common among many middle-aged professionals. All this made it okay for Tanner to bring up male friendships, or lack thereof. He'd been ribbed so long for being in touch with his inner female he wore each jab like an Eagle Scout badge of honor.

Poor son-of-a-bitch, Jack thought to himself, looking at the smartly dressed Tanner as he crossed one leg casually over the other. The guy could be a model, what with that cashmere camel blazer and charcoal gray flannel slacks. Do his socks actually match his tie? Pain, pure pain, Jack grimaced silently, but he guessed a guy who can still bounce a dime off his stomach at sixty can get away with wearing a matching sock-and-tie ensemble if he wants. Glancing at his own tired ragg-wool socks, Jack didn't need to bother with a comparison. He wasn't wearing a tie. He didn't even own one. No, wait, he had his dad's hand-me-downs like a navy and red paisley silk tie—timeless, trendless numbers from the '40s, '50s or '60s. Jack was not the black-olive-yellow-green geometric-pattern tie type. He was strictly wedding and funeral. A navy sports coat, a pair of charcoal flannels for winter and khakis for summer, white button-down shirt, spit-shined penny loafers, and he was good to go, anywhere, anytime, any season. His mom called it "sanity wear" in reference to the salvation of her own sanity each time she had to herd Jack and his five brothers into dress clothes.

Half-listening to the conversation of his cronies, Jack noticed Ellen as he did every morning. She didn't look her calm, friendly self, but still looked as great as ever, even with that funky, scarf bandana thing on her head. Like every morning, she gave him her usual seemingly-absent-though-friendly smile that he interpreted as, "Yeah, hi, how are you?

Uh huh, that's nice," all without missing a beat working the morning crush of empty stomachs. And as usual, Jack simply nodded back and quickly looked away. And as usual, he felt the thump of disappointment toward the perfunctory greeting. Dang, he thought with frustration as he tried to tune back into the morning group-talk.

It didn't take long to catch up. The wily sociologists, though weak in their methodology, had confirmed men are by and large incapable of having authentic friendships similar to those of women. Hiding his regret that Ellen surely would never consider him anything but one of the coffee boys, Jack pulled out his Teflon demeanor.

"So men don't have men friends. Is that a problem?" he asked, with a certain acidic tone.

With that, everyone at the table suddenly started examining their coffee cups as if they'd never seen one before or headed for a refill. "Hell no, there's nothing wrong with that. We're guys!" Jack proclaimed loudly after everyone had returned to the table. Once again, The Jack Doyle School of Emotional Solitude brought the moment back to solid ground. "How did the Mariners play last night, anyway?" he continued. He wished Ellen could hear his pronouncements.

Jack felt as smug as he did back in his third year of medical school when he'd finally achieved near perfection in avoiding emotional discomfort. This morning, just like the morning after his first and last girlfriend had called off their year-long romance, he proudly wore a grin that masked his feelings splendidly. He'd been a late bloomer in regard to women, too busy focusing on the satisfaction he experienced attaining academic success. He was as surprised as the next guy when he fell hard for Lisa, a second-year medical student from Hawaii. He was equally as surprised when Lisa fell out of love with him. The night she announced she felt their relationship was paralyzing her, Jack sat up until dawn nursing his ego before heading to class the next morning suffering from a major no-sleep hangover. He hauled himself onto the bus feeling as though he'd contracted polio, and it frightened him that he wasn't in top form for his usual no-hitter game. This had to be remedied. He wondered if he'd gone temporarily insane by even dating Lisa. What had he been thinking? Medical school doesn't allow for distractions and therefore neither should Jack. By the time he walked into his first lab, he'd pasted a smile on his face, buoyed by the fact he knew a woman would never again jeopardize his hold on his professional and emotional life. Since then, Jack, a smart kid from a big demonstrative, raucous Catholic family, found life safer and easier with his emotional switch securely in the off position. After medical school, he tried dating a few times, but he never let anyone else in past the shallow end. It was easier that way. And now, after all these years, sometimes, like every morning when he walked into The Manito, Ellen managed to flip the switch on for a nanosecond. He wasn't sure which bothered him more, Ellen's apparent disinterest in him or the fact he felt disappointment because of it. Regardless, he felt the now-expected sting that preceded that loss of control and vulnerability, but in a flash was able to flip the switch back to off. Other than this early-morning kick in the gut, Jack did okay without romantic attachments of the committed variety and all the pitfalls that came with them. He had his brothers, nieces and nephews, and sister-in-laws, and that was all the emotional foundation he needed.

He even accepted proudly the "Mr. Darcy" moniker the coffee guys stuck on him; though the first time he heard it he did a Google search to make sure it wasn't an insult. He discovered the character from *Pride and Prejudice* actually suited him—successful and aloof. After a moment of uncharacteristic self-reflection, Jack found he had no problem with "Mr. Darcy."

Yet, as comfortable, relatively uncommitted, and uncomplicated as his life was, Jack was surprised when he'd wake up in the morning looking forward to seeing Ellen.

He got up from the table and was putting on his old London Fog jacket when he noticed Ellen had retreated back to the kitchen. By now, she was normally ensconced behind the counter with the rest of crew. She looked exhausted and preoccupied. In spite of himself, he wondered what had thrown her off kilter.

. . .

So did Lillian Johnson.

When Jack Doyle and his brothers were growing up on Overbluff Road, Miss Johnson was the neighborhood enigma. She had never married. Instead, after attempting a brief career as a singer in San Francisco night clubs, she came home to take care of her parents and was still living in her childhood home.

Of all the kids on Overbluff Road, she wisely chose Jack to be her weekend handyman and summer gardener. He was by far the most accountable. In turn, Jack's earnings helped pay for his college tuition and set him on the path to becoming a physician. Much later in life he guessed, correctly, that Miss Johnson had seen something promising in him—a serious loner amongst the local teenagers. Jack clearly remembered when Lillian's father died. He was a senior in high school, and Miss Johnson asked him to be a pallbearer at her father's funeral. He felt honored, considering he was really just a punk-kid. Shortly thereafter, her mother died. From then on, Miss Johnson lived in the huge house by herself. Jack worried about her for a while after he left for college, but his fading worries were needless. Miss Johnson's life was very small and orderly. Like Jack, her routines were set. No surprises. Jack wondered if now, at nearly ninety, Lillian may be feeling as though she missed an episode or two in this mini-series called Life.

Observing the cat-and-mouse game Jack was playing with Ellen, Miss Johnson wanted to shake some sense into the two youngsters. She didn't know Ellen well enough, but liked her spunk. She recognized her as a woman working very, very hard to survive financially and emotionally. She admired her quiet strength.

Lillian had mildly encouraged Molly's efforts to get to

know her. It was impossible not to like the energetic, younger Kirkpatrick woman. Molly was oblivious to her own rather severe demeanor and just plopped herself down at Lillian's table one morning pretending—or choosing—not to see The New York Times privacy curtain. And, she admitted, she saw a lot of herself in Molly and soon welcomed the opportunities when she would ask to sit down for a quick chat. Their conversation started out as polite, cursory, and brief, but morphed into more personal talks over the last few months as Molly grappled with her plans for the future. She never presumed to tell Molly what to do, so she listened and only gradually offered kernels of wisdom.

"I don't know, Miss Johnson, I've loved this time with mom and getting the bakery going, but I know I need to move on, at least for a while," Molly said with more passion than she probably intended. "I'm still in my twenties! I need to experience more than Spokane has to offer at this time in my life."

If only Molly knew how well I understand her desire to leave Spokane, Miss Johnson thought to herself. Hadn't she had the same feelings over sixty years ago? Sixty years. Imagine that. It felt like yesterday.

"Molly," Miss Johnson said in her gravelly voice. "Would you like some advice from someone who, believe it or not, had a similar experience to yours?"

Molly nodded.

"You've given your mother the best a daughter can give, love and support, and that's all anyone really needs. Those things won't change if you leave."

"I know that, but I don't know if mom does," said Molly, her eyes starting to sting with tears.

Ellen always told Molly that her bladder was too close to her eyes, and she was so right. Her eyes made her the personification of an open book, which was okay with someone like Miss Johnson, but a real handicap when she wanted to exude serenity. Never able to master the art of being mysterious, Molly cleared her vision with a few dozen

41

rapid blinks and picked up on what Miss Johnson was saying.

"Give your mother some credit. She may not like it, but she wants you to do what you need to do. She raised you that way. She's a mother, and by practice, most mothers are very familiar with unconditional love. Perhaps the uncertainty you're experiencing is the fear of change mixed with excitement, and the wisdom to know that it's time to forge ahead. For heaven's sake, don't confuse those feelings with deserting your mother."

Molly gave Miss Johnson's last advice some thought, which was hard not to do with the older woman's sharp eyes boring into hers. Wow, I pity the poor sucker who tries to pull a fast one on her, Molly thought. She quickly gave Miss Johnson's forearm a gentle pat of appreciation, knowing the gesture might be rebuffed. It wasn't. Miss Johnson returned the gesture with a warm, subtle wink.

. . .

Watching Miss Johnson situate herself behind the newspaper, Ellen was surprised at the bond she felt toward the statuesque woman each morning when she glided into the bakery. It had taken some time to figure out the connection, but Miss Johnson's subtle likeness to Peggy Duncan, her own mom, was becoming startlingly obvious.

Of course there were the obvious differences, like Miss Johnson didn't show any indication of being the raging alcoholic Peggy had been. But Ellen sensed in Miss Johnson a certain by-the-book discipline mixed with a healthy dose of humor that together masked a deep kindness she had loved—and still missed—about her mom. Not knowing if she could survive another Peggy Duncan, Ellen warned herself to keep her distance as she lifted a fresh thermos of cream onto the massive oak breakfront housing the necessary evils to please today's finicky coffee drinkers: Splenda, Equal, raw sugar, cinnamon, nutmeg, skim milk, skinny straws, fat straws and, of course, a lot of real cream. She discreetly peered at Miss

Johnson, as though she were eyeballing potential sanctuary or possible prey.

From her comfort zone behind the counter, Ellen heard it, the laugh. She snapped her head around, jerking her scarf cap, a tie-dyed bandana headdress, askew. Tucking some of her shoulder-length, slightly wavy chestnut brown hair back into hiding, she blinked unbelievingly. Miss Johnson's laugh— more like a hardy, audible warble—was her mother's unmistakable laugh reincarnated! Since the first time Miss Johnson's size eleven-AAA feet carried her into The Manito, her laugh sent a shiver of apprehension through Ellen. It was a déjà vu moment from childhood. On closer inspection, the panic was really just a dull thud in her core, mixed with a dash of hope that her mom had somehow slipped unseen into the bakery, to check up on her. But, of course, it could only be Miss Johnson. Oh, what memories that vivid laugh brought back into focus.

Aside from Jack, Chuck Robinson, the tall, red-headed, gangly retired newspaper editor—and official top dog of the coffee boys at The Manito—was the only man in the daily mix that could pull such uninhibited self-exposure out of Miss Johnson. Turning toward the walk-in freezer, the cost of which was equal to a semester of college for Molly, Ellen wondered what astutely cynical observation (most likely from Jack or Chuck) was rewarded with such an honest, genuine laugh from the lily-white octogenarian this morning.

Later that evening, she and Molly were in her apartment watching a Food Network Channel dessert competition— which they both undeniably agreed that Ellen could win with one arm tied behind her back. During an ad for a weight loss program, Ellen muted the television and off-handedly mentioned to Molly how many similarities Miss Johnson shared with her grandmother.

"Look at her, Molly. She's tall and willowy. She had to have been quite an athlete in her day, or could have been, just like mom. She plays her cards so close to her chest she could be an ESPN channel poker champ. And her clothes! She's stunning! She has to be incredibly smart or else she's one heck of a fraud."

Instinct and observation told Ellen that Miss Johnson was no teetering old woman who needed caring for, proven by the fact the woman had a sizeable fortune she'd managed herself since her parents died.

"Geez, mom, you sound a little manic here," Molly laughed.

Molly never knew her grandma personally, but from the stories she'd heard, and from what she knew of Miss Johnson, what her mother was saying was probably a compliment to them both. "I've always thought grandma was cool, except maybe when she got drunk and fell into the bushes. But, you've always said when bright people get screwed up they do it better than anyone, right?"

"Oh yes, and my mother was a stellar model for that theory," Ellen said. "Maybe if I made more of an effort to get to know Miss Johnson, I'd appreciate the similarities and not be so freaked out by them."

"Why don't you?" Molly suggested. "And, try to stay away from the dark side, okay?" The last thing her mom needed right now was a meltdown over Peggy Duncan's mixed nuts and bourbon days.

Ellen picked up on her daughter's concern and quickly reassured her. "I don't go there much anymore, Mol. If anything, I'm finding this mystical connection to Miss Johnson comforting in some odd way. Honestly, no worries here, Molly. Since your dad died, I've become surprisingly proficient at vagrant unexpected life events. I just soil my britches a little and carry on with the tremendous grace I've never had, but can fake as well as the best of them. And now I have to throw this graceful bag of bones into bed."

"What? Here we are spending quality mother-daughter time together and you want to go to bed?" Molly yipped.

"Yes, deary. My alarm clock starts barking at me, it seems, before I close my eyes."

"Night, mom, love you!" Molly said, and headed off to

bed herself.

"Likewise"

Ellen was going to miss their nightly chats. So was Molly. She was leaving in a week.

. . .

Molly looked around her apartment and reluctantly admitted how much she would truly miss the little paradise, a Shangri-La, she'd created for herself. When her mom sold the only home she'd ever known and bought the tired, old Manito Grocery building, she cautiously went along with the idea. But given carte blanche to design the interior of the bakery and the two apartments, Molly found an excitement and a latent talent.

For months, with the dogged determination of a Jack Russell terrier on the hunt, she scoured second-hand shops, flea markets and garage sales for bona fide antiques, unique retro decorations, mildly distressed wooden chairs and tables, and leather sofas for the two large seating areas. The front of the old grocery had floor-to-ceiling windows, so awnings were installed to keep the sun from blinding customers on sunny days, but still let in enough natural light for seasonal affective disorder-afflicted, sun-starved Spokanites in the winter. Acoustically, the high ceilings were a problem. It could be incredibly loud when the bakery was jamming. But, as she found out through experience and observation, people liked the din. It gave off an edgy buzz of excitement, like attending a special gala event without the hassle of a ticket and a tux.

Molly chose a mocha espresso shade of paint for the walls that oozed a soothing vibrancy. Kind of like a latte. The perfect coffee drink that perks you up in the morning and then mellows you out—all in one cup—for a mere three dollars and fifty cents, plus tax.

She restored the store's three-inch crown molding and stained it a dark cherry red, adding Old World charm to the fifteen-foot ceilings and matching chair rail molding. The solid brick wall on the east side of the bakery was her favorite feature. It continued up to the second floor and was the focus of the apartment Molly had so devotedly made hers.

Her apartment had become a palette of personal expression. Molly began with solid, comfortable furniture in earth tones. Loving the challenge of color, she added peacock blue vases, pomegranate and tangerine paisley pillows, retro-classic movie posters—a variety of styles and pieces she chose because she liked them and not because she had any theme in mind. Yes, leaving this comfortable cocoon she'd created would hurt, but her decision was made. No turning back now.

Chapter 6

A single aluminum goose-neck lamp was among the list of scant furnishings Molly could expect in her room at Providence House. She would have just enough space for a few clothes and personal belongs and was instructed not to bring anything larger than a lap top, which left her apartment at home completely intact. The arrangement more than pleased Ellen. Just seeing to the tasks of watering her plants and feeding Swimmy (the Goldfish) helped Molly's impending move seem less permanent. The apartment would feel like Molly had merely run to the store and would return at any moment. Hopefully a year wouldn't seem as long as it sounded.

Ellen couldn't leave the bakery for more than a few days so they collectively decided Lou would fly down with Molly and help get her settled.

"Promise you'll come home after your year is up?" said a tearful Ellen.

"I promise, Mom," said an equally weepy Molly.

But unlike Ellen's sense of culminating sorrow, Molly was full of anticipation, like waiting for the clap of thunder after a colossal flash of lightning. This is a good move for me, Molly thought, and resolutely boarded the Southwest Airlines flight to LAX.

Lou took a seat beside Molly on the plane and looked fondly at the young woman who was like a daughter to her. Sure, she'd had lots of "kids" as a teacher. As a coach she was able to create a team family, a bond between herself and the girls she helped guide through the ups and downs of high school by way of the softball field. This was different because Molly was chosen family, and she unconditionally loved her. Lou remembered Molly as an inquisitive, precocious toddler; a gangly, pimply teenager; a rebellious, outspoken college student. And now look at her. She was athletic, charming and blessed with those killer Black Irish good looks. Most impressive of all to Lou was that Molly was smart, savvy, kind, and genuinely unaffected by her physical beauty. This girl is nobody's fool, she thought to herself. Okay, sure, well, except in love. Molly had a history of attracting more than her share of eccentric, deadbeat boyfriends. Starting over in Los Angeles was a way to reinvent herself just as her mom had done with The Manito. Things happen for a reason, Lou mused.

"How's Molly's Big Adventure so far?" Lou asked as she flipped through the SkyMall magazine.

"You know, not too bad. I have a good feeling about this detour in my life. It feels like when you decide to get off the freeway and take the country roads for a change of pace."

"Comparing a move to LA with taking the rural route is a stretch of the imagination," Lou observed jokingly.

"Ha-ha. What I mean is if I stayed on the academic highway, I would be heading to the University of Washington to get my master's. What else do you do with a dead languages major besides teach or go to law school? Maybe I'll end up going back to school someday, but now is definitely not the time."

"Right. That's how Liam O'Connor turned his degree in the classics into a law degree from Harvard!" Lou reminded her.

"Who? Oh yeah, him. Remember, you promised to put your matchmaking skills on hold for a year, Yenta." Molly rolled her eyes and thought how much Lou annoyed and endeared her with such dogged tenacity. Dear God, she was like a freaking bird dog about this Liam cat. "Right," Lou smiled.

A brilliant game plan was starting to formulate, and it had

nothing remotely to do with Lou's high school softball team. She needed to call Father Joe at Notre Dame and run an idea by him. A combination of divine and secular intervention was in order.

Chapter 7

An ice cold beer and a little late evening weeding in the Sisters' hearty vegetable garden was all Molly thought of on her commute home. That and peeling herself off the plastic bus seat at the next stop. Needless to say, Molly found LA's late-summer September heat, humanity, traffic, and smog overwhelming, uncomfortable, and very un-Spokane. However, she had become quickly immersed in the work at El Centro Community Center and made herself a promise to concentrate on the positive. Remember, she told herself, this is only a one-year assignment.

At El Centro, Molly was surrounded by poverty and its consequences. The Sisters of Providence, who by choice not birth, devoted their lives to relieving misery in others less fortunate. Molly soon found herself admiring not only the Sisters' work but their lifestyle as well. From the spare simplicity of her room to the quiet harmony of their day-to-day life, Molly felt herself recognizing a work ethic and character she'd always had an awareness of, yet never fully explored. And so, with each passing week, Molly found herself speaking the language of a wider world. "Amazing" she would often say to herself. "This is learning, and, as trite at is sounds, I can't get enough."

The room she was assigned was bare of any decorations. That was fine for the Sisters, but soon Molly filled her room with a few tasteful, yet personal touches as she fell back on her old habits of visiting second-hand thrift stores on Saturdays.

Before long, she discovered each Sister had distinctive preferences and interests. On Sundays, she quietly delivered a gift to one Sister for whom she'd bought the day before. They were simple gifts, but it spoke of Molly's understanding that each woman was unique. They were special not only to God, but to her, too.

It started with Sister Aracelia whom, in particular, Molly had struck up an immediate friendship. Growing up in migrant camps, Sister Aracelia had an understanding of street life, language, and problems of Mexican immigrant families. She was born in America, although her parents were illegals from Mexico. As a child, her family traveled the migrant worker circuit moving from crop to crop, from lettuce in the fields of central California to the apple orchards of the Okanogan Valley in Washington state. One year, when she was about ten, they traveled as far as Traverse City, Michigan, during the cherry picking season thinking the family could make more money—which they did, if you didn't count the added travel expenses and the unreasonably-high rent charged by the orchard owners that erased any extra income they might have made. Thereafter, picking cherries at Flathead Lake in Montana was the furthest point east in their seasonal circuit.

Molly discovered Montana was a place that held special memories for Sister Aracelia. Urban mining one Saturday, she found a small creamer with an image of a cowboy throwing a lasso and the accompanying words, "Montana, Land of the Shining Mountains." Molly gift wrapped the creamer and gave it to Sister Aracelia the next day. Sister A, as Molly sometimes called her, was visibly touched by the gesture. Seeing how something so small could do great things, Molly began her quest to find something unique for each of these special and dedicated women who had accepted her unreservedly.

When Molly had a particularly challenging case, or needed some street-savvy, Sister Aracelia stepped in as interpreter and guide. Occasionally if a tough, young Latino created an ugly scene at El Centro, she could be called upon to adjust his attitude and miraculously find a way to communicate and finally make positive progress.

Molly walked into a huge caseload at El Centro.

Managing a challenging work schedule was an expectation of the job from Day One. Nevertheless, she was surprised when each case was like a multi-vitamin building her strength to tackle the next one. Molly felt good and garnered strength from being a person for others. What wasn't expected was how involved she would get in the lives of the people who defined her caseload. The circumstances of one family in particular were not only keeping her occupational muscles pumped up, but were keeping her awake at night. The Raigosa family had been in the states for twenty years. The federal government, under the current Immigration Customs Enforcement administration, was on a deportation binge and real people were targets in the crosshairs; case in point, the Raigosas.

. . .

Les Schwanbeck had been chasing down illegal immigrants for more than thirty years and had seen all the bullshit and heartache even a perceived tough guy like himself could handle. Back in the day, with a whopping six years in the Los Angeles Police Department under his thirty-two-inch belt, he was naïve enough to think that working for immigration was a step up to a place where his keen intuition and so-called people skills wouldn't be wasted on petty street thugs. His reputation for working well with people stemmed from the simple fact he didn't like beating the shit out of people, a habit most young street cops thought translated into bravado.

Now, what felt like centuries later, sliding behind his desk was like squeezing into a booth at Denny's—a booth that was far too small for his cumbersome girth. He took a quick look at piles of "urgent" cases needing review. He also thought about making a quick run to Sears for some suspenders and assigning his now forty-inch belt to the round file. He chastised himself for letting his body go to hell, but his gut had been killing him lately, and his damn belt didn't help any. His former, slighter circumference was a shadow fading in the rearview mirror.

"Shit, I've got this barrel of a gut, skin pallor that looks like I've been on ice for the last ten years, and a crew cut best suited for a Marine. I might as well complete the look and give this paunch of mine some breathing space. No one said this was a fashion show," he mumbled to no one in particular.

The Raigosa case wasn't helping any, either. He'd been popping anti-acids like candy from a Pez dispenser the past couple of months trying to undo the miserable knot the family's life had become. It wasn't that the Raigosas' situation was all that unique. In fact it was a situation that was becoming overwhelmingly common. Raigosa, Rodriguez, Chavez—they were all eating at him. Literally. He wished he could trace his declining attitude back to when the Immigration and Naturalization Service became part of Homeland Security and was assigned the heavy-handed new name: Immigration Customs Enforcement. But the organization had become political long before 9/11. Now it just had more bipartisan heft. Immigration was intense election and legislative fodder. The administration was watching the numbers like Nordstrom watches month-end sales figures, and since 2004 the numbers were good, depending on your political preference. Managers of high-level production houses were being arrested regularly and so were the people they hired with illegally-obtained papers, or no papers at all.

The Raigosa family was caught up in this new enforcement strategy, and so was Les Schwanbeck.

"What do you think?" he said, looking over at Graham, his office mate of six months. Graham was half Les's age and still far too much of a Boy Scout eager to earn his next badge, which usually meant doing whatever ICE policy dictated. Les kissed that manual goodbye about five years ago. He was pretty sure the kid had it tattooed on his ass.

"What do I think about what?" Graham asked cautiously. He was never quite sure when Les was going to pull his chain.

"Let's see, I wanna know which glitzy martini bar you and

your dipshit friends are thinking of going to after work," he said sarcastically. "For some reason—oh yeah, it's our job, I wanna know what you think about these people, the Keystone beer crowd," Les said, nodding toward the stack of manila file case folders with color-coded tabs that denoted urgency.

God, I should quit yanking this kid's chain, but it's so entertaining. How else is he going to learn how this three-ring circus really works?

"They're breaking laws, the least of which is not paying taxes. They take advantage of this country's open-door policy. They need to go back."

Les cocked his head. The kid made it all sound so simple.

"Well, that's a plucky idea, Graham! I mean, really, look at all the fine, upstanding American citizens begging for all those below minimum-wage jobs these people steal from them. Jesus, if only I could find a decent lawn mowing job, with no health care or benefits, I'd retire tomorrow!" He'd seen some joker running for governor of California on television last night say he was against minimum wage because it was never meant to support families. Les had gone ballistic wondering if that colossal jerk knew how many families actually lived off minimum-wage jobs these days. He refused to let Graham get him riled up. He'd learned long ago that dumb-ass-stupid was an incurable human condition.

Instead, Les settled for letting his belt out to the last possible notch.

"Look, Les, I know the script has changed since you started, but the law is the law. We're paid to uphold immigration laws. No one has a gun to your head forcing you to keep this job."

"No, just a wife who is a half-rabid canine, a house payment I just refinanced, oh, and the obvious fact I like to eat," Les was laughing, which was a lot easier to do now that he could breathe.

"Just try to remember it isn't my fault it's not the old days," Graham said defensively.

That said, Graham effortlessly lifted dozens of files and

headed for the vault, a drab windowless room where minions would scan, shred or file the closed cases. He looked more FBI than ICE. Way too clean cut. There wasn't a hair out of place. His pants always held a crease and the kid even had freckles, which really didn't add to his tough guy image.

Les took the one-two punch because the kid was right. The glory days were over. These days high-profile, so-called glamour cases were handled in Washington. The LA bureau had morphed into a detention and deportation unit. Gone were the days of sending back smug, moneyed-up, big hitters entering the U.S. to expand their line of work, which included fraud, money laundering and avoiding arrest in their native country. A guy got a real rush nailing those flagrant sons-a-bitches. Today is different. Today, there are over twelve million undocumented immigrants in the U.S. It sure makes it hard to plan your day.

Opening the file on his desk, Les leafed through the past week's work on the Raigosa case, one that had become standard issue since Mexico's economy began sinking into the crapper. With no hope for economic or political survival, poor and even once middle-income Mexicans were flooding over the border into Arizona and Texas like dead leaves in a strong wind. California had become for them what it had long been for thousands of Americans, a land of opportunity. Los Angeles in particular had become a Mecca. It was where everyone went to become something better—a movie star or a McDonald's fry cook. Everyone fit in. No one stood out in the crowd. The Raigosas fit in, maybe for a little while longer. Unfortunately, one member of the family refused to stay under the radar. The kid, Hector, was in trouble with the law, and the entire family was red-flagged because of him. Les was weary of history repeating itself. More accurately, he was getting tired of playing the same tedious role as immigration history played itself out over and over again.

Chapter 8

"Hi Lou! It's great to hear your voice. How's mom? Is everything okay?"

"Relax, Molly. Everything's fine. Are you doing anything this weekend?"

"No, why?"

"Peyton and I are flying down for the Notre Dame-UCLA game and I have an extra ticket. Can you come along?"

"You bet I can." She would gladly cancel her Saturday thrift store shopping date with herself. Molly never realized how exciting a football game could sound. And a visit from her Spokane family sounded even better. The LA heat and the seemingly insurmountable social problems could seriously dampen the cheery co-ed side in a girl. Other than hearing the Rosses talk about their annual pilgrimage to Notre Dame Football games in South Bend, she'd never actually attended one.

"We're staying at the Westin Hotel in downtown LA with all of the other rabid ND fans. Do you want us to book you a room? Or are you becoming too spoiled at the Sisters of Providence Hotel and Spa?"

"Proceed with the booking, please and thank you! Otherwise I'd spend most of my time commuting and never see you. This city is nuts to get around in."

"Consider it done. We arrive Friday about five. We'll be looking for you in the lobby at six. Get a kitchen pass because I'm going to keep you until Sunday. Our flight out of LAX leaves late afternoon. Until then, you're all mine."

"Thanks, Lou. Can't wait to see you and Peyton. Any

chance Mom can come?"

"Nope. I tried. She's married to that bakery now."

"OK. I'll call her tonight."

"She'd like that."

"See you Friday."

Chapter 9

The black market hip-hop version of the Notre Dame fight song bantered from his cell phone.

"Coffee tomorrow?" barked at him.

Father Joe O'Brien instantly recognized Clare McGuire's husky voice, which contradicted her perky, pixie-like looks. She'd arrived on campus as the new dean of student affairs a year ago, and since then, the two of them had seen eye-to-eye on virtually everything. Barely reaching five-foot-two, she had short, spiked red hair and a tendency to wear anything that would distinguish her from the nuns on campus. Everyone assumed any single female over thirty—she had about eight years on that milestone—was a nun.

"No nun shoes for me," she announced shortly after her arrival at Notre Dame, referring to the stereotypical sensible shoes worn by most of the good sisters—as if her proclivity for dropping the ef-bomb and other choice profanities weren't convincing enough that she wasn't a nun. Soon after they became friends, she and Joe started having what would become their standing Monday morning Starbucks session. One particular Monday morning she proudly showed him her new red patent leather Dansko clogs. It was the first time Joe saw the almost childlike side of Clare, and he loved it. From the moment she stepped foot on campus as a new dean, she had been sure to wear a serious game face informing everyone, that despite her youth and size, she was good at her job and would be treated accordingly.

"What is the deal with these nuns?" she laughed, tucking her clog-clad feet back under the table. "Vatican II frees them from having to wear twenty pounds of black wool, but they continue to wear dowdy shoes! Didn't they get the memo?"

No, Clare wasn't one for cutting anyone much slack. Students recognized the way she shed her outer shell if the reason or person merited the effort, and they were nuts about her. Some faculty, like Joe, knew she parceled out trust cautiously, and although she had a long list of friends around campus, she kept her small inner circle close.

Clare snapped Joe back to the moment. "Hello? Coffee? Tomorrow?"

"Why is it you sound like a staccato mob boss when you get all fired up? Complete sentences are expected on this prestigious campus."

"You know me, always the rule breaker." She sounded proud.

"Sure, I wouldn't miss our Monday coffee for anything. See you tomorrow," Joe said, preparing himself for Clare's predictable sign-off.

"Okay." And that was it. Click.

The woman does not waste words, Joe thought as he turned off his phone.

He admired the purposeful, willful, and sometimes bombastic approach to living Clare executed in her world, even if it disrupted the serene, slack-water calmness of his academic life. Admire? No, what Joe felt was more than that. Joe flat out envied, even coveted, Clare's independence that presented a bold-faced happiness his life lacked for far too long. He wondered if the loud turbulence thrashing around inside him about his life at Notre Dame—as a priest—was apparent to anyone but himself.

Joe knew Clare would never tolerate this kind of unsettled, questioning existence.

"Lord, why me and why now?" the priest asked his omnipresent almighty boss as he plugged his cell phone in its charger for the night.

Studying his small monastic two-room dwelling, he felt a lump the size of a communion wafer seize up in his throat.

The oak-trimmed room was home, and its sparse but comfortable furnishings were the sum of his material, worldly belongings. His grandfather's cherry wood desk and a funky bookshelf he'd taken from his parents' home when he left Cleveland to attend college in South Bend over thirty years ago dominated the space. One could hardly consider these treasures signs of blatant disregard for the vow of poverty. His books, however, were copious. There were hundreds of them, each one a diary of his constant quest for understanding the real and spiritual world and how the two inexplicably came together, or not. C.S. Lewis was squeezed between the writings of St. Ignatius Loyola and Jon Krakauer, who neighbored volumes exploring Darwinism. He couldn't recall how many times he'd read Durant's *History of Civilization*. He learned early as an academic priest the importance of portraying oneself as being academically, spiritually, and socially well-rounded. He'd been quite successful accommodating this expectation, but he knew for at least the past two years the effort was tearing him apart. For a short while, he took weak solace in observing countless other priests face their own struggles. Younger priests, himself included, called it mid-priest crisis. His conversation with Liam punctuated his feeling of being at loose ends and he felt very much the fraud by giving the kid advice.

"You there, Lord?" he asked again, staring hard at the Crucifix that had once hung in his parents' bedroom. "Are you forsaking me? You know about that first hand."

Mindlessly, he picked up a tennis ball and initiated a game of catch with the wall behind his desk. Normally, when these waves of questioning hit, he'd haul his six-foot, one hundred seventy pounds of skin and bones out on a run. It kept him at his fighting weight, and the rhythm of his feet acted as a metronome for prayer. But tonight he knew prayer wouldn't remedy the mood that hung over him. Never mind he didn't have the energy to change out of his black suit and white priest's collar he'd worn all day. Against his almost white blond hair and blue eyes, he always thought his black suit made him look like a surfer at a costume party and avoided wearing the uniform whenever possible.

"Okay, Lord, throw it at me. Give me all you've got. It can't get any worse than it already is. How about a good old-fashioned flood? That caught everyone's attention back in the day."

He gave the tennis ball one last whap, which would surely make his neighbor, a mild-mannered, anemic academic wince, and then crossed the room to pour another scotch. He sipped his drink, studying the richness of the Turkish rug covering the worn pine floor of his room. He got the rug for almost nothing while teaching at a university program in Greece. The students had been more into ouzo than his Greek mythology classes, but it had been an exhilarating year studying and teaching about the great philosophers on their home turf. His bouts of doubt, followed by self-chastisement and fear, began before Greece and escalated to full gale force when he got back to South Bend. Turning the almost empty glass in his hand, he felt the liquid ease him away from today's episode.

. . .

Just a few blocks away, in an old neighborhood crowded with small, tidy brick homes traditionally occupied by Notre Dame faculty, Clare also plugged her cell phone into its charger, turned off the lights and got ready for bed. She liked her home and the privacy it promised after long days surrounded by needy students and demanding faculty. She enjoyed the job, but her disappointment in the university was simmering. She'd left Northwestern after five years with the naïve hope that not all universities suffered from severe elitist tendencies and faculty paranoia. Wrong again.

"I'd hoped God would be channeling through the priests or something, and maybe this place might be a little more real," she confided in Joe a couple of weeks earlier. "Boy, I missed that putt by a mile."

The University lobbied hard to get Clare. Highly

credentialed with a business degree from Yale and a PhD in psychology from USC, she'd carved an unprecedented niche in student affairs. She was well published and way ahead of the game when it came to tackling frightening and unexpected situations now popping up on college campuses. Academia had been broadsided by societal malfunctions like suicide and domestic terrorism.

"My God, intellectuals can be so ostrich-like! How could you not expect the shit to hit the fan here given what's going on all over the world?" She was talking to a group of deans, many who reacted to her as though she were a Pentecostal television evangelist speaking in tongues. Joe tried to temper her frustration, explaining the expectation that, for the most part, colleges were and should be off limits to certain human blundering, to which Clare literally called bullshit.

"I'll bet Northwestern is really mourning your departure," Joe retorted in an effort to lighten her intensity.

Clare laughed at herself, which was a rare attribute among Notre Dame faculty. Joe maintained she had more humility than any priest on campus, including himself.

Lights off and doors locked, Clare headed to bed with the latest *Utne Reader*. She liked Sunday evenings, especially after weekends like this one where she spent time outdoors. She and some friends had cycled out into Indiana's hinterlands enjoying the long rides before they would be forced to hang up their bikes for the winter months. She was ready for the week and looked forward to starting it over a cup of coffee with Joe.

Sitting in bed, intent on getting at least one article read, she tried to remember when she'd first met Joe. The memory was fast to surface. He was conversing with a student outside her office, gesturing wildly as though he was leading a hundred-piece orchestra. Right then she decided to get to know this character, which wasn't hard to arrange since they sat on several committees together. Their Monday morning coffee sessions ensued and before she knew it, her trust in Joe was solid as the proverb about building your house on rock instead of sand. She could count on his honesty, which she first attributed to the fact he was a priest. In time, they accompanied each other to mandatory functions and frequently shared late dinners where they gossiped like stereotypical academics. Their friendship grew into a deep and heartfelt companionship.

Clare especially came to enjoy what they now referred to as friendly-fire showdowns.

"So, Clare," Joe said in his rarely heard priest-serious tone. Clare had been in South Bend about six months when Monday morning coffees had progressed to every-so-often dinners. One particular evening, they were having a late-night glass of wine after seeing Casablanca at the small, ancient theater near campus that ran campy, classic films.

"What have I done now?" she rolled her eyes, expecting to receive yet another heads-up about Notre Dame do's and don'ts.

"Nothing! But, you know how faculty can talk, right?"

"Really? I had no idea," she replied dripping with sarcasm."

"Well, it's about men."

"Men?" She leaned forward, not quite believing she'd heard what he said. This topic certainly had not come up before. She set down her glass. "Let's cut to the chase, shall we? People, including you, I presume, are wondering about my love life." Clare remembered Joe actually blushed like a Southern belle at Cotillion.

"Not me! Forget me!" he raised his arms up defensively. "But faculty, you know, they talk. Always the questioning, inquiring minds and all that jazz."

Clare knew this line of questioning was bound to come up, but somehow felt awkward talking about her love life with Joe.

She rushed into it headfirst. "Okay, here's the Cliff Notes version. No, I don't have a history of multiple failed marriages. No, I didn't run away to South Bend to heal a broken heart. No, I'm not gay, lesbian, transgender, or a cross dresser. And no, I'm not searching for a husband. Got it, pal?" Her voice was pencil sharp.

Feeling bad for imposing an explanation on her, Joe fell into a verbal backstroke.

"Who said you were running away or married or, I mean, not married or whatever? Are you? Were you?" Good Lord, I'm in over my head, he thought to himself. She just stared at him, incredulous, not uttering a word.

"Well, isn't this uncomfortable?" he said, raising his arm to signal the waiter for another glass of wine. "God as my witness, I didn't mean to upset you."

"Augh, no worry," Clare waved him off unconvincingly. The fact of the matter was she felt a bit let down. "Never mind, really. I'm sorry. I'm overreacting."

"Maybe a little, but I've certainly pressed the wrong button."

Clare leaned toward Joe with both hands resting flat on the table. "Here's the 411, Joe. I hate gossip, about me anyway. But for you, and only you, here's the straight skinny. I came close to marriage once, but let's just say, well, I bailed. He was too traditional and needy. I was too independent. I probably still am, which in case you haven't noticed, a lot of men do the 400-yard dash as soon as they meet a strong female."

"I don't," Joe said in a very matter-of-fact voice usually reserved for homilies and confessionals. "It's what I love most about you."

A dead silence pulled itself up to the table like an unexpected guest they both wanted to ignore but couldn't. Joe felt as though he'd just passed an emotional kidney stone and expected to feel sweat dripping off his upper lip. All he could do was look at Clare McGuire helplessly and grin.

Clare slowly leaned back, afraid Joe would hear the New York Philharmonic blaring away in her head. Did he just put the words love and you in the same sentence? The bridge of his nose was the closest she could get to looking him in the eye.

"You have no idea how often men attempt to get the

slightest bit of attention from you, do you?" he asked.

"No, I don't. And quit sounding like a romance novel." She hoped he didn't notice she had started doing some sort of origami thing with her cocktail napkin. "You're a priest, for God's sake! You shouldn't be noticing those things. What do you know about matters of the heart, anyway?" As soon as the words were out of her mouth, she knew she might as well have slapped him.

"Good point." His eyes had shifted from kindness to coolness. "But don't underestimate this priest, Clare. I'm fully capable of observing a variety of emotions—and have a few myself—that would surprise even you." He was sliding from hurt to angry. Sweet Jesus, they were a pair.

Clare was uncharacteristically thrown off guard. Her best friend—a priest, mind you—had just divulged something quite profound, and she didn't know what to do with it.

"I'm sorry," was all she could muster.

Where do I get off ripping into Clare like this? Joe thought. He gave her forearm a reassuring, though not terribly convincing pat. "Not to worry, Clare. I take myself too seriously sometimes. I'm a little at loose ends right now. I guess best friends bear the brunt of that."

Clare wanted to leave, to be by herself and figure out what had just transpired between her and the priest. She stood up, muttering something about needing to get her beauty sleep—a phrase she had never used in her life. Joe stayed seated.

"You go ahead. I think I'll stay and finish my wine," he said.

"Oh, okay. Well, I'll see you tomorrow, then. Thanks for the movie."

He stood up to give her a quick hug. "Right, thanks."

Now Clare lay in bed staring at her unread magazine. That late-night conversation seemed so long ago. They ended up clearing that first hurdle clean and, as strong-minded best friends do, went toe-to-toe plenty of times since then, which solidified their relationship into something she cherished.

Back to the present, Clare turned off her night light leaving the latest *Utne* unread. Again.

. . .

The next morning, Clare gave her yellow Nike running watch, which closely resembled a grandfather clock against her tiny freckled wrist, an impatient glance. Joe was a no-show. Not one to languish by herself in the Monday morning Starbucks crush of students, she put on her jean jacket, grabbed her worn leather satchel and left for her office.

Was she worried? Maybe a little. Slightly irked? Yes, very. If she had time, she'd show some maturity and give the good priest a call to make sure he wasn't dead in an alley or conked out in the shower bleeding to death. It was, after all, not his style to stand her up. He knew all too well how ticked off she'd be. When she spoke to him on the phone the night before, he sounded almost melancholy, but she'd dismissed it. He'd been a little whiney lately, or as her dad back in Wyoming would put it, off his feed. But it wasn't Joe's style to stay that way for long.

The first golden leaf on an oak tree caught her eye outside Starbucks, and the air felt cool and refreshing when she stepped outside. It was most certainly the beginnings of autumn in Indiana. She was glad she got in that bike ride over the weekend.

Her office had two temperatures, freezing and jungle hot, which is why Clare always dressed in layers. The central boiler in the prehistoric building that was her home away from home hadn't quite adapted to the change of seasons and was feverishly hanging on to summer. Hence, cold nights lingered in every room until about two o'clock in the afternoon when the boiler finally hit full stride and everyone commenced their afternoon peel down. Clare didn't find the seasonal climate change as quaint as everyone else did. But then, these days, she wasn't finding a lot about Notre Dame as quaint as everyone else did.

She picked up her phone and called Joe. "Hey, where were you? Bye," qualified as a long message for Clare, but it was all she had time for. She had a butt-numbing day of back-to-back meetings, and if she were to be ridiculously honest, which she always was, she was glad Joe didn't pick up his office phone. She was in work mode now and knew she didn't have the patience for any explanations.

The day delivered as promised, and Clare crashed back through her office about five-thirty, just long enough to grab some work to go over after dinner and then hurry over to the fitness center. Her primary focus was to get circulation back into her lower extremities. Today, that would be her ass in particular. She much preferred running outdoors, but her blood was still too summer-thin to handle what was turning out to be a chilly evening, so she hit the treadmill. After thirty-minutes of intervals, she passed on a shower and headed for home. A baked potato smothered in vegetables, topped with gooey globs of the sourest yogurt dressing imaginable, had been dancing in her head since early afternoon.

The phone chimed "Mack the Knife" just as she unlocked the front door and Wallace, her thirteen-year-old German shorthair, galloped out to the front lawn to do his business.

"Yo!" she demanded, simultaneously turning on her oven and shrugging out of her jacket.

"Shoot me now. Just get it over with. I'll bring the gun," Joe offered.

"Hey! Where the hell were you? Remember me? I'm not a priest—or a nun," she corrected herself. "I don't have to be forgiving, but I may be heavy on the penance."

"I overslept."

"What? No way! Try again."

"Honest to God. Hey, you want to grab a bite?"

"No way. I'm an unshowered piece of rancid pork, but I'll meet you halfway. How about I pick up a pizza—no anchovies—and come over to your place?" She'd only been in his living quarters a handful of times for faculty or alumni dinners and had only been in Joe's room once or twice.

Usually, they met at Starbucks or some other coffee joint, lunched on campus, or dined at their local favorite, Anton's. Sometimes Joe would come over to her home to watch a movie and devour popcorn, but public venues were their standard.

"That would be great. Head over whenever."

"Half an hour. See you then." So much for potato fantasies.

Joe enjoyed the few times Clare visited his little enclave. It wasn't unheard of for some faculty priests to have female colleagues visit, but it also wasn't a run-of-the-mill occurrence, and everyone understood it shouldn't be.

He took a quick swipe at cleaning up his already tidy front room and changed from his black and whites into a pair of jeans and a gray John Carroll University sweatshirt. He'd thought about Clare a lot during the day and was relieved she wasn't angry about his no-show, or at least wasn't in his face about it. The calm he'd felt the night before after talking with her had waned quickly, and he'd spent a sleepless night ruminating over his future. A relaxed evening with Clare would set him on firmer ground again.

In all honesty, she'd become his lifeline, though he was sure she'd cuff him smartly on the back of the head if he told her that. She was an independent spirit and might feel smothered if she felt responsible for a needy priest. Needy students were one matter, priests another. He ran down the five flights of stairs to the makeshift wine cellar and returned to his room when Clare's arrival was announced over the relic intercom system that made every word sound as though it contained no vowels: "Cl..r.z...r..bl."

He gave his room a quick three-sixty and realized he felt like a college kid. "Good Lord, what's with me?" he mumbled to himself as he headed downstairs.

Clare was standing in the vestibule trying to look casual when she nodded hello to passing priests, some of whom looked older than Methuselah.

"Follow me," Joe said from the top of the stairs. "I hope

you don't mind paper plates and plastic cups."

"Wine on a week night?" Clare commented when he handed her a plastic cup and before she even said hello. "You must really feel guilty."

His functional, yet cozy, living room impressed Clare, and she made herself at home, plopping on the floor where most pizza at any college was properly consumed. They sat cross-legged facing each other and dove into the pizza. The audible portion of pizza dining consisted of the occasional mouth-filled muffled, "This tastes great," or "You've got a thing of cheese on your chin."

After her third slice, Clare stretched out flat on the floor with a long exhale and small burp. "Do you realize we spend a great deal of time eating together? If we didn't exercise like the obsessive-compulsive people we try not to be or have the metabolisms of mosquitoes, we'd be the size of what's his name? You know, the huge center guy only a mother could love."

"Ronald. His name is Ronald. And his mother does love every starchy, corn-fed inch of him."

She rolled over onto her stomach to look at him. He was leaning on his elbow looking at her. "Not to change the subject, Joe, but what's going on? Talk to me."

"You want the abbreviated version?" he asked, trying to ignore the knot in his stomach, which he envisioned looking like a big ball of pizza. Priests usually did the listening, and the role reversal threw him.

"I want whatever version you want to give me. I'm worried about you."

"So am I," he said flatly. "I'm free-floating, Clare. You must see that."

"I see you're preoccupied if that's what you mean?"

"That too. I don't know what I'm doing. I don't know what I'm doing at this university, I don't know what I'm doing as a priest, and I'm scared to death."

"Have you spoken to anyone? You know, like someone in the priest business, I mean this must happen a lot."

"Yeah, it happens a lot, but floundering isn't something we priests like to talk about. It's a career killer," he said with a slight grimace. "This is the first time I've said it out loud, except to myself. But I talk to you about a lot of things, in case you haven't noticed."

"Oh, Joe, what am I going to do with you?" she said in her best this-too-shall-pass tone.

"Hang in there with me?"

"Of course! I've waited all my life to come to the aid of a priest. When I first got to know you, I was kind of pissed you were a priest, but I got over it. I also felt sure I'd go to Lucifer's den if I lured someone away from the priesthood," she said with a humorous open smile that never failed to make him feel like he wasn't supposed to feel about her.

Joe sat upright and studied Clare. Damn, he was fortunate for her friendship. This freckle-nosed, pixie-haired fireball had it all—with humor and intellect. She was the full-meal deal. For the first time he wanted to tell her he'd also had some unpriest-like thoughts about her early on in their friendship but had rapidly shelved the inclination. He was, at least for now anyway, a priest. And, as well as he knew Clare, he didn't know how she would react to the admission. He didn't want to jeopardize their friendship, not now.

"I'll get it sorted out," he said in a tone that was more hopeful than fact.

"Sure you will. You've got my ear whenever you want it. Okay?"

"Got it," he confirmed. "I head out to LA this weekend for the game. Can I twist your arm into coming with me? Some old friends from Spokane will be there. You've met them—Lou and Peyton Ross? Lou reminds me of you, a straight shooter. And you remember Liam O'Connor, the kid I told you about who's all torn up over his girlfriend, who is stunningly beautiful and wealthy, but also manipulating and superficial? He'll be there, too."

Clare stood up and offered her hand to Joe. It was time to head home. "Geez, Joe, you know I'd do anything for you, but one of those mutual admiration society alumni football weekends? I can't. I'd wilt and die."

Joe laughed and enveloped her in a big bear hug. "I know, I know. But you can't blame me for asking."

"Just put your magic smile on that handsome face of yours and the weekend will fly by."

"And then I'll fly right back to you." He feigned a crooner's tone, but as the words tumbled out of his mouth, he instantly registered how natural they sounded. He looked over Clare's shoulder at the crucifix on the opposite wall and quickly looked away. He was holding onto Clare in a lifeguard ring hug.

"Um, Joe?" She'd heard what she interpreted as melodramatic kidding in his voice, but with her ear against his sternum, she could hear—and feel—his heart doing double time.

"Yes?" He couldn't move.

"Ah..." what am I trying to say, she asked herself?

"Well put, Clare."

"Ah, um..." and before she could get another monosyllabic word out, Joe leaned back to look at her and kissed her. The kiss reminded Clare of her first kiss ever. Kenny. E-gad what was his last name? Oh yeah, a seventh-grade classmate had delivered her first innocent kiss and then immediately jumped on his Stingray bike and beat tracks across the city park. She ran to tell her younger and only sister that kissing didn't feel half as gross as it looked. But before Clare could make the mental shift from something that happened just shy of thirty years ago, Joe kissed her again in a way that didn't come close to pimply-faced Kenny. This time, Joe kissed her with an intensity that nearly elevated her in her Nike Airs, and she found herself willingly kissing him back.

. . .

At some point, Clare was pretty sure Joe called her watch a weapon because it scratched him twice as he was trying to extricate her from her hoodie sweatshirt. Now, the weapon's indigo light was telling Clare it was four in the morning, and she needed to leave, which she would gladly do the minute she figured out how to shimmy herself from between Joe's deadweight sleeping body and the wall. She turned her head, or tried to, to look at Joe, as if seeing him would verify what took place between the two of them. Pinned against the wall, she barely had room to blink, let alone move her head. He's obviously used to having this expansive twin-size bed to himself, she thought, and began to slide herself out the end of the bed as stealthily as a Navy Seal. She didn't want to talk to him now. She had to buy some time to wrap her head around what had happened. It was quiet in the dark hallway—so much for her belief priests got up in the wee hours for morning vespers, or were vespers in the evening, she wondered?

She left via the kitchen loading dock, not entirely proud of sneaking out, but not ready to become front page fodder for the Notre Dame Enquirer. Once home, she made coffee and picked up the phone to call her sister, Anne, in New York. Until Joe came along, Anne was her closest confidant. The two had chosen opposite life tracks—Anne was a stay-at-home mom with six children and a husband who flew for United Airlines, but their connection was symbiotic.

"Hey, Anne, it's me." She felt bad interrupting her sister's quiet time before the kids woke up.

"Holy cow, Clare, it's five in the morning there, what's wrong? Are you okay?"

"If sleeping with a priest qualifies as being okay, I've never been better."

"Are you serious? Joe?" As identical as the two sisters were, Anne was even more emphatic in her self-expression.

"Yep, as serious as that nasty bunion you had removed last year. You should wear better shoes, you know."

"It's about time!" Clare pictured her sister pacing around the island in her kitchen.

"What are you talking about? It's about time? Are you

out of you mind?" Clare's sister had only visited South Bend once and met Joe briefly. Had she talked about him that much? What train did her sister see approaching that Clare hadn't realized left the station?

"Clare, seriously, it's about time the two of you came to grips with the fact you're ape for each other."

Clare plopped down on the end of her bed. Clare of copious words was, well, speechless. What happened between them felt right in every way, but she was prepared to consider it a slip, a mishap, a blunder between friends—anything but the apparent breakthrough her sister sounded so sure about.

"I don't know what to do."

"It sounds like you already did it," Anne said with a strong tone of sarcasm.

"Anne, help! This is all wrong. He's a priest!"

"Look, sissy, you aren't one to jump into anything carelessly. Reckless is not your style. Joe's in your life for a reason and vice versa. Last night was no accident."

"I admit it didn't feel like one, but shit-oh-dear."

"Have you talked to him?"

"Hell no! I snuck out!" She felt sheepish.

"Whoa, now that's not very Clare-like! Well, toots, you need to face the good padre, and soon. Look, the beasts are starting to rumble upstairs. I've got to run. Call me. And Clare?"

"Yes?"

"Don't intellectualize this to death, promise?"

"Promise? I can't even promise I'll make it to the shower, and it's only fifty feet away, but I'll try."

. . .

Joe was still in bed unable or unwilling to open his eyes. He'd been lying like this since he heard Clare leave less than an hour ago. He knew she had her reasons for tiptoeing out without saying anything, and, truthfully, he wasn't sure he would have known what to say to her anyway. A quick inventory of his emotions provided confusing results. He couldn't feel guilty about something that felt so incredibly right and normal with Clare. And it certainly wasn't a stumble, as in a recovering drunk falling off the wagon kind of stumble. He'd jumped off the wagon feet first. Like many priests, he thought of celibacy as an antiquated use of control by the Church, but when he joined the priesthood at the ripe age of twenty, he'd accepted celibacy. And, unlike a lot of priests, he'd stayed celibate. He never had any reason not to—until now. Now there was Clare. What was she thinking? Joe hauled himself out of bed and headed for the shower. He avoided breakfast, unsure how he could sit with the other priests as though it was just another ho-hum monastic morning. The sooner he arrived at his office the better. The sooner he spoke with Clare the better, but when he tried to call her, he was sent directly to voicemail. He couldn't leave a message. He didn't know what to say. He just needed to hear her voice.

Chapter 10

Ellen saw the pile of mail on her desk and thought about skipping the daily ritual, but couldn't help sifting through it to see if there was a note from Molly. It was a ridiculous expectation what with cell phones making daily or even hourly communication the norm, but Ellen was still old school and felt a tinge of excitement when she opened the mailbox. Disappointed, she tossed the mail aside. As she did, a small ivory envelope slipped out from amongst the junk mail. It was hand addressed, not the computer-generated cursive penmanship mass-marketers use to fool the unsuspecting into opening the envelope only to find an invitation to open a new Visa account.

The upper left hand corner read LMJ followed by an Overbluff Road address. Mildly curious, she was taken aback to find an invitation to dinner at Miss Johnson's Saturday night. Holy crap, this Saturday? So much for lead time. Even though Miss Johnson was a regular customer, Ellen's interaction with her had been limited to a fairly cursory exchange of greetings. Molly, on the other hand, had sat with her for long chats and expounded about the older woman's wisdom and intellect.

A date with an octogenarian. My wild and crazy life is just getting out of hand, she thought while punching Miss Johnson's number into her cell and simultaneously putting her sarcasm on hold.

"Hello, Miss Johnson?"

"Yes," responded the somewhat-familiar refined voice.

"This is Ellen Kirkpatrick. I received your invitation for

dinner Saturday."

"Yes?"

What's with the questioning tone? Ellen thought with increasing unease. Hey, lady, you invited me, remember?

"Well, it sounds great."

"I'm so glad, Ellen," Miss Johnson responded. "Cocktails are at five o'clock. Dinner at six. I apologize for the late notice, but I've gotten lax in my old age."

Lax? Ellen thought. Glancing again at the Emily Post perfect invitation, she almost laughed. This woman doesn't know lax the way Ellen had gotten to know lax over the past year when it came to social graces. Besides, these days an e-mail invite was considered acceptable. Texting and Tweeting couldn't be far behind.

"No problem, I checked my calendar, and I can fit dinner in between whole nut bars and almond vanilla scones," she said, hoping Miss Johnson wouldn't be put off by her attempt at humor, a tact she unconsciously resorted to when she was on shaky ground. But the older woman didn't notice, or was too shocked to say anything.

"Good, then. We'll enjoy seeing you. Oh, and dress casually, dear."

"No worries there, Miss Johnson, since I spend ninety percent of my time in baker's wear, my clothing situation is limited to white t-shirts. It will be a treat to break out something different from the bowels of my closet."

"Fine!" said Miss Johnson, sounding, could it be, giddy?

"Say, Miss Johnson, do you mind if I ask what the occasion is?"

"Oh, it's nothing special, dear. I just so enjoyed meeting Molly before she left for Los Angeles. I know you must be missing her and, well, I thought it would be nice to get better acquainted."

"That's sweet. Okay then, I'll see you in a few days."

Ellen hung up the phone and buried her head in her hands. Who the heck is the we in, "We'll enjoy seeing you," anyway? We in this context clearly refers to more than Miss

Johnson and me. I'm toast, she thought, simultaneously thanking her mother for over-training her in the fine art of cordiality. Miss Johnson would never guess I'm cringing at the thought of Saturday night. Or would she?

"Shit! Why won't people just let me be a loner? I'm getting so good at it! Leave me to my muffins, all you well-intended people," Ellen said under her breath as she pushed herself up off the floor where she'd seated herself.

That little hissy fit out of the way, she headed for the shower. The thin white coat of flour slipped off her, and she could almost hear her skin taking its first deep breath of the day. Ah, life's simple pleasures.

Turning off the shower, Ellen wondered again, for a brief moment, if God was going to banish her from eternal happiness for swearing like a longshoreman. Before she was old enough to utter complete sentences, Ellen took to four-letter expletives like a fish to water. Her mom would frequently let fly with an effective, well-timed "Damn!" when she was really angry or startled. She referred to such outbursts as "tasteful profanity." Ellen obviously followed her mom's lead. Like her mom, Ellen had tried to restrict her outbursts to her inner voice. To her annoyance, however, relatively mild profanities remained too close to the tip of her tongue to suppress. Her grandmother lectured that profanity was a crutch used by people who lacked creativity. Well put, Gram, I'll remember that the next time I drop the ef-bomb, Ellen thought as she sank into bed, which—next to her evening shower—was by far her most coveted time of day. She reached for her current read, Rachael Ray's gripping instructive muse about increasing the flake in flaky turnovers.

A few blocks further up the South Hill, Dr. Jack Doyle was picking up the phone to respond to the same dinner invitation.

. . .

"Hi Jack, what can I get you?" Ellen asked,

simultaneously trying, albeit awkwardly, to secure her bandana, a black-and-white number with a little Buddha pattern. Put on in the nebulous pre-dawn hours, she was hoping Buddha's serenity might seep into her head.

"A refill, please?" Jack looked and sounded unusually hesitant, not the cool, self-assured guy she was used to. "By the way, are you going to Miss Johnson's for dinner Saturday? She told me she sent you an invitation."

That his voice sounded more tenor than baritone was a relief, Ellen thought as she handed him his coffee.

"Ah, yes, actually, I am." Jeepers, I sound as much like a tongue-tied junior high kid as he does, she thought. In a slightly twisted way, she enjoyed the ever so slight flaw in Jack's usually smooth demeanor. It made her feel a little surer of herself and better of him.

"You know, it's funny because I don't really know her that well. I mean she comes in here every day, and she and Molly became friends, but I've never had more than a brief chat with her. Now, out of the blue, it's dinner at her house? Odd, don't you think?"

"I think it's just the three of us, if you want to feel even odder. I do know that she prefers small gatherings. But really, it's no big deal."

So, thought Ellen. That answers the we question.

"Would you like a ride?" Jack asked, sounding so casual a person listening in would think the two of them carpooled together all the time.

"Sure," she said, despite the fact her inner voice was screaming, Are you out of your mind? What if I want to escape over the hedge sometime between soup and sorbet? "Okay, good. Great!" stammered from her mouth despite her urge to say otherwise.

"I'll pick you up at about, oh, ten to five? It probably won't come as a surprise to you Miss Johnson is a stickler for punctuality. Very military, in fact. When I was a kid and showed up late for my summer weeding job, she never said a word, but the looks were lethal. Still can be."

"Duly noted," Ellen saluted. "Drive around to the back door, and I'll be ready."

"Will do. You know, you've done a great job with this place," Jack said in his best conversational voice, which he wasn't quite sure was his.

"It's been fun," said Ellen. "It's consumed every nook and cranny of my life, but it's been worth the effort."

"Cool. Okay, well I'll see you later," Jack said. "Have a good one," he added over his shoulder.

Ellen watched him walk out of the bakery, relieved to have solved the mystery of who would be at dinner, and although she didn't relish the prospect of being outnumbered two to one, it might be interesting to see Jack somewhere other than the bakery. Like Lou always said, you never really know a person until you see them on their own turf. That's how you get to the substance. Ellen hadn't done much of that since Sam died, but Jack was the first man she had noticed, as in took note of more than his coffee and pastry preference.

From what Molly and Lou told her, Ellen knew Jack had never married and left a financially rewarding medical research position in Boston to come home to Spokane. He joined an internal medicine group, and she guessed he was older than she by, just guessing, five years or so. She got a kick out of the way the other men in his group called him Mr. Darcy. Every now and then she caught him looking at her with a very serious knitted brow. But when she attempted a half-smile back at him, he would quickly look away. He was very Mr. Darcy-like, perhaps using his aloofness as a cover for something? Maybe dinner at Miss Johnson's would give her a better pulse on Jack.

Chapter 11

Late Friday morning, Liam was waiting at Gate C-52 at O'Hare when Joe jogged up to meet him with just moments to spare.

"Never enough time," puffed Joe.

"I know the feeling. You have no idea what heroic feats I've had to accomplish this week to be here and make this plane—on time," Liam smiled.

The two men boarded the plane and took their seats in economy. Within minutes, a flight attendant came up to Joe.

"Father, would you two like to move up front? We have two open seats in first class."

"We'd be honored! Thank you!"

Joe whispered to Liam, "God provides for those who work hard in His name—and it doesn't hurt if the captain is a Notre Dame football fan either. He must have seen me board."

After a neat scotch and fairly decent airline meal, the two friends settled in for what they hoped was an uneventful flight.

"What was it you wanted to discuss with me last Sunday?" asked Liam.

"Nothing that can't wait. My most pressing need right now is a power nap to be ready for the onslaught of activity that awaits us in LA. Would you wake me in an hour? We're scheduled to land at three o'clock."

"Consider it done."

Joe, remarkably adept at power-napping as time allowed, closed his eyes and was out like a penny candle. Liam opened his laptop and tidied up some work-related documents. Then he pulled out *The Fountainhead* he'd promised to read.

Although the flight proved uneventful, the drive downtown in their mid-size rental was anything but. Accustomed to big-city traffic, Liam volunteered to drive, but it took all his concentration and self-control not to commit retaliatory acts of road rage. Liam decided he would rename it Lost Angeles.

After checking in at four-thirty, Joe handed Liam his itinerary.

Friday:
5:30 – Notre Dame pep rally in the Ballroom
7:00 – Dinner with the LA Alumni Chapter at Ernesto's
9:30 – Notre Dame football alumni hospitality suite
      meet/greet
Saturday:
8:00 – Alumni continental breakfast/pre-game in the
      Ballroom
10:00 – Notre Dame Alumni pre-game tailgate party at
      UCLA stadium
11:00 – Prayer for ND players/ND locker room
11:30 – Kick off

"Would you mind attending this evening's activities and tomorrow morning's breakfast and then drive me to the stadium? Once there, you'll be on your own. My duties will take me to the locker room and on the field with the team."

"Absolutely, Joe, I'm here to serve!"

"Here's your ticket to the game. You'll be sitting with Lou and Peyton Ross, very good friends of mine from Spokane, Washington."

Liam vaguely recognized the name.

"Didn't I meet them earlier this year before a pre-season game?"

"Yes, now that I think of it, you did," Joe smiled.

"I remember Lou. She was all over me to meet this nice

Irish girl from Spokane. A classics major at Gonzaga. I think I gave her my e-mail address.

"Right. Well then, let's go to our rooms, unpack, and get ready for the roller coaster ride they call Notre Dame Football."

"I'm on my way and ready for anything you throw my way."

"Perfect. See you in the ballroom in a half an hour."

. . .

Joe unpacked his carry-on and started charging his cell phone, which only reminded him he still hadn't spoken to Clare. She never returned his call Tuesday morning after "the night," and all of his other attempts to reach her failed. He didn't know if she was angry, embarrassed or just in need of time. Amazingly, they'd moved through the week without seeing each other, and more than once he wondered if she'd rearranged her schedule to avoid him. He put his shoulder into the work week and finally loaded himself on the flight to LA. He repeatedly told himself he'd see her as soon as he got back to South Bend, using the weekend to get his head together. Looking out the window of his hotel room, he saw a rock star bus pull into the parking lot, and a bevy of blue, green and gold unload. For the first time, Joe honestly admitted to himself that surviving this weekend of Notre Dame football and alumni fanaticism seemed, all things considered, pathetically trite if not emotionally impossible.

. . .

It took Molly three buses and a three-block walk to get to the Westin Hotel, but it was worth it. Leaving her current world of immigration and sparse living conditions made stepping into the luxury lobby of the Westin an out-of-body experience. Wow! It was all so grand, including the people. She imagined this was how Holly Golightly felt in Tiffany's.

Nothing bad could ever happen to you in a place like this.

She checked in and took the elevator to her room on the 22nd floor. It was heaven with a view. Molly started to feel bad about this reaction of exhilaration. Oh, forget that guilt crap, she thought, and started running a hot bath. She definitely wanted to watch a movie later in the king-size bed that was all hers for two nights. "Oh my, oh my," she sighed.

After a long soak in her own private, non-convent bathroom, she quickly changed her clothes and called the Rosses to say she'd be right over.

"I can't even tell you—no words can ever express—how absolutely wonderful it is to see you both!" gushed Molly when she entered their room across the hallway. "I could honestly sit here, in this hotel room, all weekend just looking at you and be utterly content."

"Had enough of this city? And I wouldn't blame you one bit. Los Angeles is a disturbingly acquired taste if you ask me," said Peyton. He, too, had driven white-knuckled from the airport.

"No, no. That's not it at all. I really love my work. It's just so good to see you, and that's as close to home as I can get right now."

"Hey, I really want to hear more about your job, but it's almost five-thirty. Anyone for a good old-fashioned Notre Dame pep rally?" asked Peyton. "I hate to miss any pre-game football fervor!"

"Would you mind going without us?" asked Lou. "The older I get the more annoying the cheerleaders become, and the band is too loud for me in such a closed space."

"No problem. This gives you girls a chance to get all caught up. And, the funny thing is that the cheerleaders don't bother me. Not one little bit," Peyton grinned and winked at Molly as he left the room. Lou threw a pillow at the closing door.

"What an old tick hound. How about a glass of wine or a beer?" asked Lou, opening the mini-bar.

"I'll have that little bottle of red with the screw top."

"I'd like a Corona, but there's no fresh lime," Lou pondered. "I guess I'll go with the white wine version with the screw top."

They found two wineglasses, some crackers and proceeded to get comfortable. For the next two hours, Lou and Molly talked nonstop about Molly's job at El Centro, Lewis and Clark High School, Ellen and the bakery, Spokane news, Gonzaga's basketball team prospects. They were surprised when Peyton walked in and exclaimed, "I'm starved! Anyone for dinner?"

"I definitely am, as long as we make it an early night," said Molly. "This has been a killer week at work. I have to admit that gynormous bed and an on-demand, in-room movie are looking dang good to me."

They found a Thai restaurant a block from the hotel and shared three entrees, a bottle of wine and a lot of laughter reminiscing. As they walked back to the hotel, Molly was sandwiched between Lou and Peyton, each holding one of her hands.

At the door of her room, Peyton announced, "You may have skipped the pep rally, but we're all leaving together for the pregame tailgate party/BBQ that starts at ten at the stadium. I want you both dressed and ready to go by nine-thirty. Woops...I forgot something. Wait right here."

Peyton disappeared across the hall for a moment and came back with a plastic bag.

"Molly, I took the liberty of buying you a Notre Dame football t-shirt at the traveling bookstore," Peyton said. "There is a strict dress code for the game, which is pretty much anything green, blue, or gold with a Notre Dame logo printed on it."

Molly held up a shirt matching Peyton's description exactly and yelled "Go Irish!" as she closed her door.

Chapter 12

"Hi Mom! I'm in LA with Lou and Peyton." Ellen could feel Molly's excitement over the phone. "We're just about to leave the hotel for the game. I wish you were here with us."

Ellen was on the bakery phone and feeling stressed. One of the front counter workers didn't show for her shift this morning. To hell with it, the customers could just wait a minute while she talked to her daughter.

"Molly, you sound so chirpy! I can't talk long; I'm short an employee this morning. But listen to this one. Miss Johnson invited me to a dinner party at her house tonight. Why don't I call you Sunday, and I'll give you all the tiniest of details. Okay?"

"That sounds great. Tell Miss Johnson I said hello. I'll be home around dinnertime Sunday. I'll tell you all about the football game. It's Notre Dame-mania around here!"

"Fun! Love you and kiss Lou and Peyton for me."

"Will do. Bye. Love you."

Ellen hung up the phone and turned to face the Saturday rush head on. Having to be ready at quarter to five would cramp her for time, but a little voice in her head convinced her that the change of routine would do her good. All work and no play make Ellen a dull girl.

Later that afternoon, Ellen stood in front of her closet pondering what to wear. Miss Johnson was always impeccably dressed when she came to The Manito each morning, usually wearing a lovely St. John-esque knit suit, coat, gloves and every hair in place. Ellen wondered what she owned that was appropriate for a "casual" dinner at Miss Johnson's.

"Conservative," Ellen said out loud. "Let's look in the wedding and funeral section of the closet."

She pulled out a simple black dress she'd splurged on, oh, about five years ago. It would do just fine once she draped a maroon, black and cream silk scarf around her shoulders, which would save her from having to wear pearls. She quickly slipped the dress on to see if it still fit. If anything it was roomier than the last time she wore it to a friend of Molly's wedding. She reminded herself that it was a good thing she was born with Paxton genes and rarely ate her own products.

"Not bad," she mumbled. "Not half-damn bad, if I do say so myself."

She set her alarm for three-thirty. That would give her enough time to nap, shower and primp for her first formal outing with a man since Sam died.

Oh, Lordy, she continued ruminating, I'm glad it's not a date-date. It's just a carpool ride. I can sit in a car.

. . .

"Oh sweet chariot, what have I done?" Jack said aloud to the small colorful tiles bordering his fireplace.

What in God's name possessed me to ask Ellen if she wanted to drive to this dinner with me? He was not the spontaneous type. It was almost as if some other Jack had taken over the controls for a minute and kicked him into saying those words. At least he didn't need to worry about what to wear. No jeans. No khakis and a polo shirt. This called for his navy blazer and charcoal pants, newly dry-cleaned and at the ready. The only choices were whether to wear the white or blue shirt? His dad's old red and navy paisley tie won virtue of the fact it was his only decent tie. The black Bass loafers or the two-toned black and ox blood Allan Edmonds oxfords? Black socks, of course, that's a no-brainer, and clean underwear, another standard instituted early on by his mother.

Flowers. He'd forgotten Miss Johnson asked him to bring tulips. He called BeauK Florist and ordered an arrangement to pick up at four-thirty. He had several hours before landing on the beach at Normandy, plenty of time for a last-minute, mind-decluttering bike ride.

. . .

Before she knew it, Ellen was retrieving the black dress from her small closet, a far cry from the walk-in she used to have in the old house. At the moment, the slight curiosity she'd felt when Jack offered a ride to Miss Johnson's had morphed to mixed feelings of fatigue and dread.

What did she, Jack and Miss Johnson have in common except to talk about the bakery and Molly? This was going to be seriously painful, she decided.

"I have to learn to say no to old ladies," she blurted out to Lou, who'd just called to check in.

"Look, El," Lou said, trying to sound encouraging and simultaneously thankful that she was not a single woman. "She probably misses Molly and knows you miss her, too. She just thinks it would be nice for the two of you to get to know each other. Consider it a sweet gesture."

"Very sweet. And in what way does Jack Doyle fit into the picture?"

"I don't know... maybe she thinks the two of you are lost and lonely souls who need a kick in the ass?" Lou was warming up to a conversation with Ellen that was a long time coming, but regrettably she sounded harsh.

"Okay, Lou, get it off your chest. You won't sleep tonight if you don't."

Grabbing the baton, Lou sprinted hell-bent toward the finish line.

"Well, look at you. Your life isn't exactly Nirvana."

Ouch! That was a direct hit, but Ellen knew Lou was right on target. Still, her feelings were hurt, and Lou's remark, combined with a long week and the stress of the pending evening, left her emotionally pummeled.

"Hey, I like my life. It's been a hard couple of years, Lou, so cut me some slack, okay?" she fired back defensively. "Maybe I'm not flying to LA for a football game or having dinner with my best friend's daughter, but here's a news flash for you: I'm trying, Lou."

Lou felt instantly sorry for initiating this conversation on the phone and tried to massage her friend's feelings.

"I know your life is fine, El. I admire the hell out of what you've done with The Manito, and God only knows Molly couldn't have asked for a better mom or Sam a better wife. But maybe there is more to life than just fine. Maybe it is time to look beyond that front counter downstairs."

"Okay, I give on that one, but I still don't get what Dr. Jack Doyle has to do with anything," she said, knowing damn well what role Jack Doyle played. She just didn't feel like admitting this to Lou at the moment.

"Jack is on the other side of that counter," said Lou.

Ellen was close to tears. Lou was telling her exactly what she'd been trying to convince herself of, quite unsuccessfully, for months. Sam was gone. She'd poured every fiber of herself into the bakery, and now Molly was trying to launch a life of her own. Yes, it was time to get on with her life, too. Note to self, it might include a relationship with a man. The thought that Jack might be that man, or at the very least get her into the starting block, was just a little overwhelming at the moment. Then again, she thought, when isn't it going to feel overwhelming?

"I don't know whether to bust you for trying to channel Dr. Phil or thank you, Lou, but you know me better than I know myself sometimes," Ellen half cried and half laughed.

Ellen was wondering why she had to go from a dead stop to a sprint. Really, what would be so bad about baby steps? Isn't that what Richard Dreyfus told Bill Murray to do in some movie she'd forgotten because she never remembered the names of movies. Oh yeah, What About Bob?

Lou had a knack for monologues. She could talk on and

on completely unaware the only one listening to her was herself. It drove some people nuts, but Ellen cherished her friend's humor and found her Jay Leno-esque crowd warm-up moments entertaining and usually insightful. They made for a kind of intermission in Ellen's coffee soaked- day. She tuned back in as Lou was saying Ellen was one of the chosen few who, like it or not, passed the saliva test and was deemed worthy of entering the inner sanctum that is Miss Johnson's home, a.k.a., Spokane's Louvre.

"Hey, at least you get to have a look at the inside of the legendary Johnson house! And be sure and check out the artwork. It's rumored to be incredible!" advised Lou, relieved that the emotional tempest had blown over.

"I will. And, I'll be nice to Dr. Doyle. You'll get a blow-by-blow account within twenty-four hours."

. . .

Jack arrived at four-fifty on the dot. She was ready. Her profuse case of nervousness created so much perspiration Ellen stuck Kotex Light Days pads on the armpits of her dress, something she hadn't done since, well, never. Situating the dainty pad strategically to protect the thin fabric of her dress, she lamented the fact these things weren't available when she was a teen. Ellen looked in the full-length mirror she had avoided for quite some time. Her black dress and scarf didn't exactly scream, "Hey! I'm a fun-loving, game-on kind of gal!" She tried to convince herself that if black and simple is the standard attire of the manor born, she'd hit the mark. Shrugging it off, Ellen headed downstairs determined to enjoy the evening in spite of her misgivings.

She hit the bottom stair as Jack was knocking on the bakery's heavy glass back door. He was wearing the conservative male version of her attire. We look like bookends, she thought, while unlocking the scant five dead bolts before opening the door, thus initiating the first test to her underarm area. Did I call that one right or what?

Then her mouth was off and running like a horse out of the starting gate. "Hey Jack, I wonder if I should get a doorbell back here? Everyone told me it would only invite strangers to the back of the bakery, but the bakery's back door is my front door, and I never know if anyone is there. Not that a lot of people come to see me, or anything, and it isn't like Jack the Ripper is going to be creeping around back here in this neighborhood. Sorry, bad example, but you could have been out here for hours, and I'd never know it, but of course I did know it because I was expecting you." Pausing for a breath, and to grab her black beaded clutch, she finally shut up. She turned toward Jack hoping he hadn't noticed her nervous rambling, but his face indicated otherwise. His furrowed brows and slightly cocked head were a dead give-away. Yep, she thought, he thinks I'm a first-rate nut case.

What Jack really thought was how nice it was to see Ellen show some bare-ass emotion. He also felt a little bad that he might be making her nervous. And, yes, shamefully, he also felt a little smug. Or was it intrigue? He never imagined he could cause such a state of nerves from the normally perfunctory, cool Ellen he observed every morning. On the other hand, he thought perhaps anticipation of having dinner with the formidable Lillian Johnson might also be at the root of Ellen's nerves, which pretty much dashed any thoughts about his magical charisma.

What Jack was sure about was that Ellen looked stunning. Stunning as in oh-my- eyes-feel-good stunning.

"Well, doorbells are kind of standard door accoutrements," Jack said, unable to take his eyes off the back of her neck. God, she has the neck of a ballerina, he thought. Long, straight and graceful. This anatomical attribute was normally hidden by the Nehru-like stand-up collar of her baker's jacket.

After hearing herself yammer on about her riveting doorbell quandary, Ellen clammed up. Clutch in hand, she bee-lined past Jack, mumbling something about the door locking itself. Ellen hoped she didn't look the way she felt crossing the gravel parking area in her two-inch heels. She felt herself teetering precariously toward Jack's Land Rover. She'd so hoped to glide. Accoutrements? Did he just call doorbells accoutrements? Who cares, she thought. Just stay upright, ol' girl. You've done enough damage to your image for now. You have an entire evening to cause more injury so, by all means, pace yourself and don't blow it all by skidding right under his damn vehicle.

Proud of herself for reaching the vehicle upright, Ellen opened the imposing passenger door and froze. Climbing into Jack's Range Rover loomed before her like the last hard pull to the summit of Mt. Rainier. She wanted to make a statement of independence by getting to and in the car without assistance. Unfortunately, climbing conditions were going to be an issue, and she would need help in the ascent unless she wanted her dress to ride up somewhere around her neck. She thought back to the countless times her father and uncles would hoist ancient aunts—whose fur coats far outweighed their frail bodies—in and out of cars for holiday dinners. Her dad compared the effort to shoving a giant bear into the car. "When you grab on, all you get is fur!" Armed with the memory of her father's deep laugh, and her refusal for assistance at her age, Ellen ever so modestly stepped up on the running board, sat her behind down on the elevated seat and swung her legs in with a semblance of style.

"Nicely done," Jack applauded, while sheepishly trying to avoid staring at Ellen's great legs and fine-boned ankles. Not that he made a habit of noticing physical attributes of women. He was a far cry from a middle-age prowler, but he found himself lingering over parts of Ellen that he usually, well never, got a chance to see. She was always camouflaged in baggy cotton pants, Birkenstocks and thick wooly socks that didn't exactly invite a second look. What he liked most at the moment was the way everything fit together in such a pleasing, interesting way.

"This isn't exactly a luxury sedan. Sorry about that. I guess a personals ad would say I'm the outdoor, adventurer type. To be honest, I don't go on dates often enough to think about feminine logistics. Thanks for being a good sport." Personals ads? Good sport? Dates? Jack firmly advised himself to shut up and drive.

With asinine comments behind him, he closed the car door, walked around to the driver's side, hopped in and started maneuvering down the back alley to tree-lined Manito Boulevard, where the huge maple trees arched to meet each other, as though spreading a blanket to keep them warm on this almost-cool early autumn evening.

The ride took all of six minutes and, by Ellen's calculations, about fifteen gallons of gas. A trip up Overbluff Road, by car, bike or foot, was always a pleasure, especially at night when a passerby could see inside the wonderful, old turn-of-the-century homes.

Spokanites had a unique habit of rarely covering their windows at night, as if they had nothing to hide. This was especially true of Overbluff Road, which was Philly's Mainline, Seattle's Washington Park or Chicago's Oak Park. Red brick graced the outsides of stately colonials with hedges that looked like they'd been trimmed with eyebrow tweezers. By contrast, untamed perennials and knots of evergreens made the immense Tudors look almost relaxed. Still, the huge wood homes were Ellen's favorite. The Pacific Northwest lumber industry was well represented by clapboard-sided homes with vast wrap-around porches. Ellen began to see Miss Johnson's home resembled Miss Johnson herself, impeccable formal gardens surrounding an imposing looking Bavarian Tudor.

"We're here," Jack announced to Ellen.

"You know, I rode my bike by this house every day growing up, and I've always wondered what the inside is like. Have you been inside before?" Ellen asked.

"Many times. I was her garden boy and errand runner growing up. I'm guessing you were probably still a schoolgirl in pigtails at Sacred Heart back then. Lillian and I had an employer-employee relationship over the years that evolved into a friendship."

"That's nice. I'm glad she has you. She seems so alone."

"I think she prefers it that way, being alone that is. I think she likes the mystery her solitary life evokes. Here, let me get the door for you," Jack said.

Ellen handed him the bottle of red wine she brought despite Miss Johnson's instructions to bring nothing. At the last minute, Ellen's better sense prevailed, and she grabbed a bottle of merlot. Her mom's instructions were to never arrive empty handed, and Ellen wasn't about to start disregarding this code of etiquette now. Jack opened the back car door and came out with a gorgeous bouquet of tulips. Ellen wondered why she was so tickled to see that Jack's mom obviously followed the same code as hers. He gave her his arm, and together they proceeded to the front door where Lillian was waiting for them.

"What have you two been talking about? I've been waiting in this doorway for ages. Jack, you really should get a decent car. Ellen practically had to slide to the ground. Now come inside. I'm not getting any younger!"

"Hello, Lillian," Jack said. "Where would you like the tulips?"

"On the table, of course."

He called her Lillian to her face! Ellen noticed. Who would have guessed?

"Jack, take that nice bottle of wine Ellen brought and open it so it can breathe before dinner. Lovely choice. Thank you, Ellen. What a sensible name. It reminds me of a dear friend I had many, many years ago in California. Hmmm... that was another lifetime, it seems."

"Thank you, Miss Johnson. I was named after my mother's sister, my favorite aunt. Your home is lovely!"

"First of all, and Jack already knows this, although I prefer to be more formal in public situations, as a guest in my home, please call me Lillian. Second, please feel at ease. I'm the one who should be nervous. This is the first dinner party I have given in years because, quite frankly, most of my contemporaries have been dead for years. Come along dear and I'll show you around. If you're like most people, your curiosity is killing you. Oh, yes, I hear people talk. I barely let the house cleaner upstairs, so don't feel slighted if we just poke around the first floor."

"I was telling Jack I used to ride my bike by your home growing up and have always wondered what it looked like inside."

"Yes, I imagine my home looks a bit imposing from the outside. But as you can see, it's really quite comfortable and warm."

They toured two living rooms, one formal and one less so. A library covered floor to ceiling with bookshelves was just off the formal living room and a stunning sun room next to the library. Ellen could swear the wallpaper had to be hand painted. The dining room boasted a table that seated twenty, at a minimum, with crystal sconces along the walls that cast a warm glow into the spacious room. Lillian's mother, or perhaps Lillian herself, had incredible taste and created a feeling of formality and comfort in every room. Inlaid woodwork, books, antiques, figurines, Tiffany lamps and huge, colorful Eastern rugs all complemented the subtle, richly-colored walls. And, of course, the paintings. Ellen was speechless and looked in awe at the jaw-dropping collection of framed canvases placed with exacting care throughout each room.

"You'll notice quite a few original works of art in our home. I still think of it as our home, my parents' and mine. They were avid art collectors." Lillian gestured toward a painting in the corridor.

"This is was my father's favorite, a Cezanne. He was particularly taken with his style. And here is one of my mother's pets, a Picasso. Ghastly as a human being, but he was a talented painter, wasn't he? I guess you could say that these works of art are my brothers and sisters, so to speak, and I'm the caretaker of this precious family."

Jack returned. "The tulips are on the table, wine is breathing, and these delicious looking canapés look ready to serve. May I pour you ladies a sherry before dinner? Lillian, you won't mind if I help myself to a scotch?"

"Yes, and no. Come along, Ellen, let's sit in the sun room while we can still enjoy the beauty of our lingering sunset and allow Jack to wait on us."

Jack chuckled. Ellen had never seen him so relaxed and congenial. Lillian either, for that matter. They seemed to bring out the best in each other. But then, old friends do that for each other, don't they, she mused? Like Lou. Everyone needs a friend like that.

"May I do anything to help?"

"Ellen, your job, first and foremost, is to sit here and converse with me. I trained this young man in his formative years. He takes direction marvelously well. You are to do nothing but enjoy yourself. Now tell me the story behind The Manito."

After a sherry, they moved to the dining room where the enormous mahogany table was set for three. Ellen looked at the place settings at the far end of the table and was reminded of three lone pins left standing, awaiting the second roll of the bowling ball. Lillian asked Jack to bring in the field greens salad with Mandarin oranges and candied pecans from the refrigerator. The salad course was followed by a chilled cucumber soup, also pre-prepared and waiting.

The conversation flowed, along with a light, white wine. Jack dutifully cleared and delivered each course and, to Ellen's amusement, seemed to enjoy playing the dual roles of houseboy and guest. After the appropriate half-time break, as Ellen always called the timely lapse between soup and the main course, Jack brought in three lovely plated dishes of Duck a L'Orange with roasted vegetables and light, flaky butter rolls from Ellen's bakery. Jack poured Ellen's red wine, which everyone agreed was the perfect complement. Dessert was a refreshing pomegranate sorbet sprinkled with shards of dark chocolate, accompanied by coffee timed expertly to finish brewing as the dessert was served. How civilized, thought Ellen, as she mulled over the seamless, effortless and delectable dinner.

Lillian invited her little party to retire to the library with its overstuffed, comfortable furniture. Relaxed and full as she was, Ellen hoped she wouldn't nod off before the evening was over.

"Sometimes it saddens me that these lovely works of art aren't shared with others," said Miss Johnson, following Ellen's eyes toward the gold-leafed framed Gauguin lighted perfectly in the library.

Coffee finished and utterly content, Ellen listened to Miss Johnson. How could I ever call this woman by her first name, she wondered? Jack chatted about everything from putting the garden to bed for winter—obviously a task not taken lightly— to making sure window screens were traded out for storm windows by mid-October.

"Well, young lady, it's time for us to be on our way so you can get your beauty sleep," Jack said to Miss Johnson with a wink at Ellen.

"Oh, hush up," Miss Johnson retorted, obviously enjoying his attention.

"He's right," said Ellen, pushing herself up from the depths of a most comfortable red leather chair. "It's been a wonderful evening, but my bakery beckons early."

"I'll accept that, Ellen, but not Jack's hogwash about beauty sleep. I'm well past that, and you certainly don't need it."

"Thanks, but I beg to differ," Ellen smiled. She was well aware Jack had his eyes locked in her direction as if verifying Miss Johnson's claim.

"I think rising before even a hint of dawn on a daily basis, combined with long, although interesting, days have taken their toll," Ellen said.

"All right then, I'll let you two go, but only if you promise, Ellen, to come again, with or without this young scallywag."

"I will, and thank you. Molly's right. You're quite a lady. I certainly understand why she's so taken by you. And your home, oh my heart, what a treat to finally get a peek inside!"

Knowing Miss Johnson's annoyance with prolonged departures, Jack had retrieved Ellen's small bag and was standing at the door of the library like a dutiful butler. Man-o-man, has she got him trained or what? Ellen observed.

Jack gave Miss Johnson a gentle hug at the front door. "I'll get right on the garden. You don't need to remind me a hundred times. I'm not in high school anymore."

Looking at the elderly lady and the much younger man, Ellen could tell Miss Johnson loved him. Jack's feelings for Lillian were equally deep and true. The coffee boys at the bakery would never believe this of their Mr. Darcy. She extended her hand toward Miss Johnson as a farewell gesture, but was taken aback when the woman leaned forward to give her a quick peck on her cheek.

"I haven't seen Jack this happy in so long, Ellen, thank you," she whispered.

Ellen had little time to absorb this surprisingly personal comment as she and Jack waved good-bye to the tall, back-lit figure in the doorway. Glancing back at Lillian, Ellen felt a dash of sadness. Really it was more poignancy than sadness, as Miss Johnson would never tolerate pity.

Ellen was still digesting Miss Johnson's whispered message as she and Jack turned onto Overbluff Road and headed back to the bakery. "The two of you have quite a friendship, Jack," she said to break the silence that was screaming over the deep rumble of his Range Rover.

"We understand each other. Sometimes I think she knows me better than I know myself. And she doesn't hesitate to tell me what she sees. Never has."

"My friend Lou is like that. It's a blessing, really, to have someone who can crawl inside my head and doesn't hesitate to tell me what she sees. Sometimes it's frightening, but usually she exposes the lint balls I've either tried to ignore or didn't see at all."

"No doubt Lillian has called me out more than a few times. When I was young, it was usually about my chores, school, career, that sort of thing. Now, it's clear to me she's headed down an entirely new road."

"As in....?"

"Relationships, or lack thereof," he said in a hardly audible voice. His clenched jaw was visible even in the shadows of the tree-lined arch over the street. "I'm now quite sure that was her ulterior motive behind tonight's dinner."

Jack's mood had suddenly flipped like a Sunday morning pancake. The life he had engineered for himself—the one with few surprises—was under fire. He had achieved professional success in medicine, mixing his practice with research, and was able to architect a move back to the part of the world that accommodated his coveted love for the outdoors. Within ten minutes, he could be out on the road cycling. In an hour he could be skiing—snow or lake.

"She's trying to get us together?" Ellen was flabbergasted, and her tone stressed the word us a little harder than she intended. Huh, imagine that, she thought. Well, well, Lillian, you little vixen. She held back a giggle, which wasn't hard to do when she glanced sideways and realized Jack was truly stressed. Suddenly, her inclination to laugh took a hard left toward hurt feelings. Well, hellooo Mr. Darcy, she thought. I was almost convinced you had taken the night off. Ellen had observed Jack the whole evening and liked what she saw. At some point during dinner, she thought she was piteously ready to concede to Lou that tonight was a good idea. Not anymore. Now, she was reserving judgment.

She opted for the fall-back position, sarcasm. The alternative option was to get really pissed right back at him, but the evening with Lillian had been too enjoyable for her to go there.

"You know she means well, Jack," she said in her most sisterly voice. "You'll just have to humor her, oh, and get the garden ready for winter. Don't forget those storm windows. Shoot, you can keep her distracted from your love life well into November. But if I were you, I'd be engaged by January or you're in for a long winter now that old Lillian has a bull's eye on your heart."

"Funny," Jack said, clearly meaning he didn't find her the least bit humorous.

"C'mon, Jack, lighten up. You just spent a lovely evening with two ravishing women. Consider yourself the luckiest guy in Spokane. You'll be the envy of your buddies at The Manito on Monday morning. And, I promise not to tell them what a good time you appeared to be having all evening. Oh, and by the way, I'm not a threat to your life of solitude. I'm in a heavy, long-term relationship with a big, fat, doughy hunk of a guy called a bakery."

That said, all Ellen wanted was to be home, in her oldest Susan B. Komen fun run t-shirt and a pair of Sam's old boxers reading herself to sleep with *The Art of Racing in the Rain*. Nothing like an emotional look at a man's tragic life through the eyes of his faithful dog to kick Jack out of her head. She'd always been a sucker for dog stories.

From all appearances, Jack may not have even heard her. He was still looking straight ahead, though she noticed he was still oh-so-slightly-thin lipped. The remainder of the short drive was silent, thankfully.

As Jack pulled in behind The Manito, Ellen had already unbuckled her seatbelt and was almost halfway out of the car, or whatever one called this bodacious thing on four wheels. Once again, thanking her mother for an athletic gene pool, Ellen slid flawlessly out of the Range Rover unassisted. She conquered the rocky parking area like a pro, and once at the back door, felt comforted in the dimly lit sanctuary of the bakery. The delightful evening had somehow ended badly.

She unlocked the back door and paused for a moment to extract her key from the lock, not quite sure if Jack was behind her. He was. Crap! she winced. Why didn't he just stay in the car? The time for manners and pleasantries was over.

"Look, Ellen,"

If she wasn't mistaken, he was shifting from one foot to the other like a nervous, middle school kid.

"I'm sorry for my less-than-stellar behavior. I know

Lillian and everyone else means well, but I'm a big boy now."

Could have fooled me, Ellen thought, but kept silent. Damn, I'm getting good at buttoning my lips, she silently applauded herself.

"I just get frustrated when people try to invade my personal life, that's all. This is the first time Lillian has injected herself into my lack of a love life. Add that to the constant barrage coming from my family, especially my sisters-in-law, which quite frankly is getting old."

"Jack," Ellen said. "I'm going to be completely honest here, which I can do because we're standing on my back porch, and the worst thing you can do to me is boycott my coffee."

"Please, continue," he said, sounding polite but much less confident.

"A nice, though admittedly obstinate, old lady loves you like crazy. It's obvious you think the world of her, too. Correct?"

"Correct."

"That same well-intentioned lady got to know my daughter and thought, just maybe, she'd like to get to know her mother. Still with me, Jack?"

"Yes."

"Is it such a big deal that she asks you to dinner with this seemingly overworked, empty-nested woman? That would be me, Jack."

"No."

"I'm going to think of tonight's dinner as nothing more than a lovely effort by a charming woman who wanted to entertain two people she thought needed a little entertaining. I suggest you do the same."

Jack's head snapped from the small herb garden he was staring at as he continued his two-step shuffle performance. He looked up wide-eyed at Ellen.

"You're right. I'm sorry." Then, to Ellen's utter amazement, he leaned forward and gave her a light peck on her right cheek. Ellen stood still and silent as a stone while he quietly returned to the beast and drove away.

Chapter 13

In *The Art of Racing in the Rain*, the dog, Enzo, observes one of the greatest tragedies of the human race, namely its inability to listen. Ellen agreed philosophically with Enzo. We humans talk everything to death! The little yappers, like toy poodles, are almost as bad, but she definitely agreed that humans are over the top. Why don't we just listen for a change? Ellen felt sorry for Enzo who couldn't get his floppy canine tongue to utter one coherent syllable, so he could explain the importance of listening to his master.

Ellen reached over to turn off her bedside light and left Enzo and his sage advice on the nightstand. It felt good to close the chapter on this bizarre day.

You're so right on, Enzo. She gave her pillow a stern adjustment and with a little luck, would now give herself over to sleep. Her head wasn't cooperating with that plan. I thought I was a listener. I used to listen to Sam hour upon hour at the end of the day. The counselor in me understood his need to just talk the day out. But tonight I was pure petite poodle. Staring at the elongated shadow of the white enamel light on the ceiling above her, she continued to let bits and pieces of the evening float through her head like shapes of a jigsaw puzzle searching for its rightful space.

"Do I like this guy, as in pitter-patter there goes my heart?" she asked herself out loud.

"Whoa, I'm not ready for this!" she whispered, as if

responding any louder would trigger the faintly familiar feeling wandering around her stomach. Butterflies? All this over a peck-on-the-cheek? Ellen covered her eyes with her forearm. Jack? No, not Jack. How can I deal with someone like Jack? He's such an emotional load. Way too Irish.

Tomorrow, she said. Tomorrow this will go away, and I'll be back to normal.

. . .

Jack opened the fridge looking for who knows what, simultaneously tossing his car keys in the general vicinity of the kitchen catch-all basket. As usual, he missed.

"How can I be hungry after that dinner?" he wondered aloud, grabbing a yogurt. The light from the fridge was the only light in the kitchen, which was small but far exceeded today's standards—everything stainless, from the Viking refrigerator to the tiny stainless cone-shaped light covers hanging over the eating bar. Lately, only one burner on his serious six-burner gas range saw life when Jack would heat up a can of soup or water for tea. He usually ate at the hospital.

Why did I act like such a jerk with Ellen? Spooning up the fruit in the bottom of the yogurt cup he didn't want, he lit into himself much the way Lillian would if she was sitting at the counter across from him.

Everyone and their best friend had been trying to get Jack established in the marriage category for the past year. He just assumed Lillian had the same agenda. God forbid I guessed this one wrong, he thought. Maybe Ellen's right, and Lillian just wanted to spend a pleasant evening with Molly's mom and me. Ellen didn't exactly throw herself at me like some others have. Quite the opposite. Cripes, she must think I'm a Class A, major league, narcissistic moron. She's obviously happy on her own. Just look at the life she's built. She's done the marriage thing. She's obviously moved on.

Yogurt stirred but uneaten, he walked to the back deck while Luke, his faithful man's best friend, darted from bush to bush. Jack liked the size and architecture of his home. It was just right—close to work, plenty of room for him, and lots of yard for Luke. What more can a man ask for?

A lot, he admitted. A lot.

Chapter 14

In spite of all the craziness, Liam was enjoying himself. The whole ND-mania thing was, to him, a re-occurring special event, though definitely not a way of life. How does Joe do this for a living, he wondered? Between yesterday's pep rally, alumni dinner and late-night reception, Liam must have personally met more than one hundred people. Amazingly, it seemed as if Joe knew every alumnus' name, graduation year, current occupation, spouse, names of their children, and the approximate year the next generation was likely to enroll at Notre Dame University. And, it seemed as if each alum felt like a part of Joe's extended family. The man was incredible.

And now (drum roll) Notre Dame football game day, bay-bee, as Dick Vitale would say. The rites of autumn turned an otherwise typical Saturday into a big-top circus. Even Los Angeles couldn't help but notice that the Fighting Irish were in town.

Dressed in this year's official t-shirt purchased yesterday from the portable ND bookstore in the hotel lobby, Liam headed down to breakfast. He spied Joe talking to a man who looked remarkably like Reverend Schuller of televangelist fame.

"Liam, I'd like you to meet Dr. Logan Rogers. Dr. Rogers and his wife, Mary Belle, are good friends of mine. I visit them whenever I can at their cabin on Flathead Lake in Montana."

Joe moved on, leaving Liam to chat with the Rogers. After a few minutes, Liam excused himself to grab a muffin and a cup of coffee before locating Joe again. Joe could move through the crowd more quickly when he and Liam deployed the ham 'n egg routine. It began with Joe engaging alums in conversation. Joe would catch Liam's eye, who would then join the conversation. After introductions were made, Liam took over the conversation, and Joe moved on to cover more real estate. It was good training for a political career if Liam decided to buy into Stacie Dearborn's prediction of their future together. And Jim Dearborn's. And Osbourne, Wainwright, Nelson's. Sitting there in a corner of his mind was a very messy pile of unfinished business. Later, he thought, no time for sorting things out now.

Joe was talking to a couple along with a young woman in her mid-to-late twenties, around Stacie's age, he guessed. She had dark, wavy hair and amazingly clear blue eyes with a few freckles sprinkled across her nose. Not the red-haired, fair-skinned Irish version of himself, but the striking features of the Black Irish. She also had a wholesome, athletic look about her. And, she was wearing the same t-shirt as he was, with jeans that fit her slender, very nicely proportioned body.

"Liam," Joe smiled. "Do you remember meeting the Rosses at my apartment in South Bend?"

"I certainly do. Liam O'Connor. Nice to see you again. If I recall correctly, it's Lou and Peyton, right?"

Liam saw the girl aim a sharp look at Lou.

"Exactly! What a memory you have for names, Liam," replied Lou. She looked at Joe, smiling like the cat that swallowed the canary.

"And this is Molly Kirkpatrick, Liam," said Joe. "Molly's living in Los Angeles and working with the Sisters of Providence in their outreach work with the Hispanic immigrant community. I think that program is an extension of the Jesuits from Gonzaga University, right Molly?"

"Yes it is, Father."

"Please, it's Joe," Joe said. "Liam is an attorney for the federal government in Chicago. He's also done a lot of work on immigrant rights—for, not against," he inserted quickly. "It seems you both have a common thread in your choice of careers, don't you think? Perhaps you can compare notes later. Right now Liam needs to drive me to the stadium. I have to make an appearance at the tailgate event before joining the team for my awe-inspiring, pre-game prayer in the locker room. And oh, by the way, here are your passes to the President's Skybox. Don't ask me how I got them. Just enjoy!"

"Nice to see you again," Liam said to the Rosses. "And nice to meet you, Molly. I guess I'll see you at the game."

As he walked with Joe to the parking garage, he decided not to ask the obvious question. Joe seemed just as content to leave the subject alone. This was definitely some sort of setup. He remembered Lou and Peyton writing down his e-mail address to give to a girl in Spokane. He was sure the name was the same: Molly Kirkpatrick. But from the look Molly gave Lou, he was reasonably sure she also knew nothing about the plan. She seemed nice enough at first glance, and he was determined to enjoy the football game. Truth known, he was sort of looking forward to getting to know her. He liked the fresh, natural, Lands End look about her.

. . .

Molly watched Joe and Liam O'Connor walk away. She couldn't help appreciating his tall, athletic build, broad shoulders, and the way his jeans fit. And his strawberry blonde hair. She hated to admit it, but he was awfully cute.

Molly had to force her attention back into sharp focus and remind herself that she was mad as hell with Lou.

"You're like a horse with the bit in her teeth. Is there no stopping you?"

Lou just smiled as Peyton excused himself to find a restroom.

"You've been planning this with Father Joe—excuse me, it's Just Joe—haven't you? Manipulating a priest, no less, to become involved in a deceitful conspiracy."

"Molly, let me start by saying I admit nothing. Except of course that he's gorgeous, a brilliant immigration lawyer and he'll be sitting with us at the game. I, for one, am looking forward to getting to know him better. I've met him only once before, but I don't have that many friends and acquaintances that I couldn't use one more. How about you? At twenty-four-years-old, you don't have room for another friend?"

"You didn't set this up for us to become friends."

"Yes, I did. He's a smart, interesting young man. That's all I know about him. And if Joe gives him a thumbs up, I know he's for real. What you do with him is your own business. My part is done, and I have no vested interest in what happens from this point forward. To play off your equine metaphor, you can lead a horse to water…yada, yada, yada."

Molly knew Lou was right. She was also a tiny bit flattered everyone involved would go to so much trouble to pull off this plan. And she knew she would have refused to come to the game if Lou had told her Liam was coming.

"Did Liam know about this?"

"No."

"Good. I would hate to think I was the only stooge."

"Time to get over yourself, Molly," Lou sighed. "Let's have a fun day, enjoy some good football and, God forbid, make a new friend or two. Life is short, and the sun is shining in Southern California. No complaints or regrets."

"I'm sure the ND and UCLA football coaches have nothing on you when it comes to a good ol' fashioned, butt-kicking pep talk. Okay, I'm in. Let's Go, Irish!"

A few loyal ND fans picked up on her cheer and started yelling "Go Irish!" Like a stadium wave, the yell spread through the breakfast crowd. Lou and Molly, laughing at the absurdity, set off to find Peyton. It was getting close to game time.

Liam loved everything about college football games. Well, everything except traffic jams, jockeying for a parking space, maneuvering through crowded corridors, climbing over

112

people to get to a seat, settling down and then immediately having the urge to go to the bathroom or to get something to eat, having some know-it-all, loud, foul-mouthed, intoxicated braggart sitting behind you, the hot sun bearing down on you in California, or the rain pouring down in Indiana. Other than the aforementioned, going to a big Notre Dame showdown game was among a few of his favorite things.

He had no complaints today. By chauffeuring Joe, Liam scored easy access to the stadium with security guards magically stepping aside when they saw Joe's collar and ND credentials, directing him to a prime parking space. Once inside, there were no lines, no jostling crowds and the Skybox was over the top with comfortable seats, a private restroom and plenty of food and booze. The social climate matched the bright 75-degree day. How can so many people have such straight, white teeth? Or is it the tan that makes them so luminescent? All these things he wondered as he accepted a bottle of Fat Tire ale. It must be a West Coast thing, he concluded. Looking around at the happy Skybox people, Liam decided that this wasn't a bad way to watch a game. He also wondered, since he was already considering taking a new job, if the ND president was looking for a new corporate counsel.

Joe had already disappeared to the ND locker room where he would deliver a Holy Mother Full of Grace/ Play Like Champions prayer to the team and coaches. He would be out on the field with the team, a constant reminder they were playing for God's football team.

Liam was engaged in conversation with several key alumni when Lou, Peyton and Molly arrived. Man, she really is quite lovely, he thought. But before he could make his way over to say hello, the national anthem began to play followed by the kickoff. The Irish received the ball and ran it back to their 48-yard line. A tremendous first play for the Irish and the sea of green in the stadium was on their feet, making one helluva noise. There was a rush to the Skybox window, and for a few moments, Liam forgot all about everything except this opening drive against the Bruins.

In the next play, the quarterback lateralled the ball to the running back who, with a fabulous flea-flicker play, tossed it back to the quarterback. He then threw the ball to the wide receiver. The wide receiver broke a tackle and followed his blockers to open range territory, running it in for a touchdown. The extra point was good, and less than two minutes into the game, the Irish Leprechaun did seven elevated push-ups. Notre Dame was in the lead seven to zero.

Pigskin passion surged through the Skybox crowd. A tsunami of high fives, hugs and backslaps ricocheted and reverberated like a pinball machine. Liam, like everyone there, was caught up in the frenzy. It was an out-of body experience and utterly contagious. When he finally stopped shouting and took a moment to find his waylaid beer, he came face-to-face with Molly.

And, like everyone else in the room, Molly's spirits were high. Who couldn't love college football from this vantage point? Her cheeks were pink, and the rest of her loveliness took his breath away. Liam felt as if he'd taken that last tackle himself and could hardly keep his eyes on the game and away from Molly's face.

Wow, he thought. She is the embodiment of the perfect girl of my subconscious dreams. Yes, Stacie is Grace Kelly blonde and classically gorgeous. But Molly is like Ali McGraw, and I'm freakin' Steve McQueen.

Reining himself in, he gave Molly a one-armed buddy hug and said, "Holy crap, Molly, we've got ourselves a ball game," and then noticed her empty hands. "Can I get you a beer?"

"Sure! I was about to get myself one, but then all hell broke loose."

She followed him to the bar, and in the absence of her favorite Canadian Kokanee lager, he ordered them two Fat Tires.

"What about Lou and Peyton?"

She spied them in the crowd. "It looks like they found the bar already. Besides, I rarely have to worry about those two." She gestured toward the four corners of the room like a ballerina. "These are merely friends they haven't met yet. By the end of the game, they'll know everyone here, where they are from, where and when they went to Notre Dame, or elsewhere, and will have at least one acquaintance in common with each person they meet. Believe me, it's a gift."

"They're teachers, right? Sounds like they missed a calling in sales."

"ABC...always be closing."

They laughed. Liam liked her honest, straightforward style and upbeat, genuine laugh. No pretense about this girl. She was the real article. Dang, and he was contemplating marriage to Stacie Dearborn. How could he feel such a strong connection to another woman? And so fast? It was like a riptide he couldn't fight. So he did what any experienced swimmer would do, he relaxed and allowed himself to be swept out to sea hoping he could swim his way back to shore if he had to.

Notre Dame held the lead and finished strong with a 36-10 victory over UCLA. It was, "A Great Day for the Irish," as Molly quickly picked up on Skybox lingo. The very same had almost emptied out, leaving Lou, Peyton, Molly and Liam waiting for Joe to re-emerge from his final blessings in the locker room. Within twenty minutes, the priest burst into the Skybox and grabbed a beer. "Hope y'all appreciated the afternoon's entertainment. I'm starved and have worked up a terrible thirst. Where would everyone like to go for dinner?"

No one had the heart to point out they had been eating and drinking the afternoon away in the lap of luxury.

"Your call, Father!" they agreed in unison.

"You know, I saw a Thai place right around the corner from our hotel. What do you say we go to dinner there so we can relax, take our time, and walk home?"

"I've been craving Thai food myself," added Liam with a disarming grin.

Lou, Peyton and Molly resisted the urge to tell Joe and Liam they'd eaten at that very same restaurant the night before. First sharing a knowing look, Peyton exclaimed, "You know,

Spokane doesn't have much in the way of Thai (a very forgivable white lie), so that sounds great, huh, girls?"

"Absolutely," said Lou, smiling.

"Done," said Joe, finishing his beer. "Liam and I will call ahead and meet you there in an hour. Everyone sync your watches. We are now T-minus one hour and counting."

. . .

Molly got into the backseat of Lou and Peyton's rental car and waited for an onslaught of questions about Liam. Instead, they drove back to the Westin Hotel in relative silence. Lou and Peyton seemed to be concentrating on traffic and directions and had hardly a word for her in the backseat. She was alone with her thoughts about the day. And, she had to admit privately, what a day. Although she had entered it kicking and screaming like her dad—heavy sigh—used to say she entered the world, it had been the best damn day she could remember in quite a while. Mainly, she was loath to admit, because it was spent with Liam. He was everything Lou said he would be, and more. Handsome, fun, funny, smart—brilliant in fact, and he had spent the entire game, between plays, hanging on her every word. Where's the downer in this scenario, she asked herself?

"Do you girls want to go up to your room and change or go right to dinner?" asked Peyton as they pulled into the parking garage. "Lou? Molly?"

"Let's go freshen up. We still have twenty minutes before we meet Joe and Liam. It's only a five-minute walk. I don't know about you, Molly, but I could use a splash of water on my face and some fresh lipstick."

"Sounds good. Knock on my door when you're ready to go."

When Molly reached her room, she saw the message light flashing on her phone. Must be mom. No one else knows where I am, she thought, except mom. She called to retrieve her voicemail and was surprised to hear Sister Aracelia's voice.

She sounded calm, but Molly could hear the underlying concern in her tone. It was about the Raigosa family. Alberto was in serious trouble with the ICE. Although Sister Aracelia assured Molly there was nothing to be done tonight, she was hoping Molly could return to the retreat house by two o'clock on Sunday and go with her to visit Maria and the Raigosa family at their home at three. There was no need to call back tonight. Just touch base with her in the morning.

Chapter 15

Maria and Alberto Raigosa believed they made the right decision immigrating to the United States from their home in Guadalajara, Mexico, twenty years ago. As newlyweds, life in their small village, with no formal schooling and little or no work available, was a bleak future staring back at two optimists who wholeheartedly believed in life's boundless possibilities.

Since crossing the border and settling in Southern California, Maria worked the graveyard shift in the nearby fruit packing plant. Alberto was a hard worker, but his employment was more erratic. He was sometimes a warehouse laborer, mechanic, landscaper, truck driver and junk hauler. Maria's steady paycheck covered the rent, groceries and necessities. Alberto's cash-under-the-table jobs made up the difference for new school clothes, furniture, support money for family still in Mexico, and paying the hospital after each of their four children was born.

Buying new school clothes gave Maria and Alberto the most pleasure. An education was a democratic right of all children born in the United States. Education was a privilege, not a right, afforded to children living in Mexico unless they were born into money and influence. The Raigosas may not have earned United States citizenship, but they were proud their children were U.S. citizens by birth. Believing the sacrifices for their children validated their lives, the Raigosas faced the risk of deportation that was intensifying in the climate of anti-immigrant politics.

In all their twenty years living in California, the Raigosas had never felt as vulnerable as they were feeling now. Alberto was working a laborer job when the ICE raided the warehouse. Three of his friends were arrested and detained for deportation. The close-knit Hispanic community was becoming more and more afraid of the ICE. Alberto would have been the fourth arrest if the boss hadn't sent him out on an earlier errand to pick up an order at the parts supply store. Yes, he was happy not to be arrested, but the boss told him not to come back looking for a job until things had settled down and the pressure was off. He needed this job. The boss was a decent man paying Alberto a decent wage. The Raigosas needed the money.

Rosa, the oldest of the four Raigosa children at eighteen, graduated from high school in June and had just started her freshman year at University of the Pacific on academic scholarship. Her scholarships, student loans and part-time work study job on campus covered Rosa's tuition. However, living on campus was more expensive than Alberto had anticipated. Rosa was an exceedingly bright, hard working kid and he wanted to give her all the advantages. Losing this job was going to set them back financially.

The two younger girls, the twins, were doing well in school. At eleven years old and in the sixth grade, Ruth and Lupe were a constant source of joy to both parents.

On the other hand, Hector, seventeen, was a cross to bear bringing concern and fear into their household. He had been sucked like quicksand into joining a street gang. Alberto and Maria suspected he was dealing drugs and God knows what else. Hector often had money but no job. He wore expensive clothes that signified gang membership. He had already fathered one child and openly admitted it was his because it gave him status in the gang. But Hector refused to marry the young mother and saw no reason to care for the child. Just yesterday, a shooting had occurred in their neighborhood when a rival gang targeted a friend of Hector's. Alberto and Maria confronted Hector, but he brushed it off as a random act.

When pressed further, he stormed out of the house.

At least while Alberto wasn't working for the next few days, he could walk the twins to and from school until the neighborhood settled down. He'd also get his "honey-dos" done around the house. And, although Maria missed Rosa, she knew her daughter was safer living on UOP's campus.

"I don't understand this violence and hatred," said Alberto. "Where did it come from? These kids have so many more opportunities and advantages than you and I ever imagined, Maria."

"But it is not enough," Maria said in her clipped English. "The quick and easy money is what they're after. Drug money. The easy money corrupts. The drugs destroy lives. Kids think they're invincible, so danger itself is a drug."

"The kid who was shot didn't make it through the night," said Alberto. "I'm expecting there will be pay backs to put right the so-called wrongs. That's how it works. I don't want Ruth, Lupe or you getting caught in any retaliation shootings. What are we going to do about Hector?"

Despite the heat, Alberto was wearing what he wore every day: a buttoned khaki shirt with long sleeves and pressed trousers. And Maria noticed, not for the first time in the past few months, Alberto looked beaten.

"He's been dropped from high school. I got the call yesterday that he hasn't shown up for school since the first week, and he's not allowed back," said Maria. "If he's not at school and he's not working, where does he go?"

"I don't know where, but I'll tell you this: Hector's going to go take my job until things settle down with ICE. I'll talk to my boss and try to set him up as a temp. God knows we need the money, and if he's going to live in this house, he can help us pay the bills and put his sisters through school."

Like a feral tomcat, Hector didn't come home that night or the next. Three days later he showed up wanting food, a shower and his bed. Alberto told him to help himself to leftovers and sleep as long as he needed to, but after he woke up they would be having a talk. Hector rolled his eyes and disappeared to the back of the house without another word.

The next morning, Hector walked into the kitchen clean, showered and looking to grab something to eat before a quick escape out the backdoor. He was surprised to see both parents at the kitchen table waiting for him. He steeled himself in an attitude of sullen indifference for the inevitable and promised lecture from the night before.

"Where are you going today, Hector?" asked Alberto. "Don't tell me it's to school because the principal called and informed us you are not welcome back. Ever."

"As if I'd ever go back to that prison."

"So you'd rather be in another prison? From the look of things, you're on a fast track to jail. What do they call that in school...accelerated?"

"Get off my case."

"Don't you talk to us like that. We didn't cross the border and work hard at any job we could get so you could be someone's cellmate. Oh, by the way, happy birthday. You're eighteen today, Hector. No juvey anymore. If you get caught dealing drugs, or whatever you're doin', you're going to jail or prison. It will make high school look like daycare."

Hector stayed quiet, but his look was defiant.

"I can't go back to my job. Three undocumented workers were arrested two days ago at work. I was lucky. I was on a delivery run at the time, but now the boss won't let me come back for at least two weeks until things cool down. The ICE has been known to show up again a couple days later in a follow-up sting. I've called the boss, and he said you can work temporarily in my place now that you're eighteen. We need the money, Hector. Your mom can't support us alone on what she makes."

"Oh thanks, happy birthday...to me."

"It's time to grow up and start living with the consequences, Hector," said his mother.

"Sure, whatever," Hector said. He was thinking, I've got to get out of here as quickly as I can, and I'm never coming back. "When do they want me to start?"

"The boss needs a warehouse worker for the three-to-eleven night shift," said Alberto. "It's almost noon now. You need to be there by two o'clock to fill out paperwork in the office and be ready to punch in no later than three."

"Si senor, sir," he said dripping with sarcasm.

Alberto was tired of the battle. "Do this for your mother and your sisters. Put others first for a change."

As if I don't know how to make money, Hector thought to himself as he walked out the backdoor. His real family, the Alaharas gang, was waiting for him in the alley in a black Cadillac Escalade. He knew he could make more money than his parents ever dreamed of when the next big deal came down. Then it'll be raining gold for this hombre. I'll throw money in their faces and then ask them how they like the consequences of their life choices, he thought.

When Hector didn't show for his shift at the warehouse, Alberto wasn't surprised. He didn't know what had made him believe or given him hope the boy had grown up enough to take on the responsibilities of a man and put the needs of his family first. Mother of God, Hector had a child, his own flesh and blood, he wasn't even interested in loving or supporting. And, although Alberto knew Hector loved his sisters, his path of selfishness and self-destruction was placing them all in danger.

Anxious for a job and money, Alberto talked his boss into letting him come back to work after one week. The same day, the ICE showed up, as predicted, and arrested Alberto in a follow-up sting. Maria, trying as best she could to appear calm and holding it together, put the twins to bed, lit a candle and prayed the Rosary before she placed a quiet call to Sister Aracelia at the Providence Retreat House.

After the longest time, she finally drifted off to sleep when she was jolted from her bed with another phone call. This time it was Hector, telling her he'd been arrested on federal charges of drug trafficking.

Chapter 16

Still feeling unsettled about Sister Aracelia's call and what the Raigosa family was dealing with on this otherwise perfect California evening, Molly tried to put her angst aside as she readied herself to join her little traveling troupe for dinner. A quick change out of her game day jeans and t-shirt into something slightly more appropriate—brown cords, a clean white shirt, a light pink cotton sweater draped over her shoulders, a swipe of pink lip gloss and a final brush through her hair, and she was ready when the knock sounded on the door.

Lou, who could read her like a book, took one look at Molly and asked her what was wrong.

"Nothing I can solve tonight, but one of the families on my caseload is in trouble with the ICE. Sister Aracelia called and left a message. She asked me to be back to the Retreat House tomorrow by two o'clock. She scheduled a meeting with the family at three and would like me to go with her to their home. I'll probably leave right after breakfast."

"Oh Mol, I'm so sorry. I hate to be selfish, but I had hoped we could go highbrow and tour the Getty, or lowbrow and go freak-watching at Venice Beach together before we have to head to the airport. Our flight isn't until six."

"I'm so sorry, too. I was looking forward to being a California tourist with you. But I just can't."

Peyton joined in. "Let's enjoy what time we have. Our dinner companions are waiting. It's T-minus five minutes and counting."

"Agreed," Lou and Molly said in unison.

The trio arrived at the Thai place to find Liam and Joe already seated. Both gentlemen stood up as the three approached. Liam was a little surprised by how happy he was to see Molly again. Her easy, athletic walk, her genuine smile, the healthy glow of her skin and hair, and the way she made her casual outfit look, well, stunning. My, oh my. He was feeling all googly inside, like a fourteen-year-old with his first crush.

However, he could tell something serious had happened between the game and dinner. He waited a few minutes until the small talk died down and asked Molly if anything was wrong.

She was never one to hide her feelings well. And knowing this crowd would be sympathetic and helpful, she opened up about the Raigosas.

"They're Mexican illegals who have been in the U.S. for over twenty years. All four kids are American born. Alberto, the father, was arrested and detained yesterday. In today's immigration climate, I don't have much hope for Alberto. If Maria, the mother, is arrested, the older two children will be okay, but the younger girls, eleven year-old twins Ruth and Lupe, will have to return to Mexico with their parents or stay in the U.S. with their siblings or other relatives. The older sister, Rosa, is eighteen and totally amazing. She's on a full-ride academic scholarship to the University of the Pacific. The brother, Hector, is seventeen, close to turning eighteen and is a known Alahara gang banger, suspected drug dealer, and although he doesn't or won't see it, is on a collision course with the law. So our choices will likely be to either send the twin girls back to Mexico where they... Well, you don't need me to tell you how dismal their lives will be. Or, we pull the daughter out of college, ask her to forego her goals, give up her hard-earned opportunities for a higher education and maybe, if she's lucky, take over her mother's job working graveyard shift."

"We'll take them," blurted Lou.

"In a heartbeat," said Peyton, wondering how those words came out of his mouth, but liking the sound of them.

"It's not that easy," added Liam, raising his hand as if to slow traffic. He and Molly exchanged a look. His breath caught at the knowing pain in her penetrating blue eyes.

"The system," Molly explained, "will put those girls in a household of relatives, even if they are pedophiles and drug dealers, before it will place Hispanic children in the loving home of an Anglo couple like you."

"And Spokane is not in the state of California," Liam added. "You're tripping over international, federal and state laws. It's a morass."

"It sounds more like a pain in the ass," Joe commented. "If I may, I'd like to bless our upcoming meal with a prayer of thanks and then ask God for special assistance in helping this family. They certainly have some excellent troops fighting on their side."

They all bowed their heads as Joe said a heartfelt prayer for mercy and guidance in doing God's work for this family and others like it. Molly was moved to tears and squeezed Joe's hand, acknowledging his kindness and words of support. She felt genuine compassion and a depth of spiritual connection through Father Joe O'Brien.

Just then the waiter arrived. Orders were taken, drinks were raised with toasts in both a light-hearted air, and more serious fortitude.

Dinner was excellent. The party continued on until almost eleven when Joe pointed out it had been a long day, and he had to be up early in time to say Mass for the Notre Dame alumni.

Peyton took up the gauntlet and announced, "All brave and pious souls will reconvene for Mass at eight in the morning followed by a nutritious breakfast in the hotel restaurant. Then, like Molly, we must go our separate ways and make the world a better place. As my great Uncle Harry once said, 'Public service is the rent you pay for the space you occupy in your community.' "

The party walked together from the restaurant to the hotel lobby elevator. All five got in the elevator together.

"What floors?" asked Joe, who was closest to the buttons.

"Twenty-two for the three of us," said Peyton.

Joe pushed twenty-two and said, "Same as Liam and myself."

Molly was considering a conspiracy theory, but then figured ND had a block of rooms, and it only made sense.

Still? How awkwardly coincidental.

"I'll walk you all to your rooms," offered Liam.

"What room are you in, Liam?" asked Lou, ever so innocently.

"Let's see. Where's that envelope thing. I miss keys. Here it is, room 2222, and Joe is right across the hall in 2221."

"Then we're almost neighbors, just two doors down in 2225, and Mol is across from us in 2226. Small world," said Peyton.

It certainly is, thought Molly, and it's getting smaller all the time. "Good night you two," Molly said over a three-way hug with the Rosses. "Thanks for a wonderful day, Joe and Liam. See you in the morning."

. . .

Liam noticed the message light flashing as soon as he entered his room. He had purposefully left his cell phone in the room. He checked it and found three missed calls and the voice message indicator glaring back at him. Who else could it be but Stacie Dearborn?

He didn't want to talk to Stacie. Not yet, anyway. He wanted this perfect day to stay intact. But inasmuch as he resolved not to call her until the next day, the phone rang, and he couldn't help himself from picking it up.

"Well, hello stranger." Although it was about one-thirty in the morning Chicago time, Liam knew Stacie very well. She'd probably just gotten home after a night out with her throng of friends. "I've been missing you and trying to get in touch with you all night."

"Is something wrong, Stacie?"

"No, lover. I'm just so lonely without you. And even if I can't be with you, I want to talk to you and want your voice to be the last one I hear before I go to bed."

"Are you interested in knowing who won the game?"

"Sure, I have the news on now, but luckily they haven't gotten to the sports report yet. I don't want to hear that particular news from anyone but you. I'm saving myself for you in more ways than one, darling."

He shuddered.

"It was a great day for the Irish. We beat UCLA 36-10. The first play was crazy. The whole game was amazing. Joe got us passes to the President's Skybox."

"Us, lover? Who's us? I thought you were just with Father Joe all day. I assumed you were on the sidelines and in the locker room after playing like champions today."

"No, Stacie. I'm not allowed on the sidelines or in the locker room. I would have to be the new legal counsel employed by the ND athletic department for that to happen."

"Too bad. But no, not really. I like the sound of your other new employer, OWN. So, back to my previous question, who's us?"

"Joe has some close friends from Spokane, Washington, who were also down for the game, Louise and Peyton Ross. The Rosses have a family friend working for a Jesuit outreach exchange. They are all very nice, and the five of us had dinner together. I just walked into the room when you called."

"What was the friend's name again? I think I missed that part."

"Molly Kirkpatrick."

"And she's how old?"

"I don't know. Probably about your age, in her late twenties."

"And she's plain, dull and wears clunky, comfortable shoes?"

"No. She's actually quite attractive in a Northwest, outdoorsy way."

"You sound taken with her."

"Stacie. I've never known you to be this insecure about other women."

"I'm hearing something I've never heard before. Anyway, lover, can you take an earlier flight home tomorrow? I'm missing you terribly. We have so much to talk about and so many plans to make for our future."

"I'll be coming home on the same flight, Stacie. Are you still picking me up at the airport, or would you rather I grab the airport shuttle?"

"I'll be there. And then I'll take you home. Be sure and plan on an overnight guest. I'm so hot for you I can hardly walk."

He couldn't bring himself to respond directly.

"Great, Stacie, my flight gets in at four o' clock. Meet me at the second baggage claim door. Oh yeah, and can you give Joe a ride to the train station?"

"Only if you say you can't wait to see me…in bed."

"Yeah sure, I can't wait. Good night, Stacie." Click.

Geez-zus Murphy. What a sleazy little tart. But that really wasn't fair to her. Only a week ago he'd have gotten a kick out of that kind of phone sex act from the Blond Wonder. Somehow, now, it sounded like what it was. Cheap.

Whoa. He was having a bona-fide Shallow Hal moment. But he couldn't help it. What a difference a day, and an entirely different kind of girl, had made on him. The thought of Stacie? Actually, he didn't want to think about Stacie at the moment. For once her timing and instincts were all wrong. Had he heard a hint of desperation in her voice?

The phone rang again, and he told himself not to answer it, but he did anyway.

"Hello?"

"Liam, it's me, Molly." Her voice had a palpable tone of desperation.

"Molly, what's the matter?"

"May I come to your room? I need to talk this situation out. I just hung up the phone with Sister A. Hector—remember, the Raigosas' son—has been arrested for drug trafficking. Add that to Alberto's arrest and Maria is now a goner."

"Just give me two minutes."

Liam quickly put on jeans and a sweatshirt and picked up the clothes from the floor.

He was waiting with his door open when Molly approached from down the hallway.

"I'm so sorry to bother you, but I won't be able to get any sleep until I have some plan of action. I'm a mess."

Molly had on gray sweatpants with a white sweatshirt and bare feet. Her eyes and brow held a look of deep concern. She was distraught, yet vulnerable and lovely. He would do anything for her. To distract his thoughts, he walked over to the mini-bar.

"Would you like a drink? How about one of these little bottles of wine? Diet Coke?"

"Unless you want it, I'd give you my left arm for that can of Diet Coke."

"It's yours. And though that left arm is tempting, go ahead and keep it. Sounds like you may definitely need it." Liam poured himself a scotch and soda and sat down in a chair opposite hers where she sat resting her chin on one knee with the other leg tucked under. This image was one he would carry with him for a very long time.

Molly shared with Liam everything she knew about the case and what Sister Aracelia had just told her about Alberto and Hector. She told Liam what she knew about the local Los Angeles ICE agency, their recent activities and cases. Liam paralleled similar situations and outcomes he was familiar with in the Chicago district.

"This is a lose-lose situation, Molly," Liam said. "I'll offer my advice, for what it's worth. I think there is one plausible way to proceed. No guarantees, mind you. But with a little luck, you'll have a chance of creating something good out of a crap-shit situation."

They talked until one in the morning exploring every legal option he could think of. He agreed Alberto and Maria were surely heading south. He couldn't see a way around that inevitability. Hector was unquestionably on an express train to federal prison. However, if the Rosses were serious about their "offer" to provide a home for the twins, this strategy would allow the twins to stay in the U.S. and Rosa could continue her college education. Feeling reasonably sure that this was the best of all options, Liam and Molly exchanged e-mail addresses, cell-work-home phone numbers, and home addresses in case she needed to contact him.

Plan set, Molly decided it was time to leave. She stood up quickly, only to stumble as one of her legs had fallen asleep. Liam quickly caught her, placing his hands under her arms. Before he could stop himself, he slid his arms around her back and pulled her close for a brief, soft kiss.

"I've wanted to do that all day."

Molly didn't pull away. "And I've been wanting to do this all day." She kissed him back with an intensity that shook him to his very core. His head was spinning. Stacie was right to be insecure. He had never felt like this in his life. So this is what the "right one" does to you? Could Molly be the "right one?"

"I'm so sorry, Liam. I know you're practically engaged. That was wrong of me."

He quickly dove in again for another kiss before the magic spell lifted. "Here's another cheesy phrase, 'If lovin' you is wrong, I don't wanna be right.'"

Did he just say love out loud?

"Okay, but I always like to get the last word in. 'Here's looking at you kid.'" And with that, she turned away and walked out the door leaving him alone. Oh, come back, he thought. He heard her door close firmly down the hall, and when he fell back onto the bed, his head was still spinning.

Chapter 17

Ellen woke up early Sunday feeling surprisingly cheerful. Refusing to mentally rehash Saturday night, she worked steadily through the morning bakery rush until it finally slowed to a steady, manageable flow. She was happily humming along with IZ and his rendition of "Somewhere Over the Rainbow" and "What a Wonderful World" thinking Don Ho ain't got nuthin' on IZ, when the phone rang.

If there is a just and benevolent God, which I've really started to doubt over the past year, it won't be Jack on the other end of this call, she thought hopefully. She didn't want his apologies or his continued pout to damper her pleasant Sunday morning.

"Hello?" she answered cautiously.

"I wish with all that's good and holy that you were down here with me!" Lou yelled at the other end of the phone. The declarative statement jerked her out of her bakery Zen, but at least it wasn't Jack.

"Lou, how's it going?"

"It's going, and I wish you were here, that's how it's going."

"You said that already. What's up?"

"Well, what would you say if I told you Peyton and I have offered to bring eleven-year-old twin girls home to live with us?"

"I'd say Notre Dame has kicked its alumni recognition to a whole new, though ethically-questionable, level. Whatever happened to just naming building and lecture halls after people, or a tastefully done commemorative plaque?"

"I'm serious, El."

"What are you talking about?" The seriousness in Lou's voice was Lou at a level of intensity Ellen seldom heard from her best friend.

"I take it you haven't talked to Molly this morning?"

"No, I figured she was busy with you, Peyton and the game. I planned on calling her later after the bakery closes."

"Well, it's possible that Peyton and I could become legal guardians of twins whose parents are being deported back to Mexico."

Ellen reached over and turned off IZ, buying time to absorb what Lou just told her.

"Back it up a little and tell me that again, Lou."

"No, you heard right. There's a family Molly has been working with, the Raigosas. The parents are illegals from Mexico and are being deported. They have four kids, one in jail, one in college, and these twin girls, Lupe and Ruth."

"Lou, are you serious?" was the most Ellen could offer at the moment. "I was thinking you were calling to interrogate me about dinner with Miss Johnson and Jack. This is way out of left field."

"Oh, don't worry, I haven't forgotten about that. Never fear, I'll get the blow-by-blow from you. But you had to be the first person I told about the twins. Granted, it's a long shot, but Peyton and I were serious when we put the offer on the table," Lou said.

"Sweetie, I'm psyched for you two. Geez, I can't believe this. These could be two very lucky kids."

"I hope so. Gosh, El, you don't think we would screw them up too bad, do you?"

"Never! You and Peyton got the short straw not being able to have kids of your own. Just look at how good you've been with Molly. Sometimes I think you've been a better mom to her than I have."

"Oh, shut up. You know that isn't true. You're just kind

enough to let me play surrogate mom once in a while. But this is different because we've offered to step up to the plate for real this time. There is no possible way we would let these kids go back to Mexico, and if their parents agree to them staying in the U.S., like I said, we've told Molly to offer 'us' as a guardian family."

Ellen still hadn't fully taken in the news that eleven-year-old twin girls could be entering Lou and Peyton's, up until now, childless life, but she wasn't about to second guess Lou. No way in hell was she going to jeopardize the happiness she heard bounding through the phone.

"What can I do at this end?" she asked.

"I really don't know. Just talking to you is reassuring. We have the guest room the girls can take over for now. My gut tells me they'll want to share a room at first. So there isn't really any preparation. But, Molly tells me that Ruth, one of the twins, has a serious eye issue, which is a compelling argument for them to stay in the States. Ruth's medical problem may prove to be a blessing in disguise. There isn't a snowball's chance in hell she could get the health care or surgery she needs in Mexico."

"How advanced is her problem?" Ellen asked trying to hide her worry.

"I don't have details, except it's pretty severe because technically she should have had the surgery long before age eleven. Hopefully someone in Spokane has the expertise she needs. Hey, now I know how you can help. Could you talk to Jack and get a referral for us?"

Ellen silently dropped the ef-bomb. Why didn't Lou ask her to do something easy like add on a room to their home, install a new sprinkler system, stock the fridge or cut off her right arm? But there was no way she could deny the request. Oh dear, oh damn!

"I'm sure the Spokane Eye Clinic has someone who can handle it," she said, hoping that would appease Lou. But she underestimated the tenacity with which her friend had grasped motherhood.

"I don't want an unknown," Lou said with the foot-down tone only a mother can muster when it comes to her children's health. "Just do us all a favor and ask Jack, okay?"

"I'll call him today, and if I can't reach him, I'll ask him tomorrow morning, Monday, and first thing. Do you want me to get an appointment?"

"Just get a couple of names. If this move comes together like we hope, it will be hugely hard for the girls to be separated from their mama and papa. We'll get them used to Peyton and me and their new home for a couple of days before Ruth gets thrown into the warm and fuzzy U.S. health care system. All things considered, though, I wouldn't want much time to get away from us either."

"Got it. Consider it done," Ellen said. If she sounded suddenly absent from the conversation, she was. Calling Jack so soon after his prize-winning performance wasn't creating a great urge from within to do cartwheels across the bakery. Hopefully he'd take her call as it was intended, purely professional.

She pressed the "end" button on her cell phone and stared at the communication device, wondering if she should just bite the bullet and call Jack now. It was still early, and looking out she could see a brief lull in counter traffic. She knew there wouldn't be much time later in the day to call since The Manito was usually slammed, nonstop, all day on Sundays. So she put on her big girl panties and called Jack. Blessedly, he had his phone on a short leash and the leave-a-message instructions came on after just three rings. Ellen hung up before the beep, relieved to put Jack out of her mind until tomorrow.

For the remainder of Sunday, as predicted, neighborhood families overran the bakery like Coney Island in July. Dads and kids with uncombed hair, and some still even in their pajamas, gave their moms a much-deserved Sunday morning sleep-in. No sooner did the first shift amble out the door, the after-church crowd arrived. These folks were usually a little older and fully dressed. Throughout the rest of the day students would settle down with their laptops for hours. Families drifted in from the park for an afternoon snack. It was hard not to like Sundays.

Ellen found herself looking forward to Sunday night even before she got invited to her fancy pants dinner Saturday night. Cocooning, she thought, rather proudly. Ha! I've been cocooning since I was five. Who said it was a XYZ generation trend? As usual, Ellen showered after putting in an inordinately long day in the bakery and was just about to call Molly to find out more about Lou and Peyton's possible parenthood when the phone beat her to it. She was fully expecting to hear Molly or Lou's voice on the other end.

"Ellen, it's Jack. I see that I missed your call." Ellen turned statue-still when she heard his voice rather than Molly's.

"Hi," she said. The dang caller ID ratted her out. Ring and run is gone forever!

"You did call, didn't you?"

"Yeah, I did. Um, I need a referral." Stammering, now that's a nice touch, she cringed.

"Okay."

"Well, I don't need one for myself, per se. My friend, Lou, needs one for a little girl coming to Spokane. She's eleven. She's Mexican." God, I sound like a stammering idiot, Ellen chastised herself. A quick reminder of Jack's arrogant behavior last night gave her a blessed sense of serenity. Thank you, mom, she said to herself before continuing.

"Anyway, this little girl apparently needs to get into an eye surgeon. She's crossed-eyed. Lou asked me to call you to ask for a referral. She'd like to get Ruth, the little girl, on deck to see someone."

"Eleven? Is this something new or something they've known about since birth?" Jack said matter of factly, very doctor like.

Ellen wanted to explain to Jack that poor medical care was one of the bummers about being the daughter of an illegal immigrant. But for Ruth and Lou, she took the high road and kept her sarcasm in check.

"That's what I understand, Jack, from what little I know from talking to the Rosses this morning. Regardless, they'll need to get her into someone good. Can you recommend anyone?"

Ellen's shift in tone wasn't lost on Jack, and he knew he was getting the back-draft from his performance last night. He was simultaneously embarrassed and angry by the emotions Ellen evoked in him twice in twenty-four hours. This woman is something else!

"Right off the top of my head, I'd say Mark Stuben is your man. He may not be taking new patients, but that's where I would start. I'll call him in the morning and give him a heads-up. Don't know if it will help, but maybe. We've worked together some." He couldn't help but hope he was winning a few points back with Ellen, but he couldn't tell by her fairly expressionless response.

"Thanks, Jack. I'll call Dr. Stuben tomorrow and see what he can or can't do."

"Sure, okay." Now it was Jack's turn to stammer when all he really wanted to say to Ellen was that he enjoyed dinner and was sorry he ended the evening by acting like such a putz. At the very least, that might put them back on their awkward, yet friendly, ground they shared before he trampled it Saturday.

"And Ellen, I enjoyed last night. I was going to call you earlier but ended up taking someone else's call shift with back-to-back patients."

In her head, Ellen wanted to spout forth with some expletive-peppered statement about his having a weird way of showing her what a swell time he'd had, not to mention the quaint diatribe he offered on the way home about people leaving him alone was a real mood killer, but instead—damn—she took the high road with a polite reply. "Well, now I know why Molly feels so much affection for Miss Johnson," Ellen said, purposefully excluding Jack from the equation. "She's quite a woman."

We really are creatures of habit, Ellen thought to herself after she hung up from talking with Jack. We work all week savoring the prize of having a weekend. And then what happens? By Sunday evening, we're eager to catapult back into our work-a-day routines. Silly us. Lying in bed listening to the last birds reluctantly packing up to head south, Ellen was relieved to chalk this weekend up to history.

Chapter 18

As immigration focused more on entire families than rogue kids, Les Schwanbeck learned he had to work with people, not against them. Thinking about illegal immigrants as enemies only got you as far as homes and buildings vacated just minutes before you arrived with deportation papers. Hard-ass threats so convincing just ten years ago didn't bode well when children were involved like they are today. Families are willing to risk their lives, so their children can live in the U.S., and organizations had sprung up like dandelions after a spring rain to help them. Like the Raigosas, most illegal immigrants today have American-born children. At first glance, no one would guess Les recognized how traumatic it is to separate children from their parents because of the mother or father's illegal status. The complexities and emotions tied to tracking and deporting all or part of a family had become a huge network of victims, advocates and the ICE. Les had mastered it like a mouse seeking cheese at the end of a maze. The bottom line, though? He had a job to do. He just went about it differently than some of the other agents.

Les had Sister Aracelia to thank for making him feel more comfortable shifting from his "us versus them" paradigm. The nun was unlike any of the musty smelling, thick-ankled women he'd grown up with in Catholic schools. She gave up teaching over twenty years ago to work with immigrants and soon became the point guard for organizations like the National Council of La Raza, the largest Hispanic advocacy group in the

U.S. She was one of the first people he called when on the trail of families like the Raigosas. The two had worked together in dozens of cases over the years. Yes, they were adversaries, but they shared a deep respect for each other. If asked, both would refuse to admit they considered each other good friends.

"How's the meanest nun in LA County on the Sabbath?" Les could never initiate a conversation with Sister Aracelia on a serious note. He blamed it on post-Vatican II nuns he had in grade school who couldn't figure out where they belonged after Rome turned the altar around to face the congregation and simultaneously turned their lives upside down. Many nuns, like Sister Aracelia, flourished under the newfound freedom. Others could never find solid ground and either left altogether, or became snarly and took it out on their charges. Mostly kids.

"Devout and forgiving of those less compassionate who call me for information I won't provide them," Sister Aracelia responded with the monotone cadence every good Catholic could emulate on demand. "And how is my heathen friend?"

"Still paving the way to hell with good intentions, Sister. I need to talk with you, and not about my salvation."

The minute Hector was arrested she expected a call from ICE. She was thankful it was Les. He was old school, but understood her position better than anyone else she worked with in the agency. Under all that huff and puff was a good man.

"Let me guess. Hector Raigosa?"

"Hector Raigosa and family. When are you available?"

Sister Aracelia exhaled slowly. "Will tomorrow work? About 4:30?"

"Thanks, Sister."

"Sure," she said. "I'll put on a clean pair of jeans for the occasion."

. . .

Try as she might, Molly couldn't mask her emotions. "You can't let them tear this family apart!" Molly begged.

Sister Aracelia called Molly at the Westin immediately after she hung up with Les Schwanbeck. She guessed correctly that Molly would react with anger and unreasonable expectations, but still felt obligated to keep her up to speed on any developments concerning the Raigosas. However, Sister Aracelia knew how easy it was for just one person, someone like Hector, to put an entire family in jeopardy. And, it was also clear that Molly had broken rule number one of working at the Center. She let herself become emotionally tied to the Raigosas. The young volunteer was learning the hard way. Yes, she should care for the wellbeing of the people she was helping, but if she immersed herself too deeply into their situation, she would lose her ability to work within the system, which was so necessary to be effective.

"Molly, you know as well as I do the odds turned against the Raigosas the minute Hector was arrested. You have to take a step back. Caring the way you do is what makes you good at your job, but getting too close also sets you up for a world of hurt. It can also make an already chaotic situation much worse."

"Sister, I may have a solution—for the twins, anyway. Please don't agree to anything with the ICE until I get back. Please?"

"Molly, trust me, there is only so much we can do when families find themselves where the Raigosas are today."

"I know, you're right," Molly said, feeling put in her place, but no less angry. She could only think of the dismal options the Raigosas faced. "When do you meet with this guy from ICE?"

"Tomorrow afternoon."

"May I be there?"

"That's probably not a good idea. Les, the agent who's coming to meet with me, doesn't take kindly to feeling ganged up on. Let me talk with him one-on-one. I'll call you right after we meet."

"Okay, but remember, I may have a solution, if such a thing exists in this case."

. . .

Lou and Peyton drove Molly back to Providence House. "He's pretty amazing, isn't he?" asked Lou, not able to stifle herself.

"Who?" replied Molly knowing exactly whom Lou was talking about. She hated to admit it, but Liam was not going to be easy to forget.

"Oh Molly, can't you admit it? When I'm right, I'm right. If he was a movie star, he'd make the top ten list of People magazine's Mr. Rights!"

"Chicago is too far away, and besides, he's already in a relationship," said Molly. "Yes, he's absolutely wonderful. Happy? Now let this alone." They drove in silence for the remaining few miles. Molly didn't want to say it out loud, but of course she had to agree with Lou that, yes, Liam was definitely, incredibly, undeniably amazing.

The neighborhoods grew more decrepit as they ventured deeper into South Central LA. Homes were run down with scabby lawns and abandoned cars. There was hardly a fence or wall that hadn't been tagged with spray paint. Shops and restaurant signs were displayed in English, Spanish, Korean, Arabic, and some of unknown origin. A mass of humanity with so much in common but, for some reason, only focused on their differences and clustered with others who on the outside looked like themselves.

Arriving at Providence House, Molly was in a hurry to see Sister Aracelia about the status of the Raigosas. "Come in with me. I want Sister Aracelia to meet you." Then she added. "Are you absolutely positive you're ready for this level of commitment? If it happens, it will happen fast, and there will be no turning back."

"Lou and I talked last night about the situation with the

twin girls. We're ready and more than willing to take the girls if you, and they, need us," said Peyton quietly with Lou nodding in agreement. "We've made several calls and covered ourselves, work-wise, for the next few days just in case. We've extended our hotel room a few extra nights hoping things will happen sooner rather than later."

Sister Aracelia came out to meet them, and Molly made introductions. As they walked inside Providence House, Sister Aracelia whisked the three of them quickly into her small, cluttered office at the retreat house. Molly explained why she brought Lou and Peyton to meet her. She wanted them to know everything.

"Confidentiality is critical, Molly."

"Please Sister, trust me. And you can trust Lou and Peyton in the same way."

"Okay, then. I've been in touch with Les Schwanbeck from ICE. Field Officer Schwanbeck and I have a meeting tomorrow afternoon," Sister Aracelia said. She then went on to explain the circumstances around Alberto's arrest and detention by the ICE agents, followed by Hector's arrest on drug charges by the Drug Enforcement Agency.

"Why the DEA and not the LAPD?" asked Molly.

"Because Hector was part of a drug trafficking ring moving illegal products from Mexico to Canada. This goes beyond LA police jurisdiction vis-a-vis it's international in scope. It's one of the largest drug trafficking busts in recent history. Hector's in deep. I don't know what we can do for him. So let's concentrate on whom we can help."

"What are the chances that Al and Maria can stay in America?"

"Not very good. We'll know better tomorrow. I've asked Les not to pick up Maria for a few days. I assured him she is not a flight risk, which she is not. However, our main concerns are keeping Rosa in college and the health and welfare of Ruth and Lupe. The Raigosas don't have actual blood relatives in California. If we don't do something fast, the girls will be assigned to the Department of Health and

Human Services for foster care placement when Al and Maria both are deported. That's what we have to plan for. Time is of the essence."

"I have an idea. It's pretty far-fetched, and we probably shouldn't even consider it, but the plan would put the girls in a good, loving home away from Southern California," Molly said, looking directly at the Rosses and then back to Sister Aracelia.

Molly went on to tell Sister Aracelia about the table conversation at dinner the previous night and how her godparents, the Rosses, had willingly offered to take the girls if the situation became dire.

"I also had the good fortune to discuss the case with an immigration attorney from Chicago who was part of our little Notre Dame weekend group. Last night, after I picked up your second message, we talked about the possible scenarios late into the night. He agrees it's a long shot and without some divine intervention, that a court would likely deny the Rosses consent to adopt the children. But he also agreed the system will destroy either Rosa's future if she's forced to drop out of college to provide and care for the girls, or the twin's lives if they are placed into foster care, even for a short time. He didn't like it but reluctantly agreed with me that sometimes you have to do the wrong thing for the right reason."

Because Molly and Liam had already discussed the probabilities of what the ICE could and couldn't do by law, she and Sister Aracelia discussed the logistics of each scenario with Lou and Peyton listening to every option and argument. By the end of the conversation, Lou and Peyton were solidly on deck, prepared to leave at a moment's notice for Spokane with the girls.

"If you'll excuse me, I have a few phone calls to make," said Sister Aracelia. "I have a judicial favor I was saving for an occasion like this. I'd like to call the judge while he's still clear headed and before he starts in on his Sunday afternoon cocktail hour. Timing, in all things, is ever so important, don't you agree?"

After a tearful good-bye overflowing with uncertainty and anxiety coupled with hope and anticipation, Lou and Peyton drove back to The Westin in downtown LA to await news from Molly and Sister Aracelia.

Good-byes said, Sr. Aracelia went immediately back to her office. She had Schwanbeck lined up where she needed him. Now she needed to talk to the judge.

. . .

Mort Zuckerman had just poured himself a much-anticipated vodka tonic when the phone rang. Wondering why he could never seem to get just one hard-earned, relaxing moment to himself, he sighed and walked over to pick up the phone. The caller ID showed "Providence House" on the display. No wonder his blood pressure was so high. The problems of this world never went away, even in his small jurisdiction. But ignoring a nun was unthinkable, especially for a half-Jewish guy from the Bronx whose Catholic mother sent him to private Catholic schools. You never dis a Sis, he reminded himself. Especially on Sunday.

"Mort Zuckerman, here."

"Hello, Judge. This is Sister Aracelia from Providence House. Am I catching you at a bad time?"

"What if I said yes?" he asked gruffly.

"Well, I guess I'd have to honor your opinion and ask when would be a better time for us to talk."

"No, Sister. Now is as good a time as any. How may I help you?"

Sister Aracelia explained the Raigosa situation to Judge Zuckerman.

"I'm taking a leap of faith, judge, by confiding in you. But we both know that I have one favor to call in, and this is the family I need your help with."

The judge was silent for a few minutes.

"Can you make it happen?" asked Sister Aracelia.

More silence.

"Bring the Spokane people, and the girls and their mother to my chambers at seven o'clock Wednesday morning. I need to think through some options.

"We'll be there," she said, elated. "Thank you, judge."

. . .

The Honorable Judge Mort Zuckerman made another attempt to drink his vodka tonic when Les Schwanbeck called.

"Schwanbeck, you're one of only two people brave enough to call me at home. I just spoke with the other. What the hell do you want?"

"Sister Aracelia, right? It's only because we hold you in such high regard."

Zuckerman and Schwanbeck were bookends in every way except that they came from opposite sides of the tracks. Zuckerman from Yale and Schwanbeck Cal State-Fullerton. One drank vodka, the other Budweiser. But after working together on enough immigration cases to fill a boatload back to Cuba, the two had developed a friendship neither of them would ever admit to. They understood the law, and they understood each other.

"Stop with the romantic crap and tell me what you want," Zuckerman grumbled.

"The Raigosa case. You're meeting with the nun, right?"

"So they say. Jeezus, there are a lot of people pulling for this family. What, do they have a fan club or something? And I take it you're the newest member?"

"I'm that predictable?" Les said, partly in jest, mostly not.

"Yeah, you've become as soft as a kitten in your old age. I also know you've agreed to grant Maria Raigosa more free time than you'd give the damn Pope if he were being deported. What gives?"

"I don't know, maybe I'm getting prissy with age. Or, maybe I'm just trying to bug the shit out of this by-the-letter dog-bright partner of mine. He's so far out of touch with what's coming down these days. It's a whole new ball game,

Judge. You know it, and I know it. He can't see it. It's huge. Tell me I was never as bull-headed as this kid."

"No," Zuckerman said. "There's too much marshmallow under that thick skin of yours."

"Thanks, I think. Look, our boy scout, Graham, is dead set to send Maria Raigosa back to Mexico. The law is with him on that. I'm with him on that. But he's looking for every loophole in the books that will send the twin girls with her. The ass wipe is even trying to pin down the fact one of the twins needs surgery as a reason for them to go with their mother so the U.S. government doesn't have to pay for surgery. Like pre-existing conditions will decide their fate. Christ!"

"They're U.S. citizens, right?" said Zuckerman, who was clearly annoyed.

"Yes, they are. Look, to be honest, I don't trust the kid. Who knows what he may surprise us with? I just know he's going to make this as difficult as possible. He's into holding people up as examples to future generations."

"Okay, I'll sharpen my pencil," Zuckerman assured Les.

"Thanks. A lot of people have been working their butts off to make the best of this crapper of a situation, especially our friend Sister Aracelia. I don't want to let them, or her, down."

"Anything else, Les? Or are you going to shut up and let me be for ten minutes?"

"Nah, I'm done. Go back to your vodka, and I'll crack open a beer."

"As always. See you in court."

Chapter 19

The flight home was agreeably uneventful. Stacie was waiting at the arrivals curb at O'Hare, on-time, to pick them up. Liam and Father Joe dragged their carry-ons to the back of a red Lexus SUV.

"New car?" Liam asked.

"How about, 'Hello, Stacie? You look great Stacie? I've missed you, Stacie?' "

"Okay. Hello, Stacie. You look great, but you always look great, so that's redundant. And did I miss you? Well, yes, I missed you. But I've only been gone a few days, and all the weekend events kept me moving so fast that I really had little time to miss you too terribly much. So let me ask again, new car?"

Stacie didn't like the tone of this conversation, so she turned to Father Joe while Liam loaded the luggage.

"Hello, Father. It's nice to see you!"

"Hello, Stacie. How are your parents, Marge and Jim, right?"

"Yes, Father. They're fine." She turned to Liam, "Darling, would you drive my new car? Daddy just bought it for me because he didn't think my Audi was big or safe enough. It's kind of an early Thanksgiving/Christmas present. And besides, I couldn't have fit all three of us—and your luggage—in my two-seater sports car."

Holy spoiled rich girl, Batman, thought Liam.

Liam took the keys from her. But instead of getting in

the front passenger seat with him, she jumped in the back seat with Father Joe. What the hey is she doing?

"Father Joe, did you hear the good news that dad has secured a really spectacular job offer for Liam at the impressive Chicago law firm of Osbourne, Wainwright, Nelson? Once Liam takes that job, and we get a few other details decided, we can start looking at your calendar for a possible wedding date. Right, Liam?"

Joe could see Liam's face wince in the rear view mirror.

"How lovely, Stacie. Liam? I wasn't aware that you had made the decision to take that position. Are congratulations in order?" asked Father Joe.

Stacie was doing this on purpose, he knew. Trying to coerce him into false confession. In front of a priest, no less. He wasn't taking the bait.

"You're getting a little ahead of yourself, aren't you Stacie? How about you take it down a notch or two and give us all a little breathing room."

Sensing the change in the wind, Stacie came about and set a new tack. She engaged Father Joe in a two-way conversation about this year's Notre Dame Football cheerleaders. Liam concentrated on driving to the train station in time for Joe to catch the five o'clock commuter to South Bend in time for dinner. Otherwise, Joe would be stuck at the Chicago train terminal for another hour.

His brain kept obsessing on a dark-haired young woman, like a computer with its pop-up ads and subliminal messages. Each time he thought of Molly, it made him physically sick to be in the car with Stacie. Something had changed, irreversibly, with Molly's last kiss. And Stacie? Well, she was making it so easy for him to see the shallowness of their relationship.

Fortunately, traffic was light with no accidents or construction delays. Liam pulled up to the train station with twenty minutes to spare. Stacie said goodbye to Father Joe and offered to stay with her new car so Liam could walk Joe to the ticket booth. After saying their good-byes, Liam and Father Joe promised to touch bases later in the week.

"Be careful how you handle Stacie, Liam. It's at times like these you must lead with your best and kindest self. Take a few days to think the situation through and explore your emotions before you plan your next steps."

Father Joe gave Liam a one-armed buddy-hug, they shook hands, and he walked away.

"I'll try," Liam said quietly.

Liam stood where he was, rooted to the ground, for several minutes. He was going to have to stand up to the Blond Wonder and, as her parents should have been doing all along, tell her no. The thought of spending the night with Stacie was, well, unimaginable right now. As he walked back to Stacie's car, he saw her waiting in the driver's seat.

There was a subtle message.

Sliding into the passenger seat he closed the door and looked straight ahead.

"May I have a kiss, lover?" Stacie asked with a pouty smile.

He leaned over and brushed her lips with a perfunctory kiss.

"Well, that will do until we get to your place. Remember, I told you to plan on a guest tonight."

"You aren't staying over, Stacie. I've got an early meeting tomorrow morning and work to do tonight."

Stacie looked straight ahead and waited a few seconds before asking, "Should I be worried about us?"

Think fast, bucko.

"Stacie, I'm just tired and very cranky right now. This weekend totally wiped me out. Add to that, as a result of the trip this weekend, I'm in the middle of a situation with Father Joe that includes a family in California in danger of being deported, and there are small children involved. My mind, to point out the obvious, is on overload. I need a little space to clean out the cobwebs if you can find it in your heart to understand."

"Well, no. I don't understand. Not at all. But I'll go along with it. If we're going to spend the rest of our lives together, I guess I can wait a few more days to have you—all of you—to myself."

The rest of the drive passed in an awkward silence. Stacie stopped in front of his apartment and pushed the button that automatically opened the tailgate. Liam got his suitcase and walked to her driver's window.

"Just give me some time. I have a lot to think about."

"I've already made my decision, lover. You're it for me. I'll wait as long as you want me to."

As Stacie drove away, she made a vow to her Lexus, "I'll fight little Miss California Sunshine if I have to, and I'll win."

. . .

At the station, Joe wondered why he'd stifled his instinct to advise Liam to move on from Stacie. Probably because Joe knew he was heading toward his own emotional showdown. After a short wait, he boarded the train and wondered if this might be the last time he'd travel back to South Bend. The ride was blessedly quiet, which was exactly what Joe needed to think through the decisions he had to make.

The train was barely out of Chicago before he knew he would leave the university. At least that much was certain. His relationship with Clare—or whatever it was—was only part of his larger dilemma. Leaving Notre Dame was the first leap toward figuring out the rest of his life's puzzle. What had started as a spontaneous pizza dinner with Clare before he left for LA had surpassed mind blowing. He was emotionally frozen when it came to Clare. She may have consumed every other thought he'd had for almost a week, but he still had no idea what to say to her. He couldn't imagine what she was thinking and feeling. He knew he had to do something, anything. Mostly he felt the need to keep moving forward. Sitting around throwing a tennis ball against the wall while having one-sided conversations with God was no longer an option.

Back in his apartment, before he even unpacked his bag,

he called Father Tony Bennito, a good friend in Spokane. Tony had been a theology professor of Joe's in undergrad. Years later, Tony and Joe's paths crossed during Tony's frequent trips to Notre Dame as part of an academic accreditation team. Many a personal and professional relationships are formed in academia when your department's strategic plan is being examined ruthlessly. Tony scrutinized every fleck of Joe's department, and the two frequently butted heads. But to this day, Joe wondered if it wasn't Tony's pesky penchant for constantly asking probing questions that made him take note of the older man's wise way.

When Joe joined the Holy Cross Order, he had been assigned an adviser, and they had a good intellectual relationship, but it was weak in regard to spiritual and personal issues. So Joe broke ranks and frequently turned to his close friend for advice. Sometimes Joe felt as if Tony knew him better than he knew himself. It turned out that Tony had been wise to his inner turmoil for months, even though Joe had never mentioned it to him.

"I think I'm about to stretch the definition of spiritual adviser," Joe said, once the two had caught up on current events.

"I'm seventy-years-old and have taught undergraduates for over forty years, off and on. Do you think you can dish up something I haven't handled before? Let 'er rip."

"At retreat last summer, you knew I was struggling, didn't you?"

"I knew. I figured you'd talk to me when you were ready."

"Well, I'm ready."

"Okay," the older priest said in his calm, unflappable manner.

"I feel trapped," is all Joe said. He knew he needed to let the older priest guide him through this rather than pour his guts out in incoherent bits and pieces scattered like pick-up sticks in his head.

"How long have you felt this way?"

"It's been creeping up on me for about a year, probably more. For a long time, I thought it was just a side effect of being in the confines of Notre Dame. Or that my vocation had somehow become insignificant."

"In what way?"

"Tony, look at what I do! I might as well be the damn college mascot!"

Tony heard the younger priest's anger and knew better than to try and talk it out of him over the phone.

"Get out of there. At least for a while." he advised. "Go visit your family and spend Thanksgiving with them. Then, come out here. Stay as long as you like. I can get you an adjunct teaching position here at Gonzaga."

"I've already decided I'm leaving here."

"I figured as much. I know the feeling all too well."

Tony had broken HC ranks and gone to teach at Gonzaga, the Jesuit university in Spokane, about five years ago. Every time the two spoke, he encouraged Joe to consider taking a break, not just from Notre Dame, but also from the Holy Cross camp.

"Well, you are my adviser, so I suppose I should listen to you," Joe said, thankful he was suddenly given some direction. Even though it was just geographic, it was movement, and it was progress.

"Damn right. I'll get the ball rolling at this end, and you do the same. Get out here before Christmas. I'll line up something for spring semester."

"You think you can get me into the classroom?"

"That's what I'm shooting for."

"Great, I'd kill to get back in front of those empty, hung-over undergraduate heads so eager to hear my monologues."

Father Joe hung up the phone, picked up a tennis ball and absent-mindedly started tossing it against the wall. At least the wheels were finally moving. He'd figure out everything in Spokane. Distance from Clare and Notre Dame was what he needed.

He picked up the telephone again and called Lou on her

cell phone.

"Hey, Lou."

"Joe?" She, Peyton and Molly were just leaving Providence House after talking with Sister Aracelia.

"Lou, I have a favor to ask. May I come out to Spokane for a while? Could you and Peyton put up with me for a few weeks?"

"Sure, Joe. Is something the matter?"

"Nothing I can do justice to over the phone. I just want you to know that when I say I'm coming out to visit, I'm hoping you'll let me stay through Thanksgiving and Christmas. I'm taking a leave of absence for the rest of this year."

If Lou had the capacity to fit anything more into her head besides Lupe and Ruth, she would have grilled him for more information, but instead she answered with a very un-Lou like fashion. "No worries. You can tell me, or not tell me, when you get here. When will you arrive?"

"I'm thinking about driving out. I need some thinking time. My plan is to pick up my mom's old car from my sister in Cleveland and then drive out. My guess is I'll get to Spokane sometime during the week before Thanksgiving. That will give me a chance to see my sister and brother-in-law before the holidays. Sure you have room for me?"

"Yes, of course, Joe. Peyton and I will be thrilled to have you with us for the holidays and for longer if you want."

"Thanks, Lou. You're a life saver."

And he meant it.

"Before we hang up, Joe... I'll fill you in later with the details, but Peyton and I are waiting to see if we'll be given guardianship of Lupe and Ruth. We may be returning to Spokane with a couple of passengers. Do you follow?"

"Amen!" Joe exhaled. "Absolutely. I know whatever you decide to do will be the right thing. My thoughts and prayers are with you. And if there's anything else I can do, please let me know."

"We'll be in touch," said Lou. "I need to keep this line open, so I'll sign off."

"Godspeed, Lou. See you soon and talk to you sooner."

. . .

Home alone at last. Liam unpacked his suitcase and by habit started a load of Sunday evening laundry. Next stop was the refrigerator to see what he might be able to fix or forage for dinner.

Not much. Nothing that looked remotely edible.

He picked up the phone and called the local Chinese restaurant for a delivery. Ah yes, some General Tso's and fried rice would put his stomach, if not his mind, at peace.

His cell started to ring, and he picked it up, checking the number and hoping it wasn't Stacie. It was a 509 area code. Curious, he answered it.

"Hello?"

"Hi Liam, it's Molly."

"Molly! It's good to hear your voice," he rushed on. "I want to tell you again how much I enjoyed being with you this weekend."

"I did too, Liam. More than you know."

"What's up?"

"The Raigosa situation has gone south, literally, for both of them."

"I'm sorry."

"You know the travel plans for the twins we discussed?" she asked rhetorically. "Well, I'm waiting to hear back from Sister Aracelia, and the Rosses are waiting at the hotel for the green light."

"God, they must be torn apart."

"Tell me about it. And to top this off as the ultimate weekend of surprises, Lou just got a call from Father Joe. He's taking a leave of absence from Notre Dame and asked to spend Thanksgiving and Christmas with them in Spokane. Did Joe mention anything to you on the plane?"

"What?" No, he didn't mention anything to me this whole weekend! But before we left last Friday, he did say he had something important to discuss with me. He never brought it up again. Between considering this job offer, the game and the Raigosas, I guess I never asked him what was on his mind. What a crappy friend."

"Maybe he wasn't ready to talk."

"Maybe. But I should have been more aware."

Molly smiled at his admission. Besides the requisite Catholic guilt, it said a lot about his character.

"Obviously the timing wasn't right," she offered. "He'll let you know when he's ready. Lou has no idea what this is all about either."

Her generosity of spirit and understanding was sweet, unexpected salve on his guilt.

"Back to your situation. Will you be okay? Please call me anytime. I'll do what I can from my end. Even if it's just a voice on the phone rooting for the team."

"Thanks. I've gotta go."

"Right. Call any time, and I mean it."

"You may regret that offer."

"Not on your life."

"Bye, Liam."

Liam sat on the couch in a cloud of confusing emotions until the doorbell rang, snapping him out of his fog. Food first, he thought.

Liam spent the rest of the evening charting the pros and cons of his professional life. He loved his work with the federal government, but lately he felt like he was swimming through a quagmire of bureaucracy. As rewarding as his job was, a nagging voice in his head kept urging him to try pitting his intelligence and shrewdness with, and against, the big dogs. His career was defined by accomplishing a yeoman's share of work with a peasant's resources. What great things might he achieve if given the chance to do more using a king's ransom?

He briefly contemplated the tug-o-war he was experiencing with Stacie and Molly. In all honesty, he didn't want to think about Stacie, much less mix in an emotional mind-cluster with this pivotal career decision at hand. One life decision at a time, boyo. First things first. He had more time to sort out feelings of the heart. He told Mel Wainwright he'd give him a definitive answer Monday.

A nagging voice in his head kept repeating, "DENIAL!"

Liam quickly changed the channel.

. . .

The phone startled Ellen just as she was drifting off to sleep. It was Molly.

"Mom!" she yelped excitedly over the phone. It may as well have been ten in the morning. Her excitement almost jarred the fillings out of Ellen's molars. "I can't believe how everything is falling into place! Liam O'Connor has been great. He has this immigration law down. If we're able to pull this off, I—we will forever be in his debt. " From there she went on with more accolades, from his reading likes and dislikes and even-keeled manner to what Molly described as his Hugh Jackman good looks.

Ellen reminded herself to stay neutral. That she was half asleep made that easy enough.

"He sounds like a nice guy, Mol."

"He is! But, he also has a girlfriend."

"Am I hearing a dash of disappointment?" Ellen asked. She knew Molly could protect herself. She hadn't raised a wimp, after all, but she didn't want to see Molly left flat-footed with a broken heart. Again. She quickly changed the subject.

"So, Mol, call me after you know more about Lou, Peyton and the Raigosas. Sending Hail Marys your way!"

"I will, for sure. Love you mom. Ciao!"

"Ciao, Mol," Ellen said.

Ellen had to admit her Mol was turning into quite a formidable young woman, she thought proudly. Looking out her bedroom window at the hearty oak trees, she admired how their withered, yet persistent, leaves would hang on through winter. Molly's like that, she thought. Far from old and dry, but she sure hangs in there. She's tenacious. Who but Molly would think to orchestrate the arrangement between Lou,

Peyton and the twins virtually in one weekend? Even as a child playing with neighborhood kids, Molly was a connector. She brought the right people together at the right time.

Chapter 20

"Here's how I see it, Sister. Just hear me out, will ya?"

Sister Aracelia stifled her urge to laugh at how out of place Les looked in her microscopic office, which barely accommodated herself. Now, here she was, with Les and the rest of Les. She leaned forward in her chair, looked at him squarely, and said, "Fire away."

The second-hand oak chair creaked loudly when he leaned back, as was his habit before he initiated discussion. She knew he heard the creak. She also knew when Les was on a mission. It would take more than him ending up on the floor to divert her attention.

"You know as well as I do Hector Raigosa screwed his entire family."

"Yes, he did." Like at a border crossing, she didn't want to say anything more than was necessary.

"Hector stays locked up."

"I understand."

Les knew it was the rest of the family Sister Aracelia was worried about and took a deep breath before he continued.

"By the book, the parents go back to Mexico," he said flatly. "With your connections, you probably knew before I did that Alberto's in federal custody. Maria's next, Sister. I can't keep deportation on permanent hold. The only thing keeping the two of them here this long is the health problem with one of the twins. ICE doesn't want to look like the assholes they are and send a sick kid off to Mexico where the child can't get decent care, but they'll only hold off for so long."

Sister Aracelia continued to look Les in the eye. Some of the most hard core jerks in the world have tried to stare him down without success. Damn, this nun was a tough nut. Her mossy green eyes always made him squirm. He silently cursed his twelve years of Catholic education. The stare-down continued, each waiting for the other to say what they both knew would be said.

Les fell first, only confirming to himself he was getting softer, just like his waistline.

"The older daughter, Rosa, is old enough to decide whether or not she wants to stay or return to Mexico with her parents, although I have no idea why she'd want to go back there. She'll never have the opportunities there she has as an American citizen."

"How much time do we have before the ICE deports Alberto and Maria?" Sister Aracelia asked point blank, the way she asked any question.

"A week, maybe two. I have a partner who does it by the book, Sister. Kind of the way I used to."

"You sound pretty much by-the-book yourself, Les."

Her words hit Les square in the jaw. He had grown fond of Sister Aracelia and begrudged the day he started respecting her cause and the way she went about her work. A lot of immigration advocacy groups fell into two groups: borderline militants or bleeding hearts. The first had become frightening and the latter pathetic, and neither was particularly effective. Neither knew how to negotiate, which was something Sister Aracelia had taught him without his even realizing it. Here was the deal: She personally made his job harder to do. Not long ago he tried to explain to his wife how the nun was getting into his psyche, how she was making him look at cases from angles unacceptable to ICE policy. Her only response was to give him a pat on the head and ask him for Sister Aracelia's address, so she could send her a thank-you note.

"Sister, we know each other pretty well, don't we? We know our boundaries. You know the rules as well as I do. You also know how often I stretch them for you. Give me a break here, will ya? I'm stretched about as far as I can stretch on this one."

"There's nothing you can do to keep Alberto and Maria here while Ruth gets the medical care she needs?"

"Not unless they can take care of it pretty damn fast." He felt his gut strings tighten. "Or, they could leave them here."

"Are you out of your tiny mind, Les?" He hoped his grimace was undetected. Oh, God, she's up out of her chair. He sat up taller in his chair in hoping to meet her ire head on. "This family has been through hell! They're hard-working, honest people trying their damndest to give their children a future. And the icing on the cake is one of them is a child about to lose sight in one eye."

"Get creative," Les said, sounding more like the bastard ICE agent most people knew, but not Sister Aracelia.

"Get creative?" she responded incredulously. "You, Mr. ICE agent, are telling me to get creative?"

"Yep." He knew better than to press her buttons any further unless he wanted to get tossed out on his big ears.

Relieved, Les watched her sit down again, simultaneously tilting her head as though trying to read his mind. She continued to look him in the eye, her brow slightly furrowed. Her voice lost the anger it had moments ago.

"Okay. I get it. We have a week before anyone goes anywhere, right?"

"That's the best I can promise, Sister. What's going on in that head of yours?"

"I'm just thinking a week isn't a lot of time, but it's more than most people get. Thanks, Les. I apologize for flying around the office on my broom."

"I'd be disappointed if you acted any differently. Just keep this clean and maybe a little bit legal, okay? In the meantime, I'll do my best to keep my bloodhound of a partner busy scratching his hind end. And be in touch, got that? I don't want any surprises."

Showing Les to the door, Sister Aracelia was already hoping Lou and Peyton were ready to jump into their commitment sooner than later. She gave Les a hug, happy that he returned her peace offering.

Heading out the door, Les paused. "You know, Sister, we'd make a lousy married couple. We understand each other too well."

"Maybe, but it wouldn't be boring."

"No offense, Sister, but right now, I'd be happy with boring."

. . .

Molly was hip deep back into her caseload. Packed with several dozen people, the reception area at El Centro seemed too small to handle the many families, including great-grandparents and infants, all waiting with a combination of anticipation and anxiety. Molly would never get used to seeing the worry in their faces. It never failed to devastate her to see children who were far too young to wear such deep, furrowed brows. Sugar cookies and hot chocolate were the one constant in the room. However, most of her personal anxiety was focused on Sister Aracelia's meeting with Les Schwanbeck. Finally, she got a call.

"Molly, I need to speak with you, Peyton and Lou as soon as possible." Sister Aracelia could hear the clear sense of urgency in her own voice. Knowing that Les Schwanbeck was a man of his word, she also knew that this window of opportunity was not going to stay open long. No sooner had Les left her office, she called Molly.

"Is something wrong, Sister?"

"No. Things are great." She tried not to sound too sarcastic. "Les Schwanbeck just left my office. Lou and Peyton have to make some definitive decisions soon about the Raigosa twins."

"We'll be right over."

Lou and Peyton picked up Molly at the El Centro office and drove back to Providence House. "We aren't in Kansas anymore," Lou whispered to her husband. It was natural for

Lou to use humor to melt tension. "Riding shot gun takes on a whole new meaning around here."

"Only in America," Peyton responded. "Where else do the haves and the have-nots live just one street light away from each other? I feel like I'm driving a Bentley, not a mid-sized rental."

Molly was in the back seat looking and listening. She remembered how foreign and frightening these same scenes were when she first arrived in LA. Peyton and Lou were kind, strong people, but this experience was a world away from their zip code, not to mention their comfort zone. Hopefully Sister Aracelia had information that would yield positive results.

"You're still one hundred percent positive you're ready for this kind of commitment?" Molly asked again, as the threesome walked up the front steps. Molly's new home seemed like an odd oasis of calm, nestled in the middle of a simmering melting pot.

"We would never agree to taking these two children to Spokane unless we were one hundred and fifty percent sure we wanted to, and equally as sure that it was the best thing for them," said Peyton. Molly had never heard him sound or look so solemn. "Our attorney in Spokane is preparing custody papers as we speak. Hopefully the court system will have the common sense to choose us."

Molly's gloom faded several shades when she saw Sister Aracelia at her office door. This has to work out for the Raigosas, damnit!

For Sister Aracelia, Molly's endorsement of Peyton and Lou and their capacity to care for the twins was what she needed to step out on a limb for the Raigosas. Most importantly she knew—in all honesty—that she could assure Maria and Alberto their twin girls would be much loved and in good, safe hands.

Seated formally in front of the nun's huge 1940s metal desk that consumed her small office, Lou and Peyton glanced at each other in affirmation—one final look to cross-check that the other was prepared for the big leap. Peyton's eyes were calm and comforting.

"I met with Les Schwanbeck," Sister Aracelia began. "He's giving us a little time, and by little, I mean minuscule." Her audience of three nodded in unison. "We need to shake a leg, folks. Lou and Peyton, if you have any second thoughts, speak up now because once the wheels get rolling on this, there is no turning back. I will not put this family through more stress."

"We're on board," Peyton said with a tone of finality.

"Lou?"

"Sister, I may look like a deer in headlights, but I am so ready for this. No second thoughts here."

When Molly saw Sister Aracelia's eyes soften at Lou's response, she knew the plan was going to work. It took all of her self-restraint not to scream, "You rock, Lou!" She settled for quiet, yet determined, "Yes!"

Chapter 21

Like roaches in a kitchen sink, word spread fast that Father Joe was leaving Notre Dame. Clare got the news at gossip headquarters, the faculty services copy center, where faculty and teaching assistants queued up each morning waiting for handouts and tests.

"Unbelievable! Why would a guy give up such a sweet job?" a twenty-something history teaching assistant was saying to his lowly overworked and underpaid cohorts. "The guy gets to travel to every game and schmooze big shot alums all over the world. He's seriously nuts!"

"Who's leaving?" Clare asked. It was rare for her to participate in catty, copy center conversation, which is probably why every head at the copy center turned in her direction as if on cue.

"Father Joe," a still pimply-faced teaching assistant said. "Crazy, isn't it?"

"What are you talking about? He's not going anywhere," Clare said, trying to sound casual, despite the fact she felt like Mount St. Helens had just taken up residency in her larynx.

"Well, that's not what the president's secretary said."

In a rare moment of efficiency, Clare's copies appeared on the counter. She swept them up, still trying to appear casual, and bolted to her office to call Joe. An uncharacteristic sense of panic tingled through her from head to toe as she scurried across campus.

"You're leaving?" she asked before Joe could utter a

word.

"Ever the interrogator," Joe responded, cursing the party-line gossip that prevented him from telling Clare himself he was leaving. But he still couldn't say the words.

Silence lagged between them for so long Clare thought she could have painted her toenails and her house.

"Let's have dinner. Anton's? Six-thirty?" he proposed.

"Sure. I'll see you then," was all she could say. Her emotions were stuck in her throat like a massive hairball. The night she and Joe spent together was the big eighteen-wheel semi-truck parked between them.

Anton's was busy for a Monday. First to arrive, Joe grabbed a table thankful that the buzz surrounding them would be a slight diversion from the topic at hand. The tiny Italian restaurant looked anything but Italian with fluorescent lights, small white enamel and chrome tables, and white plastic porch chairs. Prints of Florence hung haphazardly in cheap plastic frames. But what it lacked in ambiance, it made up for in great food. When Clare arrived, Joe stood and enfolded her into a long hug before either of them said a word. Both wished they could freeze-frame time.

Joe held her chair for her, which usually cued a smart aleck remark from Clare, but tonight she just offered a quiet thank you. He poured house red into two of Anton's short jelly glasses. Clare tapped hers to his and said sadly, "Here's to you, Joe." Immediately, he realized Clare knew for fact he was leaving. Okay, so she knows I'm leaving South Bend, but she can't know I'm perilously close to leaving the priesthood, he thought.

"Clare, I'm leaving Notre Dame. You obviously know that, but what you don't know is I also might leave the priesthood."

Clare felt as though she'd been hit on the back of the head with a frozen meatball the size of a bocce ball. She could only stare, dumbfounded.

"I know, it's a lot to digest," Joe said, swirling the wine in his glass so fast it looked like blood in a centrifuge.

Clare remained silent, staring absently at Joe's glass. She was never good at shock and awe.

Joe reached over and gave Clare's forearm a gentle shake. "So, say something," Joe said. "I know you have an earful in there, so let's hear it."

"It must have been one hell of a weekend or else I must be really good in bed," was all Clare could say.

Joe laughed. The relief in his voice was palpable, but what Clare wanted to know—needed to know—was what role, if any, she played in his decision. She'd be lying if she tried to convince herself, or anyone else, she wasn't in love with Joe. But luring a priest away from the flock had to top the mortal sin hit parade. If she was going to go the honest route, the only route she knew to take, she also knew she wasn't ready to commit to him. These and other unknowns scurried around in Clare's brain throughout dinner like caged mice on wheels. Apparently, Joe had taken her comment about his weekend literally as each time she tuned in, he was talking about LA.

"So what's your game plan?" she asked, trying to get off the sidetrack he'd taken. They'd finished their gnocchi and were having port with bread pudding, an odd combination but one of Anton's signature desserts. Any unsuspecting passerby would easily miss the tension seated at the table with Clare and Joe. The questions she wanted to pose sat between them like an uninvited guest. The petite pixie woman and handsome guy with slightly graying hair just above his ears were failing miserably at ignoring the obvious.

"Well," Joe said, a little too slowly.

"Just get it out, Joe, before the restaurant closes." Clare squirmed at the curt tone of her own voice.

"I'm going to Spokane, Washington. The state." His tone matched hers, which he could tell was motivated by anger and possible disappointment.

"And?"

He pressed on. "Tony Bennito at Gonzaga University said he could get me some classes to teach this upcoming spring semester."

"Okay. Well, I hear it's a more than decent university. The Jesuits definitely have a laudable reputation in higher education. The Gonzaga basketball program has developed national status, which helps. Nice town?"

Score one for Clare, Joe thought. Maybe his time in LA, surrounded by so many people in a state of urgent flux, had lulled him into a false sense of relief he was making the right decision. He normally appreciated Clare's ability to point out gaps in his logic, but this wasn't some faculty senate issue, like whether to make the Tuesday before Thanksgiving a workday. This was his life, possibly their life together, damn it. He wished he could say all this to her now, but he couldn't. There were too many questions he had to answer first, but he hated leaving her out there dangling like a participle.

"Look Clare, I don't have every base covered, okay? I'll be sure and mention that in my next confession. But, I do know I have to leave here, at least for a while, and I'm damn lucky to have found a place to land. I pray that in Spokane I'll find the clarity I can't seem to find in South Bend."

Clare felt chewed up and spat out. She leaned back in her chair with one arm resting on the table, slowly turning a spoon over again and again, her green eyes boring a hole through Joe's brown ones.

"Clare, did you hear what I just said?"

"Yes, I heard. Are you leaving the priesthood?" She was shocked at the calm sound of her own voice, which totally contradicted the sinking feeling she felt all the way down to her little toe nail.

"Like I said, I might leave. 'Might' being the key word. You must know I've been struggling with my vocation. Clare, after what happened between us, how can you not know? I need to figure it out. I can't do it here." There, it was on the table. He waited for a reaction.

"I hope Spokane offers you the space you need, Joe. South Bend and the people here obviously aren't what you want or need."

And right then and there Joe pulled his head out of his

derriere and realized he was hurting the one person in the world he never wanted to hurt. The life of a priest was a solo life when it came to personal decisions, but what he was going through now obviously affected Clare. The idea scared him and at the same time made him happy. Someone, Clare, cared.

"Don't think for a minute I'm deserting you. You have no idea how important you are to me, do you?"

Clare looked around the restaurant as though looking for a waiter, buying time to think of a comeback. There wasn't a waiter in sight and just two tables were still occupied, both with couples talking quietly. I'll bet they aren't having as much fun as Joe and I, she thought, surprised—and pleased—to see her sarcasm hadn't vanished entirely.

She took a deep, shaky breath.

"Important to you?"

"Yeah, Clare, I need you."

"Well, I like to think it's been a mutual need-based, co-dependent, enabling friendship," Clare said, trying to cut the heavy air between them with a little levity. If she told him she loved him, she knew he'd end up staying, and she'd end up feeling like a black widow. She didn't want to admit it, but he was right about going to Spokane. But still, yes, she felt deserted. "No, you aren't deserting me, Joe," she said, hating the bold-faced lie. "Go do what you need to do. What happened between us, well, I don't know how to think about that night either. It is what it is, I guess. You know I'm not big on regrets, so I don't do things I might regret. And you also know I'll be fine."

Buying Clare's stand on my own line, Joe felt an overwhelming sense of undeserved relief. "The last thing I would ever want to do is hurt you," he declared.

A lot had been said, and now Clare wanted to get away from Joe for fear he'd start to accurately read her emotions. It was time to leave Anton's, go back to the small house she'd hoped would be her happiest home ever, and continue her life at Notre Dame. An awkward good-bye ensued with the usual reassurances of keeping in touch, I'll miss yous, and Clare was out the door.

Joe nodded toward the lone waiter taking care of straggling patrons.

"A Christian Brothers, please," he asked. It struck him as an appropriate drink to toast the occasion of what could be the inevitable loss of the woman who had planted herself, unintentionally on both their parts, between himself and his vocation. The brandy arrived, and Joe took a slow draw. I have to make this move, he reassured himself. Clare, or no Clare, I need this change. She may be hurt and angry now, but this is for her too. Joe shoved himself away from the table.

. . .

Monday morning Liam walked into his supervisor's office and submitted his resignation effective immediately. Then he walked to his office, sat down at his desk, picked up the phone and called Mel Wainwright at Osbourne, Wainwright, Nelson.

"Good morning, sir. This is Liam O'Connor."

"Yes, Liam. Good to hear from you."

"I'm more than pleased to accept your generous offer of employment, sir."

"Excellent!" exclaimed Wainwright. "In anticipation of your decision, we have the personnel paperwork ready for your signature as well as your fifty thousand dollar signing bonus check ready for your personal use. Can you be at our offices at, say, four o'clock this afternoon?"

"Yes, I think I can adjust my calendar, sir. I'll see you at four."

"I'd like to welcome you to the firm, son. You've made the right decision. This career move will be transformational for you, in no uncertain terms. See you at four."

As far as Liam was concerned, that fifty thousand was definitely transformational. It was two-thirds of a full year's salary with the feds. And the doubling in salary would be a welcome boost to his standard of living. Liam had weighed the options—pro and con, back and forth, right side up and upside down. He'd convinced himself this was the right thing to do. His head was taking the lead in the balance with his gut and his heart. You don't have an offer like this every day, he told himself. The money is just too good to pass up. I'll give it a year, he rationalized, and if it's not right, I'll hang a shingle out on Main Street, Somewhere, USA. And the signing bonus is mine. No payback clause, he reasoned.

There was a little voice in his head repeating, "If it sounds too good to be true, it probably is." But the fifty grand kept lowering the volume.

The desk phone rang jolting him from his reverie.

"Liam?" purred Stacie, "do you have something you'd like to tell me?"

Word travels fast.

"Stacie, you'll be happy to know that I've decided to take the OWN offer. I just got off the phone with Mel Wainwright." Funny, it had a hollow sound when he said it out loud.

"You made the right choice, lover. Let's have dinner tonight and celebrate. I have everything planned. Just the two of us. My place. Okay?"

"I'll be there at six. See you then."

Sex at six, thought, Stacie. I'll literally make you forget about anyone but me. Including little Miss Outward Bound from Northwest Poe-spunky-ville.

Chapter 22

Wednesday morning, the small troupe arrived on time in Judge Zuckerman's chambers. His court docket wouldn't begin until nine o'clock, so there was no reason for the black robes he felt could intimidate the mother and twin girls. He knew their lives were on the chopping block and the less stress, visible or otherwise, the better. The casting call included everyone involved. Why not get all the parties in one room? It would save time and energy, both of which he had very little.

"I believe I know, or can figure out, who all the players are in this room, except one. Who might you be, young lady?" he asked Molly.

"Molly Kirkpatrick, sir. I'm the Raigosas' caseworker from El Centro. I work with the Sisters. This is Louise and Peyton Ross, my good friends from Spokane who are willing to become legal guardians to the twins."

"Thank you, Miss Kirkpatrick."

Impressive young woman, he thought to himself.

"Now Sister," he continued, "you are acquainted with Mr. Schwanbeck from the ICE?"

"Oh yes, Judge. Les and I are old acquaintances. We run with the same crowd."

Judge Zuckerman chuckled at the irony.

"Good. Mrs. Raigosa, I'm sure you are aware of the seriousness of this situation and that I, as a judge in this court of law, and based on the information before me, cannot change the inevitability of your deportation. Are we clear on that issue?" Maria nodded. The judge couldn't help but notice the defeated, vacant look in her eyes.

"Les, do you see any way to avoid deportation for Maria and her husband?"

"No, sir, I do not."

"You have two children of legal age and two twin daughters who are currently minors, all of whom were legally born in the U.S. However, you and your husband were born in Mexico and therefore are not legal citizens of this country."

Again Maria nodded.

"Mr. and Mrs. Ross, have you considered all the consequences and responsibilities entailed with assuming guardianship of these two eleven-year-old girls?"

"Yes," Lou and Peyton said in unison.

"Now I need to talk directly to the Raigosa girls. Ruth and Lupe? Your mother and father have no choice but to return to Mexico, and we're probably talking very soon. Am I right, Mr. Schwanbeck?"

Les nodded.

"You girls do have a choice, however. You may return with your parents to Mexico, or you may go to live with the Rosses in Spokane in the state of Washington. However, I want to be very honest with you. In Mexico, you will probably have to forgo an education and work to help support your family. The health care is not good. Life in Mexico will not carry the same rights and privileges as your America citizenship offers you. And as I understand it, Ruth, you have need for an eye operation that could mean a sustainable difference in your ability to see out of one of your eyes. More than likely, you will not receive the operation if you return to Mexico with your parents."

Mort Zuckerman paused for a moment to allow each person in the room to absorb the finality of the decisions in front of them,

"Mrs. Raigosa—Maria, do you have anything to say to your daughters?"

"Yes, judge. This is very, very hard. Family is everything

to Alberto, the girls' father, and me. Being separated from our children is, and always has been," Maria had to pause to fight back her tears before she could continue, "our worst nightmare. However, we came to this country as newlyweds over twenty years ago to make a better life for ourselves and for our family. Our older children can now make their own choices and their own way in this world—one for better and one for worse. But our girls, Ruth and Lupe, must do as their mother tells them."

Maria looked at her girls and paused to again collect herself before she was able to continue.

"As hard as it is for me to say this, you girls must stay here in America. Your father and I did not make these sacrifices and live in fear of this very day so we could turn our backs on your future."

Maria turned back and faced Judge Zuckerman.

"It's done," she said with a sob. "The girls will stay, and I do thank God for this loving couple. My husband and I want you, Lou and Peyton, to know that you are forever members of the Raigosa family." Her eyes were sad, black puddles.

"Mamma!" cried Ruth, while Lupe shed silent tears.

"Hush now. It is done. Life is not perfection, it is adaptation. No one can deport our love for you."

"Girls?" asked the judge.

Both girls looked to their mother who was unwavering in her expression of resolve. They both nodded and dropped their eyes to a spot on the floor.

"Anyone else? Speak now or forever hold your peace."

Silence.

"All right then. My assistant, Linda, will draw up the guardianship papers for your signatures. She will need to obtain information from each of you. After that, Lupe and Ruth, you go with Sister Aracelia and Molly to pack your things. Mr. and Mrs. Ross, after Linda is through with you, go ahead and check out of your hotel, make airline reservations and any other arrangements necessary to leave with the girls for Spokane. Maria will need to wait here, don't you agree,

Les? Everyone meet back in my chambers at noon, and we will sign the papers and say our good-byes."

As the troupe dispersed, the Judge wondered if seven-thirty was too early in the day for a drink. He sorely needed one.

Molly was plum out of stoicism. Sister Aracelia said a quick prayer of thanks. Les Schwanbeck, like the judge, was ready for a beer. His partner, Graham, was royally pissed but dutifully kept his mouth shut. Lou and Ross were stunningly happy.

Lou approached Maria. "Mrs. Raigosa, we'll take good care of your precious girls. Don't think for a minute we'll ever let them forget who their real mother and father are," said Lou. She felt helpless in her attempt to comfort Maria. "We'll make sure you see them often."

"Mrs. Ross, thank you from the bottom of my heart. You and your husband are making it possible for Alberto and me to fulfill our American dream, if not for ourselves, for our children."

The two women hugged each other and parted with a world of promises to share.

Chapter 23

Jack again proved he was a man of habit. Once again, his attempt to engage Ellen in conversation at the bakery bombed. As promised, he had lined up Dr. Stuben and promptly let Ellen know, hoping his good deed might repair her tarnished opinion of him. Her plain, "Thanks a lot, Jack," didn't exactly parlay into, "You're a fabulous guy!" No, it was just Ellen being polite, and he knew, with a thud, he didn't deserve much more.

Back at the office, he started to wade through weekend updates on patients he had in the hospital. Mostly, though, he stared mindlessly at his computer. Repeated efforts to convince himself there was no way in hell Ellen was going to give him more than the cool time of day prevailed and soon he was behind schedule.

He tapped mechanically on the door of his first patient. Nothing like a good case of congestive heart failure to brighten the day. Examining the rotund patient's swollen ankles, which looked frighteningly similar to the fat end of a baseball bat, Jack pictured Ellen's shapely gams. Even before he got a full view of them Saturday night, he knew she'd have great legs.

He was adjusting his patient's diuretic when his hands suddenly became clammy, and he felt as if his size twenty-two patient was now sitting on his chest. He knew he had to get out of the room. I'm having a damn heart attack! He couldn't tell if he was talking out loud or not. Little Lotta Fat Ankle was just sitting there in the small exam room, looking out at the parking lot, so he figured the voice had to be from within. He managed an abrupt but professional exit and left the room, hoping the woman would assume his pager beckoned him to an emergency. He was standing outside the exam room like a petrified tree silently praying someone would notice him. They had to. The sweat behind his knees had to be pooling all over the floor by now. Someone had to notice all the water? Hello? Does anyone notice I'm dying here? No luck. He took one step toward the nurse's station and saw the brown and gray weave of carpet coming up to meet him. There, now someone will notice, he thought as he passed out.

. . .

"Jack, my friend, you can now count yourself among the millions of Americans who have had a first class panic attack." Jack heard his friend and colleague, Stanley Cohen, but couldn't quite wrap his brain around what he was telling him. All he knew was he'd been somewhere he never wanted to go to again. At the moment, though, he'd never felt so calm. He didn't dare move his body for fear this heavenly feeling would vanish, so he cautiously moved his eyes from Stanley long enough to see he was in the emergency room.

"You're joking, right?" he said quietly.

"Nope. Everything is clean as a whistle. You're a finely tuned machine. From the neck down, anyway."

"What's that supposed to mean?" Damn, the calm was slipping away. Jack was back.

"Look Jack, I'm a doc and friend. You know what it means. Plain and simple, you had a panic attack. Something triggered it, and I doubt it was the patient you left sitting in the exam room. By the way, she sends her regards and hopes you're okay."

"What did you load me up with?"

"Some Xanax. Not much. Just enough to get you back on the ground."

Jack covered his eyes with his forearm to hide his

embarrassment. He was ashamed and didn't like his friend and ER staff seeing him like this. Standing side by side on any other day, it was hard to imagine Jack and Stanley were anything more than professional friends. But Stanley, all five-foot-seven of him, was the only colleague he also counted as a friend. Something about the squatty, balding Jewish doctor exuded an understanding of people Jack appreciated and envied.

"I'm not going to be able to work juiced up on Xanax."

"Oh my God, shut down the hospital. His Royal Highness Dr. Jack Doyle is unable to work today!"

"Very funny."

So much for trying to take it easy on his friend, Stanley was ready to play hardball.

"Jack, exactly how long did you think you could elbow your way through life without it catching up with you?"

"I don't know what you are talking about. Fuck off."

"No thanks."

"I mean it Stan, let it go."

"No, I won't let it go," Stanley said as he printed out a prescription.

"You will fill this prescription, and you will listen to me. I'm now your doc. You and I will spend some time talking."

Jack resigned himself to re-entry into real life and sat up to face his friend.

"I'm that screwed up?" The fear in his voice wasn't lost on Stanley.

"Jack, come on!" Stanley laughed. "You're human for Christ's sake! And no, you aren't all that screwed up. You just need to get some balance. You wouldn't hesitate to suggest exactly what I'm suggesting to any of your patients."

"Got me there."

"You're a smart guy, Jack. Now act like one. And don't think for a minute I don't see how you let work devour you. Go home, eat something and sleep. Anxiety attacks can make you feel like you ran a sub-four-minute mile and then some. Trust me, we'll talk tomorrow."

Stanley stood up and put his arm over Jack's shoulders. "This may be the best thing that ever happened to you, Jack. It may have saved your life."

"Yeah, right."

. . .

Stanley didn't waste any time connecting with Jack the next morning and committing him to a long lunch outside the hospital. It was not until twenty minutes into a hummus and cucumber sandwich that Jack fully understood the psychological and biochemical tango that constituted anxiety disorders. The biochemical part was easier for Dr. Jack to digest. Fouled up serotonin uptake was logical. The psychological part was harder for him to wrap his head around, but by the time Jack polished off his raisin oatmeal cookie, he was catching on to the connection between the two. He was a quick study and knew it wouldn't take years of psychoanalysis for him to connect the dots between his heart-racing face plant and his recent behavior toward Ellen. Stan wasn't surprised it took so long for Jack to hit the wall. After all, he'd spent half his life protecting himself from emotional entanglements. Not by intention, but by default.

"I think you owe Ellen a dozen roses," Stanley said. "You've met your match. She's your wake-up call."

"Maybe so, but I think I'd end up wearing them. I don't think Ellen is particularly open to any overtures from me," Jack said.

"Don't be so sure. From what you've said, she's damned smart and kind to boot. Don't underestimate her, Jack. Remember she hasn't been living in an emotional lockbox like you. She's been through the proverbial wringer, what with losing her husband, raising a daughter and opening that bakery. She's come through all that with all her buttons intact. As my grandmother would say, she rang your bell, but good. Quit second-guessing and answer the bell."

"Well, I'm not sending her flowers. That's definitely not

me. I agree with everything you've so poignantly drawn to my attention, Stan, but I'm no flower-toting Don Juan."

"And considering how well you've done with your current course, you certainly wouldn't want to alter your chosen behavior," Stanley said sarcastically. "Look, I'm just suggesting one thing, don't run."

"I'll try," was the best assurance Stan could get from Jack, but it was better than nothing. Considering what had transpired over the past twenty-four hours, it was the most he had promised anyone, ever. Besides, despite the fact Ellen seemed to be scraping a lifetime's worth of emotional scabs off him each time they spoke, he didn't think he could stay away from her.

. . .

The first thing Ellen noticed when she glanced out at the coffee boys was that Chuck Robinson needed a haircut. More accurately, he needed someone to take a Weed Whacker to his ear hairs. He was grumbling about his old, incontinent dog, holding everyone's attention including Jack's.

"In my book, a dog who needs diapers is giving me the high sign it's time to go to doggy heaven. But, damnit, I love that dog!" This was a heartfelt admission coming from Chuck.

Ellen was laughing at the comical gaggle of men just as Miss Johnson walked in the bakery and tossed the boys a perfunctory nod. After all these years, they still reacted like parochial school sixth graders by nodding politely in return. Next thing she'll have them standing when she comes through the door, Ellen thought.

"Miss Johnson, good morning!" Ellen said, surprised she was really quite happy to see Lillian even though she still felt a bitter aftertaste from Jack's behavior. But she knew his sophomoric act had nothing to do with Miss Johnson. Ellen had genuinely enjoyed her time with the elderly woman.

"Thank you again for dinner,"

"I bored you to tears!" said Miss Johnson as she removed

her tanned kid gloves.

"Bored? Not possible! To show my gratitude, let me offer you one of my new creations, a custard pear torte. And I demand an honest critique. Why don't you go sit down, and I'll bring it with your coffee."

If Ellen wasn't mistaken, she noticed a slight flush in Miss Johnson's cheeks. Geez, she thought, that must be a rarity. She cut a healthy, yet ladylike, piece of torte and placed it with a steaming mug of coffee in front of Lillian. Ellen still found it awkward to see Miss Johnson drinking from a thick white stoneware mug, but The Manito wasn't exactly a porcelain cup-and-saucer shop. Plus, the slightly browned edges of pear, lightly dusted with powdered sugar, were a stunning work of art and more than compensated for the down-to-earth dishware.

"So, tell me what you think," she said with the anticipation of a competitor on Bravo's Top Chef.

Not one to dive into anything, not even a heavenly pear torte, Miss Johnson slowly unfolded her napkin and situated her coffee mug just so before picking up her fork. Ellen appreciated the ritual and watched the fine-boned woman take her first bite—a dainty one—and slowly chew. Her snow-white brow slightly furrowed, she looked up toward the ceiling as though searching for just the right adjective. She swallowed and took a sip of coffee before speaking.

"Satisfying," she said, both hands coming to rest in her lap.

Okay, so Lillian isn't big on extrapolation, Ellen thought, but throw me a bone here, Lilly!

"That's it? Satisfying? Nothing else?"

"No, dear, satisfying sums it up."

"I'll take that as a 'go-ahead' and save the recipe."

"Yes, you do that."

Okay then, Ellen thought with some disappointment. Geez, don't bore me with too many accolades. She'd try it out on one of the coffee boys. They were much more honest and expressive, and their critiques had helped her refine many a pastry recipe.

"So tell me, Ellen," said Lillian, clearly done with the subject of the torte, "did Jack get you home safe and sound Saturday?"

Safe maybe, but not so sound, Ellen thought but didn't say. She expected Jack to come up in their conversation but didn't know how to maneuver around her less-than-gold-leafed opinion of Jack at the moment.

"If you mean did he drive that huge truck of his up a tree? No. I was delivered home in one piece."

Ellen knew by the way Lillian's thick, perfectly plucked white eyebrows caulked upward ever so slightly, the old gal sensed something was amiss.

"Jack is a dear but very strong-minded," she said. "I often think he has a bit of a chip on his shoulder."

A chip? Try a condominium! Ellen thought. Still, she was glad Lillian recognized some imperfection in her dear, perfect Jack. So instead, she replied with a safe, "Maybe so."

Ellen glanced around the bakery pretending to be the conscientious proprietor, when in truth she desperately wanted a diversion from the topic of Jack. Dang, everything was going smoothly. Maybe someone will drive a car through the front window.

"What do you think about Jack?" Miss Johnson asked point blank.

No wonder Molly likes this woman so much. They're so alike. No time for subtle. Just point and shoot.

"Um, I think Jack is a complex fellow." Ellen realized what an utterly noncommittal answer this was but hoped not to get drawn into a critique of Lillian's blessed Jack.

"I think a lot of expectations have been placed on him," Miss Johnson continued. "As a youngster, he always acted more mature than his friends. Even I expected more from him than was fair. His parents were demanding, and his brothers, oh they worshipped the ground he walked on."

"Did they have any fun at all? Was there any love floating around?" asked Ellen, feeling reluctantly sad for the Doyle boys. Her childhood had been so opposite Jack's she couldn't help but feel sorry for anyone growing up any other way as antiquated as her life seemed by today's standards.

"Oh, I think so, but I know from experience parents' expectations can put a damper on a child's happiness."

Ellen was taken aback. She had never heard Lillian refer to herself in such a sensitive, almost personal way. She was looking past Ellen toward the front windows with wide eyes. Ellen knew this woman had a lot of memories, good and not so good, under her double-breasted herringbone suit.

Ellen interrupted Miss Johnson's far away thoughts.

"Miss Johnson, why don't you stop by for tea tomorrow afternoon? We'll have it upstairs in my apartment. Believe me, it will be a short tour."

To Ellen's amazement, Lillian accepted the invitation.

"Great," Ellen said. "About three, then?"

"Three it is," Lillian said.

Ellen walked her to the door. She let go with a small yelp when she turned to go back into the bakery and literally ran into Jack who also was leaving.

"Sorry, I didn't mean to startle you," he said.

"No prob," she said, attempting to extract her forehead from his left shoulder.

"It looks like you and Lillian were enjoying yourselves," he said, moving slightly to the side but not far enough for Ellen to get by without a half body slam. She stepped back a few feet, resigned to a forced form of chit-chat.

"She was a willing guinea pig for a new torte. I might as well try it on someone old. Her taste buds might be half shot, but if she croaks…" Ellen caught herself and shut up before her sarcasm got carried away. Jack's sense of humor hadn't proven to be his strong suit. In fact, she didn't know what his strong suit was. "Anyway, if you'll excuse me, I need to get back to work."

"Sure," Jack said, reluctantly stepping aside. "Did you set an appointment at the Eye Clinic?"

"Not yet, but thank you, Jack.

Chapter 24

Damn, that woman has an obsession with promptness! Ellen had just changed into a fresh pair of navy flannel slacks and an ivory cable-knit turtleneck sweater when she heard Miss Johnson tapping gently at the back door. Her hair, well it was still post-scarf, which meant she looked and felt like she was wearing a skull cap. She slid her bare feet into some well-worn Cole Haan loafers that refused to wear out and galloped downstairs.

"Welcome, welcome, Miss Johnson!" Ellen said, opening the door with energy that surprised both of them. But she was genuinely happy to see her tea guest. "Please, come on upstairs. I promise, it's a short climb."

"Thank you, dear. And don't you worry about me. I sometimes think I'm half mountain goat after climbing those stairs in that big, old house of mine all these years."

She followed Ellen up the brightly lit staircase, impressed by the fine woodwork and beautiful staircase runner. At the landing, she paused for a moment to look at the huge window surrounding a cozy window seat. Ellen noticed she wasn't the slightest bit out of breath.

"That's as far as I get some evenings," Ellen said.

"It's a beautiful view of the park and a perfect reading spot."

"If you open the window seat, you'll see oodles of books," Ellen admitted.

"Ah ha! I should have guessed. A reader. You're a girl

after my own heart."

Ellen gave Miss Johnson the cook's tour of her apartment, and then they settled into two over-stuffed chairs for tea.

Ellen set her grandmother's pale pink and white Wedgewood teapot on the table and tucked her now shoeless feet cross-legged up into her chair. "I hope you don't mind, but by this time of day, my feet are screaming for freedom."

"Not at all! If you can't be comfortable in your own home, it isn't home. I spent half my life trying to convince my mother of that. I hate to admit it, but I did not succeed."

The sun cast a warm shadow across Ellen's apartment, turning it into the nest she and Molly had in mind when they went to work on the once lonely, empty space. Indeed, Ellen felt relaxed and delighted at having an afternoon guest. While Sam and she used to frequently have people for dinner, her life as a widow and single business owner changed her social calendar markedly. Lou was perhaps the only regular visitor to her secret fort.

"I envy you," Lillian said. "I lived in my own home, once. It was a cozy apartment much like this. It was such a good time in my life."

The wistful tone of her voice struck Ellen with a deep sense of melancholy, and she felt a growing affinity toward Lillian.

"When you and Jack came to dinner last month, it reminded me of the little dinner parties I would have for a few friends. I had so much energy then."

Last month? Ellen thought. It had been less than a week since she and Jack had dined at Lillian's. She let the slip pass. The woman had earned a right to slip up from time to time, even though Lillian didn't seem prone to confusion.

"When was that, Miss Johnson?" Ellen prodded, anxious to hear more about her past.

"Call me Lillian, dear. It was the late-thirties, in San Francisco. Before the Second World War. "

"San Francisco?"

"Yes, San Francisco, Ellen, and don't sound so surprised," Lillian laughed. "As starched and proper as I may appear, there was a time in my life, though brief, when I was a free agent, so to speak. I made a mean Gibson in my day."

"Oh, no, I didn't mean, well, you know what I mean," Ellen stammered, embarrassed she had offended Lillian. "It's just that I've always pictured you living in Spokane, in the home you grew up in with your parents. You were so close to them."

"Oh, I was, especially my father. I worshipped him. I was probably too close to them both. They were far too protective of me. You know how parents can be."

Ellen only had to think of Molly for a nanosecond to kick her motherly worry and protectiveness into high gear. She hoped she never let these feelings impede Molly's spirit for adventure.

"What took you to San Francisco?" Ellen gently prodded. God, Lou would be so proud of her for asking all these questions, she thought smugly.

"Sometimes it seems so long ago, and sometimes it seems like yesterday. I went there to sing."

"Sing?"

"Your face is an open book, Ellen, so don't try to hide your shock. It's quite all right. I'm used to it."

"Well, Lillian, I have to admit you could have said you went to San Francisco for a lot of reasons, and I probably wouldn't blink, but sing? I mean, it's not like you walk into the bakery belting out a Broadway tune every morning."

"Quite right and for good reason. I have a horrible voice, now. But, back then, I was fairly good."

"Really?"

"Yes, really," she said.

"So, tell me all about this adventure of yours."

Ellen replenished their tea and placed a still warm slice of cinnamon raisin bread on Miss Johnson's plate. Then she sat back, all ears. It was slowly getting darker outside, and Ellen's apartment wrapped around the two women like a well-worn down comforter. Fearful any distraction would end this rare opportunity to hear a story Ellen was sure very few, maybe not even Jack, had ever heard, Ellen concentrated on staying still and attentive.

"Well, I arrived in San Francisco scared to death but equally determined. I was so full of myself. I was going to get out from under my mother's expectations with one suitcase and a dream. Oh, my mother. Growing up, she made all the decisions for my sister, Nancy, and me. She sent us all the way across the Spokane River to Holy Names Academy as boarders. In high school—can you believe it, boarders who lived just three miles from school?"

Ellen knew the school well. It was one of two Catholic, all-girl high schools in Spokane, and a lot of her friends had gone there. Thankfully, she hadn't. Back in the day, Lillian's day, Holy Names was where all the wealthy young girls went to school.

"Mother liked the idea of boarding school. It provided an illusion of grandeur. After graduation, she sent us to St. Mary's just outside San Francisco, which at the time was more of a finishing school than a college—just two years. She had gotten wind of the fact that some of Spokane's more elite families sent their daughters there. None of them were my friends. Nancy was always the social one. Oh, she loved a party. Too much, I'm afraid. But she was a beauty and received invitations almost every weekend to Pebble Beach with girls whose families had homes along the coast. I rarely left school on weekends, though. I spent hours taking private voice lessons or practicing with the choir. Most girls went home to marry, which was the thing to do, for them anyway. But after two years, even though it was a very strict school–nothing like today, I was just becoming accustomed to living my own life rather than my mother's. Marriage was the furthest thing from my mind. Our little choir had performed at various parties around San Francisco, and I'd taken to performing like dry sherry to an old lady. I convinced myself that I was destined for a great singing career, so I got my dear father to lobby my mother for me, and he convinced her to allow me to stay in San Francisco."

"Are you kidding?" Ellen exclaimed. She had become completely caught up in Lillian's autobiography. "You were a generation or two ahead of yourself! You were brave!"

Lillian had been looking out the window as she spoke, and when she turned to look at Ellen, she almost seemed surprised to see someone else in the room.

"Oh, you shouldn't let me go on about myself like this. I'm as boring as watching the paint dry! I rarely think about those days, and I certainly don't talk about them. Speaking of old ladies and sherry, you wouldn't have any would you, Ellen?"

Ellen felt somewhat flattered Lillian was comfortable enough with her to ask for a sherry. "As a matter of fact, I do," said Ellen. She walked over to a small mahogany breakfront Molly had found in Seattle. She poured two glasses of sherry and hoped it hadn't turned to…whatever sherry turns to with too much time on its hands.

"Please, continue," Ellen said softly as she handed Lillian the small ruby red crystal sherry glass that had been her grandmother's. She was afraid to break the spell.

Lillian took a small sip of sherry then held her chin up high and returned her gaze to the window.

This is good. The sherry didn't kill her, Ellen thought with some relief. That surely would have been awkward.

"Back then most people, my mother in particular, thought I was more idiotic than brave," Lillian continued. "She thought life—life as she understood it—was passing me by. I was supposed to return to Spokane, join the Junior League and marry. Doesn't that sound like riotous fun?" she said with unmistakable sarcasm. She had settled down further into her chair as though she'd found more memories, like spare change, lurking in the depth of its cushions.

"Father rarely stepped in where my mother's directives were involved, but he intervened and supported my choice to stay in San Francisco. So I took a small room at the Fairmont

Hotel up on Nob Hill. I had a wonderfully entertaining circle of friends whom I spent time with when I wasn't in voice lessons. We'd go down to Monterey for weekends or further down the coast to Santa Barbara. California back then was paradise. A Mecca."

"How long did you stay there?" Ellen asked.

"Not long enough." Lillian said. Ellen was saddened by the flat finality in her voice.

"I was able to secure a few singing engagements at small clubs, but I was no Ziegfeld girl. Nothing convinced my mother I should stay in San Francisco, so I was there for just over a year. By then, even my father agreed it was time for me to return home and settle down. Talk of war had started, which I know made him worry."

The regret in Lillian's voice was palpable and Ellen filled the ensuing silence with a quiet question.

"Why didn't you just stay?" Ellen asked quietly.

Lillian gave Ellen a sharp sideways glance.

"It was a different time, Ellen. Women didn't just go off on their own like they do today. But believe me, I wanted to. Not just for the singing. You see, I had fallen in love."

Ellen felt as though her carotid artery just burst. Good Lord, she thought and simultaneously asked herself if she was really hearing correctly. Lillian's voice brought her back to Earth.

"Ellen, I wasn't always the aging fossil you are having sherry with today," Lillian was saying.

"No, of course not," Ellen stammered. Oh my, shut up, she told herself. Did I just call her an old fossil?

"Will was a trumpet player at one of the clubs where I sang. He had a sort of Robert Mitchum look, very suave, alluring and equally kind. We fell head over heels for each other, and I couldn't have given a hoot that he didn't have more than a few dimes to rub together. Of course I didn't dare tell my parents about Will. Had I even hinted I was in love with a horn player five years my senior, they would have brought me back to Spokane in a snap."

A quiet, "Whoa," was all Ellen could offer.

"But I wasn't strong enough," Lillian sighed, almost as though Ellen wasn't in the apartment. "I returned to Spokane. They brought me back to bridge at the Spokane Club and golf at Hayden Lake during the summer."

"So you left everything. You left Will?" Ellen sounded disappointed and sad.

"I did. I left Will. I left my friends, my singing, the fun—everything. I left all of what I loved, so I could be what my parents wanted me to be. A day doesn't go by when I don't regret my weakness."

"And Will didn't try to stop you?"

"He did. We went to Carmel one weekend, and I told him my parents expected me to come home, that they wouldn't provide financial support if I stayed in San Francisco."

"And what did he say?"

"He asked me to stay. He said he'd quit performing and get a steady job, so he could support me the way my parents expected, but I couldn't ask him to give up his music. It was his life. That weekend was the last time I saw Will. I packed my few belongings the following Monday and left without even saying good-bye. We never communicated with each other again."

Ellen looked out the window at the silhouette of branches. Lillian Johnson, who would have thought? She wondered who else knew this story.

As though reading her mind, Lillian suddenly said, "Jack is the only other person who knows about Will."

Of course he does, Ellen thought. She wondered if he was as touched by it as she was. Probably not. Ever the Teflon-coated man.

"So, here I am in Spokane. I lived the life my mother expected and outlived both of my parents. I've had a comfortable life. But yes, I've always wondered what could have been—what should have been." Her voice once again held a tone of finality.

"You never met anyone here? Never fell in love again?"

Ellen asked cautiously.

Lillian looked at her dismissively. "I'm far too proud. No, for some reason I chose the stoic, independent road, which isn't terribly attractive to men. Independence can make you strong, but it can also leave you lonely." With that she stood up and brushed the front of her camel hair pencil skirt. This conversation obviously was over.

"I've talked your ear off, dear. Now I'm getting tired. It's late and I should be getting home."

"Oh, Miss Johnson, I need to thank you. I've enjoyed every minute."

The two women walked downstairs, and Ellen helped Lillian put on her boiled wool Eisenhower jacket.

"Are you okay to drive home?" Ellen asked protectively.

"Dear me, I'm fine. My car practically drives itself around the South Hill after all these years. I'm just along for the ride."

The older woman was standing at the door when she turned to Ellen and reached to give her a brief hug. "Don't let your independence get the best of you, Ellen," she said.

Ouch, Ellen winced. Is this woman always going to offer me advice when she gives me a hug?

"Not too worry. I'm too much of a wimp. Any independence you see here is all smoke and mirrors."

"I wish I could say the same for Jack," said Lillian over her shoulder as she walked toward her car. Ellen was becoming accustomed to Lillian referencing Jack out of the blue.

"You know, Ellen, Jack cares for you. If I didn't know better, I'd say he could be in love with you."

Ellen surprised herself. She typically would have expected Lillian's observation to put her in the fight-or-flight starting blocks. Instead, she was more than mildly, well, giddy.

"I didn't know you were such a romantic," was all Ellen could manage to say as she helped Lillian into her land barge of an automobile.

"Oh, I'm not. You know me well enough now to know I can't help commenting on the obvious."

I think Jack has a lot more issues than independence, Ellen thought, as she shut the door, turned off the back hall lights and headed upstairs. She wondered if Lillian gave Jack the same advice about independence. Had she talked to Jack about his feelings for her? Was he in love with her? With that last confusing thought banging around her head like a moth against a summer porch light, she realized she hadn't heard Miss Johnson's car pull out of the parking lot. Double checking, she went down the stairs again and peeked out the back door. Lillian's dark blue sedan still sat where she parked it earlier. The Lincoln Town Car sat idling quietly. Her heart pounding, Ellen ran barefoot across the gravel parking lot to the driver's side where Miss Johnson's head rested against the steering wheel.

Chapter 25

Ellen was in the back of an ambulance screaming down yet another tree shrouded street toward Sacred Heart Medical Center when Miss Johnson opened her eyes.

"Where am I?" she sounded angry and confused.

Ellen looked wide-eyed at the six-pack paramedic and gave him her best "You tell her!" look. Thankfully, he responded.

"You're on the way to the hospital, young lady."

Oh please, if you know what's good for you, you won't patronize her with platitudes of youth! Ellen thought too late.

Lillian's look prompted Ellen to speak up.

"You passed out, Miss Johnson."

"Where?" she snapped, sounding demanding and annoyed, which Ellen suspected was a cover for fear.

"In your car, behind the bakery."

"What bakery?"

Ellen looked across to the paramedic who kept writing. No help from him.

"The Manito, Miss Johnson. Remember, we had tea?"

"Who are you?"

Oh man-o-man, Ellen thought. Why me?

"I'm Ellen, Miss Johnson, Molly's mom. I'm Jack's friend." Or whatever.

Jack was the first person Ellen saw when the back doors of the ambulance opened. He was also the first person Lillian saw.

199

"Jack! What is going on here?" Lillian sounded more like someone who, for some inexcusable reason, hadn't been seated at her customary table at her favorite restaurant.

Ellen may not have finished medical school, but she figured Lillian's attitude was encouraging, plus she recognized Jack. Of course she recognized her precious Jack who gave Lillian a light but reassuring kiss on the scared woman's porcelain smooth forehead as paramedics wheeled her into the ER. Ellen clamored out the back end of the ambulance, still barefoot, and caught up with them.

"It looks like you had what you would call 'a spell,' " he said. His voice was deep and soothing. "We'll get you checked out."

Jack's caring voice drew Ellen up short. Maybe Lillian is right about Jack.

With that, Lillian, Jack and a cadre of scrubbed-up people performed a highly choreographed dance through the door of a brightly lit exam room. Now that she had been retired from first-baseman to right fielder, Ellen wondered what she was supposed to do. She was worried about Lillian, but clearly her trauma work was done. Jack had picked up the ball and was down his home field. And, crud, doesn't Jack's look cute in scrubs?

"Please ask Dr. Doyle to call Ellen Kirkpatrick when he has a minute," Ellen said to the harried looking woman seated at the hub of ER central. She got a nod, called it good and went outside to catch a cab.

. . .

Ellen felt as though she'd been on a three-day bender by the time she arrived home from the hospital. It was late. She was starving but eating was out of the question. Her tongue felt hairy enough to braid.

I should call Molly, she thought, but couldn't muster the gumption to explain the evening's events to her, not right now, anyway. She needed to get horizontal, bad. She padded upstairs, yearning to stretch out on her deep green, body-friendly, nine-foot couch that Lou lovingly called the Green Dragon. Lou, where are you when I need you? she appealed to the universe.

Ellen began to wonder if she should have noticed any odd behavior by Miss Johnson and then remembered Lillian had been confused about when she and Jack had been to her home for dinner. Miss Johnson usually didn't make those kinds of chronological slips or any other kinds of slips. But she had been so awed by her self-revealing story she probably wouldn't have noticed anything was amiss, short of Lillian doing a swan dive into her tea.

Before going prone, Ellen headed to the shower to wash ER germs off her feet. She'd read somewhere that hospitals were the most germ-infested places on earth when she felt her cell vibrating in her pocket. It was an unknown number, something she normally would ignore, but considering the day's events, she took the call.

"Hello?" she said, simultaneously visualizing her feet as Petri dishes.

"Ellen, it's Jack."

"How's Miss Johnson?"

"You left."

"Left? Oh, you mean left as in left the hospital. Yeah, well, you seemed to have everything under control, and I didn't want to be in the way."

"But you brought her in. She asked for you."

Damn, Ellen thought. She was embarrassed and could barely miss what she interpreted as a "You coldhearted wretch"-tone in Jack's voice. How could she explain her mom's lifelong instructions that one never hung around hospitals unless they were needed desperately? On the rare occasion her mom would take Ellen to visit anyone in the hospital, Patty would nod toward a room filled to capacity and shake her head with disapproval. If she could have it her way, the stringent visiting hours of the old days would be re-initiated. Ellen always considered her mom's view on hospital visits as being a little cold but obviously hadn't forgotten them. Jack's voice made her feel foolish for following childhood instructions purely out of habit.

"Oh no, she asked for me? I feel horrible! In the ambulance, she didn't even know who I was, so I figured once she saw you she'd be okay. How is she?"

"I'm on my way home, just a couple of blocks from your place. Mind if I stop by?"

Ellen quit picking at her left big toe nail and sat up abruptly. She reminded herself she needed to try a pedicure one of these years. Dang, she thought. Do I mind? It's midnight by bakery time! In the past six hours, I've gone from listening to Lillian spew forth with her rather unsettling life's story to finding her conked out in the car. All this was followed up by a fascinating trip to the ER, barefoot, and Jack wants to know if I mind if he stops by?

Guilt and concern, as ever, prevailed.

"Sure, come on by. I'll unlock the backdoor. I'm jumping in the shower so just come on upstairs."

"Okay. Thanks. I'll be there in a minute."

Was that fear she heard in Jack's voice? The third face of Jack? This guy is complicated.

Ellen heard Jack in her living room just as she began scrubbing Mersa-infested dirt from her feet.

"I'll be out in a second!" she called down the hall, feeling almost revived and germ free.

"Take your time, but don't yell at me if I fall asleep on your couch!" Jack was busy scrutinizing everything in her living room like Inspector Clouseau, particularly the photos of Ellen with Molly from birth and a handsome guy who had to be Sam. There were photos of Lou and Peyton and copious other friends or relatives. Most pictures were group shots of tanned, smiling-faced families on ski trips, camping and river rafting in which the adults looked as exhausted and content as the red-cheeked, freckled kids. Ellen wasn't the most beautiful woman in the photos, but her smile had them all beat. He was jealous of Sam. And he thought for a moment what it would be like to be that happy and relaxed with someone.

Ellen stood in the doorway of the living room observing Jack looking at her Rogue's gallery. The shower washed away germs and most of the day's stress. Watching Jack examine the photos, she suddenly felt any anger and frustration she had harbored against him fade, ever so slightly. Be nice, she told herself. He's tired and stressed, and you're just running on fumes.

She spoke quietly not wanting to surprise him. They'd both had enough surprises today. "To a person, everyone in those pictures has been with me through the best and worst times in my life."

Jack turned to look at her. The dark circles under his eyes looked like hockey pucks, and the blue-green scrubs gave his pallor the glow of day-old dough she wouldn't think twice about tossing into the trash. My God, he's a car wreck, Ellen thought.

From his vantage point, Ellen couldn't have looked more stunning. Few women could look so beautiful in gray sweats and an old olive green fleece pullover. He wanted to reach up and undo the top-knot hiding her dark, wet hair.

"You're fortunate," was all he said.

"Don't I know it? I wouldn't have survived without them," she said, looking at the photos. "So, tell me, how is Miss Johnson?"

"She'll be okay," Jack said as he fell back into the middle of the couch rubbing his hands over his eyes. "We'll know more in the morning, but initial tests show signs of a slight stroke. Tonight's may not have been the first."

Ellen told Jack about Lillian's confusion earlier and the way she'd just brushed it off.

"Don't blame yourself. Strokes are sneaky and insidious, especially with someone as sharp as Lillian. She's far from feeble, so it's almost impossible to see little slips. You don't expect it. More than likely, she isn't even aware she's been having them."

"So it wasn't my tea?"

Jack let the corners of his mouth bend upward ever so slightly. "No, I can assure you that whatever tea and crumpets you served this afternoon were in no way harmful. She's just, well, old."

He sounded so resigned. Ellen sat down at the end of the couch facing Jack with her feet curled up under her. She looked at his profile and wanted to give him a motherly hug, pat him on the back and tell him everything was going to be okay. Remembering his proclivity for shoving people out of the way like an old horse with a swift kick, she held back.

"Lillian and I had quite the conversation this afternoon," Ellen said quietly. "I don't know where it came from, but she told me things about her parents, her aspirations and dashed dreams. It nearly broke my heart."

Jack gave her a sideways glance but didn't say a word.

"She gave up everything, Jack. Her singing and the love of her life. It's so..." Ellen felt a boulder roll into her throat, cutting off her sentence abruptly.

"You know, she told me her story just after I got out of college," he said. "I think she was trying to warn me. Even though I was probably too young to really appreciate the message she was conveying, I knew there was a lesson there somewhere. I told myself I'd never let anyone's rules stop me from doing what I wanted in life."

"If only I had a nickel for everything I promised myself I would or wouldn't do," Ellen said. "But it's so much easier said than done."

Jack shut his eyes with a long sigh. Ellen still wanted to give him a hug. He looked like he needed one and so did she. She couldn't tell if it was her motherly instinct or something more. She cautiously set her right hand on Jack's knee, moving her thumb back and forth in a steady, reassuring pattern. She knew he was thinking how alone he was. A hard pill to swallow for someone as self-assured as Jack Doyle.

"You know, Jack," she said so quietly she could hardly hear her own voice. "We aren't—either of us—Lillian. We may feel as if life is careening by like a series of Formula One race cars, but we have a lot of tread left in us. No one's the boss of us. We're our own boss, like it or not."

Jack opened his eyes, stared at the ceiling for a moment and then turned his head toward her. He felt a tsunami of relief overtake him. She's right, he thought. This woman with admirably clean feet is dead right. Ellen was silent, hoping she hadn't overstepped her boundaries. They looked at each for a foolishly, awkwardly long time.

"I've been so busy trying to cleverly catch and avoid eye contact with you every damn morning I've never really noticed your eyes," he lied. "Now I can't tear mine away.

"Yeah, well, I'm quite the artful dodger in my own right."

"Cat and mouse," he said. Stan's advice about trusting others, and more importantly his own emotions, were front and center.

"Something like that, I guess."

"You've been wise to me for a long time, haven't you?"

Ellen smiled broadly. "I'll admit it, there have been times I thought you might be just a bit too big for your loafers, but you're so kind to Miss Johnson. And the boys at the bakery, hey, nothing gets by them. They would have blown you off long ago if you weren't the real deal."

"I'll take that as a compliment," Jack laughed. "And Lillian, well, she means the world to me."

"That's pretty obvious. Everyone needs someone, Jack."

Jack looked down at Ellen's hand still resting on his knee, her thumb like a metronome, back and forth, back and forth. Huh, he wondered. It's amazing how the slight touch on the knee by the right person can soothe the soul, even his.

"Do you plan on wearing a hole in my scrubs?" he asked quietly.

"Oh! Sorry!" Ellen jerked her hand away as though she'd been stung by a wasp, the moment between them lost. "I come from a long line of touchy-feely types. No one gets out the door without at least two hugs."

"You're lucky, Ellen Kirkpatrick," he said almost enviously. "And on that note, I better let you get some shut-eye." He stood up and stretched his arms high above his head. "You have a bakery to open in the morning, and I have a dear old friend to check on first thing."

"Right," Ellen said as she unknotted herself from the couch and walked to the door with Jack.

He stepped out on the porch and stopped. "Thanks for letting me stop by. It helped. You helped."

"No problem." Even though her early morning wake-up loomed just a few hours away, Ellen didn't want Jack to leave. Now that's amazing, she thought, considering how she coveted her sleep. Instinctively, she reached out and put her hand on Jack's shoulder pulling him toward her into a big bear hug reminiscent of her mom's.

"Don't forget for a minute you can get away without the aforementioned hug."

Jack wrapped his arms around Ellen like a man who'd just been introduced to hugging and immediately took to the concept. He didn't know exactly what to do next, but he liked where he was right now, a lot. "You have good family traditions," was all he could come up with.

Ellen gave him one last reassuring squeeze. She wanted to tell him that as much as she cherished her familial hugs, none of them compared to his at this moment. The moment Jack's arms encircled her, her motherly instinct vanished. So much for brotherly hugs, she thought.

Jack stepped back and turned toward his car.

"I'll see you in the morning," he said without looking at her.

Ellen tried to sound as casual as a woman can when a swarm of butterflies takes up residence in her tummy. "Okey doke, Jack. Tomorrow." And then he was a set of taillights disappearing into darkness.

No sooner had Ellen begun brushing her teeth, an oddly enjoyable end-of-the-day ritual, when her phone chimed. She held her supersonic toothbrush while it splattered toothpaste on her mirror, wondering if she could pretend she didn't hear it. Forget that idea. She knew the minute Molly was born that the days of ignoring phones were over.

Dang.

"Hello?" she said, wiping toothpaste from her cheek.

"Hey."

"Jack? Is that you?" she asked while simultaneously trying to put the toothbrush back in its stand.

"Yeah."

She could hardly hear his voice.

"Are you okay?" she said. She tried to sound like a worried mother but knew motherly instinct was still the furthest thing from her mind.

"Ah, not so much."

"Is it Lillian? Is she okay?

"Yeah, I checked just after I left your place. She's sleeping."

"Jack, where are you?" Ellen felt a little freaked.

"Sitting in my kitchen." What he wanted to tell Ellen was he wanted to be back in her apartment holding her. That his tough guy demeanor was nothing more than an eggshell a la anxiety attacks and that she'd cracked him wide open and dumped him into an emotional frying pan he'd avoided for a lifetime. He wanted to tell her he was scared shitless for feeling so vulnerable. He wanted her to know he was scared of losing the old, feisty broad resting alone in a room at Sacred Heart Medical Center, and he never wanted to be an old guy by himself in a hospital room.

But he could only offer a prolonged silence.

"Jack, what's wrong? Why did you call?"

"I don't know, and I'm not sure." Cripes, he said to himself, just be honest for once!

Ellen was starting to feel like a crisis hotline operator without a script.

"Jack, why don't you hit the hay? It's been a long day. Shoot, it's been a long week. It will all look better in the morning."

"You're right. I'm sorry. It's been a hell of a day for you, too. I shouldn't have called so late. It's just that…"

Jack wasn't the kind of guy who let his thoughts trail off to nowhere. Metaphorically speaking, Mr. Darcy had left the building.

"No, it's okay, Jack. But it's late. Get some sleep. I'll see you in the morning." She tried to sound firm. Glancing at her half-dollar size black sports watch, she realized her morning was a mere five hours away.

The idea of seeing Ellen in a few hours was all Jack needed to hear to wipe away the sense of free-floating anxiety. He could let her go for a few hours before seeing her again.

"You're right. We both need some sleep. Man, Ellen, I don't know what's going on with me, but if I call again, hang up on me. Better yet, don't even answer."

Relieved that Jack sounded more like himself, or at least less like someone walking the ledge, Ellen said goodnight and pressed "END" on her cell phone. Okay, she wondered, how embarrassing was tomorrow going to be? During the last few hours, she'd witnessed a Jack she'd have bet millions no one had ever seen. Was he going to be back to Mr. Darcy tomorrow? Rolling over in bed trying to get comfortable, she hoped he wouldn't. She knew her feelings for him were too fragile and would only be hurt by any Darcy-isms. She and Jack had crossed a line. No more cat and mouse games.

Chapter 26

Liam walked into his office at Osbourne, Wainwright, Nelson with three weeks under his belt and the fifty grand still in his pocket. He wasn't sure what he wanted to do with the bonus money yet. For now it would stay in the dumbest place anyone could keep an investment, in his checking account.

He didn't lust for a boat or a new car. He'd just recently paid off his Saab. He didn't want a penthouse condo or a house with a yard. His apartment was just fine, and he was happily not tied down to a long-term lease.

Stacie was putting some low-key pressure on that front. Just last weekend, she insisted they stop by an open house near her parent's home in Oak Park.

Ah, Stacie. Try as he might, for him the bloom was fading from the "Yellow Rose of Chicago." He knew he was not being his best self as Joe had beseeched him to be. He was constantly having hot flashes of a darker-haired variety that captured his imagination and subconscious. The it girl thing wasn't there for him any longer with regard to Stacie, and the more he pulled away from her, the more desperate and manipulative she became.

Liam picked up a file on his desk he had been working on the day before. Better earn my inflated salary, he thought. Working at OWN was a walk in the park compared to the workload he had been carrying with the feds.

He opened a manila file folder that looked the same on the outside as it had when he'd studied it yesterday. However, the inside contents weren't the same at all. What the hell was he looking at? There were confidential stamps on most of the pages. Immediately, he knew he should turn it in to the Ethics and Compliance Department, but his Irish curiosity got the better of him.

The phone startled him away from reading further.

"Hi, Liam!"

"Stacie, I was just thinking about you."

"As it should be, lover. I'm the sun and the moon to you, right?"

More like the setting sun, he thought.

"You're an incurable romantic, aren't you?" he said.

"Love, romance and sex fuel the world economy. And I, for one, thoroughly embrace that as a positive world view. Speaking of which, let's go shopping and out to dinner, and you can stay at my place tonight. You desperately need to buy a new suit, et al, and I would love to help you pick it out. This way you don't even have to go home to that dreary apartment of yours. We have so much to talk about and a lot of planning to do, don't you think? Anyway, we'll start with some new clothes. I'll pick you up at work. Just leave your old Saab there, and we'll go out in my new car. I like the way it drives, don't you? How about trading in your car on a new Lexus? I saw a really cute two-door coupe that would be perfect for you. What do you think?"

"Which question?"

"All of them, silly. I'll pick you up at six o'clock out front. I'll be the cute blonde who looks like she can't wait to get you home. Bye!"

I've really got to figure out a way to end this, and soon. He felt like such a hypocrite because he had to agree with her on the sex part. With a bizarre twist of fate, their sex life had intensified, thanks mostly to the fact that Stacie was working hard at being really good at it. But, as of late, the only room he could stand to be in with her was the bedroom. What kind of sick human being had he become? The thought of spending his life with Lexus Barbie was, in all honesty, unthinkable. But the thought of spending the night was definitely do-able. When sex was over, it was over. Why not enjoy the ride while it lasts? Another Shallow Hal moment, he admitted. He was less than proud of his Jekyll and Hyde behavior.

Liam placed the confidential file in his briefcase for later. He spent the remainder of the day throwing his shoulder into solving the problems of a corporate client because he knew the firm was billing that client an exorbitant hourly rate.

"Good night, Mr. O'Connor," said his secretary, as she poked her head in his office door.

"Good grief, is it that time already?"

"It's a quarter to six. Have a nice evening!"

"You too, Marissa."

Liam's unique filing system of piling papers transferred with him to his plush new office. He had triple the shelving and desktop space and took full advantage of every inch of the available real estate. He coveted the space and relished the staff support absent at the fed job. Yes, there were some definite perks here.

Stacie was waiting for him in her red Lexus. As he got in, she leaned over for a quick kiss. It didn't seem to bother her outwardly that he didn't kiss her back.

"Yum! Let's put shopping and dinner on the fast track. I want some more of that good stuff. Must we go to Brooks Brothers? How about the Hugo Boss store on the Miracle Mile followed by dinner at the Eclectic Cafe?"

"I've never been to either. I literally turn myself over to you. I'm all yours."

"I adore an open invitation. I'll make it worth your while," she promised.

Later that night at Stacie's, Liam's body was game, but his mind resisted sleep. He kept thinking back to the file in his briefcase. When he was sure that Stacie was in deep REMs, he quietly crept out of the bedroom and sat down at the kitchen table to spread out the papers for further study.

An uneasy feeling washed over Liam. Who put this file on his desk? Was the "Ghost of Christmases Yet to Come" warning him of what life would be like if he bought into the firm and the Oak Park Country Club life? Or, was the firm testing his loyalty and commitment to "the man?"

It was eleven o'clock Chicago time, which meant nine o'clock LA time. He picked up his cell phone and called Molly.

"Hey there."

"Hey there, yourself," replied Molly. Her straight forward greeting, sans clichéd-Stacie jargon, was refreshing.

"I haven't talked to you for a few days. How are the girls?"

"The girls are cold. Spokane had an early snowstorm, and now most of the local population—and the landscape—is white. Ruth and Lupe have never seen snow before. Can you believe it? Lou and Peyton are taking them sledding at Mt. Spokane this weekend. Then, when the ski slopes open at Thanksgiving—cross your fingers, they're committed to making downhill skiers out of them."

"Lucky girls! Do you think they're happy? What I mean is everything working out okay, as well as can be expected anyway?"

"I think so. They desperately miss their parents. That's the tragedy. But here's some good news, Ruth's eye surgery is scheduled. The specialist in Spokane feels certain it will be a success. That's the happy part."

"Any word from Maria and Alberto?"

"Sister says Les Schwanbeck is watching their backs. I definitely feel better knowing he's on their side. Don't you? Oh, that's right, you never met him. I forget that you weren't there in the judge's chambers. I felt like you were there. You were such an important part of the planning and decisions we all made."

"I felt like I was there too. Thanks for the virtual inclusion."

Silence.

"Molly?"

"Yes."

"I'm coming down to LA on business next week. Would you have dinner with me?"

"Sure, I'd love to."

He heard the toilet flush in the other room. Stacie.

"Okay! I'll give you a call when I have more details. Great talking to you, Mol."

"You too. Bye!"

Liam shut off his phone when Stacie walked into the kitchen.

"Who were you talking to?" she asked suspiciously.

"Oh, no one. I was reviewing a work file and leaving a few reminder messages on my voicemail."

He hated to lie. It made him feel cheap and sordid. He didn't want to feel that way, especially with anything associated with Molly.

Stacie knew it was a lie. Liam was a horrible liar. She decided to let it go for now and check the recent calls on his cell phone later. Her intuition told her that it had everything to do with a certain Molly Kirkpatrick, the granola bar bitch.

"Come back to bed, lover. I'm not through with you yet," said the naked woman in front of Liam. He followed her beautiful body and forgot all about the file and the cell phone left exposed on the kitchen table.

. . .

Liam pulled up to Providence House. Driving in LA was an out-of-body experience and he tried to blame his sweaty palms and racing heart on the traffic. But he knew freeway driving was only half to blame for his anxiety. Molly Kirkpatrick was responsible for the other half. He was anticipating seeing her again with feelings of nervousness and apprehension redolent of high school.

You're thirty-three years old, pal. Get a grip, he told himself.

He walked in the front door and informed the woman in the office—a nun, he wondered?—that he was here to see

Molly Kirkpatrick.

"You must be Liam O'Connor," the woman said. "My name is Sister Aracelia. I was hoping to meet you, so I could personally thank you for all your help with the Raigosa case. Let me call Molly for you. She is very special to us, Liam. It's so nice to see her going out on a date. She is very devoted to her work here. Perhaps too much so."

A date, thought Liam. Well, okay. That would explain my adolescent symptoms. Other than the Raigosa strategy session in the hotel room after the ND game, this is the first time we've been together—just Molly and me—alone. He warmed at the thought of that idea.

He glanced up, and there she was, looking breathtakingly beautiful with her dark hair, vivid blue eyes and arresting smile. His racing heart literally skipped a beat.

"Liam, how nice to see you!" she said. Then seeing he was wearing a business suit, "Oh dear, I guess compared to you, I'm underdressed." Molly had on a pair of dark jeans, a crisp white button down, and riding boots, a combination considered dressed up for almost any occasion, short of a black-tie affair, back home in Spokane.

"Not to worry. Really! I came here directly from my meeting and it was easier to pick you up first and then swing by my hotel and change. Do you mind? You can't believe how much I seriously want out of this suit and tie. Okay?"

"Okay."

After wishing the couple a lovely evening, Sister Aracelia watched Molly and Liam walk to the car. He opened the car door for her. Hmmm, manners. That's a good sign. He seems like a nice young man. And handsome, too.

The first few minutes in the car were awkward until they started talking about the Raigosas, the twins, Lou and Peyton, and Father Joe, and before they knew it, Liam was pulling up to his hotel. She agreed that it would be best to wait for him in the bar. He found a nice quiet table and ordered her a glass of red wine and himself a beer. He went to his room and came back several minutes later wearing khakis, a polo and topsiders.

"That was fast," Molly observed. "You almost beat the waitress with our drinks."

"I didn't want to waste any time. Sorry to say but I'm flying back to Chicago tomorrow, and I don't want to miss a moment with you."

Molly didn't say anything but felt very flattered at the attention and the sentiment behind his compliment. She knew he was practically engaged, so she changed the subject before reading too much into it. Distance, Molly. Keep your distance.

After the waitress asked if she could bring them another drink, they both decided it would be best to get some food into their empty stomachs. Since neither of them had a clue where to go for dinner, the waitress suggested they have dinner at Burnell's directly across the street from the hotel.

When they came to the crosswalk, Liam took Molly's hand protectively in his. Surprisingly, the simple sensation—the physical connection—of holding her hand was exhilarating. He felt as though he was floating across the street. Whoa, if it feels this great holding her hand walking across a street, I'm a goner. They took a corner table and the candlelight muted the evening into soft focus, casting an ambience of other worldliness. Three hours, and two bottles of wine later, Molly looked up and was surprised to see that they were the only ones in the restaurant.

"Look at the time," she said, clearly embarrassed that she'd lost track of her surroundings. "I'm sorry, but I really should be going."

"I'm sorry too. I can't remember when I've enjoyed myself more."

"You know, Liam, why don't I call a cab? We drank a lot more wine than I'm used to drinking. I don't want you to take any risks by driving me home."

"No, I'm fine. I really want to drive you home." I want every last drop of time with you, thought Liam.

"Let's take a walk and talk about it first?" Molly wasn't

exactly sure how steady she would be on her feet.

Liam reached for her hand again and led her across the street, into the elevator and up to his room. "I'll just get my keys and a jacket," he said.

Molly allowed herself to follow him into his room but stood close to the open door.

"Liam, I really think I should call for a taxi. It's just not worth wrapping your rental car around a light pole."

She was right.

"Trumped by logic. You win."

Liam picked up the phone and called the front desk for a cab.

Molly, now visibly relieved, entered his room and perched on the edge of the desk. "Thanks, that makes me feel much better."

Liam walked over and pulled her up to stand directly in front of him. He slid one arm around her back and with the other he tipped her face up to his.

"Déjà vu, don't you think?" Liam brushed her lips with a light kiss.

"I'm not thinking straight right now. Must be the wine. And last time we were in this situation I took advantage of you. I'm sorry. I won't do it again."

"Damn!"

"Liam, we've avoided the obvious all evening. You have a girlfriend. You're unofficially engaged to her. You took a job as a corporate attorney because of her. You…"

Liam kissed Molly again. This time it was a long, lingering kiss that rocked them both.

"That was lovely," she said, breathlessly, and looked down. "But what does it mean?" After studying the polo pony on his shirt for a minute, she continued, "That we are attracted to each other? Attraction fades, let me tell you. Plus, I'm on relationship sabbatical for at least a year."

Liam kissed her yet again with increased intensity.

"Molly, I don't know how to tell you this—I think I'm experiencing the real thing for the first time in my life, but I think I'm falling in love with you."

"With me? What about Stacie?"

"It's over," he sighed. "It's been over for some time. I'll sadly confess that I've been too weak and selfish to face the truth and break it off. But now, with how I'm feeling about you, it's over with Stacie. I'm ending it."

The phone rang and Liam picked it up, telling the front desk he'd be right down.

Molly's head was spinning from more than the effects of wine when he turned back, pulling her close.

"I'd give anything—my right arm—if you would stay with me tonight. But I'm not going to ask you to. As a matter of fact, I'm going to insist you go. I have some important tasks on my to-do list. First and foremost, I want to be free of entanglements and come to you without any baggage. And when that time comes, don't be surprised if I ask you to marry me."

Molly, in a wide-eyed state of shock, said nothing.

He kissed her lovely, sweet mouth once more. Wordlessly, he led her to the lobby, said goodbye, and pre-paid the cab fare home to her nun space at Providence House.

. . .

Stacie sensed the change in Liam over the phone and was pretty sure it had a lot to do with Molly Kirkpatrick. She'd done a bit of Molly sleuthing while Liam was in Los Angeles, going so far as to bribe the front desk clerk at the hotel for information.

She knew the two had gone out to dinner together, and Molly had gone home in a cab. What else happened, she had no idea, but Stacie planned to find out. She called Liam.

"So, how was LA?" Stacie asked in her sweetest voice.

"Fine."

"Were your meetings successful?" she tried another tack.

"Yes."

"Is there something wrong?" she asked. "You seem

upset."

"No, I'm not upset, just tired. I didn't sleep well in that hotel room. My room faced the freeway. And, contrary to popular belief, New York isn't the only city that never sleeps."

Up all night with Molly Kirkpatrick, she thought, but didn't dare say anything yet.

"How about if I come over tonight and give you a massage?"

"How is that supposed to help me get some sleep? Not tonight, Stacie."

For the first time, the thought of sex with Stacie was, well, unappealing. His mind and his body had finally reached détente. The consensus was no.

Deciding to play this on the down-low, Stacie replied, "No worries, lover. I'm dreadfully tired too. We had a huge photo shoot at work, and I was on my feet all day. I'll talk to you tomorrow, and we'll plan dinner out, okay?"

"Sure."

"Good night, Liam."

And good-bye, he thought as he hung up the phone. Tomorrow night is the showdown. I've got to end this relationship. Nothing's holding me back.

Unfortunately, he knew ending it with the Blonde Wonder was going to be like getting gum out of your hair. Although there are several methods, a cut-away with scissors is the cleanest, simplest and most effective option.

Also weighing on his mind was the information he'd uncovered at OWN. From his cursory review of the files, he knew already his days were numbered at the firm, and his position was assuredly in jeopardy the minute he cut Stacie loose. He didn't harbor any false illusions the firm was so enamored with his legal skills they would keep him on if Jim Dearborn raised the hue and cry after finding out Liam wasn't his future son-in-law and father of his grandchildren.

Liam called Stacie the next day to make arrangements for dinner, on his terms. He took the lead, choosing EL Grille because it was usually busy and loud. He also made certain they each drove to dinner so they could leave separately. Would Stacie allow the relationship to end respectfully and quietly? Not likely. He could only hope for the best and prepare for the worst.

Liam consciously arrived first and chose a table in the middle of the restaurant. He was hoping that Stacie would know several people there, thereby avoiding a scene.

"Hi, darling," she said kissing him on the lips. She sat down and gazed around the restaurant. "Oh look, there are the Olivers and the Crews. I think I'll go over and quickly say hello. Do you mind? What a great choice for dinner. I love the decibel energy at EL Grille. I should let you choose more often!"

Stacie got up and walked across the room. She paused and turned back, grazing her lips across Liam's cheek. "Order me a dirty martini, okay lover?"

Every man and woman in the room watched her performance. Liam had to admit she was one of the most beautiful women he had ever known. She attracted admiration like a firefly on a warm summer's night. She was mesmerizing. But, he was sad to admit, it was just a window display.

Liam had just finished his martini and was ordering a second when Stacie retraced her steps. "Oh, my goodness. I had another day on my feet. Did I tell you about the magazine spread I'm working on? The fashions are so…."

"Stacie?" he interrupted.

"Liam," she whined. "I was just sharing my day with you. It's what couples do. It's what people in love do."

"Thanks for the perfect segue," he said. He paused a few seconds, took a deep breath and forged ahead. "It's time I come clean, and—hard as it is to say—it's over, Stacie. I'd hoped what I felt for you early in our relationship would develop into something more. I thought I might grow to love you in a deep and profound way. But as fond as I am of you, as much as I adore you, I honest and truly don't love you. And that's not fair to you or to me."

"Is there someone else?" she asked already knowing the

answer.

"It's too early to tell, but I have found someone who I have feelings for… feelings I've never experienced before."

"Is it the Molly person you met at the Notre Dame game and had dinner with two nights ago?" she said matter-of-factly.

"How did you know?" he looked up, startled and angry. She knew about his dinner with Molly. "Let's get something straight. What we are discussing now is a separate issue, and it will stay that way. As for you and me, I repeat, it's over."

"Why are you telling me this in a crowded restaurant? This is like the firing scene in *Jerry Maguire*. Why couldn't we have had this conversation in private? I want to scream and throw things," she said quietly, her eyes and lips drawn back as tight as a pit bull pulling at its chain. "Because I'll be honest with you, it's not over for me, lover," she said in a warning tone.

"I'm sorry I can't help how I feel or how you feel. It is what it is, Stacie."

His second martini arrived, affording a welcome diversion.

"What is it with this woman? I'm crazy about you, Liam. I always have been and always will be," she pleaded, changing tack with a tear rolling down her high cheekbone.

"Do you want to order dinner or just call it a night?" he asked, again taking a different off-ramp from the conversation. He hated tears, and she knew it. Leave it to Stacie to turn on the waterworks. His only protection was that they were in a very public place.

"I've lost my appetite. I just want to go home. With you, Liam, and talk about how we can make us work. Please?" she pleaded with a pretty, yet practiced, pout.

"Talking won't make a difference about how I feel, Stace," he said with firm resolve. "I really think I'd better go now. I'm sorry. I am truly and very, very sorry things didn't work out. I'll get the tab on my way out."

He got up and walked toward the door.

Stacie stared after him, dumbfounded. Her mind raced

with conflicting emotions. No one dumps me. I'll get him back, if for no other reason than to drop him like a hot rock.

But as angry and hurt as she was, she knew she was still in love with him. A quote that had something to do with wrath and woman scorned flashed through her subconscious. No retribution. Not yet, anyway. What she needed now was a plan.

Liam stopped by a bookstore, bought a few groceries, and picked up his dry cleaning on the way home. He opened a beer and microwaved a frozen dinner before checking his land line for voice messages.

The first one was a welcome breath of fresh air. "Hi, Liam. It's Molly. Thank you again for a truly wonderful dinner. And guess what? Sister Aracelia wants me to attend a conference in Chicago. I'll be there a week from Thursday. Could I return the favor and invite you to dinner? Give me a call."

The second message sucked the wind right out of the room like a *Harry Potter* Azkaban Dementor. "Hi, lover. I didn't say anything at the restaurant because I wasn't sure and was hoping we could share this experience together. I'm late. You know, late. So, on the way home I bought a pregnancy test, and, well, it's showing positive. I realize the timing is not the best, but we are definitely pregnant. Call me. We need to talk, don't you think?"

Oh God. Holy shit. The rabbit died. What the hell am I going to do now?

Chapter 27

The more he researched the contents of the confidential file assigned to him by Mel Wainwright, the more he hated this kind of cover-your-ass business law. No wonder lawyers were placed in the genus of reptiles, a.k.a. snakes, and prehistoric underwater killing machines, a.k.a. sharks. What he'd uncovered was avarice and greed that made him physically sick. And it involved his future father-in-law.

After not speaking to her for a good thirty-six hours, Liam resigned himself to doing the honorable thing and decided he would marry Stacie. What else could he do? She was pregnant. He put his game face on, reconciled with Stacie and decided that his brush with what might have been true love was exactly what it sounded like, pure flight of the imagination. The luxury of envisioning what life might have been with Molly was pointless. The course was set. The flight plan was registered. There was no looking back now.

However, he hadn't told the two people, Molly and Joe, who both deserved to know his decision. Was it cowardice or avoidance? Or were they the same thing in this case?

Molly first. She was arriving at O'Hare later that evening. Offering no room for discussion, Liam had informed Stacie that he would be picking Molly up at the airport and taking her to dinner. Stacie was visibly less than pleased, but he wouldn't abide any arguments from her, and she diplomatically backed down. Could he get through this evening intact, thereby wiping his emotional slate clean? Damnit, this was the rest of his life he was talking about.

Focus, Liam, focus, he kept prodding himself. The file in front of him was loaded for bear. It seems that Dearborn Manufacturing was involved in a U.S. Navy contract, and the whole thing reeked of insider trading. Although there was no concrete evidence to prove criminal intent took place, there were allegations Dearborn Manufacturing received advance notice of the contract award and several members of the corporate board, Jim Dearborn included, purchased unusually large amounts of the company's publicly held stock. When the contract was officially granted, the stock increased significantly in value, and shareholders became the beneficiaries of a ship-shape profit. The case was under review by the Security and Exchange Commission and the Justice Department. Both were licking their chops.

After tracking down the lawyer who no longer worked at OWN, but was the last attorney to work the file, Liam placed a call. He figured the guy might avoid communication with anyone from the firm, so he used his old moniker.

"This is Liam O'Connor with the federal immigration department calling for Eric Miller."

"Speaking," replied Miller

"Hi Eric, first let me be up front with you. Until recently, I was with feds. I just started working at OWN. Now do you still have a minute?"

No response.

"Eric, I'd like to ask you a few questions about a file I'm working on. I think you can guess which file I'm referring to."

"I can't talk to you here," Eric said very quietly.

"Can you meet me today at Snug Harbor on Pine at eleven-thirty for lunch?" asked Liam.

"No."

"Tomorrow?"

No response.

"Eric, let me assure you that our conversation will be strictly off the record. I'm conducting research and was hoping you could help me fill in a few details. It will be strictly a casual conversation, if you know what I mean."

No response.

"Tomorrow then? Eleven thirty, Snug Harbor?"

"Yeah. I'll be there."

"Thanks, Eric."

Click.

Liam didn't like the hint of paranoia in Miller's voice. He had a bad, bad feeling about this. Would the guy go to the mat for Jim Dearborn? He didn't want to think that far ahead. Decisions should be made after the facts were accumulated, not before. Innocent until proven guilty. Liam closed the file and straightened his desk.

"Take a deep breath, pal. Be strong," he said giving himself a pep talk. "Time to head to the airport."

The season's first snow, a light one, was falling as he pulled out of the parking garage. He wasn't paying close attention, too distracted to see a red Lexus SUV parked on the opposite side of the street.

He turned on NPR and listened to Marketplace to take his mind off Molly and the reaction his heart and body experienced when he remembered their last encounter and the promises he made. No wonder she was on a relationship sabbatical for a year. Men were assholes, and he was a standard flag bearer.

Liam pulled in front of the US Airways terminal and saw Molly. Man, she's the opposite of Stacie in every way, complete with her dark hair, California tan, and faded straight-leg Levis. She looks so beautiful. Maybe this wasn't such a good idea after all.

"Hi Liam!" she said all smiles as she jumped in his car. "You are soooo good to pick me up and save the Sisters cab fare. If you have plans tonight, you can just drop me off at my hotel. I truly don't want to impose." Dang, he looked good. The attraction she felt was stronger than expected.

"Molly. No imposition at all. Believe me, this is my pleasure," he said in all honesty. "However, I do have to be somewhere at nine o'clock. But seeing as it's only five now, let's grab a bite first. Does that sound okay?"

Hmm. Molly thought that was pretty standoffish for a guy who dropped the "L and M" words very recently. She'd noticed Liam sounded off kilter on the phone the last few times they talked. Remember your oath to waive off men for a year, she reminded herself. It was a solid plan, so stick to it.

"That sounds great," Molly said agreeably. "The conference starts at seven o'clock tomorrow morning. And since moving into the Providence House, I'm usually in bed by nine. With the life I've been leading, too much social activity could induce a coma," she joked trying to lighten the odd tension in the car.

Liam chose a quiet little Italian café tucked in a trendy shopping area near Molly's conference hotel. Being alone with her was agony. His conflicting emotions were slapping him around like a prizefighter. He felt like a certifiably emotional mess.

"What's wrong, Liam?" Molly finally had to ask. She was concerned, bordering on pissed off. Why did she always fall for men's bullshit? But, before she allowed her head to take her to the darker places, she wanted to hear what he had to say. However, it was becoming obvious to her that his earlier declarations of "L and M" were missing a few letters: LAME. Why did she think he would be different? Oh boy, just wait until she saw Lou at Christmas. Yenta must die.

"I need a drink before I can explain."

"Fair enough," she replied flatly without any of the emotion and turmoil roiling inside. The waiter came by, and Molly ordered a double scotch with no ice.

"Make that two and don't be a stranger," Liam added.

"You look fabulous," he said to her with all honesty. "I've been looking forward to seeing you."

"Thanks," Molly said with a smile that Liam noticed didn't quite reach her eyes.

"Two double scotches, no ice," said the waiter. "I'll keep an eye on you. Just wave at me when you're ready for round two."

Liam nodded.

"Okay, shoot," Molly said, cutting to the chase.

Liam knocked back half of the glass and let the alcohol effect shimmy down his spine. He closed his eyes, took a deep breath, reached over, put his hands over hers and took a deep breath.

"Stacie's pregnant," he bluntly confessed.

"Oh," Molly responded, quickly pulling her hands and eyes toward her lap.

"I've decided, and I'm just going to say it, that as deeply as I have fallen for you, there's a child to consider, and I'm going to marry Stacie."

Molly looked up and saw the anguish in his eyes. She was stunned into silence.

"I won't blame you if you end up hating me, but please forgive me. I wish we had never met because then I wouldn't feel this compulsive desire to spend a lifetime getting to know and love you," he said sadly. "Enough. I'd better stop right here."

Here's a good time for a pregnant pause, if there ever was one, she thought. Oh, dear God. She had to say something.
"I'm sorry too, Liam. I was starting to feel something I've never felt before. But now I guess I, too, am glad I haven't had enough time to find out what it is."

She paused and took another sip of scotch as a diversion. Time for an exit strategy, she thought. "How exciting for you! A challenging new job and a family with a child on the way. I wish you all the best. And I mean that," said Molly more enthusiastically than she truly felt.

Liam's back was to the door, and he didn't see the striking blonde woman who entered the restaurant. Molly noticed that the woman was looking at her and walking directly toward their table.

"Hi, lover," Stacie bent down to kiss Liam on the cheek. She looked over at Molly and offered her hand in gesture of greeting. "I'm Stacie Dearborn. You must be the famous Molly Kirkpatrick I've been hearing so much about."

"Likewise," said Molly shaking Stacie's hand but looking at Liam in total bewilderment.

"Stacie!" Liam looked up at her like she was some kind of freak. "What are you doing here?"

"Merely a coincidence, darling. I saw your car parked out front, so I thought I'd pop in to see if it was actually you. And I really wanted to meet Molly. I've heard so much about her. How was your flight, Molly?"

"Fine. Thanks for asking."

Wow. This is first-class weird, thought Molly.

"Isn't anyone going to invite me to sit down?"

"Stacie, will you take a walk with me? Excuse us, Molly."

Liam stood grabbing Stacie's upper arm and escorted her out the front door.

Holy Jerry Springer, Molly thought to herself. She didn't remember signing up for the lead in a psycho-drama. She clearly wanted to remove herself as a member of this unhappy little love triangle, and the sooner the better.

How do I get myself into these messes, she thought? Once again, she thought of Lou and performed a virtual dropkick in her mind's eye.

Molly looked up to see Liam walking back to the table, alone.

He sat down, visibly embarrassed. "I'm sorry, Molly. That was awkward."

"You know what, pal? I've just written myself out of this scene. How about you drop me off at my hotel, and we'll call it good."

"I can't even start to explain what is happening or what just happened in this restaurant."

"No explanation needed. Just a ride would be great. Can we go? Now."

Liam stood up, pulled out his wallet and left a wad of money on the table.

"Sure, Molly."

They rode the few miles in silence. The air of regret was palpable.

As he stopped the car in front of her hotel, Molly started to get out. Liam placed a hand on her arm and looked as hard as he could into her tightly guarded face. He memorized every feature and every flicker of shock, hurt and control that fought so hard and showed so clearly what he was losing.

"Molly, I don't know what to say other than I'm sorry. I meant everything I said to you."

"Liam, this is where I bow out gracefully. And please don't call me again. Let's make this clean and tidy, okay? Just stay right where you are."

The bellman retrieved her bags. She walked into the hotel and didn't look back. Liam watched her until she disappeared and then drove away.

Chapter 28

The next day, Liam snagged a back booth at Snug Harbor. It was a popular lunch restaurant, and the booth was the perfect spot for the type of conversation he was planning to have. A few minutes later the hostess arrived followed by a tall, slender young man in his late twenties with a prematurely receding hairline and horned-rimmed glasses. He had on the requisite lawyerly dark suit and, Liam noticed, was wearing a wedding ring.

"Liam?"

"Hi, Eric. Thanks for meeting me. I was a little worried you might change your mind."

"My wife asked me not to come, but I'm here."

"Have you been married long?" asked Liam.

"Since before law school," he replied. "We have a seven-year-old daughter and a three year old son."

"Wow. You don't look older than thirty."

"We got pregnant just after graduation. I'd already been accepted at Northwestern, and my wife had a teaching job lined up at Fenwick Catholic High School. She put me through law school. It was tough, but we made it, kids and all."

"Was OWN your first job after graduation?"

"I summer interned for them. When they offered me a job, I grabbed it. I was up to my armpits in student loans and debt. I didn't know then how much I would hate their brand of partner-track hours and pressure."

Eric stopped when a waitress arrived, and he ordered an iced tea. Liam followed suit.

"Tell me what you can about Dearborn Manufacturing," inquired Liam.

Eric hesitated at first, but once he started talking, he seemed relieved to purge what he knew about OWN, Dearborn Manufacturing and the Securities and Exchange Commission investigation. Eric's narrative matched the research Liam had already uncovered. Client-attorney privilege notwithstanding, Dearborn Manufacturing would be ruined, and Jim Dearborn would serve time if an investigation uncovered the truth.

Eric got up to leave.

"Thanks for lunch, Liam. But, if I am called in connection with any investigation, I will deny this lunch and conversation ever occurred.

"Eric, believe me. I totally understand. I'm already missing my fed job. I was poorly paid, but I sure slept better at night." They shook hands, and he watched Eric walk out of the restaurant. He finished his iced tea, paid the tab and went back to his office.

Liam was surprisingly productive the rest of the day, considering all he could think about was Molly, Stacie and the pregnancy. Reality was ever-present, especially with today's check-up with Dr. Larkin, Stacie's OB-GYN, to medically confirm her pregnancy with a blood test. She hadn't, in all honesty, invited Liam to go with her, but he decided he would meet her there and be supportive. He didn't want to think Stacie would lie about being pregnant, but like the old saying goes, sometimes the apple doesn't fall too far from the tree.

Liam arrived at the doctor's office at just before four o'clock. He didn't see Stacie's car in the parking lot but went in anyway and sat down in the waiting room. A room filled with estrogen-based life forms. He was the recipient of a few questioning stares from various women and children. But Liam remained steadfast. This was, after all, the new millennium.

After about twenty minutes of waiting, there was still no sign of Stacie. He walked up to the receptionist.

"I was to meet Stacie Dearborn at four o'clock for her appointment with Dr. Larkin."

The receptionist smiled blandly and checked her computer screen.

"I'm sorry. I don't see Stacie Dearborn on Dr. Larkin's schedule. Let me see if she rescheduled her appointment to another day," the woman said and continued searching the computer screen and tapping on the keyboard. "No sir. I don't have record of Stacie Dearborn making or changing an appointment. It looks like we haven't seen her for over six months and haven't made any recent appointments for her. With HIPPA regulations, that's all I can tell you."

"Thank you, anyway."

Liam walked out to his car and sat in stunned silence. "I'll be damned if she didn't play the pregnancy card to manipulate me into marrying her after all," he said out loud. On the other hand, that surprise performance in front of Molly last night reeked of desperation. Was she doing a Glenn Close *Fatal Attraction* rerun?

Liam went back to the office to wait for Stacie's next move. He, too, could play his trump cards close to his chest.

A little after six o'clock his direct line rang at his desk. The display showed Stacie's cell number.

"Hi, lover. Can you come over tonight? I want to apologize and make up for being such a pain. I shouldn't have dropped in on you and Molly. Please know that I'm incredibly sorry. I really am. Oh yes, and I want to tell you about my appointment with Dr. Larkin today," she ended excitedly.

"I'll be there at seven."

"You still sound upset, Liam."

"I can't help it, Stacie. Last night was a real loser move in my book."

"I know, I know. I admit it. For the first time since we've been together, I was jealous of you being with another woman."

With good reason, he thought. "See you at seven," and he hung up.

. . .

When Stacie answered the door, she had her hair pulled back casually in a ponytail and was dressed in ND sweats. She put her arms around his neck and kissed him softly.

"I'm so sorry, lover. Can you forgive me?"

"I'll try," he said noncommittally. "Could I trouble you for a beer? It's been a day."

"No trouble. I'll be right back."

He had to admit it, she looked damn cute. She knew Liam liked her when she appeared dressed to go nowhere. Liam shrugged off his suit coat and loosened his tie. Other than that he resisted getting too comfortable. He wanted to stay focused and handle his next cast like a skilled fly-fisherman.

Stacie walked to the kitchen and returned with a Corona, lime and a plate of chicken nachos. "Will this do?" she asked affectionately.

"Perfect!" he sighed and took a long pull from the Corona.

Stacie watched him, choosing to wait and follow his lead. She knew he was still upset with her. How she handled their next conversation could be the deal breaker. Damn that Molly Kirkpatrick. Because of her, I had to lie and mislead Liam to get what I want. And I want Liam, she reminded herself.

"So, tell me about your day," he said in a low-key manner. "Other than the doctor's appointment, did you go into work?"

"I'd planned to take the day off, but I had tons of paperwork to catch up on. So, I went to the office this morning and then met my mother for a late lunch."

"Did you tell your mom about the baby?"

"No way!" Stacie said, alarmed at the idea. "Until I confirmed with Dr. Larkin, I didn't want to get Marge's hopes up."

"So she didn't go to the appointment with you?"

"No, I went by myself."

"Stacie, I would have gone with you."

"In retrospect, I wish I'd asked you to come with me. But you were so mad at me, I just didn't."

Smart call, Stacie, he said to himself. Hang on, boyo. Don't give it away just yet.

"So tell me. What did Dr. Larkin say?"

Stacie placed her hands on her very flat abdomen and smiled conspicuously. "The blood test confirmed what the over-the-counter test showed. We are pregnant, my love!"

"What time was your appointment, again?" he asked coolly.

"Four o'clock."

"At Dr. Larkin's in Lincoln Park?"

"Yes, why?" Stacie asked, feeling a queasy sense of foreboding.

Liam looked at her sadly, his voice void of emotion. "Because I was there, Stace. I sat in the waiting room waiting for you. Finally, I asked for you at the front desk, and the receptionist said there was no appointment for a Miss Stacie Dearborn."

Stacie stood up and walked to the kitchen. After a few minutes, she came back with a glass of wine and said in a sad ironic tone, "I guess there's no reason for me not to have a drink."

Liam looked at Stacie for a long moment and then stood up. He picked up his jacket and walked out her front door.

Other than obvious relief, Liam felt like he'd unloaded the weight of the world he'd been carrying around. That weight had been accumulating since he'd gone to the ND-UCLA game, taken the new job and most of all, since meeting Molly. Did he have the guts to call her after that macabre dosey-doe-hoe-down he and Stacie performed last night? I don't know if she'll ever speak to me again after that, but I've got to try, he decided.

Grabbing his cell phone, Liam dialed Molly's number

before he could analyze the situation any further. Shit. Voice mail. She's probably screening my calls. He tried again. Voice mail again. He hit redial.

"Hello?"

"Molly, it's Liam. Don't hang up, please."

Silence.

"Molly?"

"Yes," she replied with no inflection.

"She was lying about the pregnancy. It's really over now between Stacie and me."

Silence.

"Could I see you before you fly back to LA tomorrow? You've got to eat, right? Could I buy you the dinner we had planned for last night?" Come on, he thought, throw me a bone.

"No, Liam. Not interested."

"Not interested in dinner or not interested in me."

"Both."

He shivered. A cold wind blew through his ribcage. But he wasn't giving up. Low pressure steadily applied, he thought. Just keep her talking.

"Okay, I understand. How's the conference?"

"Good. I'm late for an appointment, Liam. I really must go."

"Early breakfast?" he tried again. "Ride to the airport?"

"I've already lined up a shuttle. Thanks anyway. I have to go, Liam," trying to end the conversation while she still had some composure. Well, I'll be. Stacie's not pregnant! she thought.

"Molly, I still feel the same way about you. I know you probably need some time and definitely space. I know I do. Take all the space you need. For God's sake, I'll give you the Louisiana Purchase if you need it. But don't write me off. Please?"

"I'll think about it, Liam."

"That's all I can ask for. I'll be in touch."

"No. Maybe I'll call you later, but for now, just leave me

alone. No calls."

"Deal."

Molly hung up without saying goodbye.

Liam's head flopped back on the headrest of his car seat and let out a heavy sigh. It wasn't the way he would have written this scene, but at least he still had his foot in the door. Joe. I've got to call Joe.

"Hello?"

"Joe, it's Liam. Where are you?"

"I'm in Cleveland. What a coincidence, I was just about to call you. Are you sitting down, my friend?"

"Why?"

"What I'm about to tell you is quite certain to blow you away."

"Pile it high and deep, Joe. I'm already dealing with so many issues nothing could surprise me."

"I'm leaving Notre Dame and possibly the priesthood and moving to Spokane, Washington."

"Hmmm, my last comment suddenly sounds a bit blasé. Wow, Joe. I don't know what to say. 'I'm sorry' seems inadequate. Shit o' dear."

"Listen, I'm in Cleveland visiting my sister and brother-in-law. I'm picking up mom's old car and leaving Monday to drive to Spokane. Are you up for an adventure?"

"You bet I am. But first, real quick, let me give you the Cliff Notes on the Life of Liam. I hate my new high-falutin' job. It was a huge mistake. I don't know what I was thinking. I can't work for this alligator-loafer firm. Who was I trying to fool? Stacie tried to pull the fake-pregnancy-guilt-marriage ruse, and I caught her red-handed in her bald-faced lie. Jim Dearborn has committed serious securities fraud, and I have the solid proof, yet another reason to sever ties with all three. And the saddest part is Molly got caught in the middle of this cluster-chaos and just gave me that famous old line, 'Don't call me, I'll call you.' Oh, and did I mention I think I'm in love with Molly?"

"Sounds like a road trip will do us both a world of good.

Do what you have to do to get away. Plan on being gone through Thanksgiving weekend at least. I'll be at your apartment a week from Monday night. We'll leave Tuesday heading North by Northwest.

"This couldn't have come at a better time."

"Too right. See you soon."

His head cleared somewhat, Liam started the car and headed back to his apartment. At least he had plans to make and a timeline with a short leash. Any kind of action was a tonic for his nerves. Not to mention the fifty grand in his bank account. He felt like he didn't deserve the signing bonus. But he didn't want to give it back to OWN either. What was chump change to the firm was decent starter money for a new career. Maybe he would like Spokane?

Chapter 29

He could hear her before he saw her. Lillian was back.

"I knew you'd be hard to corral for very long, Lillian," Jack teased as he walked into her hospital room. Clad in his white doctoring coat, well-worn Levis and a pair of old running shoes that looked like they'd been delegated to bad weather runs, he was pushing his crumpled, relaxed look to new limits.

"And what did you expect, Jack?"

With a quick glance, and considering the institutional lighting of her private hospital room, her color looked good and her eyes bright. Her wit was certainly intact, but Jack knew all too well how crafty people like Lillian could be at disguising serious underlying symptoms with humor. Something she couldn't hide, however, was her lack of appetite. Her breakfast of Cream of Wheat, toast and coffee was untouched. Granted, hospital food sucked, but even the pickiest of patients could handle breakfast.

"You're neglecting this fine breakfast in hopes I'll bring you something of Ellen's?" he teased in hopes of covering up his concern.

"Exactly!" she said. Despite the improvement in color and clarity, she looked tired, like a piece of Silly Putty that had seen better days.

"Well, just about every type of 'ologist' in Spokane's medical community has worked you up and down. From the looks of it, the original diagnosis, which I don't mind stressing again was mine, still stands. You had yourself a textbook stroke."

Listening to himself, Jack thought he sounded like an airline pilot using that all too familiar Chuck Yeager drawl. All hell could be breaking loose, yet a smooth southern voice calmly announces, "Ladies and gentlemen, I just want to let you know we're dropping out of the sky like a melon from a rooftop. It's been a pleasure flying with you today, and we hope you'll fly with us again soon. We know you have choices when you choose a hospital, and we hope you'll have your stroke with us again, soon."

"Of course I had a stroke. I could have told you that on the way to the hospital."

Lillian was not to be one-upped.

"Oh, and would that have been just after they peeled your head off your steering wheel or just before you didn't recognize Ellen? C'mon, I trump you on medical issues. You have to give me that."

"All right, Mr. Know It All. Now, when do I get out of here?"

"First, it's Dr. Know It All, to you, and I'd say you'll be enjoying the fine care here for at least a week and then onto St Luke's for physical therapy and rehab. We aren't skimping on any tests or follow up procedures."

What he wasn't telling her was he also wanted to make sure in-home care was set in cement before letting her go home. The news that she was going to have live-in company was bound to land like a lead brick right on Jack's head, but he had to tell her, so she'd get used to the idea by the time she was discharged.

"Oh, by the way, you'll need some home healthcare when the time comes," he mentioned, trying to sound casual.

Plop. There it was, part of it anyway, right on to her scrawny lap.

"Baloney."

He couldn't believe her wimpy response. He'd expected a hellacious uproar.

"Come again?"

240

"Baloney. Not necessary." Still no lead brick. Maybe she was just winding up for the throw.

"Lillian, I'm afraid it is necessary, and there is no room for discussion on this."

"Do I have any other choice?" she asked, her voice still disturbingly calm.

Christ, did they give her a lobotomy without my knowing? Jack wondered. He'd prepared for such a huge argument.

"Well, you can go to a care center. St. Joseph's has a bed available."

Silence was followed by more silence. Lillian had mentioned her dread of ending up at St. Joseph's, a very adequate full-care facility where she had visited friends either recouping from surgery or in for the slow slide from this universe. Jack knew she'd agree to anything to avoid that fate.

"All right then, let's get me home as soon as possible, so I can meet my new roommates. I haven't had one since college."

"I'm all over it," Jack said. He bent over and lightly kissed Lillian's brow that was knitted into a tight knot. He felt heartbroken.

"This is all going to work out, sweets," he said, turning to leave the room. "See you this evening."

Jack leaned against the wall in the hallway, looking upward to offer thanks to the hospital gods.

"Lose something up there?"

The voice was a welcome sound from the nursing station buzz and constant beeps. How long had it been since he'd last seen Ellen? It seemed like eons ago, Jack thought. Was it just last night? First the ER, then sitting with Ellen in her apartment, followed by his baffling late-night call.

Thanks, Stanley, he thought sarcastically to himself, simultaneously looking at Ellen's slight smile showing a hint of confusion. Doesn't she have the greatest eyebrows? How have I missed those before? Over the past several days, he'd read everything he could get his hands on about anxiety attacks and talked through what seemed like ten years of therapy with

Stan, who told him Lillian's stroke was, though sad, a prompt for Jack to display some soul-stripping feelings. Stan told him he could and should feel good about his efforts to be open— and did he say intimate?—with Ellen. Sweet Jesus, Jack thought. If that Wednesday night was a good thing, how horribly embarrassing would full-fledged healthy behavior be for him?

"Hello? Ellen to Jack. Jack do you read me, come in, over."

He sprang back into the here and now.

"Oh, sorry, I was thinking of..." No he wasn't about to tell her what he was thinking.

"Thinking of what?" Ellen asked, not entirely convinced she wanted clarification, particularly after their last exchange. She wondered, would that be when he politely asked me if I was trying to rub a hole in his scrubs or when he called me later sounding like a despondent meth addict?

"About Lillian," Jack said, proud of his quick recovery but not so proud of his tone of voice. Jack, distant and guarded, was back.

"And how is she?" Ellen asked, sneaking a peek past Jack into Lillian's room. Lillian's eyes were shut, and she looked calm but frail.

"She's okay. Still waiting for some tests but everything leans toward a stroke."

"How bad?"

"Bad enough but she'll be okay. Within a few days she'll be so over pricked and prodded, she'll tap dance out of here."

"Terrific," Ellen said hearing a nervousness in her voice. "That's good. That was a quite a scare."

Jack studied the hallway tiles for a few minutes and then looked up resignedly and said, "Next, I need to get things set up for Lillian at home. She's going to need assistance."

Great, just great, Ellen thought. She knew she was going to step up to the plate. "Do you need some help with that?" She heard the words before they were out of her mouth. "Hey, I have a friend, Lynn, who works for an in-home care

242

agency. I'd trust her with my own mother, if she wasn't dead, if you know what I mean." My, my, that was smooth. "Anyway, if there's a good fit, she'll find it. Introducing a foreign body into that house is going to be a dicey endeavor." Ellen visualized Lillian clad in a black t-shirt and jeans bouncing innocent caretakers off her front porch.

"No kidding? Great! I'd appreciate it," said Jack.

"Okay, then. I'll make a call and see what I can line up by....when?"

"I'm thinking in about two weeks or so. I'll need to see all the test results, but I want her in St Luke's for rehab first."

"Okay, I'll hup to."

"Thanks. Really. What little family Lillian has won't be much help, and it would take them forever to set this up without driving Lillian bonkers."

Jack needed to get on with his morning rounds but would have been just as happy to stand in the bleak hallway talking with Ellen. Her eyes exuded compassion. Care giving comes naturally to her, he knew it. This was only the second time he'd seen her in anything but a bakery coat. He liked the way she'd paired a chocolate brown cashmere V-neck with well-worn Levi's. Casual but not too casual.

"Okay, well I better get back to the bakery," Ellen almost stammered. She noticed his brief head to toe inspection and started to feel self-conscious. I hope I'm not shifting from foot to foot, she prayed. "I'll let you know as soon as I have something going."

"Look, Ellen...." Oh boy, he thought, I'm choking up!

"What?" asked Ellen, now looking more worried than curious.

He pressed on. "Look, Ellen, about me showing up at your place the other night..."

She could feel her shoulders sag. Yep, there he is. The old, step back, way back, Jack. She didn't want him to downplay the night he came to her apartment, which she found comforting and, well, attractive.

"...And then that call after I left. I'm sorry about all

that."

Refusing to be the fool, Ellen quickly put the Jack she was finding so likable aside and slid her guard ever so carefully back into place.

"No prob, Jack. You were tired and stressed. Don't worry about it. Call it a moment of emotional digression. It happens—to some more than others. In fact, I think I'm rewriting the book on that subject." Her grown-up voice irked her. She really wished she could pop out with Lou's favorite, "Oh, go poop and fall back in it!" And then she'd add something like, "Welcome to the emotionally rocky road world the rest of us live in, Jack. Wake up, Jack, you narcissistic boob! You have no idea what and whom you are missing out on in this world. Get over yourself and your digressions."

Jack watched Ellen walk down the long, gurney-lined hall until she turned the corner and out of sight.

. . .

It took Ellen one phone call to Lynn to set up three interviews for the following Friday afternoon. She immediately called Jack.

"Sorry for the short notice, but I hope you can meet with three lucky candidates Friday at three at Miss Johnson's."

"You don't know what to call her, do you?" Jack laughed.

"Excuse me?" she was confused by the change in tone of voice since earlier in the day. Jack seemed to have a strong habit of doing this.

"Miss Johnson, Lillian, you go back and forth."

He was teasing her, which was something she could handle a lot better than his moody darkness. "Well, don't think I don't notice you do the same thing! One minute I feel like I should be bowing in her presence, and the next minute I'm dealing with her personal affairs and wanting to call her grandma! Next thing you know, I'll be referring to her as Lilly, for short."

Jack laughed. "Here's a tip. I decided years ago she likes

to keep people guessing. But I'd refrain from Lilly. That's definitely crossing the line."

"Not to change the subject, and thanks for the heads up, but can you meet with these people tomorrow? I know the time of day probably stinks, but guess what? The rumors are true. It's hard to find good in-home care. Lillian, Miss Johnson, whatever, is fortunate she has a cache to draw from aside from Medicare."

"Here's another news flash. Miss Johnson doesn't view herself as financially well off. She still thinks of the money she has as being her parents'. Odd, I know, but kind of humble, too. Anyway, she's as tight as a tick with the dollar."

"Humble, yes, but also weird," Ellen said. "She may have to loosen her purse strings. So tomorrow is okay? It should take about two hours."

"I'll make it okay. Will you be there?"

"I guess I can." Ellen was baffled by her sudden intimate involvement in Lillian's affairs, and Jack's for that matter. But she did have a growing affinity for the woman, and, besides that, she had conked out in her driveway.

Jack could hear the twinge of hesitation in Ellen's voice and hoped if he ignored it she wouldn't change her mind.

"Perfect. It seems like two sets of eyes and brain matter might work better. And besides, I've never interviewed anyone except nervous residents who hardly qualify as normal people."

"Sure." There, she was committed. She'd ask Zack, her most trusted employee, to close for her.

"I have a key to the house, so I'll be there by a quarter to. Whup, I'm being paged. Thanks again, Ellen, and see you tomorrow."

. . .

Lou, Ruth and Lupe paid their usual late afternoon visit to the bakery. The two girls were out front devouring some of Ellen's rich chocolate Midnight cupcakes drenched in white seven-minute frosting, along with cold milk and good books, while Lou visited back in the kitchen. Ellen blanched almonds for almond pudding, and Lou picked at the discards.

"Eye problems aside, those two are read-aholics," Ellen said.

"Isn't it wild?" Lou agreed, bending her head around the kitchen corner to check on the girls. "I'm scared to death to see what happens once Ruth's vision improves. Thank God for libraries. Okay, I'm exaggerating a little when I say we'd have to take out a second mortgage to keep them in books."

Zack stuck his head around the corner. "Hey, Ellen, I'm good for tomorrow. I'm here as late as you need me." He was a gangly twenty-two-year old with frizzy black hair and beautiful olive skin. Zack was the most solid, reliable member of her team.

"What's up tomorrow?" Lou asked.

"Oh, I told Jack I'd help him interview some caregivers for Miss Johnson." Ellen knew Lou was going to grill her to well done over this one.

"Really?" Lou may as well have said, "Now isn't that an interesting development?"

"Lou, don't let your imagination run amuck. I'm doing this for Miss Johnson, not Jack. Well, kind of not for Jack."

"Ah ha!" Lou exclaimed as though she'd struck pay dirt. "Spit it out!"

Ellen was reluctant to talk about Jack, but if anyone could help her unscramble her mixed feelings, Lou could, or at least die trying. So she described the turn of events between Jack and her from dinner at Miss Johnson to that morning at the hospital. She ended with her chin resting in her hands and her elbows on the mammoth stainless steel counter.

"Sam was so easy, so predictable. He was an open book," she sighed. "Jack, well he's the antithesis."

"Whatever he is, he's got your attention," Lou said. She gave Ellen one of her looks that translated to Don't try to tell me it ain't so, sister.

"How could he not have my attention? We've been tripping over each other at every turn, and I never know what to expect. There's the aloof Jack, and there's the kind Jack who is as faithful and dear to this old lady as the day is long. There's Jack who made it clear he didn't want his life complicated by relationships, and by the way, this is the same man who shows up at my door in the middle of the night and proceeds to pour his heart out. And now this self-proclaimed, self-sufficient man is relying on me. Why me?"

"Why you? 'Cuz he's stuck on you. Duh, anyone can see that," said Lou.

"He has a funny way of expressing it."

"El, that guy fell for you the minute he walked into this bakery."

"Get outta here!" Ellen laughed. "This is high school stuff! We're too old for that."

"Quite the contrary. It's the one constant in relationships between men and women. It's the same game whether you're twelve or sixty. It's the chase. It's one or the other pretending they don't care when they really do. It's the mixed signals. It's the same butterflies in your stomach. It just is."

"Swell," Ellen said flatly. "Just what I need."

"Admit it. You feel a little something for Jack."

"Okay! Okay! When it's the Jack that isn't all hung up on whatever he's hung up on, I like him well enough."

"Well, sorry to break it to you, but you're what he's hung up on," Lou pointed out.

"So, I'm the one who brings out his less charming side? What a compliment."

"Oh, I wouldn't give yourself so much credit," Lou laughed. She got off the counter stool she was sitting on and walked over to Ellen and gave her a big hug.

"I know it sucks to go through this after you've done it once and ended up with the perfect guy, but it's the dance we do—with two left feet."

"That's so reassuring."

"Just roll with it. There is something very vulnerable about Jack, and you too, deary. You know, Sam wasn't as perfect as he seemed. He was just really good at putting his weak spots in the back seat. Jack puts it—whatever it is at the moment—out there."

"Yeah, you're probably right. It isn't like we're married. We aren't even, augh, I hate to use the word, dating. At the moment, we're just two people who have been tossed into this somewhat awkward place. But, he's obviously rung a bell in me that hasn't been rung in a while."

"Are you okay, then?"

"Yep. I am, and I don't know what I'd do without your ear, Lou."

"You'd do fine. I'm just a busy body who loves her best friend to pieces. I'm also a new mom who needs to get two little girls home."

Lou packed up the girls' books and half-eaten cupcakes and maneuvered them out the door.

"Let me know how tomorrow afternoon goes," Lou called back from her car.

Chapter 30

Liam, in his own right, had partially purged his cluttered life of unwanted baggage. Along with resigning his position effective immediately at Osbourne, Wainwright, Nelson, he provided a succinct, albeit monumentally persuasive, synopsis of the Dearborn Manufacturing fraud he'd uncovered and retained the original documentation. He gathered his few personal items, said good-bye to Marissa and walked out the door. He prepaid two months worth of bills, shifted some cash from his checking account into a three-month CD, and made a generous withdrawal of travel money. It's amazing, Liam thought, how simple things become when you get off the crazy train and start using some common sense. Brought up to be penny-wise, he had some cash to see him through until he got another job, but he knew Joe's vow of poverty didn't leave him with much of a cushion. His life temporarily collated, he packed his suitcase with mostly casual travel clothes and was ready for their adventure to begin by the designated scheduled departure. Joe arrived at Liam's apartment about dinnertime. Getting ready to leave Chicago, Liam hadn't gone to the market to buy groceries. So he just opened a couple of beers and ordered a pizza.

Other than being a little road weary, Liam noticed Joe looked healthier than ever. Deciding to leave Notre Dame must have relieved a tsunami of stress.

Over a meat-lovers pizza and several more beers, Liam gave Joe a quick rundown on recent life-altering collisions of the heart and the professional tightrope he'd attempted to walk. As Liam heard his own words coming out of his mouth, he felt ashamed. His choices paled in comparison to Joe's. Liam had a lot of questions for Joe but now wasn't the time. They had a long ribbon of highway to cover. Somewhere along the route the time would be right to ask.

"I can't think of any better medicine for our sorry selves," said Liam with a yawn. "This road trip is a Godsend."

"On that note, let's hit the sack, so we can get an early start tomorrow," said Joe.

"You take my bed, Joe. I have a few last minute computer tasks to take care of. I'll crash on the couch tonight."

Joe put his hand out to shake, and Liam gave him a double pump.

"Yes, we're a sorry pair," said Joe with a tired, but happy, grin.

The next morning, they were up, caffeinated, showered, bageled and ready to head northwest on I-94 then due west on I-90. Liam took the job of navigator with Joe in the driver's seat.

"Looking at the map, I'm estimating about three days on the road. It'll be butt-numbing but not over the top. Let's shoot for Sioux Falls, South Dakota, tonight; then on to Billings, Montana, the next night; and finally into Spokane. About eight or nine hours of driving each day," Liam suggested.

"Sounds reasonable to me."

"Where are we staying when we get to Spokane, Joe?" asked Liam.

"The original plan was to stay with Lou and Peyton Ross. But Lou told me yesterday that she's made arrangements for us to stay with a friend of theirs."

Joe thought it best to keep the fact they would be staying with Molly's mother to himself.

"Hey, I bought a few books on tape that I've been meaning to read. Your choice, *Loving Frank* about the life of

Frank Lloyd Wright's Chicago mistress, or this one called *Citizen Vince* by a Spokane author named Jess Walter."

"When in Rome. I vote for the Spokane author. Pop it in."

Listening to a book on tape made the miles fly by. They pressed on like horses heading for the barn. Finally, Joe pulled into Sioux Falls' finest, The Brimark Inn (which they agreed the name must have been chosen by default when the sign maker misspelled Bismark). A few deep knee bends around the parking lot, and it was lights out.

Joe arranged a wake-up call that came at six in the morning. Liam didn't crack an eyelid, but Joe jumped up like a Jack-a-Lope and made coffee before heading for the shower. No sign of movement from Liam. He got dressed and packed his overnight bag. Liam was still dead to the world.

"Hey, buddy, time to saddle up and get this herd-a-moving," Joe said as he shook Liam by the shoulder.

"Huh? What time is it?"

"It's time to hit the road again. It's seven, and there are 700 miles ahead of us before we reach Billings. Rise and shine!" Joe prodded Liam, whose night hair made him look as though he slept with a finger in a light socket. Huh, he thought, Stacie must've loved that look.

"I'm up! I'm up!" Liam mumbled as he shuffled toward the shower.

"I'll check out and circle up through the local chuck wagon, a.k.a, Mickey Ds, for our breakfast, and then it's on to the Land of the Big Sky. Meet you out front."

"Sure trail boss. Give me fifteen minutes."

Joe walked outside and was slapped in the face with a gust of cold wind. He was clueless to the expansive reach of the Alberta Clipper cold front predicted to stretch as far east as Minnesota. Hank, the front desk clerk wearing a belt buckle the size of both of the Dakotas, asked Joe which direction they were heading. He quickly suggested getting a serious move-on because of the impending snowstorm. Since they were driving west, Hank thought they could probably outrun the weather but not to take the storm for granted. Joe signed the Visa receipt, thanked Hank for the advice and drove through McDonald's for breakfast to-go.

As promised, Liam was ready to roll. The still unwrapped breakfast had the delectable, unmistakable greasy coffee smell that got Liam's full attention. It's amazing how great junk food tastes on the road, especially when it's South Dakota-cold outside. Joe accelerated onto the highway heading west. It was a crackling, clear day free of the dust haze so common on the east plains.

Day two of Joe and Liam's road adventure passed much the same as the first. The second audio-book narrator voiced over endless miles of feral plains and sculpted farmlands interrupted by occasional truck stops to refuel. Sometime in the late afternoon, their bodies cried out for relief. Changing into running gear at a truck stop, they went for an hour run (during which they received more than a few strange looks from the locals). Afterward, they celebrated their healthy decision to go for a run with some chicken fried steak and enough black coffee to break up the grease and provide motivation for the last push to their destination, Billings.

Over coffee Joe led the conversation from the thirty-thousand-foot level back down to ground zero. With a little persuasion, Liam went a little deeper into the Stacie-ectomy and the Molly-wanna-be-with saga.

"I wonder if all those dudes who left for the west back in the day were leaving as much baggage behind as I feel like I've left," Liam said. "It feels good getting away, even if I don't know what's ahead of me. Thanks for bringing me along, Joe."

"If the movies are correct, those dudes back in the day were most certainly running from something—usually the law. And never underestimate the promise of four simple words: head west, young man.

"Yeah, well, I'm not running from the law, just Stacie, who I know is scarier than any lawman, and that Molly is west. Maybe there's some promise in that. I guess I'll find out soon enough, or not."

"You know, Liam, I could say I'm in the same boat."

Liam knew enough to keep his mouth shut and let Joe talk.

"I have a catch-22 of my own I need some help with," admitted Joe.

"This is about Clare, right?" He could hardly believe he had asked Joe about a woman and hoped to God he hadn't overstepped his boundary.

Joe sighed and said, "Yeah, it's mostly about Clare. You know, she and I have been the best of friends from the time we first met on some Dame committee. And then, out of nowhere, something changed. I changed, and I'm pretty sure she felt the same way."

"Joe, do you mind if I ask you something?"

"Sure, fire away," Joe said.

"Are you leaving South Bend because of Clare? Are you blaming her? I mean do you blame her for your indecision about the priesthood?"

"It's more complicated than that, Liam. I've been struggling with my life or calling, my job—however you want to describe it—since I taught overseas. It changed me. Clare didn't change me. It started long before Clare. I suppose you could say she is just further verification of the evolution of Father Joe."

"What happened overseas?" Liam asked.

"This is going to sound like total therapy bull, but it was the first time I truly felt like I was part of the real world. I don't think I'll ever be able to fully describe the transformation that occurred. I felt like someone had given me the lead role in life. I wasn't just a stagehand being told what to do and how to do it. It was pretty heady stuff."

"The priesthood doesn't feel center stage anymore," Liam said.

"No, it's as far Off-Broadway as you can get."

"I get it," Liam assured Joe. "As much as I respect what priests do, I never have really understood how you do it. I've just put it in the 'higher calling' category and had faith that I wasn't supposed to question or understand it."

"Very wise of you," Joe laughed.

"So back to Clare. You don't blame Clare for your doubts about being a priest, but are you in love with her?" Liam kept his eyes focused out the truck stop café window at a distant windmill, wondering where in God's name he got off asking Joe such a personal question.

"Are you in love with Molly? Do you blame her for leaving your fancy-pants, big time lawyer job in Chicago?"

"Touche, but how are you going to pull the two pieces together—Clare and being a priest, I mean?"

"I'm taking one step at a time, Liam. For now, I'm focusing on getting to Spokane. Oh, and prayer. I may have my doubts about my vocation as a priest, but I'm still a strong advocate for God and the power of prayer." Joe paused, sighed and then continued quietly, "Look, Liam, I care for Clare more than I could have ever anticipated, but right now I need to keep Clare and the priesthood separate and allow my life to unfold. I can't, and I won't, force things to happen."

"Sounds impossible to me," Liam said. His desire to see Molly was never far from his mind.

"Nothing's impossible," Joe said as he stood up. "Next stop, Billings. Are you ready?"

. . .

Just as Liam was wondering if I-94 would ever end, Billings came into focus. To the south, the majestic Absorkee Mountains heralded the east entrance to Yellowstone Park. To the north the rock bluffs looked like Hollywood stereotypes. One expected to see the silhouettes of Crow Indians ready to attack on the unsuspecting pilgrims at dusk, which pretty much described Joe and Liam. Again, they found a decent looking motel that called itself The Lucky Shamrock. And again, the traveling duo hit their respective pillows, dead to the world.

Joe's wake-up call wasn't nearly as annoying as the previous day's because, remarkably, Liam got himself up and at-um. Both were eager to get the last pull to Spokane behind them. With no more books on tape, the two scarfed down their Egg McMuffins, McCafe lattes and began discussing books and movies to pass the time and the mileposts. For Joe, the former English professor, his literary taste ran deep and wide from Chaucer to Conway and Keats to Kingsolver. Liam was more of a movie buff. He rated *On the Waterfront* and *Harold and Maude* as two of his favorites. However, they both agreed *To Kill a Mockingbird* made the top five lists for both a book and a movie. And, of course, *The English Patient.*

Montana's Big Sky country spread out like a vast ocean. It seemed awesome and never ending. Bozeman, or as the locals call it, Bozangeles, flew by and was followed by Butte with its famous open pit copper mine (boasting elevation that's a mile high and a mile deep, where everyone's "on the level"). In succession they crossed the Continental Divide, zoomed past Missoula, scaled Lookout Pass and Fourth of July Pass, descended into Coeur d'Alene, Idaho, and finally arrived at their destination, Spokane, just as it was getting dark.

"Are you nervous?" Liam asked, simultaneously looking for the directions to Lou and Peyton's.

"Sure am," said Joe. "And you?"

"Scared shitless."

"Well hang on pardner, this turn in the road may end up being quite a ride."

Chapter 31

One of the great things about a college campus is there's always someone in the middle of a crisis available to divert you from your own. Whether it's a nineteen-year-old over-achieving junior chemistry major staring down the gullet of his first sub-4.0 or a faculty member whose been assigned fifteen overload students in a 14th century lit class, there was always someone or something to keep Clare from self-contemplation. Make that a Joe-contemplation.

The last time they'd seen each other was that miserable dinner at Anton's. And to think, Anton's was usually such a happy place. Well, no more. Clare could hardly hear the name without getting severe cramps in her stomach. Their goodbye had been stiff and painful. No words of encouragement from her about a bon voyage or better luck in the future, things she would have wished to even a casual acquaintance. She was disappointed in Joe and royally pissed that he'd make her feel so small and petty. She hated acting like a jerk.

No one contacted her about Joe's abrupt departure. That was so like the priests who rarely, if ever, admitted that life at Notre Dame was anything but perfect. She hadn't communicated with Joe since he left and imagined him cozily surrounded by family and old friends, readying himself for his sojourn to Gonzaga. Still, she was worried, and the only person she could think of to call was Joe's good friend in Spokane, Lou Ross. So she did.

"Have you heard from Joe?" Clare asked Lou, trying to

sound calm. "No one here has any idea where he is. I know you and Peyton are close to him, so maybe he's contacted you?"

"He has. He and Liam are coming to Spokane for Thanksgiving," Lou said.

"Good for them," said Clare, wishing she didn't feel so alone but relieved to hear Joe was at least alive.

"He's staying in Spokane. He's hoping to teach at Gonzaga next semester."

Lou wanted to be up front. From what little she knew of her, she really liked Clare, and she knew Joe did, too.

"Clare, look, I'm not trying to dig, but Joe is a good friend to me, and it's obvious you are important to him. So please forgive me for prying, but what gives?"

Sometimes she hated it when people were as direct as she was! Normally an alto, Clare's voice stretched tightly toward soprano, which to anyone who knew her at all meant the wall had come down, or more accurately, crumbled. Berlin all over again.

"I wish I knew what gives, Lou. But the fact is you probably know more than I do." Damn, I'm going to cry, she cringed.

The disarmed sound of Clare's voice was obvious to Lou.

"Yeah, I probably do," said Lou. She felt bad for Clare. "Hey, give me two seconds, Clare. One of the twins is trying to extract a fresh bone from the dog's mouth. I'd hate to see her lose a finger after we went to all the effort to get her here. I'll be right back."

Clare needed the break. She was stuck somewhere between laughing and crying, which always resulted in tears and snot flowing profusely.

"Okay, I'm back. That old dog has the patience of Job. So, based on what few words I did get, here's my take." Lou took a deep breath and continued, "Padre Joe is in mid-priest crisis, and I think it definitely has something to do with you."

"Did he say that?"

"No, of course not. I just know. It's my infallible Lou-

258

Lou intuition."

"Lupe!" she turned away from the phone. "Last bell! Quit teasing the dog and give him the bone back."

"Oh." Clare said.

"It's obvious. Look, Joe's been seriously questioning the priesthood for over a year, at the very least. I know he's struggling with the whole Notre Dame juggernaut. I knew from the first time I saw the two of you together at that alumni event his devotion and Hail Marys were taking a sharp turn. And you think the world of him, too. Am I right?"

Clare was taken aback at how happy, maybe even relieved she was by the accuracy of Lou's insight. She always thought she knew herself so well, but perhaps she'd had to present that self-actualized face so long she'd started to believe it was real. Ugh, I'm so full of shit, she thought.

"You got me there, Lou. I don't know whether to thank or kick you."

"No thanks are necessary. It's my unique calling to inflict myself into other people's lives. Some people hate it, but they can't hate me. I'm too lovable. I just want to know what your next move is."

"My next move? Why would I make the next move? Joe's the one globe-trotting around trying to find himself."

"Pride is the work of the devil, or something to that effect. And Clare, he's going to just keep trotting until you let him know where you stand, so he can figure out where and when to stop."

"I can't do that. Maybe I'm too proud, but I can't do that."

"Can't or won't?"

Clare felt herself backslide and reached for another Kleenex.

"Both."

"Do me a favor."

"What?" Clare was hesitant to commit to anything more than blowing her nose.

"Think about coming out to Spokane for Thanksgiving."

That brought Clare up out of her chair like a rocket.

"Are you out of your mind?" she blurted.

"Maybe, but look, at the very least it would be an educational experience."

"For you maybe, at my expense."

Ignoring Clare's protest, Lou pressed just ever so lightly.

"Think about it. You'll love Ellen. It's the twins' first Thanksgiving with us. There's a huge cast of characters here. And Clare, you need to make a choice. Either open or close this chapter in your life. Coming to Spokane may help you do that."

"I can't promise I'll even think about it, Lou, but thanks for the invite. Thanks for the concern. And with that, I'm headed to yet another meeting. They love to pack them in just before holidays."

Lou hoped her invitation hadn't fallen on deaf ears. "If you change your mind, call me. Call even if you don't change your mind."

Chapter 32

When Molly returned from Chicago, Sister Aracelia noticed she was pensive and withdrawn. Her usual sunny disposition was shadowed by an unseen dark cloud following her every footstep. Molly put in a string of inordinately long work days. She seemed to avoid interactions with the other women at Providence House, preferring to stay cloistered in her room. How do you solve a problem like Maria? Sister Aracelia metaphorically thought to herself.

In the spirit of Mother Superior in *The Sound of Music*, the nun decided to call Molly into her office and have a chat, skipping a "Climb Every Mountain" aria. She kept watch until Molly returned from work, after missing dinner yet again, and stopped her before she could slip by undetected.

"I'd like to speak to you in my office right away, Molly," Sister Aracelia said pointedly.

"Absolutely," she replied a little warily. "Have I done something wrong?"

"No, dear. Just drop your things in your room and come right back. We need to chat."

Molly walked down the hall, did as she was instructed, and headed back, all the while wondering what she had done, or not done, to warrant a speak-to with her boss. God almighty, she'd been working day and night and plowing through backlogged files like a Clydesdale under harness. She certainly couldn't be criticized for being a slacker. Oh well, she thought, I'll find out soon enough.

Molly stopped in the hallway bathroom, and as she was washing her hands, she looked with alarm at the haggard image gazing back at her in the mirror. Yikes. Her hair was dull and in need of a good cut, or at least a brush, if she could get one through it. Who was this woman with deep dark circles around her eyes and quite possibly sporting the most unflattering outfit known to womankind? Was that a food stain on her blouse? Yeah, yeah, whatever, she told herself, and headed down the hall. Molly walked into Sister Aracelia's office, closed the door behind her and sat down without saying a word.

Sister Aracelia set an egg salad sandwich and a glass of milk on her desk.

"You missed dinner," she said matter of factly.

"Thanks Sister, but I'm really not that hungry tonight."

"Or last night or the night before. You look like you've lost about ten pounds. I'm ordering you to eat. You're not going down on my watch."

Molly did as she was told and took a bite of the sandwich. It tasted pretty dang good. After a few more bites and a long draw on the glass of milk, Molly looked up and saw a look of care and loving concern on the nun's face. All her bottled up emotions and frustrations bubbled to the surface. The water main broke. A flood of tears started rolling down her cheeks, and once they got started, she couldn't stop them. What is it about people being nice to me that turns me into a puddle? she wondered.

Sister Aracelia grabbed a box of tissues and walked around her desk. She sat down next to Molly and pulled her head onto her shoulder while they both waited for the storm clouds to pass. Molly regained her composure and did her best to mop up her teary-eyed mess, blow her nose a few times and heave one more tremulous sigh. Finally, she sat back in the chair.

"Well, I'm glad that's over."

"Can you tell me what that was all about?" asked Sister Aracelia.

"Not really. It was about everything and nothing. I don't know, and I don't really want to think about it either. I just want to work and forget."

"I'm thinking this has a lot to do with someone by the name of Liam. Am I right?"

"Probably, but I don't want to think or talk about him."

"What do you want to think or talk about, then?"

"Honestly?"

"Yes, honestly and truthfully."

"Okay. Here it is. I want to go home for Thanksgiving next week. I want to see my mother, drink her great coffee and eat the best huckleberry scones in the Northwest. I want to see my fish, Swimmy. I want to smell pine trees and look out to snowy mountains on the horizon. I want to stuff myself at a big holiday turkey dinner with Mom, Lou, Peyton and experience a new family tradition, the first Thanksgiving we'll have with Ruth and Lupe. Honestly and truthfully, that's all I've been thinking about. I'm so homesick I could die."

"All right, then. Consider yourself homeward bound," Sister Aracelia said quietly.

"Personal time off is not in my lucrative contract, Sister," Molly pointed out, half smiling.

"I like seeing that smile and the fact it almost reaches your eyes. However, I repeat, go home, find your full smile. We'll see you after Thanksgiving."

Molly reached over and hugged the nun for a very long time.

"Thank you. I'm going to go call my mom right now!"

Molly called Ellen and told her the great news, then booked a ticket on a Southwest flight leaving two days later on Saturday afternoon. The forecast was calling for snow in Spokane by Sunday. Perhaps she could even fit in a day of skiing at Mount Spokane or Schweitzer. It felt so damn good to be going home.

Chapter 33

Prompt and on time as usual, Jack's Range Rover was in Lillian's driveway when Ellen pulled her old Volvo wagon up behind it. He'd left the front door ajar, and she felt like a third-rate burglar just walking into Lillian's without ringing the bell.

"Jack? You here?" she quietly called out from the front hall.

"In the sunroom." His voice sounded as though it was coming from the next county.

"Keep talking and I should find you within the hour," Ellen called back to him as she wound her way in the direction she remembered being the sunroom.

"Hey, how you doing?" he called to her as she walked into the sunroom, which wasn't all that sunny on this autumn day. Jack was stretched out on the chintz couch patterned with violets. "And please, make yourself at home. I've never been alone in this house." He sounded amusingly giddy. "I've always wanted to put my feet up on the furniture. Lillian would shoot me."

Ellen was imagining the lecture Lillian would unleash on Jack about respecting furniture when the doorbell rang.

"That will be contestant number one," he said. "Let hope this works. I'm moving Lillian to St. Luke's Rehab today, and, if we are successful, she'll be happily sleeping in her own bed by next week."

Two hours and three interviews later, Ellen and Jack had

twenty-four hour care on board. Whether or not Lillian would keep the three young caregivers was an unknown, but at least the plan was in motion.

"This could be wild," Jack said after saying goodbye to the last interviewee. "The old girl is either going to make it easy on herself or she's going to suck us through a skinny straw."

"I think she'll balk at first and then come around, figuring out that this is her best option," Ellen said with some encouragement.

"I like your spirit," said Jack.

"It's a cover. Man, I dread getting old. As formidable as she is, Lillian has to be afraid."

"Fear isn't an emotion I'd easily attach to Lillian, but you're probably right. I hope I'm doing the right thing."

No matter which way the wind blew, the vulnerability Jack displayed the night of Lillian's stroke was still forefront in Ellen's mind. Again he'd solidified the fact the aloofness he'd so successfully employed since he entered The Manito almost a year ago was mostly for show. Today, that façade had all but disappeared.

Neither Ellen nor Jack was in a hurry to leave, and somehow they had wandered into the vast living room. The late afternoon sun was reflecting off the huge maple trees outside, casting a haze across the room and its big, inviting furniture. Jack was glad he'd asked one of his partners to cover for him tonight, and although Ellen knew she should make sure the bakery was tucked in for the night, she let herself trust Zack had done his job. Ellen sank into the deep down cushions on one of two large dark blue velvet davenports.

"Interviewing for a caregiver is a lot more exhausting than interviewing baristas," she said, resting her head against the high back of the couch. She felt like Lilly Tomlin's Edith Ann character sitting in this enveloping furniture.

"I'm whipped," Jack said. "How about a glass of wine?"

Without moving, Ellen gladly accepted the offer; but

when she heard Jack leave, her head snapped to attention. Looking across the room at Mary Magdalene, she wondered what in the world she was doing lounging in Lillian Johnson's living room while Jack Doyle fetched her a glass of wine. I'm an imposter, she thought. She wasn't sure if Mary on the wall winked, or what, but her next thought was that she really didn't care. She was too drained to worry. She kicked off her brown Frye boots and settled back into comfort. Lou would be shocked. No, Lou would be proud.

"I think we make a great interviewing team," Jack said as he walked into the room with two glasses of wine in the most stunning etched crystal wine glasses Ellen had ever seen. Ellen took a glass from him wishing she could use a plastic tumbler instead.

"We'll find out soon enough, but let's not pat ourselves on the back until we're sure all the silver is still in the house after the first week."

"Or, if no one quits," Jack laughed. "Here's to Lillian and what we hope will be a long-lasting friendship between her and her three new friends." He reached his glass toward Ellen's as he sat down next to her.

They each took a sip of the dry wine and rested their heads against the back of the deep couch. "I think it will work as long as she doesn't feel trapped or abandoned, which is a tricky line to walk," Ellen said. "We'll need to check in on her a lot more for a while."

"Not a problem. You've probably noticed I don't consider Lillian a burden." Jack was touched by the way Ellen included herself in Lillian's well being. He kicked off his well-worn loafers.

"I know you don't think she's a burden, but Lillian isn't as tough and independent as she would like everyone to believe. None of us are," Ellen said. Silence bounced off the walls while they sat sipping their wine, letting their eyes wander from masterpiece to masterpiece. Ellen avoided Mary Magdalene.

"You never seem afraid, Ellen," Jack said as a statement of fact and compliment rolled into one.

"Really?" Ellen turned her head toward Jack and found her nose was about five inches from his right ear. She felt like she'd just stepped off a curb she didn't know was there.

Jack turned to look at Ellen. And for a moment they just stared at each other. It was as if they were kids having a stare-down. Neither was going to look away first. Neither of them wanted to look away.

"Really." Jack finally responded without moving.

Ellen now was quite sure she was having an out of body experience because her fourteen-inch rule had gone right out Lillian's French window.

"Smoke and mirrors," Ellen said, unable to get her vocal cords to sound calm and as ah-gee-ish as she'd hoped. Actually, she couldn't hear her own voice but was pretty sure words came out because Jack had cracked a slight smile. She stepped off another curb.

"I don't buy the smoke and mirrors. I know people inside and out—literally and figuratively, and you're the real thing. You just don't know how strong you are."

"I think if you were to do a MRI, you'd find oodles of fear in me. Case in point, I'm scared right now."

Ellen's eyes were wide open, and she looked somewhere between the beautiful woman he'd fallen for almost a year ago when he first walked into the bakery and a scared ten-year old sitting in the ER waiting to get stitches.

"Afraid? Now? Why? I mean you know Lillian is going to be fine," he said.

"I know that," she said. "It's just that so much is up in the air right now, what with Molly, Lou and Peyton, Lillian." She heard how wimpy she sounded. "God, I sound so dramatic! I guess I'm feeling a little at loose ends. Maybe today was the last yank. It's stupid! I better get going." She started to push herself out of the deep couch, which was no easy task.

"And me?" Jack asked, not entirely sure he wanted to hear the answer. Ellen had experienced every side of Jack Doyle—the good, the bad and the ugly. He was genuinely worried about which side stood out in Ellen's mind.

Floundering about, trying to secure a vertical position in the all-consuming couch deflated Ellen's intent to be completely honest and admit that, yes, she was inexplicably afraid, or more accurately, inexplicably afraid of how she felt toward him. She was too tired of analyzing. All she had left was laughter, which started as a slight air-laugh through the nose and soon developed into her mom's from-the-toes laugh. Dear God, she hadn't laughed like this in years. She'd forgotten how liberating a good, unintended belly laugh could be.

Ellen snorted, trying to catch her breath. "I feel like a beached whale! What is this couch, anyway, Lillian's flytrap? I can't get out of this thing!"

"You don't look anything like a beached whale and quit avoiding my question." He reached for Ellen's arm, gently settling her back into the couch next to him.

Ellen gave up her fight with the couch and looked at Jack close up and personal the second time in less than ten minutes. Having served its purpose of deflating the high drama, her laughter subsided. A frankness her mother had so easily expressed but rarely adopted was stepping forward.

"Am I afraid of you? You really want to know, Jack?"

"Yes."

"Okay, yes, there are times you scare the heck out of me, Jack." The horse is out of the barn.

"For almost a year, I'm the first person you talk to nearly every morning, and you act like every day is the first day. You lavish genuine care and warmth on Lillian, and I love that about you, but then, click, it's gone. All of the sudden I'm the bad guy because people who, mind you, I don't even know expect you to be Ward Cleaver with a wife and two children. Then, bam! You arrive on my doorstep in the middle of the night, so you can pour your heart out. You're all over the map, Jack. And, yeah, that's a little scary. But you know what scares me the most? I look forward to seeing you in the morning, and as baffled as I am, I'm glad you feel like you can call me in the middle of the night. I'm scared by the fact you, of all people, have pulled me out of months and months and months of sadness. And there you have it. Kind of. I'm sure there is more, but that should do for now."

If Jack had blinked any harder, he would have taken flight. Ellen sat dumbfounded by her own words. The colossal mahogany clock Ellen remembered seeing somewhere in the house let out a subtle reminder time was not standing still.

"I really need to do something before I say anything, okay?" Jack said quietly.

Ellen didn't hear a word he said. "What?" she asked louder than she meant to.

Now it was Jack's turn to laugh. "I said I need to do something."

"Oh," Ellen was analyzing the glass of wine she'd picked up after her lengthy diatribe.

"Are you okay?"

"Yes, why?" she asked, her attention still riveted on her glass of wine. She didn't trust herself to elaborate on the fact she felt bad for letting fly on him, while at the same time oddly pleased and amazingly happy with herself.

"Because." He gave Ellen a soft kiss on her cheek, which served its purpose of drawing her attention away from the intensely interesting wine glass. When she turned her face toward him, her look was one of utter confusion. Before she could say anything, Jack kissed her lightly on each side of her mouth.

"That's why," he said.

"Oh."

"Now, may I say something?"

"If you think you have to."

Jack lifted Ellen's chin and looked at her as seriously as he'd looked at anyone in his life. "Thank you."

"You're welcome, but for what?" Ellen felt like someone was clogging on her solar plexus.

"Look, there's no way I can make up for the way I've behaved, although Stan says I might be able to and should."

"Stan?"

"Never mind Stan. You just have to know I'm crazy about you. How could I not be?"

"Oh, I think I could come up with a few reasons. Let's see, oh yes, it was you I just lambasted not more than two minutes ago. Yes, come to think of it, that could be a reason not to like me very much."

"Oh, I like you all right. What you said two minutes ago is exactly why I like you. And you?"

"And me what?"

"Do you like me? Do you care for me?" Jack asked in a playful tone, letting his hand slide from Ellen's chin to her shoulder.

And at that moment, Ellen realized she liked Jack very much.

"Do you really think I'd say what I did if I didn't like you? Jack, everything I just said is frustrating and true, but I'm no simpleton. I know good when I see it and you're good. I like you very much."

Jack's kid-like smile stayed right where it was until he kissed Ellen again.

"Would it scare you if I said I love you?" he asked after the kind of kiss Ellen had forgotten existed.

"Yep," she said, reaching her arms around Jack's neck. "It would scare me to death, so I better say it first. I love you, Jack."

He kissed her softly. "You know what I'm thinking?"

"No."

"I'm thinking all the paintings in this house are smiling at us."

"You are, are you?" Ellen felt more sure of herself than she had in a long time. Sam, Molly, Lou, Lillian, all of them, were lost somewhere in the incredible rush of happiness she was feeling.

"Yeah. And I'm thinking we should give these old painting some company tonight," he smiled and kissed her again.

. . .

Without opening her eyes, Ellen knew what surrounded her, aside from Jack, that is, and it sure was a far cry from where she was supposed to be—the bakery. She bolted upright and did a 360-degree look around her. Eggshell walls, English country scenes framed in simple wooden frames as brittle as Lillian's bones. She could see the light pouring through shear curtains lining the northeast-facing windows. She hadn't been in bed when the sun was so high in the sky in over a year. She usually always arose before it did. Jack's voice brought her closer to reality.

"I wonder what Lillian would say if she knew we're languishing in one of her back bedrooms?" He felt like he'd just won the lottery, never mind happier and more content than he'd felt in his entire life.

"Shit!"

"No, Lillian doesn't use words like that," Jack reached up to draw her back under the covers.

"No, I mean shit, the bakery! And I don't think we want to know what Lillian would think," Ellen said trying to scramble in the general direction of her carelessly tossed clothing.

Jack leaned back against the intricately carved wood bedstead, his hands laced behind his head. "Happy. She'd be happy. Like I am. And you? Are you happy?"

"Amazingly so," Ellen said, half serious and half amazed how oblivious Jack was to the fact she was supposed to be at the bakery hours ago. It was hard to focus on her immediate happiness with one arm searching blindly under the bed for her stray sock. But, she was very, very happy. Last night with Jack was like nothing she'd experienced. Their lovemaking had been spontaneous and unexpected. Somehow, this surprising development had blown her socks off, literally, under the bed.

"I love you, Ellen. You know that, don't you?"

Ellen felt her tear ducts start their engines. "Me too," she squeaked from halfway under the bed, her eyes brimming.

Jack reached over and drew Ellen up into his arms. His heart landed in his throat when he saw her teary eyes. "I have the distinct impression your words are heartfelt, but your mind is elsewhere." He gave each eye a quick peck.

Ellen's face broke into a wide smile. "You're a mind reader, Einstein! Now, I've got to scram. The crew must be in a panic wondering where I am. But this," she tapped him on the nose, "is to be continued."

"Get a move on. I'll close up the house."

Ellen raced into the hallway and down the stairs. Jack heard a quick, "Love you!" just before the front door slammed shut.

Chapter 34

It was already dark when Joe and Liam pulled into the Rosses driveway at the end of their long road trip. The three-day haul they'd endured spanned half of the continent. Liam made Joe promise they'd do this again someday when they weren't in such a big-ass hurry.

Getting out of the car, it was cold, but surprisingly unlike the cold Liam was accustomed to. The air felt refreshing and light, not bone chilling like a damp thirty degrees blowing in from Lake Michigan then dropping a wet blanket over Chicago-land. Stretching his stoved-up muscles, he admired the towering shadows of pine trees standing stalwartly at guard over this South Hill neighborhood. Liam drew in a deep breath of clean, fresh air and decided he was already impressed with Spokane.

They arrived just in time for dinner. Lou met the exhausted road warriors at the door with excited shouts and hugs. She showed off the girls' homemade welcome signs and Thanksgiving decorations—complete with orange, brown and gold crepe paper streamers hanging from every doorway.

Peyton got home about the same time and immediately poured himself and Joe generous glasses of single malt scotch. Liam and Lou had Kokanees, which Liam remembered as Molly's favorite beer, and the twins had glasses of sparkling cider as they sat down to a meal of meatloaf, mashed potatoes and green beans, which—next to mac n' cheese with hotdogs—was the twins' new favorite meal.

At first, Ruth and Lupe were shy and held back from the table conversation. Sensing this, Joe turned all his questions toward them. He was a charmer by nature. And before long the girls were telling him about school, teachers, homework, sledding, movies and even that proverbial pre-pubescent, off-limits subject—boys. Lou, Peyton and Liam sat back and enjoyed watching the master at work.

Peyton served everyone generous slices of homemade apple pie that Ruth and Lupe made especially for their guests topped off with huckleberry ice cream and coffee. It was a midriff-expanding experience.

Lou reminded the girls that it was homework and reading time. Dishes were cleared and goodnights were said all around. Peyton stayed to clean up after the meal while Joe and Liam followed Lou to Ellen's where they would be staying for the Thanksgiving holiday.

The drive took all of three minutes, tops.

Lou handed them off to Ellen, who was waiting for her guests at the back door of The Manito. Joe and Liam gathered up their bags from the car and followed her up the back stairs to Molly's apartment.

"I'm so happy to meet you. I think there's plenty of room for you both. You can toss a coin for who gets the roll-away and who gets the queen bed."

"I'll take the smaller bed," said Joe with a wink. "I've been sleeping in a single bed most of my life. Occupational hazard, don't ya know."

Ellen laughed.

"You know my daughter, Molly?"

"Why yes, Liam and I met her during a recent trip to Los Angeles," explained Joe.

"I just got some great news, this evening as a matter of fact." Ellen beamed. "Molly's coming home day after tomorrow. Her boss decided a trip home will do her good. She hasn't been at the top of her game. Exhaustion, most likely, because she works way too hard. And there's something else going on with her that I can't quite put my finger on."

Liam's heart started pounding, and his complexion lost color. Molly home? Here? Holy crap, this was somewhere between a nightmare and too good to be true. He stole a quick glance at Joe who held a Cheshire cat grin. Damn him.

"Are you feeling alright, Liam?" asked Ellen with a look of concern.

"Uh, yes. I guess it's just been a long couple-a three days. Um, does Molly know we're staying here? I feel just awful that we're taking over her apartment."

"Molly can stay with me. Mine is the mirror image of this apartment right across the hall. I'm so excited to have her home! Actually, these arrangements couldn't have worked out better. I can truly say that with Molly coming home, the twins settling in with the Rosses and you two handsome men as my house guests, this may be the best Thanksgiving I've had since, well, let's just say for a very long time."

Joe walked over to Ellen and gave her a warm hug. This gesture of kindness brought Ellen to tears.

"Oh, I know I just said it, but it bears repeating. I'm just so happy and thankful to have you two staying with us for the holidays," she said wiping a tear. "But right now I need to get to bed. Customers are expecting my seasonal variety of pumpkin, cinnamon and apple baked goods to go with their morning caffeine. And, by the way, come down after you wake up for rolls and coffee. That's part of your bed and breakfast deal!"

From tears to laughter, Ellen bid her boarders goodnight and walked across the hall. So this was the Liam O'Connor. The very one Lou picked out to be her son-in-law. He was tall and handsome enough, yes, and very polite. She liked him. Maybe Lou has finally hit one out of the park? Still, something had happened between Liam and Molly in Chicago, and Ellen was sensing this was the reason for Molly's funk.

She picked up the phone and called Lou who answered on the first ring.

"Hey."

"Yeah. What the 'hey' is going on between Molly and

Liam? And I know you know more than what you've been telling me, Miss Lou-Lou-Belle. Liam's very fetching freckles just turned the whiter shade of pale when I mentioned that Molly was coming home for Thanksgiving."

"Ellen, my dearest friend in all the world, I sincerely don't know. You're better off asking Joe. But I will tell you, as I have from the get-go, I think there is mani-fricking-fest-destiny in the cards for those two."

"Come on, Lou. Molly is literally on her lips and bummed to boot. I told you she's coming home to rest and recoup. You know I'm going to have to call and tip her off that Liam's staying in her apartment."

"You'd rather have her stay in LA?"

"No! Yes! I don't know."

"Just let the thing unfold, Ellen. It sounds like she's running, and we both know it's better to walk toward the barking dog and face it head on."

"If Molly never speaks to me again, it's all your fault."

"I'll risk it. So, count to ten, take a deep breath....and CHILL!"

Ellen did as she was told.

"Thanks, Lou. Te amo."

"Me too."

Ellen hung up the phone and tried to clear her head. She thought of Jack and the recent development in their relationship and smiled. Why do things have to be so complicated? And why, for heaven's sake, does everything have to happen at once? She decided to watch Liam and give him the benefit of the doubt. Molly didn't love lightly or easily, and this guy had thrown her in a huge tailspin.

Geez o'Pete. The Manito had the feel of a Big Top three-ring relationship circus coming to town.

. . .

Joe was up early and tiptoed down the back stairway to the service entrance to The Manito. Once in the bakery, he experienced a pleasant, sensory overload—sugary smells and rich coffee beans, a cacophony of quiet conversation, outbursts of laughter and the clanking of silverware on ceramics.

Note to self, Joe thought, ask God if there's a coffee shop as good as this up in heaven.

When Ellen saw him, she smiled. She took his coffee order as he chose a cinnamon roll from the bakery case and then led him over to the coffee boys' table. Jack jumped up as though he'd been poked with a cattle prod as Ellen approached. She tried not to laugh and introduced Joe all around, so she could get back to the counter leaving Joe to run the gauntlet. The coffee boys defaulted to their favorite subjects of Notre Dame, Gonzaga, and why Spokane is The Last Best Place on Earth. Joe immediately fell in love with the group who welcomed him home like the Prodigal Son. If there had been a fatted calf in the vicinity, she'd have been a goner.

Joe noticed Jack's jumpy reaction to Ellen. There are some electric currents flowing between these two, he mused. When Jack stood up to leave, Joe noticed the way he looked for Ellen. He also noticed the subtle nod from her in return. As Jack walked out the front door, there were a few knowing looks and eye rolls from the guys confirming Joe's observation.

When the last of the coffee boys left for work, or wherever they bided their daylight hours, The Manito hit a neutral post-morning-rush lull. Ellen brought two fresh cups of coffee over to Joe's table and sat down for a rest and the chat she and Lou had discussed the night before.

"How'd you sleep?"

"As always, like a man without a conscience."

"Joe, may I ask you something? I might need some advice."

"Yet another occupational hazard," he replied kindly. "Absolutely. What's on your mind?"

"It's Molly. She doesn't know Liam is here, and although I don't know much about their relationship or friendship, or whatever it is, I think he's the reason she's out of sorts and working herself 24/7. I didn't put two and two together when

Lou asked if you could stay in Molly's apartment. Hells-bells, I didn't even know Liam was part of the package deal until last night."

Joe started looking uncomfortable and opened his mouth to say something, but Ellen cut him off.

"Just let me finish. I know you're going to offer to move out, but 'no' is my answer. Everything happens for a reason. This, well, whatever this is, will run its course. You're staying right where you are. End of story. My only question is, do you know how Liam feels about Molly? The mother grizzly bear in me needs to know."

Just then Liam walked up behind Ellen, unseen.

"Why don't you ask him yourself? Liam, I'll get you a cup of coffee and one of Ellen's amazing cinnamon rolls."

"Sounds great! Ask me what?" Liam smiled at Ellen.

Now it was Ellen's turn to shift uncomfortably in her seat as Liam took his.

For a few minutes she looked at the freshly showered and shaved young man with the intensity of a proctologist. Liam had no choice but to wait patiently for her to speak.

"I need to know what the situation is between you and Molly. Suffice it to say she's not been herself since Chicago. I don't know what happened, but I couldn't help but notice your reaction when I mentioned that Molly is coming home Saturday. She's only told me that she wants to rest and recoup. But, I'm pretty sure it's not just work that has her so maxed out. So, like it or not, I'm her mom, and I'd appreciate a little insight into what's going on with her including your part in the picture."

Liam felt blindsided. Cold-cocked. On the inside he was creating enough steam to foam a latte. He didn't see this one coming and didn't have time to prepare a solid argument as any good lawyer would before facing judge and jury.

His blue eyes searched hers for a hint of understanding. Liam found it and made a spontaneous decision to put his trust in her. He would be completely honest with this woman and proceeded to spill his guts.

Liam told her the story of his relationship with Stacie and how he met Molly. He explained how he fell headfirst for Molly, the circumstances around Stacie's duplicity and how it all blew up when Molly was in Chicago. He tried his best to convey his hope of all hopes Molly would forgive him and the pilot light hadn't gone completely out on the possibility of building a relationship together.

Ellen took several moments to absorb and process this revelation.

No wonder Molly was a mess over this man. Ellen had no doubt about the truth of his words and feelings. She put her hand on his arm and offered a warm squeeze.

"Okay. Lou's right, again. We'll just let things unfold and see what tomorrow brings. Molly doesn't know you're here, Liam, and I'm not going to tell her. My gut tells me she's a flight risk at this point, and the less said the better. Let's get her here first, wheels down, and worry about the details later."

Standing back, Joe waited for an opening. When he saw Ellen reach out to Liam, he walked back over with Liam's breakfast and sat down.

"Thank you, Ellen," Liam said, taking a bite of roll. "Wow, this is wicked good!"

He took another big bite and a sip of coffee.

"Did you get your question answered, Ellen?" asked Joe.

"Yes, I did, thank you."

"Ellen," Liam asked, "would you be okay with me helping out around the bakery? If I don't have something to keep myself busy, I'll leap out of my skin. I'm not used to going from one hundred miles an hour to a dead stop."

"Actually, I could use some help. Follow me."

Joe stood up and apologized, "I have an appointment with my friend at Gonzaga. I hope you don't think I'm a lazy so-n-so for not offering to help like Captain America here, but I'm hoping this teaching post pans out to become a bone fide job. Spokane is growing on me by the minute."

"Me too," agreed Liam as he followed Ellen in the direction of the Hobart commercial dishwasher.

Chapter 35

Molly's plane arrived at Spokane International Airport at four o' clock. Ellen was there to meet her with a big smile and warm hug as she walked out of the security area.

"Oh, Mom, it's so good to be home," she said with her eyes welling up with tears.

"I couldn't agree with you more, sweet pea. Let's get your luggage. We're heading straight to Lou's for dinner. Ruth and Lupe are so excited to see you!"

Driving from the airport down Sunset Hill, Molly saw the first of many familiar sights and probably her most favorite, the panoramic vista of downtown Spokane. This is my city, she thought nostalgically.

She finally understood why her friends who left Spokane to "live the dream" eventually pulled the full circle and returned home. Erma Bombeck once said, "The grass always looks greener over the septic tank," and in Molly's opinion, LA was literally a septic tank compared to her beautiful Northwest.

"You're awfully quiet, Mol," Ellen observed.

"Not inside my head. I'm soaking up the landscape and the memories associated with every mile marker we pass."

"Good ones?"

"About ninety-nine percent good ones."

"Hey Mol. I hate to spring this on you, but Lou asked if we could house some visitors for the Thanksgiving holiday. Would you mind staying with me in my apartment?"

"Not at all. Anyone we know?"

"Well, yes, as a matter of fact you know both of the gentlemen."

Pulling away from what was outside the windshield to focus on Ellen, Molly had a premonition of anxiety. This "going to Seattle by way of San Diego"-method Ellen was using to deliver a message meant she was trying to avoid the direct route.

"Do I even dare to ask who these two men in my apartment might be?"

"Father Joe and Liam."

"Oh my God! Turn around. I'm catching the next flight back to California."

Ellen continued driving.

"Mom, how could you?" Molly said with a quiet but level voice.

"I can honestly say I had no idea Liam was coming with Joe—who, by the way, has left Notre Dame—until they both arrived on my doorstep. Lou doesn't have room for them now that the twins are living there. It is what it is, deary. You'll just have to make the best of an odd situation. I'll grant you that much."

"Have you talked with Liam?"

"Yes, and I like him."

"Score one for Liam."

"He's been helping me in the bakery since they arrived, and, I must say, I've appreciated the extra help."

Ellen pulled the car into the Rosses' driveway to find Ruth and Lupe shooting hoops. As Molly jumped out of the car, hugging the girls, she was shocked to see a large white bandage over Ruth's eye.

"Ruth had her eye surgery last week," said Lupe, pointing out the obvious, which is job #1 for eleven-year-old girls.

"Yeah, and I get to get this big, dumb bandage off before Thanksgiving. I'm super-stoked!"

"Hey Molly, did you know that Father Joe and Liam are staying at your place? Liam is really hot," added Lupe.

Molly just smiled and suggested that they all go inside. A

few snowflakes began to fall, making her suggestion all the more appealing.

After a dinner of roasted chicken, orzo, green salad, and asiago bread sticks, Lupe, Ruth, Molly and Peyton played Scrabble. Lou and Ellen cleaned up and afterward watched them play while trying to keep Peyton from making up nonsensical words, Ogden Nash-style. Ruth won.

With the game over, goodnights and sweet dreams were wished all around. Peyton escorted the girls upstairs to get them ready for bed, serving as a watch guard to discourage pre-teen procrastination. That left Lou, Ellen and Molly in the family room to finally discuss the two men occupying Molly's apartment.

In true Lou fashion, she lost no time getting to the point. "So Molly, how are you going to handle the Liam situation?"

Molly felt so vulnerable and sad that she could only respond, "To be honest, I really don't know. I came home to get over Liam, and now he's sleeping in my apartment right across the hall. Co-conspirators, that's what you are. I feel like the whole world is against me right now." Even so, it was hard to stay mad at these two charmers.

"Deary," Lou said, "I remember giving you a pep talk earlier this fall before the Notre Dame game that basically went like this...cry me a river...build a bridge...and get over yourself. I just learned that snappy little saying from Ruth. Anyway, I also remember you removed the chip as heavy as an anvil from your shoulder that day and ended up having a wonderful time."

"He's crazy about you," said Ellen. "He told me his side of the story. I, for one, believe in second chances. Plus, as Lupe says, he's hot."

"Mother!"

"Well, it's a fact," added Lou.

"Shut up! I'm changing the subject. But I will concede to your collective points, which are well taken. Can you two be satisfied with that?"

"Yes," Lou and Ellen responded in unison.

During the short drive home Liam wasn't discussed. Lou, quick thinker that she was, called ahead, and the Kirkpatrick women found Liam waiting at the back door, offering to help carry Molly's luggage up the stairs. Damn her traitorous heart for flipping cartwheels the minute she saw him. Lupe, Lou and Mom are right, she thought. He is hot.

"Would you like to take a walk?" asked Liam as he placed her suitcase in her mother's apartment.

"Thanks, Liam, but I don't think so."

"Just once around the block?" he tried again. "There's nothing like a walk right after a fresh snow."

Oh well, Molly thought. I'll be very Lou-esque in the face of fears and trepidations.

"Okay. Let me get my coat and boots from my apartment," she pointed across the hallway. "Do you mind?"

"Mi temporary casa es su casa."

Molly, temporarily disarmed, laughed, asked for a few minutes to unpack, settle in and then said she'd be right over.

Although it had snowed fairly hard during dinner at the Rosses, only a few scant snowflakes swirled around them as they walked through the snow toward Manito Park. Crossing Grand Boulevard, Liam reached for her hand. He didn't let go until they passed the sledding hill crawling with parents and kids. Arriving at the large covered gazebo, he dusted off a park bench and asked if she would sit down.

When he let go, she missed his hand. Touching him again had felt good and right. The same way it had from the first time they were alone in his room at The Westin in Los Angeles strategizing the Raigosa crisis. Try as she might, she would never forget their first kiss. It was pure magic. Over the past few weeks she tried to tell herself the magic had disappeared when Stacie sucked all the fairy dust out of the universe. But Molly had overestimated Stacie's power. Like the Wicked Witch of the West, Stacie had no power here in Molly-Land. Someone dropped a house on her.

Liam sat down on the park bench next to her and took both of her hands. Looking at him—really looking at him, she thought he could inspire lyrics for a sad country western song: dog just died, truck wouldn't start, and missed the outbound train.

"Can you forgive me, Molly? Can we start from scratch with a clean slate? I could come up with a few more metaphors, but hopefully you understand what I'm trying to say."

"What about Stacie?"

"I'm not going to throw Stacie under the bus. I was fond of her. I would go so far as to say from time to time I adored her. But I've only truly felt love for one person in my life, and she's sitting right here. I'm a goner, Molly. I'm putting it right out there for you and God and everyone. If you'll have me, I'm yours. Beginning of story."

Molly felt very Dorothy-esque. That weird Technicolor dream was over, and she had come home to find her heart.

Liam placed a familiar, soft butterfly kiss on her cheek. Turning, she looked into his eyes and threw her puffy Northface jacketed arms around his neck, kissing him long and hard. The glorious magic was still there.

A couple of teenage boys walked by and yelled out, "Get a room, why don'tcha?"

Chapter 36

Lillian walked through her front door under her own steam. Any more time spent in the hospital made the prospect of having caregivers in her back pocket almost palatable. All she wanted was to be home.

She stood in the front hall, Jack and Ellen on either side of her. Ellen looked at Lillian and made a mental note to never discredit the value of a strong gene pool. After her stretch in the hospital, Lillian walked regally through her front door wearing a simple navy cashmere straight-fitting dress looking as though she may have just as easily been arriving for a bridge game. As if Lillian ever had the patience for card games, which she didn't.

Jack had given the caregivers the run down on Lillian. That they'd listened to him was evident in their subtle disappearance into the kitchen. Only one of the three would be staying, but Jack thought it was important they all be on hand to meet Lillian together. From the sounds coming from the kitchen, one was preparing a late afternoon tea. Maybe, just maybe, this was going to work out, Jack thought. He leaned slightly behind Lillian and caught Ellen's eye. He wanted to take her hand but settled for a thumbs up.

"We'll have a sherry," Lillian announced.

"That's what I like, Lillian—patients who blow off doctor's orders before they've even clipped off their hospital ID bracelets!" Jack laughed.

"I don't take orders, and you know that. What's the

worst thing that could happen? I could die. Oh my!" Lillian's episode, as she so inaccurately called it, hadn't put a dent in her spirit. Ethel Merman would be proud.

"I'll have to pass on the sherry," Ellen said. "I should get back to work. Thanksgiving is upon us, and I have an unexpected houseful. And Miss Johnson, Molly is home."

"It's Lillian to you, Ellen; now don't forget it. And I'm tickled to hear about Molly."

"Well, you'll see her Thanksgiving at the very least. That is, if you would like to join our ever-growing, hodge-podge of people sharing Thanksgiving dinner at The Manito. Won't you?"

"You're sweet to include me," Lillian said, sounding very touched. "I've always wanted an excuse to duck out on my milk-toast nephew and his spoiled family."

"I'll take that as a back-handed compliment. Even Jack is going to be there for part of the festivities when he can get away from the Doyle clan, aren't you Jack?"

Jack was temporarily preoccupied with memories of the upstairs back bedroom; consequently, Thanksgiving dinner wasn't at the forefront of his mind. "Yes! Sure! Sounds great!" He sounded like an idiot and knew it. Ellen was looking at him with the most beautiful Got ya! grin, while Lillian looked at him as though he'd lost his marbles.

"Jack, are you all right? You sound as though you need that sherry more than I do."

"I'm fine, just fine," he said looking cross-eyed at Ellen, who was half-way out the door waving good-bye.

Settled in the sunroom with a small glass of sherry, Lillian studied Jack, who was fidgeting like a teenager. She watched him over the brim of her glass with a steady eye.

"You and Ellen. You've finally quit dancing around each other, haven't you?"

"You know me too well, Lillian."

"Well good for you. I couldn't be happier."

Neither could Jack. He also hoped to God that Lillian never found out what had taken place upsatirs.

Chapter 37

Stretched comfortably backwards over her large red exercise ball, Clare praised her core strength for working so cooperatively the past few months. When she'd first attempted this backward stretch, the getting there had been easy, but getting up was another story and typically resulted in a flop to the side off the ball and a bad case of the blind staggers. Now her core strength pulled her upright with ease. And then she barfed.

A shaky hour later, she walked into the Counseling Center and pulled her assistant, Grace, into her office and shut the door without saying a word.

"I hurled again this morning."

A knowing concern washed across the beautiful black woman's face. Grace had been Clare's assistant since she arrived at Notre Dame. She'd also managed to bear four children in five years.

"Oh, darlin'. You know this ain't no flu," she said in an uncharacteristic Southern slang she hoped exuded comfort.

"I know, but what the hell am I going to do, panic?"

"Call Joe?"

Clare stopped and let her arms to her side.

The tears spurted, and her face was as red as the cashmere scarf around her neck.

"How can this be happening to me?" she said followed by a short sobbing hiccup.

Grace enveloped her boss and friend, which gave Clare

the go-ahead to cry in earnest.

"I'm old, for Christ's sake! I quit worrying about getting pregnant a long time ago. Shit! Wouldn't you know one fertile egg would hang around? I feel like such a fool."

"It happens, Clare. Do you think I was planning on my last baby at thirty-nine?"

"And won't I just make one heck of a June Cleaver mother?" Clare laughed and cried at the same time.

"Maybe not June Cleaver, but you will be a great mom. This is one lucky baby," said Grace.

"I don't know how to …"

Grace finished her sentence, "Tell Joe?"

"Well, yeah, that and a million other things. But, yeah, that little task is probably at the top of my 'to do' list."

"You did a test, right?"

"Yes! I bought the damn kit last week. I stood in the Walgreen's checkout lane right behind two seniors. That was a proud moment, to say the least. I let it sit on the shelf for a day or so but finally took the test after I threw up this morning. I think it showed positive the minute I took it out of the box!"

"Okay, now go see your doctor. Make sure all is well. Then you need to tell Joe."

"He left, Grace. He left me! He's gone off to fulfill a new life while I'm here hatching one! I won't lasso him back here."

"I know, Clare. So maybe you'll decide to have this child and raise it on your own, but he still needs to know."

Clare took a deep, shaky breath and sat down behind her desk. She put her face in her hands. "Okay, I'll see my doc. I'm having this baby, Grace. There are no doubts about that. But the next step, telling Joe, I need to think about it some more."

"Fair enough," Grace said, relieved to see the determined Clare start to surface. "But remember, he's the father of this child, and he deserves to know."

Clare walked out of the South Bend Family Physicians

Clinic and shivered in the twenty-five-degree-plus wind-chilled air whipping around her. She got in her car and, for the third time in less than an hour, started crying. This time it was a mixture of relief, excitement and fear. Fear in that she was, in fact, with child. (Yikes, that sounded so Virgin Mary!) Excitement in that every day she woke up increasingly more in love with the wee one growing inside her. Relief because all the tests indicated she and baby were healthy.

She was over a month along but still made certain to settle her seatbelt low across her lap—she'd heard Dr. Oz say something about proper placement of seatbelts on pregnant women—and wondered what other pregnancy advice she'd missed over the years. "Don't ever plan on getting your driver's license," she said to her stomach. Geez, she thought, if I'm this neurotic now, imagine when Hoo-Hoo is out in the open air. God help us both, she thought, liking the "both" part of that thought. She drove back to work and ate her hummus, wheat bread and fruit. For dessert, she took the supplements her doctor had given her. This was going to be a painfully-healthy pregnancy, she pledged.

And now she was supposed to call Joe. If only she'd stumbled into this pregnancy the same way most Notre Dame co-eds stumbled, literally, into it. Too much beer, too many hormones and presto, she and Joe would be pregnant. But this was Joe, whose status as soul mate had just moved to a whole new level. After he left, she'd tried to balance anger with understanding but ended up missing him even when she was praying to the porcelain god.

She drove home and laid down on her bed for a rest assuming the fetal position, which ironically seemed to keep nausea at bay. Clare picked up her cell and dialed.

When the enthusiastic voice picked up, Clare stalled, still unsure of her decision to make this call.

"Lou?" Clare asked hesitantly.

"You got her. Who's this?"

"It's Clare, Lou." What do I say now? Clare thought. She fought the urge to hang up. Augh, she silently cursed the unfamiliar hesitancy that had suddenly taken root in her head.

"Clare! I didn't recognize the number. How are you?"

Clare paused. She held back the voice in her head screaming, How the hey do you think I am? I've been impregnated by your buddy, the holy freaking priest! Instead, she inhaled slowly to buy precious seconds needed for self composure. Silence bounced between cell towers while Clare tried to shrink-wrap her emotions. Surprised to hear Clare's voice, Lou was simultaneously fighting the urge to blurt out questions she wanted to ask since Joe arrived in Spokane like, What the heck is going on with Joe? And are you the luggage he forgot to bring with him to Spokane?

"Never been better, thanks," Clare finally said in a voice she'd never heard before. The voice was wimpy. It wasn't her. It scared her back to reality. "Lou, I don't know how to say this other than to say, I'm pregnant." She was relieved to hear that familiar to-the-point voice again.

"Congratulations?" was all a very stunned Lou could articulate.

"You're probably wondering why I'm calling you."

Duh! Lou thought but didn't say. "Ah, well, maybe a little."

"Joe. Joe's the father," Clare said matter of factly.

"Holy Canola!" Lou muttered in a long whisper. "I guess that answers why Joe's acting like a lost lemming."

"No, he doesn't know, Lou. Joe's dealing with a lot, but being the father of this child isn't one of them. I guess that's why I called you, Lou. I wanted someone who cares about Joe to know what's going on. I'm not sure he's ready to add fatherhood to the list of his worries. I'm okay, Lou. I'm going to be fine regardless, but I don't want to influence any decisions Joe is trying make right now."

Well, isn't that just a heap of poop piled high and deep, Lou wanted to pronounce. But didn't. This was Clare's decision to make.

"Okay, Clare. I mean, you know what is best for you. I'm glad you told me, though. Is there anything I can do? Any chance you might come to Spokane?"

"Oh, Lou, I barely know what I'm going to have for dinner. I can't make that kind of decision right now. I don't know how I'm going to give Joe the news, but it seemed like a good idea to let someone close to him know."

Lou's heart was breaking for Clare. If only she could be the boss of everybody and orchestrate their lives the way they obviously, to her anyway, should be lived.

"I'm happy for you Clare," Lou said. "I know you're at sixes and sevens right now, but you're having a baby! Believe me, having the twins here convinced me everything happens for a reason, and your baby is no exception to the rule. You'll figure out how to tell Joe when the time is right for both of you."

"Thanks, Lou," Clare said almost cheerfully. Calling Lou was the right move, she thought.

"No thanks necessary. Just take care of yourself and stay in touch. We'll keep an eye on the dear father."

"Okay, bye Lou and thanks."

"Bye little mama."

Chapter 38

Much to the chagrin of a few uninformed patrons, a boldly lettered SORRY, CLOSED FOR THANKSGIVING sign posted on the front door of The Manito announced just one of two annual closures, the other being Christmas day.

For her family and friends alone, a latte at The Manito had been the carrot that prodded them through the three-mile-fun-run, the Turkey Trot, held each Thanksgiving morning in Manito Park. Hidden away from the errant customers in the kitchen, noshing on sinful cinnamon morning buns and sipping a latte, Ellen felt like a high school snob ditching her best friends.

"Mom, quit peeking out front, you aren't withholding food from the needy. Besides, I get you all to myself for the next eighteen hours. Not that I'm counting," Molly said, winking at Liam.

"You're right, sweet pea, and thank you, Lord, for Starbucks!" Ellen raised her arms up in the air in gratitude. "Let them serve the masses while I take the day off! I've missed you so much, Mol." She pointed a friendly finger at Liam. "You, buster, seem to make my little girl very happy."

"It goes both ways, Ellen," Liam said, giving Molly's ponytail a playful tug.

"Please, don't make me feel like an aged old prune," Ellen laughed, handing him another latte. "We're going to need a caffeine buzz to kick us into gear. Dinner, my friends, isn't going to prepare itself."

Molly used Liam's knee for balance as she reached for her second morning bun dripping in butter-honey. She gave his knee a gentle squeeze, silently remembering the, "Get a room, why don'tcha?" comment made by the kids in the park.

"And where was the good Dr. Doyle this morning?" Molly asked. "Why didn't he join us for the Turkey Trot?"

"He drew the short straw. He's on-call, but he'll try to make it to dinner. Speaking of which, I'm heading to the shower and then its hup-to. We have a turkey to cook!"

Ellen headed upstairs, and Liam and Molly started washing coffee mugs. He looked at Molly out of the corner of his eye. "Do you believe in love at first sight, Mol? 'Cause I do."

"Are you talking about her and Jack?" she paused. "Maybe? I do know that the first time Jack walked in this bakery he fell for mom like a Douglas fir on a Christmas tree farm. That was love at first sight, but I'm more like my gram, the cautious type." She gave Liam a gentle elbow to the ribs. "But, when we fall, we fall hard."

"Oh yeah?" Liam smiled. "I must be more like Jack because I fell in love with you the minute I laid eyes on you."

"Did you, now?"

"Come to Chicago with me, or I'll move to LA. Whatever you decide. All I know is that I can never be away from you again."

Molly opened her mouth but remained wordless.

"I'm serious," Liam said, and Molly could tell by the square set of his jaw he was as serious as she had ever seen serious.

"Liam, isn't this a little fast? I mean, you were just engaged to a woman who couldn't be more flip-side different from me."

Liam stood still with his soapy hands dripping at his side. "Tell me something I don't know."

. . .

It was Molly's job to set the Thanksgiving table while Ellen ran the kitchen. She started by moving the odd assortment of tables and chairs together in one long formation to seat ten guests. With the addition of Rosa—whom Lou had flown up from California, Ruth, Lupe, Peyton, Joe, Liam, Lillian and possibly Jack, this was shaping up to be a big inaugural Thanksgiving gathering at The Manito. Over the past few days, Molly and Liam explored her favorite second-hand thrift stores and found a large red tablecloth that, as it turned out, seemed to fit the table arrangement just right. She added a smaller brown square cloth down the center for variety. Then came her signature mismatched silver flatware and Spode blue, pink and brown dishware supplemented, as needed, with various plain white ceramic dishes Ellen used every day in the bakery. Molly unboxed her grandma's stemware that hadn't seen the light of day since Ellen and Molly moved out of the Comstock rancher and into The Manito. She gathered an eclectic assortment of cloth napkins from Ellen and Lou, and with an eye for the dramatic, she chose from solids, stripes, and floral prints to individually complement each place setting. Finally she created a centerpiece from snowberry, Hawthorne berry and pine tree cuttings in a large center glass bowl.

As she stepped back to admire the arrangement, she thought to herself that it looked like Martha Stewart had collided with Jackson Pollack. "And, if I do say so myself, it works," she commented aloud.

"Lillian is going to love this," Ellen said with a dash of sarcasm over Molly's shoulder. "Sterling and white linen are so passé."

"Speaking of Miss Johnson, who's bringing her over?" Molly asked.

"Jack will, if he's not pumping undercooked turkey out of someone's gullet," Ellen laughed. "Otherwise, I'll run over and get her."

"She's bounced back pretty well, hasn't she?"

"Yes, she really has, thanks in part to your recent visits.

She enjoys spending time with you and Liam. I think the two of you bring back some long-forgotten memories of happier times. It was a rough start for her having caregivers in the house, but she's adjusted like a trooper. And she comes in here every morning, moving a little slower, but still on her game."

"Hey, mom, what's the deal with Joe? Whenever I ask Liam about him, he says he's a great guy going through a difficult time. As crazy as I am about Liam, he's not giving me much 411 when it comes to Joe."

Ellen tossed Molly a bag of sweet potatoes. "Here, Ann Landers, chop these up, and Mol, I'm brilliant in a lot of areas, but I don't know Joe's entire story. He's a priest, for God's sake. Who knows anything about the private lives of priests?"

Chapter 39

Joe stared at the frail, lace-like sheets of ice clinging to the edge of the Spokane River as it wove itself through downtown Spokane. For the first time in a long time, he didn't feel as frail as the thin ice looked. He estimated this trip to Spokane was, in fact, a step toward solid ground. He'd passed on the Turkey Trot, choosing to unpack boxes of books that arrived the day before from South Bend. Lou, Peyton, Ellen, Jack, Molly, even the good old boys at the bakery, made him feel at home and that was a start. I need this, Joe thought, as he looked across the wide river toward the Gonzaga campus. Father Tony had started introducing him to people at Gonzaga, and he felt the awakenings of affirmation he needed. He'd even thought about moving into a big, old house near campus renting dirt cheap, compared to South Bend rates. Joe kept reminding himself to take baby-steps; after all, he'd just taken one huge leap by leaving South Bend in the first place. Moving from his dorm-like apartment on South Bend's campus into a three-story four-bedroom home, alone, might be biting off more than he could chew.

As much as his decision to leave Notre Dame was making more sense, unfortunately there was one significant factor missing from his happiness equation.

Clare.

A slice of his soul was empty real estate, and he knew it belonged to her. Before he left South Bend, he'd all but told her she didn't factor into his quest. For one hell of a smart guy, I'm a complete fool, he chastised himself.

As he entered the light ash-paneled lobby of Gonzaga's Jesuit House, it struck Joe as humble but more than comfortable. Very Jesuit. He started peeling off layers of polar fleece down to a long sleeved t-shirt. The temperature was perfect for gardenias and old priests.

Outside, the day had yet to climb out of the low teens and he wondered, though briefly, why he hadn't chosen to do his personal and spiritual homework at one of the country's Catholic country club schools in Santa Clara or San Diego. Tony greeted him with a strong hand shake and led him to a darker paneled library overlooking the river. Alice, whom Joe knew as the housemother to this Jesuit frat house for at least 25 years, arrived with tea.

"I need to talk with Clare," Joe said as he ladled three spoons of honey into his Earl Grey. Father Tony's ability to stay levelheaded in virtually any situation always amazed Joe. He needed a level head today. This attribute was solidified with Joe years ago when Tony managed to keep a straight face as Joe sneezed wine through his nose while saying one of his first Masses. "Then do it," Tony said.

"You think so?"

Tony was a thin, all arms and legs Italian, and when he spoke he looked like a corpsman directing F-18s on and off an aircraft carrier. His gestures added significance to everything he said.

"Look, Joe, do you want me to call it exactly as I see it?"

"I always have."

"You haven't fallen out of the priesthood as much as you have fallen in love with Clare. It's become abundantly clear your feelings for her need to be acknowledged. You're delusional if you think this is just about your calling to the priesthood. You can't move forward without dealing with your feelings for her, no matter the outcome."

Joe digested Tony's honesty in silence.

"No one, not me and certainly not God, is going to strike you dead for being in love. It's the most beautiful gift God gave us."

Aside from the fact that Joe wanted to ask, Why, if the Church thought love between a man a woman was so beautiful, why didn't it allow priests to marry? there was nothing more to discuss. He'd save the Church versus woman and marriage debate for later.

"Thanks, friend," Joe said

"You, my good man, are sincerely and profoundly welcome."

Joe stood up and walked to the expansive window overlooking Gonzaga's soccer fields. "My mother is going to spin in her grave," he said. "She was so happy to have a son who became a priest." He added only half jokingly, "So, now what?"

"Pray, for starters. I'm no Dr. Phil, but it sounds like Clare is a formidable woman."

"Okay, and then?"

"Enjoy Thanksgiving."

"Now that I do. Thanks again, friend."

Joe left Jesuit House with just enough time to get himself up to Ellen's. He also wanted to call Clare immediately.

. . .

Lou and Peyton's Suburban looked like a '50s college phone booth when it pulled into Ellen's back parking lot. Four doors opened simultaneously and out spilled the twins, Rosa, Peyton, Lou and two chocolate Labrador retrievers, Iggy and Squiggy—the only dogs ever granted entry to the bakery unless they were in someone's purse. Everyone carried at least one contribution toward the Thanksgiving celebration.

"The Clampets have arrived!" Lou called out, herding her new brood through the bakery's back entrance, simultaneously balancing a ring of her mother's gorgeous tomato aspic filled with fresh shrimp, green olives and artichoke hearts in one hand and a dish cradling scalloped potatoes in the other.

Ellen looked at her friend and smiled ear to ear. Lou was

so utterly happy. She gave Lou a hug. "Happy Thanksgiving, my sweets," she said.

"Back at you, El. The word Thanksgiving doesn't capture all the good things that have happened to each of us this year, but it'll have to do for now."

"You've got that right, now go pour yourself a glass of wine and then get back here to help me. Oh, and while you're at it, let me know how Lupe and Ruth like my Mexican hot chocolate concoction."

Lou found Molly, Liam and Rosa cozied up in a far corner laughing hysterically about something. Peyton had the twins engaged in an artistic version of Where's Waldo using the photos covering the bakery's wall. By the chocolate lip mustaches the twins were wearing, the Mexican chocolate was a hit.

"Lou, I've got to hand it to you. Bringing Rosa to Spokane for Thanksgiving was brilliant."

Jack picked up Lillian fifteen minutes before they were due at Ellen's. Jack wanted this day to be as pleasant and stress-free as possible for Lillian. She'd been through the old-fashioned ringer, and he wanted this day, in particular, to be perfect.

Lillian looked like Mary Astor herself. Gray hair was pulled tautly from her face into her standard, neat bun. For a woman sneaking up on ninety, her skin was still lovely and needed minimal make-up, except her signature lipstick. A deep red St. John knit fit her like a glove and gave her cheeks a warm, healthy glow. Even Jack, normally oblivious to jewelry, couldn't help but notice her giant diamond and pearl brooch and matching bracelet. He helped her into her beaver coat and walked her to the car. She looked like a million bucks.

"Don't tell me you got rid of that giant, monstrous car of yours," she exclaimed. "You're finally listening to me?"

"It's my brother's," Jack said, admiring the nearly silent door closing of the BMW sedan. "I knew you'd rear back if I showed up in my Range Rover. And no, I'm not taking your advice. I'm just thoughtful. Now, let's go eat some turkey,

Miss Daisy."

"This is quite a treat for me, Jack," said Lillian as they pulled out of her driveway. "After my mother and father died, I began spending holidays between my pathetic relatives and my contemporaries, most of whom are dead or infirmed." Jack choked back laughter at her blunt, pithy statement. She's baaack, he happily confirmed to himself.

"I'm no fool, though. I know I'm using up the extended warranty my parent's sturdy genes gave me. That, along with my thanks to you and Ellen, is why I'm not eating a lonely meal of mashed potatoes with a bib this Thanksgiving. I do like that woman."

"I do too, Lillian. I do too."

"I'm glad to hear you say that, Jack. It gives an old woman hope."

Jack pulled up to The Manito where Ellen was waiting to help Lillian inside. At night it was a delightfully different visual experience, and Lillian didn't hesitate to announce her approval with a quiet, "Oh, my." Adding to its natural old-world warmth and charm, Molly and Liam rearranged the furniture in the front room to create a living room atmosphere with sofas and chairs in a conversational style. Little white lights were strung across the front window and around several ficus trees, giving them a holiday glow. The room lighting was limited to a few small lamps and candles. The tables at the other end of the room formed a long, elegant dining room table.

. . .

Joe showered, threw on a pair of charcoal pants, red plaid Brooks Brothers shirt and black lamb's wool sweater vest. But before he beat tracks down the stairs, he picked up his cell phone and punched in Clare's cell number. He had no idea how he was going to break the glacial shelf he had pushed into their relationship before he left, that is, if she answered her phone. When he got her perfunctory message to leave a name and number, he tried not to let his voice reveal the fear mixed with excitement he was feeling.

"Clare, it's Joe. Hi!" Oh Lord, this is hard, he thought. "Happy Thanksgiving," he added, trying to buy time. "Look, I need to talk with you. I want to talk with you. I'm guessing with the time change you're in the middle of dessert somewhere, but call me, okay? Bye Clare."

He flipped his phone shut, took a deep breath and slowly walked down the stairs into the bakery. "The last to arrive does dishes with me, Joe," Ellen said, giving him a welcome hug. "And I can't think of anyone I'd rather clean up with than you!"

"Likewise, Ellen, and thanks for including me today."

"Oh, yeah, you're a real burden, Joe!" Lou piped up from behind. "Do you have any idea how much you've done for just about everyone in this room?"

"It goes both ways, Lou," he said, leading her away from the others after Ellen returned to the kitchen with Jack. "I just tried to call Clare. She didn't answer." Lou could hear the alien nervous stutter in his voice. "I...I love her, Lou."

"I could have told you that, Joe."

"What?" Joe yelped back in surprise.

"You heard me," Lou grinned.

. . .

"Joe, would you say grace before we dish up dinner?" asked Lou. "The thing about buffets is by the time everyone gets seated and grace is said, the food is usually cold. If we say it now, everyone can dive in while it's hot. Do you mind?"

"Not a bit," Joe answered. Everyone gathered in a circle, and Joe knew technically this small group was the last he would pray with as a priest. He wished Clare were here.

The traditional Catholic grace is said, day-in-day-out, with the speed of a hummingbird. Joe was moved to break the unwritten Canon Law of speed prayer and took the liberty of a little preaching. After all, it had been quite a year for everyone standing in The Manito on this Thanksgiving evening. There was so much to be thankful for—and to hope for.

"Thank you, Lord, for this tremendous meal we're about to share, and thank you, Ellen, for opening your door to us."

Jack gave Ellen a kiss on the cheek, and she squeezed his hand in return and smiled. "Okay, time out, Joe," Jack said. "I have to say this now. Sorry, my timing has always been lacking, but I want to say how thankful I am for this bakery," which earned him raised eyebrows from everyone. "Without it, I would never have met this beautiful, flour-infested woman who has given me not only a deep appreciation for fine pastries and la-dee-daa coffee, but also for life itself." He bowed toward Ellen. "Okay, the floor is yours again, Joe."

Joe laughed and continued. "I'm almost afraid to continue, but here goes. Thank you, Lord, for our health, especially for Ruth and Miss Johnson." Lillian winked at Ruth, who returned the wink with her now nearly-perfect eye. Lou and Peyton patted each other's fanny, their long-time silent message that they'd always have each other's backs. "And thank you for your much-needed guidance through the challenges set before us."

"I'll second that," Liam interjected. Misty-eyed, Molly took Liam's hand. "Sorry for the interruptions. Go ahead, Joe," Molly beamed.

Joe smiled broadly and continued, "And finally, thank you, Lord, for giving us each the capacity to be open to change, but most of all to be open to love. Amen."

"Speaking of which," Lou said, nodding toward the front door. Like a marionette, Joe's head followed her eye. The silhouette of the one person he had the most to be thankful for in the world was outlined against the lightly falling snow.

"Clare?" Joe mumbled, stunned.

"For a soon-to-be-ex-priest," Lou said, "your prayers still carry some kind of weight. Go let Clare in before she freezes to death."

ABOUT THE AUTHORS

Sarah Porter was born and raised in the more rugged, dry side of Washington state in Spokane. Once launched from the all-girl Mary Cliff Preparatory High School, she attended six colleges and universities. Sarah was a news writer for the Sandpoint Daily Bee and The Spokesman-Review in North Idaho and currently works in marketing and public relations for a community college system in Spokane. Aside from her journal, this is Sarah's first effort at fiction writing. In her spare time, she rides her bike, snowshoes, skis, golfs and fully expects to face knee replacement in the future.

Judy Rogers was born in Virginia Beach, Virginia. Her family moved every two years until she was 14, staying in one place long enough for her to graduate from high school in Troy, Ohio. She taught World Geography and American History at Scottsdale High School and coached the Badminton team (1981 Arizona AAA state champs!). She later transitioned into the world of nonprofit development. She currently works for Gonzaga University as the director of planned giving. She and her husband, John, have one son, Logan. This is also Judy's first novel.

Made in the USA
Charleston, SC
30 June 2013